Praise for *Escape from Differe*

Mikelyn H. Bolden has crafted an imaginative, arresting, and intriguing tale that will both engage and influence readers. She brings to life believable and accessible characters who, as they face their fears and flaws, invite us to join them on their critical journey toward truth and awakening. It's an exciting story at a breathtaking pace that is sure to leave the audience eagerly anticipating the next book in the series.

—**Hannah Miller**
Singer/Songwriter, Highlighted by Lilith Faire, MTV, The International Songwriting Competition, and iTunes' "Indie Spotlight," www.hannahmillermusic.com, Nashville, Tennessee

Bolden has tapped into a unique world that young people and adults alike will not want to leave. Once started, the only disadvantage to the reader is knowing that the journey must come to an end. Not only does it engage you from the first page, but it makes you think beyond words and imagination. A mystery, a coming of age tale, a dystopia and a utopia, a quest for freedom, and a glimpse into the vulnerability of being human, *Escape from Differe* is prime reading material. The characters teach us about who we are, about the communities and people that bind us and define us and ultimately the ones who set us free.

—**Rachel Hendrix**
Actor/Photographer, Lead Actor in Feature Film *October Baby*, www.rachelhendrix.net, Winterthur, Switzerland

Mikelyn H. Bolden's debut fantasy novel, *Escape from Differe,* is nothing short of a remarkable adventure. The compelling characters leap from the page and grab you by the imagination, driving you to a place of decision about faith, family, and friends. It's clear from the opening pages that Bolden loves to spin a yarn. This seemingly dark and thoughtful tome is more like a graphic novel for the mind than a mere book. It's a movie waiting to be made, a delightful romp with a substantive message. You cannot be indifferent about *Differe* once you begin reading it … so hold on tight to every page.

—**Tom Kimball**
Filmmaker and Author of *That's How I Remember It!*
www.TomKimball.com, Littleton, Colorado

From its opening sentence, *Escape from Differe* grabbed both my heart and mind, drawing me immediately into a compelling adventure and causing me to care deeply about its characters. More importantly, I began to see facets of myself in Joel as he learned potent life lessons that inspire my own growth. Mikelyn is a born storyteller with a powerful message, fast-paced yet deep. But I warn you—this book will hook you for the sequels!

—**Jerome Daley**
Leadership Coach and Church Consultant, Author of *Soul Space*,
www.iThrive9.com, Summerfield, North Carolina

In *The Waiz Chronicles* we get a wonderful picture of the power of relationships. The conflicts and choices presented to the characters reinforces the principle that our future is determined by the current relationships that we have. Joel's journey teaches us that God often loves and speaks to us through the people around us. This is a great thing for any generation of young people to know and understand.

—**Troy Fountain**
Lead Pastor, Wiregrass Church, Dothan, Alabama

ESCAPE FROM
DIFFERE

Escape from Differe

The Waiz Chronicles
Book One

Mikelyn H. Bolden

WinePressPublishing
Great Books, Defined.

WinePress Publishing (PO Box 428, Enumclaw, WA 98022) functions only as book publisher. As such, the ultimate design, content, editorial accuracy, and views expressed or implied in this work are those of the author.

ISBN 13: 978-1-4141-2277-9
ISBN 10: 1-4141-2277-2
Library of Congress Catalog Card Number: 2011963641

This book is dedicated to those who hear voices in their heads and have the courage to fight them.

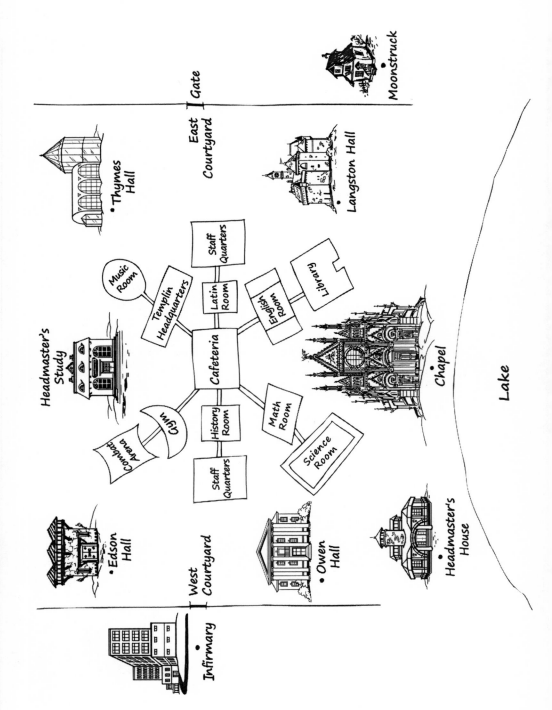

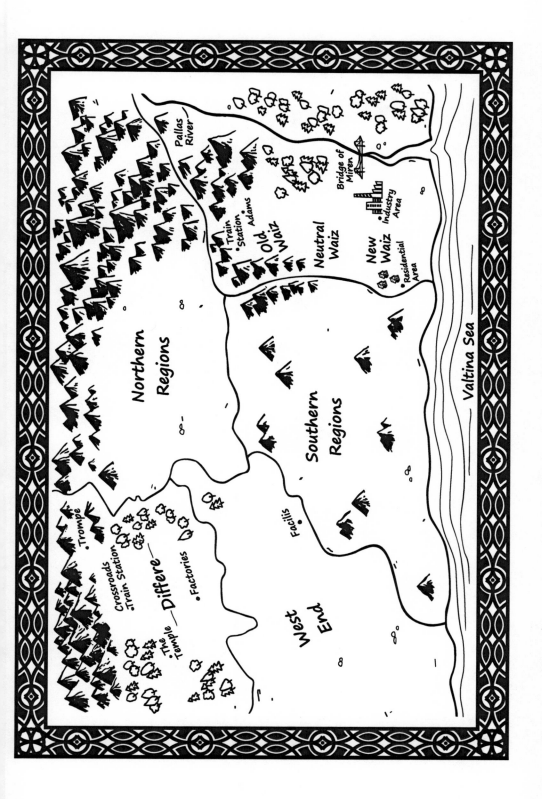

Pronunciation and Terms Guide

Bridge of Miren: (Mer—in) Waiz landmark serving as the dividing line between Old and New Waiz

Caychura: (Cay—chur—uh) Legendary places used to connect with the Majestic's presence and power

Differe: (Di—fear) Region of indifference containing the Temple of Differe School, Trompe, city, and factories

Facilis: (Fuh—sil—lus) Politically neutral city located in the West End

Kalona: (Kuh—lone—uh) Village communities located throughout Old Waiz

Majestic: Old Waiz's Deity

Norrac: (Nore—rack) Vehicle used in Old Waiz made from part-wagon and part-carriage

Northern and Southern Regions: Lands separating Differe and Waiz

Teneh: (Tin—ay) Object used to pay homage to the Majestic

Trompe: (Trom—pay) Medical facility in Northern Differe

Rhydid: (Rye—did) Weapon used by those following the Majestic

Waiz: (Wise) Region of wisdom containing traditional Old Waiz in the north and progressive New Waiz in the south

CHAPTER 1

JOEL SLOWLY BREATHED in, trying not to cough as the crisp night air filled his lungs. He couldn't remember the last time he had been outside long enough to breathe in such open air. He moved as silently as the falling snow across the heavily guarded property. His adrenaline surged as he dodged the spotlights, being careful to stick close to the shadows. His senses were pricked for any sound or movement.

He soon saw her, standing close to the edge of the courtyard. Joel had not realized how hard his heart was beating until now, and he felt a rush of relief. Sarah stood there calmly in a beautiful silver-hooded robe that glistened in the dim light. He thought she looked angelic, and, as far as he was concerned, she was an angel delivering him from ... well, many things. She held out a sealed piece of parchment when he approached. He nodded his thanks.

Taking the scroll, Joel held her hand long enough to see tears form in the corners of her dark brown eyes. He flashed her a sympathetic smile and released her hand. As if on cue, she moved to the side, revealing a wooded path that Joel knew all too well. The gate had been left open for him. Neither exchanged words as Joel hurried past her down his path to freedom.

Joel managed to catch a cab from the outskirts of the city toward downtown. Slamming the passenger door as he exited, he realized it was already half past the hour.

"Great, I hope I haven't missed it," he muttered under his breath as he slung his belongings over his shoulder. Joel gritted his teeth nervously and with some regret, wishing he had not come alone. *There wasn't enough time*, he thought as the ice and snow crunched loudly beneath his shoes.

As he stepped onto the sidewalk of downtown Differe, the city was as dreary as he remembered it. The streets were cluttered with expressionless faces and the endless color of black. Joel caught himself before saying, "Excuse me," as he pushed his way through the silent crowd. All that could be heard was the tapping of shoes against the pavement.

For reasons Joel had never understood, the people of Differe rarely spoke in public. He had nicknamed these citizens "Black Coats" as a small boy, figuring their silence came from being old and boring. Today, however, he was glad the men and women in black would not stop to question him. He clutched his bag tighter as he broke away from the sidewalk. With several others, he began his ascent to the place he had feared for over a decade.

He shuddered a little as he eyed the black flag of Differe hanging against the smooth, white brick that encased the building. The Renaissance windows covering the front and sides of the building were a popular architectural feature. *And goodness knows they're proud of their architectural accomplishments.* He stuck a finger inside his mouth and gagged to symbolize how he felt about them. After waiting in a very slow line at the revolving glass doors, he was finally inside.

Crossroads Train Station had apparently been the main means of travel for some time—or the only means of travel, for all Joel knew. Old portraits and statues from famous scenes in history were the first images that welcomed him into the station's enormous lobby. As he glanced up at the mammoth archways holding colossal lantern-like chandeliers, he noted the bricks were inlaid with ornate historical and religious designs. The heavily curtained windows robbed the room of natural light, creating a grim and unfriendly atmosphere.

As Joel ventured across the marble tiled floor, he realized that he stuck out just as blatantly as a scream would have on the crowded sidewalk outside. His heart pumped vigorously as each passerby eyed him suspiciously. He sighed out loud, "This is not good." He hated the feeling of being watched, yet he hardly blamed the men and women for staring at someone who so obviously did not match the rest of them.

The place was crawling with Black Coats. They were mostly men who wore black caps, suits, and long coats that reached the floor. Joel was not quite certain if it was the dark color that aged these men or if indeed the entire place was filled with only old people. Gray and white protruded from beneath their hats, unless there was no hair at all. These ghostly colors stood in stark contrast to his auburn hair and adolescent, freckled face. He cocked an eyebrow as he observed this overwhelmingly drab, geriatric population.

"Sarah missed the black memo," he thought aloud, smiling. He looked down at his charcoal-colored coat, thankful that the color of it, at least, was close enough to what the others wore.

Though Joel had never been in a museum, he imagined this place resembled one—big, white and old with the proverbial "do-not-touch" look about it. Though pretentious, the station's intricate decor was no contest for that of his former residence.

"Well, Sarah, where are the trains?" Joel asked as if she were standing right there. Now he wished he had gotten her to describe more of the station. He didn't want to attract attention by asking questions. The numerous hallways and staircases extending away from the grand lobby served only to confuse him further. He glanced around at the flow of Black Coats, trying to discern a general direction. He had anticipated some form of excitement from the future passengers or from those arriving yet saw none. No anticipation about going on a trip, nor about

3

seeing a loved one. This was just a means of travel for them—getting from one place to the next—not an adventure or, as in Joel's case, an escape.

Joel glanced at several unhelpful signs hanging overhead and heard an old gentlemen bark at another one, "The train leaves in ten minutes—South Side. Let's hurry!"

His companion grunted, picked up his cane, and escorted himself to the South Side. Joel hesitated, uncertain whether to follow them, but time was short and these men were the only ones who seemed to be heading to an actual train. He discretely pushed after them.

He had no difficulty catching up; the man with the cane was moving beyond slowly. Leaving the massive lobby, Joel followed the old gentlemen at a distance down a white marble stairway that led to what must be called "the South Side Train Stop." He noted more of the alcoves full of old statues and portraits as he continued down the stairway. Joel eventually could not help but catch up with the older men.

When they offered to let him pass, Joel quickly covered his uncertainty with an intelligent facade. "No, sir, after you. I'm a student—uh—currently studying history, and well, I can enjoy these ancient statues in greater detail at this pace." He wanted to say, "at this snail's pace."

With much practice he had mastered the art of communicating the opposite of what he really thought. Some would call that "lying," but Joel called it "avoiding conflict." Sometimes he stumbled on the first couple of words, yet he usually concocted a verbal masterpiece to appease most audiences. This is not to say that Joel did not have occasional outbursts. He did, particularly when he was angry.

The blast of an approaching steam engine interrupted his thoughts. His spirits lifted as he rounded the stairway, and, after what had seemed like a million minutes, he finally entered the train stop. Perhaps his journey had begun. There certainly was a train.

"Hey, you!" shouted the old gentlemen with the cane. "Is this the ten forty-five to Facilis?"

"No, sir, you just missed it," replied a young porter. "Another one should be along in the next half hour. This one here's not for passengers." He motioned to the whistling train.

"Blast! We just missed it," said the old gentleman, as he looked at his watch. Not wanting to miss his own train, Joel quickly approached the uniformed man.

"Sir, Sir. *Excuse me, sir,*" Joel yelled to be heard above the background noise. "I'm looking for the train to Waiz?"

The twenty-something-year-old employee shot him a quizzical look. Joel also felt the attention of several Black Coats turn his way. The young man motioned him away from the train.

Once both were far enough to be heard without yelling, the young man spoke again, "Waiz, you said?"

Joel nodded, and the fellow rubbed his chin.

"I haven't heard of that city, but there are many destinations at this place. Do you have your ticket?" he asked politely.

Joel shook his head, still wondering what exactly he was going to do about that.

"Well, you could check at the inquiry desk. They regulate all the departures and arrivals of the trains. Take that set of stairs," said the young man, gesturing to a stairwell to the far right. "Once you get to the top, you'll be in the conference hall. Take the staircase at the end of the hall with the sign 'Travel Planning' seen overhead."

He started walking back towards the train when Joel called out to him, "Thank you, sir. Uh … is there anything else by the staircase to the inquiry desk? You know, in case the sign is missing?" Joel asked, trying to look confident.

The young man scratched his head. "Just look for the sign. Come to think of it though, I've heard there's some famous horse statue by the staircase." A piercing whistle sounded from the closest train. "Got it? I have to unload the train now."

Joel nodded and hurried from the South Side stairwell to the second floor of Crossroads Station. Dashing up the stairs, he enjoyed the fact that he was no longer stuck behind two old men. After he entered the conference hall, Joel spotted two staircases at the far end of the hall and then sighed in dismay, "Great, no signs, but hundreds of statues."

Indeed, statues of all sizes filled the hall; some were encased in glass while others were mounted on marble pedestals. Finding a large horse would not be a problem, but locating a small one would be quite challenging. He looked to see if he was the only one in the entryway, then started scanning the statues to his left and right. He first checked the large mounted statues and then examined the smaller encased ones.

After a few minutes he grew impatient and decided to speed things up by listing the objects aloud. "Okay, birds, swords, dragons, shields, kings."

He grimaced at some of the intense battle scenes. "Okay, I'm looking for a statue of a horse," he coached himself aloud, even though the task seemed impossible at this point. He sighed and looked to the far end, noticing a thick green curtain like the one in the front lobby. It covered the entire wall in front of the staircases. Joel paused, wondering if perhaps the curtain was concealing something.

As he walked toward the curtain, out of nowhere he heard Sarah's voice in his head. "Joel, don't give trouble an excuse to keep finding you." He smirked, thinking of how many rules he had broken over the past few months. In his mind some actions were well worth what she categorized as "trouble."

He approached the curtain carefully, hesitant to disturb it. He cautiously bent down to grab the bottom edge and peek his head under the curtain.

He had just pulled the curtain high enough for him to see behind it when a deep voice shouted, "Just what do you think you're doing?" This voice also grabbed the back of his coat collar and turned him around.

"Sorry, I was looking, well, I was looking for a horse," Joel answered breathlessly.

"You were looking for a horse," repeated the guard. His words were slow and deliberate. "I think you'll find only trains here."

Joel straightened and pulled away from the officer before mumbling, "I was actually on my way to the inquiry desk."

Thankfully, there was only one place to go once he reached the top of the second floor—down a long, narrow hallway with office doorways on each side. About a third of the way down the hall, he passed the elevator and made a mental note to return that way; he was tired of climbing so many staircases. Joel hated to ask for help, but he was getting desperate.

Stopping at a glass front, he peered inside the travel planning department at a stark white room with a few locked cabinets and a glass counter. He grasped the metal door handle, the only colored object amidst the glass, and looked around for a moment. When he turned back toward the counter, a woman in a crisp black suit, her dark hair in a tight slick bun, appeared.

"Welcome to the inquiry desk," she chirped. "Our job is to success-fully address any of your travel needs. How may I help you today?" She sounded as if she were playing a recording straight into the microphone of the headset she was wearing.

Joel furrowed his brow, trying to take the woman seriously, and responded with, "Uh, yeah, well, thanks. I'm looking for the train to Waiz."

The woman's glazed-over expression quickly changed upon hearing the place's name. Snapping to attention, her eyes narrowed in response. "Do you have your ticket?" she asked hurriedly.

"Well, no, not exactly," Joel paused to get his thoughts together. "See, I'm meeting some people here—my family," he lied.

"Hm, I have never heard of that destination," she stated as she pulled a clear box marked with a "W" and full of index cards from a nearby cabinet and placed it on the glass counter.

As she stood before him, Joel suddenly realized that this woman must be more than six feet tall. She was now not only eyeing him with curiosity but also peering down at him.

"Is it a city or county?" she asked, while placing a calculator with a red button next to the box.

"I was told it was a city."

"By whom?"

Joel stiffened as the woman pressed for more information.

"It may be helpful if you tell me more about how this place was described. Perhaps the name of another city was confused with Weeze."

"Waiz," Joel corrected. "It's pronounced *Wise*, but I believe it's spelled W-a-i-z."

"Fine. What else can you tell me about this city?" she said as she thumbed through the index cards. Something about her eager smile made Joel feel slightly uneasy.

"I heard it's warmer there, not as much snow," he replied, noting the woman's index finger as it hit the red button on the calculator.

"It must be south. Are you traveling alone? You didn't say where you've arrived from?"

This question and the red light that suddenly glared overhead cued Joel that his time was running out. "Like I said, I'm meeting some family in—oh, several minutes." He hastily glanced down at his watch. "I should probably be going. They'll be expecting me."

He started towards the door.

"Wait right there," said the woman sternly.

Joel caught her change in tone, then noted she swiftly softened. "I mean, please wait. My manager will help you locate the train."

Joel did not look back as he grasped the door handle. "Forgive me for taking your time," Joel said, as he was halfway out the door.

She continued to call out after him. "Wait!"

As the door was closing he was sure he heard the woman say the word "security" into her headpiece, and the red light began to flash. He had to find that train! And he had to find it quickly.

Joel ducked into an empty doorway at the center of the corridor. Dropping his bag on the floor, he frantically rummaged through his knapsack. He caught his breath and whispered, "Perfect." He pulled out a wool cap to cover his red hair. There was not much he could do about the freckles splashed across his face, but at least he could cover his most identifying feature. Thankfully, the cap was black. He was almost smiling about this fact as he burst out of the shadows and ran smack into something moving quickly past him.

There was a loud crash as Joel fell over, slamming what appeared to be a wheelchair into the opposing wall. After recovering from his fall, Joel quickly scanned the scene. A little, wide-eyed boy lay turned over in the wheelchair that Joel had somehow managed not to squash in the collision. A girl who apparently had been pushing the wheelchair from behind had fallen flat on her back.

Joel caught his breath. "You okay?" he asked, glancing at the little blond boy. The boy nodded silently and gave him the "okay" sign.

He looked next at the girl, who seemed to be about his age. As she climbed to her feet, Joel heard her mutter something about a "stupid boy" under her breath. He shot her a defensive look as she brushed a mass of dark curls from her face. A girl with such an attitude is not worth addressing, he decided. But before he could snub her, a door slammed ahead and all three looked up.

Afraid he was being pursued by Security, Joel nodded to the little boy, jumped quickly to his feet, and started running towards the elevator. The young lady, now almost to her feet, looked puzzled as he ran past. As he darted by, he heard a sound of exasperation escape her lips. *That's the very sound that, for some reason, females are only able to make when putting their hands on their hips and rolling their eyes.*

As he reached the elevator, he heard a voice call out behind him. "Hey! Do you want your bag? I know you're in a hurry, but you may need this."

Joel glanced back to see his knapsack dangling from the girl's gloved hand. "Argh ..." Joel closed his eyes and clenched his jaw; he knew he had to turn back. He slowly traipsed back to her and the little boy. She stood there glowering up at him with her big blue eyes as she held the bag in her hand. The little boy was quiet, looking back and forth from the girl to Joel.

As Joel reached out to take the bag, the dark-haired girl suddenly snatched it behind her back. "You want your bag? First apologize for jumping out of a doorway and then running off without helping us."

Joel looked her squarely in the eye and in a low voice said, "No."

"No?" she mimicked him. "Well, then, no bag," she said as she narrowed her eyes and clutched the bag tighter.

"Give me my bag," hissed Joel, as he took a step closer towards her.

The little boy tugged at her red coat pleadingly.

In hopes of breaking her confidence, Joel moved until he was right above the girl's face. He thought his height might intimidate her, as he was at least a head taller than she. If this did not work, Joel figured he could take the bag by force. Her thick wool coat appeared to be hiding a fairly slender figure.

Sure enough. He saw her eyes flicker with fear as he held out his hand.

She glanced at the little boy and sighed in defeat. As she released the bag she huffed, "Fine! But know that I think you are a rude, selfish, reprehensible, and atrocious boy."

"You know, I may be all those big words, but I do have my bag now. If you'll excuse me, I have a train to catch."

Joel grinned as he tipped his hat for effect. The girl brushed past him and repositioned herself behind the wheelchair.

"Oh, well, we shan't keep you. I believe you were running away, weren't you?" she said while motioning towards the elevator.

He felt his disdain for the girl rocket even higher as he turned around to leave.

As he walked off, he could hear her consoling the little boy about how sorry she was that the "stupid boy" had frightened him. *Boy?* Did this girl not have eyes? He would be turning eighteen at the beginning of the year.

He was almost back to the elevator when he could have sworn he heard her say something about "getting to Waiz" and the "inquiry desk." As much as he disliked the young woman, it was the first mention of Waiz he had heard by someone other than himself.

He hurried back down the hallway, "Wait! Please, wait!"

The girl continued on her way.

"Wait!" yelled Joel. *Dumb girl.* He would have to run to catch her. "Are you deaf?" he yelled at her.

"You have your bag. Now what do you want?" she asked, avoiding eye contact as she continued to push the wheelchair down the hall.

Joel thought quickly. He had better fake some remorse in order to gain her trust. He rounded in front of the wheelchair.

"Listen, I'm sorry about that back there. I didn't mean to scare him." Joel glanced at the little boy. As the wheelchair stopped, she looked up at him with raised eyebrows as if there were more he needed to say.

Joel gritted his teeth, "And I'm sorry for scaring you, too."

"Is that all?" she implored with her big, blue eyes, "Anything else you can think of?"

All the muscles in his arms contracted. *Who does this girl think she is?* "Listen, I know you don't like me very much right now, but I think we can help each other."

"Yes, oh, that's exactly what I'd like to do. Help you after you knocked me on my back. Move out of the way," sneered the girl.

Joel ignored her, "I heard you say something about Waiz." Joel saw her exchange glances with the little boy.

"So what, you've heard of it?" she asked casually, as she moved a wavy, dark strand from her face.

Joel could sense she knew something when she bit her lip. He looked around the hallway then motioned the two into a nearby doorway.

"Yes," he said quietly. "I'm trying to get there. I came up here to the inquiry desk, but—I don't know; something's not right." Joel then recounted his story.

"So you think someone is after you now because you asked the inquiry desk about Waiz?" the girl asked, obviously puzzled. "That's ridiculous. You must have done something wrong. Where are you from?"

Joel cast her a stone-cold look that let her know she was not going to find out.

"Augie, he told us not to mention Waiz to anyone," said the little boy for the first time.

"Hush, Sebastian," she replied hastily.

"Who? Who told you that?" Joel asked while "Augie" shot him back the same look he had given her a moment earlier. "I'm warning you. Don't go to the desk."

Augie looked down at Sebastian's pale, apprehensive face. "Okay. Okay, we won't go, but you," she pointed at Joel. "You cannot stay with us. No one is looking for us."

"What?" he said stiffly. "I just helped you!"

Augie shook her head. "No, you gave me a warning I already had. Now go away. Go. Go away." She shooed him, then shifted her eyes away as if to ignore his presence.

Joel was furious. He could not believe how horrible and ungrateful this girl was. He walked away steaming. *I hope she never finds the train to Waiz.*

Joel made his way back to the main lobby via the stairs. The other two took the elevator after Augie strongly expressed there would not be enough room for the three of them.

Though cautious to remain hidden, Joel tried to look for other young people who perhaps might be looking for the train to Waiz. This was a useless task, and every time he thought he might be catching a glimpse of someone, he would realize it was Augie. *What kind of a name is that, anyway?*

When they did catch sight of one another, she would silently round her lips and mouth the words, "Go away." It appeared that both were looking for something and were, in fact, completely lost. He envied the two of them for having each other as he sat alone on a hard marble slab across from them.

As much as he tried not to, Joel's eyes kept drifting back towards them. So when Sebastian frantically started shaking Augie's coat sleeve, Joel followed the little boy's gaze. The hair on the back of Joel's neck stood on end as a pair of guards entered the lobby from the same direction they had just come. Joel bowed his head low to hide his face as well as the red hair that was poking out from underneath his cap. He held his breath as the uniforms moved steadily toward him.

CHAPTER 2

JOEL NERVOUSLY WATCHED the black leather boots march past him toward the revolving doors. When he lifted his head again, he saw Augie walking toward the ticket counter, leaving Sebastian behind. After a few minutes, Sebastian's and Joel's eyes finally met, and though he seemed a bit nervous, Sebastian nodded him over. Since Sebastian was seated near the entrance with people still trickling in and out, Joel felt confident he would remain safely concealed.

Sebastian flashed Joel a weak smile when he approached. Joel returned the smile halfheartedly. Neither said a word for a few moments. Eager to break the silence, both boys started speaking at the same time. The second time this happened, Joel let out a short laugh and nodded towards the little boy.

"Sorry about Augie. She doesn't trust people very easily. She's also very protective of me now since Mom and Dad put me in her care."

"You're brother and sister then?" Joel asked, looking puzzled. The two looked nothing alike.

Sebastian's straight, sandy-blond hair and fair skin hardly matched Augie's olive-toned complexion and dark brunette waves. Sebastian seemed to understand Joel's reaction to this, but only answered with a short "yes."

"I've been here all day long and only seen one train and about a thousand statues. How long have you been here?" Joel asked.

"Since early afternoon. We were supposed to meet someone here that would take us on to Waiz."

Joel then remembered something and asked, "Like a guide or something?"

"Well, I guess he's a guide, but really, he's just a friend of our parents who knows the way to the city."

"So, Waiz is a city. I wasn't sure." Joel watched Sebastian shift nervously in his seat at this comment. Sensing the little boy's uneasiness, Joel quickly added, "I know it's warm there with a mountainside and a valley."

Sebastian's jaw dropped. "Warm? Really?" They both relaxed at this exchange and smiled a bit more genuinely at one another.

Joel tried hard not to concentrate on Sebastian's condition, as each passerby seemed to notice that the little fellow was obviously handicapped. Joel was curious about his age, too, for although Sebastian's size indicated he was about six years old, his face looked several years older. The way Sebastian spoke also made Joel think he was older than he looked. Joel figured that Sebastian could have picked up his elegant vocabulary from his sister, remembering the tongue-lashing he had received on the second floor.

Joel then noticed that Sebastian had turned his attention to the ticket counter.

"Augie's getting close to the front of the line," Sebastian motioned in her direction. "Dad said it'd be best if we didn't tell anyone where we were going. He didn't think I could hear, but I heard him say it would cause suspicion if we mentioned the city to anyone here." Augie was the third from the front of the line and now glaring at the two of them.

"I'm not supposed to say anything, but it's getting late, and we're supposed to meet our friend at the train stop for Waiz by eight o'clock. I have a picture Dad drew for us to help us get to the train platform."

"Like a map?" Joel asked.

"Yeah," Sebastian said as he took the drawing out of his coat pocket. "He drew it because ... well, he can't read or write," he said sheepishly, as he cautiously opened the drawing, careful to conceal the map from any other eyes.

Joel looked on with interest. The drawing itself was remarkable for someone who seemed to have had no schooling. He studied the drawing for a moment before pulling the piece of paper closer to his face. His eyes soon widened in recognition. "Oh, my gosh, I've seen this—I know where this is. This arrow here, is that where you're supposed to meet your friend?"

Sebastian nodded.

"I think I can remember how to get there," Joel said excitedly. The two looked at each other and then to Augie. The difficult part would be convincing her to trust Joel and not bite off Sebastian's head for showing Joel the drawing.

"Come on," said Joel as he grabbed the back of the wheelchair and picked up Augie's suitcase.

Joel was careful to stay in the crowd as he pushed the wheelchair toward the ticket counter. Augie's mouth dropped open in surprise as the two approached her in line.

"What do you think you're doing?" she whispered as others in line began to stare at the odd trio.

Joel spoke under his breath, "I know how to get you to your friend."

"What are you talking about?" she hissed while angrily glancing down at Sebastian.

"On the drawing, the place where the arrow is—I was there earlier today. I can take you there," Joel whispered back.

"You can't stay with us. Why should I trust you?" said Augie, obviously becoming more uncomfortable with the stares of the onlookers.

"Probably because I seem to be the only one here who's heard of a train to Waiz. Doesn't that count for something?" Joel replied earnestly. "Listen, it's getting late. The line is dying down, and if your friend's not there you can come get back in line. Come on, Augie!"

She looked startled at hearing him say her name for the first time. "If you take us there, do you promise to leave us alone after we find our friend?" she asked stiffly.

Though slightly irritated at her attitude, Joel nodded and managed to mutter a "yes."

She then got that same look of distrust in her eyes he had seen on the second floor. "I don't even know your name," she said.

Joel shrugged, "I won't be with you long enough for it to matter."

Joel easily navigated his way back to the hall of statues up from the South Side Train Stop. *The three of us are the only ones in the silent hall,* he realized—*that is, except for the army of statues.*

"This is a very strange room," said Augie, breaking the silence.

Sebastian nodded, "Uh, yeah. It feels like the statues are watching us."

Even though Joel had been in the room earlier, he couldn't help but feel an eerie presence as he walked past the ancient characters toward the green curtain again. He almost wished that the statues were real, as he was starting to feel paranoid about being found. He knew the inquiry desk was only one flight above him, and he could use a little extra cover.

Joel watched as Augie shuddered at some of the images and noted that Sebastian's teeth were chattering by the time they reached the end of the hall. Suddenly a loud bang echoed throughout the place. Instead of looking around, all three reacted in sheer panic by scrambling for a place to hide. Joel pointed toward the curtain that now stood directly in front of them.

They raced forward but stopped abruptly when a large lump unexpectedly protruded from beneath the thick drape. The lump made all three jump back and look at one another in complete terror. There was nowhere else to hide. Joel's temples began to throb and his heart felt

17

like it was going to pound out of his chest. The three remained frozen in fear as a large brown heap emerged from underneath the curtain.

A towering man with a warm smile and a tan, bearded face scanned the room, taking in the surrounding statues. He looked at the figures, then to the three of them, then back at the curtain. He appeared puzzled but simply shrugged his shoulders and walked toward them.

"Hello. Well, this is excellent timing," said the bearded man as he reached out to take Sebastian's hand. After giving Sebastian's hand a firm squeeze, he took the same hand and tenderly touched Augie's face.

As he watched these exchanges, Joel was still recovering from the shock of the "lump" being his new companions' friend. His mouth gaped open when the man eventually looked over at him.

"And who is this?" the man asked politely.

"He is property of Differe," shouted a cold female voice from the top of the left staircase. All four looked up to find the woman from the inquiry desk along with the guard Joel had encountered in the hall earlier.

"Don't try to run," the woman commanded as she glided down the staircase with the guard at her heels. Though his mind was racing, Joel noticed the guard squinting down at him as they approached.

The guard turned to the woman. "This is who you're looking for? I found him snooping around here earlier."

"Figures," the woman muttered. "Joel, isn't it?" she asked, while looking directly into his eyes.

"No ma'am. It's Fred," Joel answered hurriedly, pretending to look puzzled, while also trying to piece together an escape plan.

"Oh, really? Then who are these people?" the woman asked suspiciously while eyeing the rest of the group.

Joel managed a ready response. "This is my family and our friend," said Joel as he pointed to the large man in the brown coat. "Remember? I told you I was meeting them here."

Joel's insides were shaking, for he knew his companions could give him up anytime they, or rather she, wished.

"Hmm ... using a fake name *and* a fake city? Your authority doesn't treat escape lightly, young man," said the woman sharply.

The "lump" interjected at this point. "With all due respect, ma'am, I am a friend of these children, and I have met them here."

"Oh, really?" she said again, still obviously unconvinced.

"Well, it is not merely a coincidence that we are both here in the same room at the same time and happen to be friends," said the man as he smiled at Joel. "Also, I know the place from which you think this young man escaped, and I would think it highly unlikely that someone of his age could manage such a feat. Wouldn't you agree, officer?"

The guard scratched his head. "It would be quite difficult. The security there is fierce." The guard turned toward the woman, "You're sure you have the right kid? This one looks older."

While she stood thinking, the man with the brown coat continued. "Furthermore, I would find it even more unlikely that any young person from that facility could find this station. I can assure you, I have been expecting these three to accompany me on the train today."

The woman's eyes narrowed at this statement. "The train to Waiz?"

The man drew back and grinned with an odd smile. "Have you heard of a train to Waiz?" he asked respectfully.

"Well, no," the woman said, looking a little embarrassed.

"Then there is your answer. We are headed south for health reasons," he said while gingerly gazing down at Sebastian, who appeared to be turning a bright shade of red. "He," motioning toward Joel, "has not traveled by train before. I hadn't had the pleasure of meeting him before today, yet since arriving in Differe, he has fought hard to find his family and bring them here." The man then turned and nodded with respect to Joel, who was trying to keep his face from showing any sign of emotion.

"Please," the man continued, "our train leaves in fifteen minutes. Do you have any more questions for us? Would it help if I showed you our tickets?" he asked while reaching into his pocket.

The woman turned to the officer, who shook his head, then turned back to the group. She paused as she bit her lip. "You sure you're family?

None of you look alike." Joel shrugged his shoulders at her remark, and the other two said nothing.

She sighed in defeat. "Well, I suppose you're right. Most young people wouldn't even know how to get to the station, and you certainly don't have brown hair," said the woman as she studied a piece of paper in her hand. She then looked up at the tan, bearded face and smiled. "I'll let you get on your way."

"Thank you," the brown heap tipped his hat at the lady. "Gather your things now," he motioned to Augie and Joel.

When the woman and guard moved out of earshot, the man held a finger to his lips. "Come, we must hurry," he said urgently. With a stern expression on his face he looked directly at Joel and Augie. "Not a word," he said in a low voice. "There will be time to talk later."

He escorted the three down the elevator, and Joel was surprised to find himself back at the South Side platform when they exited. Joel and Augie followed the man in silence as he wheeled Sebastian onto the platform. Though a passenger train blocked his view of the railroad tracks, Joel noted at least four tunnels at the far end of the platform boarding area. As Black Coats shuffled toward the boarding train, Joel couldn't help but wonder if Facilis would be their first stop.

Instead, their mysterious guide took a sharp left around the platform's brick wall, and Joel figured the man must be attempting to secure an empty compartment for the group toward the back of the train. They walked single file down the narrow walkway, and though questions began to form in Joel's mind, he knew his voice would not be heard over the screeching of the train beside him.

Joel saw Augie startle when the train eased off in departure. The guide stopped suddenly, looked back at them, then pointed upward. Joel watched as the lights from the departing train illuminated two metal structures on either side of the tracks. The top of the two iron-framed towers approached the high arch of the ceiling and supported a bridge across the train tracks. Upon closer inspection, Joel noted that a set of stairs located inside the metal frame led to the top of the tower nearest him.

After the train entered the tunnel, the guide suddenly stooped down to pick Sebastian up out of his wheelchair. He then gestured for Augie to close the wheelchair and then for Joel to carry it.

Thankfully for Joel, Sebastian's small frame meant that the wheelchair was fairly lightweight. He curiously watched the man beckon them forward up the rickety, iron staircase. As Joel entered the cage, he thought of how he had completely missed seeing the entire structure on his first visit to the South Side Stop. *But I never thought to look up, either. This man has to be a guide to the city.*

Joel's thoughts were distracted by a jolt that shook the entire tower. He wasn't sure if this was due to the structure's age or from the vibrations of the nearby trains. Hefting the wheelchair, his knapsack, and the guide's handbag proved to be cumbersome, and the shaking staircase didn't help matters. Joel quickly fell behind the pace of the others as the random jolts continued. Augie dragged behind the guide as well, daintily making her way up the staircase with both her bags and Sebastian's. For his part, Joel found himself stopping every few steps to allow her time to get ahead of him. Unfortunately, it seemed the higher they climbed, the less sturdy the steps under their feet became.

By the time the two reached the top of the tower, the guide was already across the bridge. When Augie paused for what seemed an unusual amount of time, Joel finally peered over her shoulder to discover what the holdup was.

He was alarmed to find that the bridge was swaying wildly, almost swinging, from the jolts of the shaking towers. He heard her squeal when she attempted to take her first step. The swaying bridge flung her into the side and rocked her back and forth between the two sides as she moved forward. Joel shook his head at the predicament but realized it must be the only way to get across the tracks. Before he took his first step, however, he noticed something in the corner of his eye. He swiveled his head around and saw a bright light moving toward him. *A train?* He hurried to get on the bridge behind Augie.

Joel rushed onto the swinging bridge and was instantly thrust into the nearest side railing. At first, he felt paralyzed on the moving bridge, but when he caught sight of Sebastian's head bobbing down the tower across from him, he ordered his body, *Move! The guide's almost to the bottom!* After several awkward moments, he began to adapt to the bridge's swinging rhythm, skillfully shifting his weight and keeping himself upright.

By the time he reached the middle of the bridge, he had caught up with Augie again. While they continued the battle for their footing, both turned their heads toward the sound of a loud whistle and found themselves looking straight into the light Joel had seen earlier. A train was rapidly approaching and from their perspective it appeared too tall to pass under the bridge.

Joel sensed Augie's nervousness and watched as she attempted to quicken her pace. She instantly fell forward, catching herself on the grated iron with her hands.

With his own hands full, Joel felt powerless as he watched her try to get up. He grimaced as his mind flashed to scenes hours earlier—him knocking her down in his haste and her restraint at not betraying him to the inquiry lady. He started to put his bags down, but was blinded by the bright light of the coming train bearing down on them. Augie scrambled to her feet, and both anxiously glanced toward the train, which did not seem to be slowing down. Joel reasoned with himself that there was no way the train could be as high as the bridge, but, as he eyed the top of the speeding object every few seconds, his conviction waned.

When Joel began to hear the clanging of a railroad crossing, he felt the iron grate right beneath his feet begin to separate. He nervously jumped forward, nearly knocking Augie down again. She shot a furious glance back at him, which turned to terror as she watched him begin to rise above her. Joel glanced behind to find the bridge breaking apart in the center just like a drawbridge. The iron arms were lifting to make way for the train barreling nearer. Though this action guaranteed that the bridge would not be smashed into oblivion, it raised another problem: the drawbridge was pivoting them high above their exit and into its anchoring spot. *We're about to be wall mounts or fall all the way down to the door!* He panicked as the sound of the train engine churned louder.

As he figured was bound to happen, the increasing incline and swaying of the metal arm knocked Joel off balance. Just before he thought he was doomed to fall backwards onto the tracks, a force yanked on the wheelchair he was clutching. After Augie pulled him forward, she was instantly sent sliding to the bottom of their arm, with Joel swiftly following. He pushed them into the stairwell just before the arm anchored into the tower, closing off the entrance. Pausing to catch his breath, Joel let out a gasp of relief while Augie hurried on. *We barely made it!* he breathed, as they watched the train speed by, causing the surrounding air to whip through the stairwell with loud, ghost-like noises. Sweat dripped from his face as he made his way down, stumbling from the vibrations of the passing train and the random jolts of the old tower.

He soon found himself on Augie's heels again, and this time when she lost her balance he was ready—catching the back of her coat's belt loop. She gripped the railing, and as Joel jerked her upright, a tiny pink bag slipped through her fingers. Joel caught her look of horror as she frantically craned her neck over the railing to locate the small item. Neither could see it as they peered below.

As they neared the bottom, Joel made out the guide's and Sebastian's outline. They were motioning something to him. *What now?* Joel thought, completely unnerved as he squinted to see what they were pointing at. But he didn't have to look long as the movement of an iron gate soon obstructed his view.

His muscles tightened as he watched the gate slowly sliding down over their exit. He started skipping steps two and three at a time, but realized they wouldn't have enough time to reach the bottom before the gate closed completely, locking them inside. Joel threw his bags to the bottom of the stairs, then snatched Augie's and threw hers down, as well. He motioned for her to jump. She obeyed and scrambled to duck under the gate.

Joel scanned the area before launching himself after her and, just as he had hoped, he saw the little pink bag near the bottom step. He leapt down and shoved the wheelchair and bags under the gate, now just a few feet shy of the floor. Heart racing, he reached around the steps to swipe the bag. When the bag didn't budge, Joel swore softly, "You've got to be kidding me." He slid under the steps to free the bag from a piece of broken grate and, in one swift motion, rolled under the gate as it dropped to the ground.

The bridge had led them to a middle platform where the guide and Sebastian were now waiting. Joel gasped for breath as he got to his feet, recovering from the unbelievable task of crossing the tracks. *Who would've thought it'd be such an obstacle course?*

The train beside them was now stopped and silent. Augie and Joel looked back at where the bridge had been. At a quick glance, it just appeared to be workmen's scaffolding. *It's practically camouflaged,* Joel realized, eyeing the remains.

The guide, acting quite unaffected by all their efforts, motioned for Augie and Joel to continue following. He walked toward an object carved into the cement platform. Joel watched as he pulled something from his pocket. *A key, maybe?* The man stuck the object into the floor and pulled it open.

A dark hole was revealed underneath the trapdoor. Their guide, still carrying Sebastian and Sebastian's suitcase, descended into the depths. Augie started to follow and then surprised Joel by stopping sharply. Since he was right on her heels, he almost stumbled over her suitcase. When she turned to face him, she did not look at his eyes but down towards her tiny bag, still clutched in his hand. Joel followed her gaze and mouthed the word "Oh"—he had completely forgotten he was still holding it. He raised his hand to give it to her. She took it without a word and turned back to enter the darkness. The guide did not direct Joel to shut the door behind them, so he left it open.

Joel was getting weary of carrying so many items up and down endless stairs, and this staircase proved to be the most difficult yet, pitch black as it was. Though the door remained open, the platform had not been well-lit. Soon after they entered, Joel heard the door close, locking them inside the inky void. As cautioned by the guide earlier, no one said a word.

The air inside felt damp and cold, which caused a chill to run across Joel's sweaty brow. The steps were slippery, wet even, and the sound of trickling water echoed around them. Because his hands were full, Joel's feet were his only method of feeling his way down the stairs. The steepness of the angle made carrying everything that much more difficult. He tried his best not to run into Augie, but sometimes he just could not help it.

The stairs went on for what seemed an eternity. After they reached the bottom, Augie could not contain herself any longer.

"Quit touching me," she hissed.

"I can't see!" Joel cried out in rebuttal.

"Hush!" commanded the guide. He pulled out a light, which cast its dim flicker a few feet ahead. With the stairs complete, the passageway opened up slightly and stretched evenly forward.

Soon a light was seen ahead, hanging on the side of the wall and illuminating an old railroad track. The guide stopped in front of its glow, and all waited in silence. A minute later a man with a dirty face and a crooked nose popped his face through an opening no larger than a small windowpane.

"Corwin?" he asked in a gruff voice.

"Yes, it is I," replied the guide.

"Back so soon?" asked the man, exposing a row of missing teeth.

"Indeed. I've seen enough of this place. Train on time today?" the guide inquired, indicating he was not in the mood for small talk.

"About, yes. Got your tickets?" replied the man while sticking a grimy hand out of the window.

"Yes, I have them here, all four of them." The guide turned to look at Joel. Joel felt both surprise and suspicion. *How did he know I was going to be here?* A part of him did not care, and he was glad enough for the ticket. The other part screamed at him, *Templins are everywhere.*

The man behind the window closed it without a word and then opened a large door. "Going in to eat?" he asked their guide.

All three companions raised their heads at the mention of food.

"No. We'll grab a bite on the train."

Joel tried to catch a glimpse of what was behind the door. He could tell it was large, very bright, and packed full of people. Yet none were Black Coats.

Getting on the train was uneventful, except for the fact that, like everything else they had encountered that day, the train was old. Joel crossed his arms as he sat opposite from the others in their compartment. Augie kept giving him a look that made him feel as though she had sized him up and made up her mind about him. He despised her judgment, but knew that he had not "left them alone" as he had agreed. He greatly appreciated the guide asking so few questions before allowing him to accompany the troupe as "family." Sebastian appeared glad to have another boy join the group and would flash Joel a shy grin now and then.

Joel hadn't had time to get a good look at the young fellow until now. Joel was still unsure of his age. He sat propped up on several cushions when in or out of his wheelchair. His bright green eyes lit up his pale face when he smiled, and his small frame wore a simple black coat and gray trousers.

Augie, on the other hand, exuded the opposite. She had a foreign look about her, with olive skin and long, dark, wavy hair. Her blue eyes were set off by a bright red coat with a cream scarf. Both brother and sister carried matching black hats, though neither appeared to have worn them. Joel sat staring at Sebastian, and the little boy seemed to be eyeing Joel with just as much curiosity. The realization caused Joel to shift in his seat and turn his gaze toward his shoes.

Their guide sat back observing this whole scene, then spoke for the first time since they had left the station. "Joel?"

Joel looked up at him.

"So, that is your name … I'm Corwin. This is Augustine and Sebastian." Joel nodded as Corwin motioned to the other two. "Have you been traveling long?" Corwin inquired politely.

"Well, no, sir. Not exactly," Joel replied.

Although Corwin's quick acceptance had created a yearning in Joel to tell this mysterious companion his story, he was still unsure of Corwin's motives. Joel decided to divulge as little as possible about himself and stayed quiet.

"Well, I have been traveling for several weeks now. On my way back to Waiz, I stopped through Differe. Just three days ago." Corwin stopped to take a breath and eyed the siblings. "Augustine's and Sebastian's parents"—Augustine shot Corwin a concerned look—"they asked me to take their children to Waiz, as it can obviously be difficult to find if one has never traveled there before."

Joel was not sure why Corwin was telling him this, but if it was a ploy for Joel to explain himself, Corwin had better try another tactic. Joel shrugged, "Lucky I found you, I guess."

Corwin smiled, "Hmm … lucky? I don't think so, and, if I remember correctly, I found you."

Joel wanted to argue that fact, but maybe Corwin was right. Something had found him and helped get him out of there, but whether it was friend or "trouble" remained to be seen. Joel noticed that Augustine smirked at Corwin's remark, and he turned his eyes away to the window. As he watched the wintery landscape sail by, now lit by moonlight, his heart leapt inside as he finally realized that he had escaped. He was free. Well, free from Differe.

CHAPTER 3

DINNER CAME SOON after the introductions were made, and if the meal cost anything, Corwin made no mention of it to Joel. Joel had not realized how hungry he was until a steaming plate was put before him. Suddenly ravenous, he literally shoveled food into his mouth. When he noticed the others staring at him, he drew back and tried to savor his first taste of freedom.

Before they had gotten on the train, Joel had been forming a ball of questions in his mind for Corwin. He pondered whether or not to ask them as he grabbed his fourth piece of bread, which drew an absurd expression from Augie. He knew he had already displayed his own hesitancy in answering Corwin's questions. As he chewed his bread, Joel longed for answers but continued to keep quiet.

He soon reached forward to grab a round of seconds. With a mischievous grin Sebastian asked, "Like the food?"

"He must, since he's eating like a starving animal," chimed in Augustine before he could answer.

"I just can't help myself," Joel replied, sticking an overflowing spoonful into his mouth and purposely chewing with it wide open across from her.

"Disgusting," Augustine remarked.

Corwin turned his head toward the compartment door and cleared his throat. Joel was sure he did this to keep from laughing and appreciated that Corwin at least had a sense of humor.

Thankfully, Sebastian began a tirade of questions after finishing his dinner. Though she kept her cool demeanor, Augustine also seemed to have a looser tongue on a full stomach. Joel pretended not to show any interest in their questions and acted engrossed in his meal, as he was the only one still eating.

"Corwin, Joel and I were talking at the station, and we both heard that the weather's warmer in Waiz. Is that true?" Sebastian asked.

"Yes, it is true. In fact, you'll find a great deal different in Waiz in comparison to Differe. There are blue, sunny skies, and it's mostly green this time of year," Corwin smiled.

"So it's cold sometimes, too, then?"

"Yes, of course, but it doesn't stay cold."

Joel wondered why Sebastian was so interested in the climate and looked up to catch Sebastian's reaction to this statement, but instead caught Augustine's face. She smiled for the first time, and he imagined snow melting off her icy exterior.

Corwin explained that there were two distinct parts of the city, "Old Waiz" and "New Waiz." The older section resided in the hills and mountainside, whereas the new section was located to the south in the valley that extended out to the sea. Each eagerly took in the information.

Joel could imagine the wheels turning in Sebastian's mind when he asked, "Do the old and new sections get along all right?"

"For the most part, yes. They most certainly have their differences, but they strive for peace. They even have a—"

"Bridge," Joel said, interrupting Corwin mid-sentence.

Corwin nodded and continued, not skipping a beat, "to symbolize their commitment to maintaining peace with one another … though it also serves as the dividing line between the old and new city. What else do you know, Joel?"

"Oh, well, really not much. There's a big river that runs through the city. So, really the bridge may stand for peace or whatever, but that's actually the only way across the river," said Joel, as he cleared his throat.

Corwin nodded, choosing not to comment, which made Joel feel slightly insecure about his information. He was not sure what had made him open his mouth in the first place.

"Well, what are the people like?" Augustine asked excitedly, pretending that Joel had not even spoken. Though he was sure she meant to spite him, the change in subject helped put him back at ease.

"They are, well ... you'll just have to see for yourself. You will definitely enjoy the clothes." Corwin winked at her.

"How high is the mountain?" Sebastian asked.

Corwin took a sip of coffee. Joel noted that he seemed to enjoy being the one who knew all the answers. "The mountain is steep, treacherous even in some parts, but a handful of people still manage to live in the high places. Most of Old Waiz has stayed in the hills in kalonas."

"What's a *kalona*?" Sebastian asked.

"It's a kind of village, yet it's ..." He paused, reaching for the right words. "The kalonas are communities which remain extremely cohesive in their belief system and way of life."

"No free thinkers allowed, huh? The opposite of New Waiz, I assume," Augustine mused.

"Yes, to the second observation, but not necessarily to the first. Those who live in the kalonas find their boundaries very freeing."

Dinner was cleared, and the questions stopped for a while. Silence lingered over the compartment for about half an hour before the train suddenly came to a halt.

Joel looked around, feeling uneasy. "Are we already to Waiz?" he inquired.

"Oh, no," said Corwin, "it will take all night to get to Waiz. This is just one of the stops along the way. People getting on and off."

Joel couldn't stand it any longer. "How did you know how to get on this train?"

"I've traveled to Waiz many times before," was his simple reply.

"Well, yeah, I know, but what I mean is, how did you know how to find it? It seemed, well, a pretty unusual way to get on a train," Joel stammered.

Corwin leaned forward. "Joel, you're not telling us much, so I will not ask, but my guess is that you haven't been on a train before, and if that's true, then how do you know if my way was unusual?"

Joel could not tell if Corwin was being serious or just avoiding the question. Frustrated, realizing Corwin was right to assume he did not want to tell more than he had, he again decided to say nothing else.

Since the train would be traveling throughout the night, Corwin recommended they all try to sleep as best they could.

Augustine awoke to sunlight beginning to peek through the window. She glanced around at the sleeping crew and quietly gathered her two small bags. She had not seen any other passengers around their compartment, so when she reached the ladies' washroom, she laid out her bags on the vanity and locked herself inside.

She stood before the mirror half-dazed from a fitful sleep due to Corwin's loud snoring and the rocking of the train. *Who is that?* She winced at the girl staring back from the mirror. Her dark hair was a tangled mess of curls, and her face shone with the glossy "morning glow." She smiled, inspecting a straight row of unbrushed teeth and decided she would tackle those first.

With the toothbrush in her mouth she thought she actually didn't look half bad, considering the bizarre events of the past twenty-four hours. She could almost hear her mother's soft prim voice. "Augustine Bennett, your father and I may not have a lot, but what we do have, we need to care for properly. Please excuse yourself, as your appearance needs attention." Her mother's tone was neither mean nor caring, just matter-of-fact.

Before she left yesterday morning, her mother had made her change three times before she gave her approval to Augustine's apparel. Augustine remembered how annoyed she had been at her mom once she finally arrived at the station in her red coat amidst all black. "Ridiculous," she sighed through a mouthful of toothpaste.

In fact, it was the same word she had used the night before, when her parents had her spout out every left and right turn of the plans her father had mapped out.

"This is ridiculous. I can find the place. I'm sixteen years old, and, unlike you, I can read and write." She grimaced as she recalled the memory.

As usual, the words had slipped from her lips before she even had time to filter the thought. Augustine had braced herself for her mother's slap. To her surprise, she watched her father catch her mother's arm before the blow and let out a soft, "Stop." Augustine noticed his posture stiffen as he turned back toward her.

"That's enough," he said firmly. "I just want to make sure you can find your way around. I don't want anything to happen to you." He paused thoughtfully.

She waited for his next words, which always followed: "Or to Sebastian."

"Sir (as she addressed him when heated), I've cared for Sebastian his entire life. Has anything ever happened to him?"

"No, but Augustine dear, sometimes you have difficulty controlling your emotions and—"

She cut him off. "Not with Sebastian."

That comment had ended the discussion.

She spit in the sink and opened the smaller bag. Taking a moment to study it, her eyes traced the lines of the pastel pink leather, cracked with age and holding about a quart. "It's all there," she breathed in relief as she looked through the contents. She'd been furious at Joel for causing her to drop the bag but was shocked when he risked getting trapped inside to rescue it. In fact, the whole escapade of getting on the train had been surreal, an absolute nightmare. She had never experienced such a harsh adventure.

She had wanted to ask Corwin the same question Joel had, about how he had known where the train was. Corwin's evasive reply to Joel had been so gratifying that she had decided to hold the question for a later opportunity when they had more time.

Brushing her hair, Augustine thought back to their first meeting. She saw herself dangling Joel's bag in her hand, then snatching it behind her back while trying to manipulate an apology out of him. Her mental film skipped to the bridge, and she blushed, remembering Joel with streams of sweat flowing down his face as he returned her bag freely to her. She had not even thanked him. *And why should I? He used me to get to the train. He's obviously in some sort of trouble.* But she had no mind to get involved; she had enough on her plate caring for Sebastian.

"Joel, if that's even his real name, is not only untrustworthy but a bit peculiar," she stated in a tone, much like her mother's, to the girl in the mirror.

She thought he must be about eighteen or so. *Even though he acts like a thirteen-year-old,* she sniffed, recalling his table manners. She herself was a little over five-and-a-half feet tall, and Joel was a least a head taller. It was hard to tell with his coat on, but he appeared to have a slim figure. Though it was obvious he had a face full of freckles, his eye color eluded her. *Who cares, anyway? He'd better keep his word and leave us alone once we get to Waiz.* Though his shaggy hair made it hard for her to know for sure, she could have sworn she saw a piece of darkish jewelry in his ear. *What kind of boy wears an earring?* she thought, as she continued to pick him apart in her mind.

While washing her face, her thoughts continued bouncing back and forth. *He did help us find Corwin and had somehow known to wear dark clothes ... so I suppose he's not a complete imbecile.* In fact, she realized, he seemed to know a little about the city. "I wonder if he could be useful," she murmured. Then her father's face came into focus. *Stop being distracted,* she chided. She was determined to focus on her brother and needed to make sure Joel knew he was not welcome to accompany them in Waiz.

Her mind flipped back to the task at hand. She clicked her tongue in frustration, realizing she had left her change of clothes back in the compartment. She took another look in the mirror. "Whew, let's get to work."

Joel was having a quiet dream about reading a book in a peaceful place he did not recognize when he was awakened by the slamming of the compartment door. He rubbed his eyes as he sat upright, noticing that only he, Sebastian, and Corwin sat inside.

"Joel, would you care for some breakfast? It's complimentary, as was the dinner; it comes with the ticket."

Joel nodded, wondering why Corwin had made the latter remark. He then asked the obvious. "Where's Augustine?"

"She went to change clothes," Corwin smiled. "Not to worry, she'll be back soon."

Joel stretched his arms, groaned, and muttered, "Oh, goody." Sebastian and Corwin both laughed.

As Joel finished his bowl of oatmeal, he saw that Corwin was staring at him intently. Joel looked over his shoulder then back at Corwin. "Joel, before Augustine gets back I must speak with you about something."

Joel raised his eyebrows and then nodded towards Sebastian. "It's okay. Sebastian knows what I need to say." Joel put his fist under his chin and leaned forward to listen.

"Joel, Augustine feels very responsible for the safety of her brother. As you know, she can be very distrusting and suspicious of others."

"So I've heard," Joel said as he and Sebastian exchanged looks.

"Though her pride would not dare ask you again why you were running away"—Joel's eyes widened—"She told me while you were sleeping how the three of you met." Joel realized he must have been sleeping hard and hoped he hadn't drooled or done anything embarrassing.

Corwin interrupted his thoughts. "I know you two are not very fond of each other, but can you put yourself in her shoes for a moment, viewing her as a sister caring for her brother? How would you react if you met a complete stranger who appeared to be in trouble yet offered to help you?"

Joel understood his point but could not care less how Augustine felt. He stared back at the man in silence. *I have no intention of changing my perception of her.*

Seeing that Joel had no comment, Corwin continued, "In any case, Augustine and Sebastian have been entrusted to my care by their parents. I have been honest with you, and I ask you to be as honest as your situation will allow. It's fine with me if you continue on with us, but I need to know right now if there is anyone or anything after you that would put these children in harm."

Joel sat quietly as the other two waited for his answer. He tried to think of a way he could be honest but was not yet prepared to trust this man. Joel felt his issues were only a danger to himself. *Yeah, those things are definitely after me but so are the headmaster and his Templins at this point.* In fact, the fact that the lady from the inquiry desk already knew his name was a sure sign the Templins already knew he was gone. *Why would they even bother looking for me?* He searched his head for an answer.

He was not a stellar student and had been told on several occasions how unspecial, untalented, and unwanted he was at the most prestigious school in the country. He had not imagined the headmaster, his elite faculty, and his prize students (referred to as the "Templin guards") would spend much time in search of him. *I didn't take anything that belonged to the temple ... well, not exactly,* he thought, while silently noting the scroll in his knapsack. In response to Corwin's question, Joel felt a part of him thinking he had no other choice but to go on alone. *Why not? That was the plan all along.* He had escaped from the temple grounds by himself. You don't need these people, he heard his head say, yet another voice rebutted, You would never have found the train without them.

Joel saw Sebastian's little shoes on the floor. He had enjoyed the camaraderie he had formed with the little boy. He had seemed to care little about Joel's past before accepting him. *Corwin has to know I escaped from the temple.* Joel had gathered that from the way Corwin had spoken to the security guard. *He wouldn't have let me come this far with him if he thought I was a danger. I'm not a danger! There's no way the Templins can find a city they claim is only legend.*

Still second-guessing himself, he thought of Augustine. Joel had only a sackful of belongings and his word, which he had already broken, going for him at this point. *I have to keep it.*

Sebastian looked puzzled at how long it was taking Joel to give an answer. Corwin, too, seemed to have noticed his reticence, yet Joel suspected he knew all too well the debate going on inside his head.

Joel finally looked up and saw Sebastian's and Corwin's patient faces. "Well, I'm meeting some people there. I—I really won't be able to stay with you."

Corwin responded with a smile and said, "Hmm … yes. I think you've said that before."

"I told Augustine I'd leave her and Sebastian alone after we found you … but I wasn't exactly able to keep my word," Joel said defensively.

"I'm sure Augustine was glad to have you there to carry the wheelchair."

"And save her bag," chimed in Sebastian.

Joel smiled, "Well, I owed her one. Now we're even."

Joel had a nervous feeling in his stomach when the train came to a halt. He wished he could take Corwin up on his offer but was still unsure of his intentions. *At least I would know where I was going.* Joel sighed as the thought skipped through his mind. He watched Augie excitedly collect her bags. He knew keeping his word and leaving the group would be the safest option for all of them.

Before Joel could bolt, Corwin asked him to help Sebastian off the train, to which he readily agreed. He then asked Augustine to come gather their checked bags, and, though she looked hesitant to leave her brother, she obediently followed.

While getting off, Sebastian looked back at Joel. "I want to see the whole station. Can you push me to the middle?"

Joel pushed Sebastian to the center of the station and spun the wheelchair slowly in a circle so the two could take in the entire building. Joel leaned down by Sebastian's ear. "Huh, doesn't look like much."

The station of Waiz was a simple affair—a small, plain, tan brick house. It was hardly crowded, but the people who were there seemed to decorate the room. Each was scurrying around with looks of excitement on their faces and attire to match. Some were dressed like Corwin, in basic browns and khakis, while others wore vibrant, vivid colors that made Augustine's red coat seem drab.

"Do you think the different colors signify in which part of the city the people live?" Sebastian asked.

Joel was amazed at the young fellow's intuition. "That's a good guess … um, just another guess, but I'm assuming that would put Corwin in the Old Waiz category. Is that where you're planning to stay?" Joel had not meant to probe but was definitely interested in the answer.

"At first, I think," said Sebastian, not letting on any more than that. "Whew, it's hot," he let out, changing the subject.

"Yeah, it is," Joel agreed. "Here let me help you," he said, noticing Sebastian trying to take off his coat.

After the two had removed his coat, Sebastian asked Joel to push him over to the water fountain. Joel watched Sebastian take his first gulp, then shrugged his own coat off and tied it around his waist. He jerked back around, alarmed to hear Sebastian spewing his water. "Sebastian, you okay?" he asked as he gave him a whack on the back.

Sebastian cleared his throat and motioned for Joel to quit thumping his back. "Fine. I just got distracted."

Joel watched Sebastian's green eyes lock on something to the left and turned to follow his gaze.

Joel's jaw dropped upon finding the source of Sebastian's distraction. There stood a woman in a vibrant blue dress. The woman was so large that, though she was several yards away, he was able to make out the ocean print on her dress. She started walking towards them. Sebastian could not keep from giggling when he caught Joel involuntarily backing up. As Joel watched her move, he imagined two small cows being trapped inside her dress trying to burst through the fabric. After she passed by them, the two were able to see that a wave was printed horizontally on her dress against her backside. The "wave" crashed with her every step.

Joel and Sebastian stood in awe for a moment, then burst out laughing.

"Now that's what I'd call a rough day at sea," Joel quipped.

Augustine approached to shush them, though she was snickering a little herself.

"Joel, will you take me to the window, please?" Sebastian asked.

"Are you sure? There's plenty to look at in here," he joked, as he pushed him.

"Where's Corwin?" Joel asked Augustine.

"He's figuring out something with the tickets and getting the rest of the luggage."

Joel nodded. "How long have you known him?"

"Long enough," she responded briskly.

"Just asking a question."

"And I answered," stated Augustine.

Joel saw Sebastian shake his head in annoyance.

As Joel looked out the window, a sudden surge of doubt arose. *I don't have a clue where I'm going, and I'm out of money.* Suddenly, he began to rethink his plan. *Maybe I should stay with them. I've been somewhat helpful.* He decided to check his odds, and if nothing else, he would enjoy aggravating Augustine.

"You know, Corwin told me I could stay with you if I wanted."

She did not respond for a moment, but he could tell she was forming a rebuttal.

"Don't you have family to meet here?"

Joel thought it best to be truthful, as the answer was now obvious. "No."

As she turned to face him, something in her eyes said she knew that he was telling her the truth. "Well, then you should stay with us," Sebastian piped up.

Since Augie did not immediately oppose him, Joel gathered confidence. "I figured I might, since Corwin seemed to be expecting me."

"What are you talking about?" replied Augustine, who seemed to have been pulled out of deep thought.

"He had a ticket for me, didn't he?"

Augustine let out a breath of hot air. "Is that what you think?" she huffed. Joel was not sure how to respond to her accusation. "Did it ever occur to you that he was expecting someone other than you?"

Joel had not and felt stunned at the thought of it.

"That ticket wasn't for you. It was for—" She stopped short, and her eyes narrowed. "It was for someone in our family who had a prior obligation. So quit thinking you're so special."

He saw Sebastian lower his head, indicating that what Augustine had just said was true. Joel flinched at his idiocy. He had been right not to trust Corwin; this stranger cared nothing for him at all. Their meeting had been merely by chance. He then noticed Sebastian's bottom lip beginning to quiver. Joel, though furious, liked the little boy and feared upsetting him because he knew neither the cause nor the severity of Sebastian's condition. *I'd best give my regards before making any more embarrassing assumptions,* he decided.

He smiled down at Sebastian. "Hey, it's okay. It's about that time, anyway. My very best to you." Turning to Augustine, he gathered his pride. "I'm leaving now as I promised, and I hope you realize what a difficult, demanding, arrogant, obstinate, and ridiculous *girl* you are." Joel emphasized the word "girl" since she had referred to him as a boy several times now.

Sebastian's mouth fell open, and Augustine's eyes widened, as she stood there apparently speechless. As Joel brushed past her, he was not sure if her shock was from his being so rude or from surprise that he actually knew a few big words of his own.

The sun hit his face like heat from a warm flame as he walked out of the little station. "Wow, it's hot," he said aloud while pushing up his sleeves and unwrapping his coat from his waist. He squinted through the bright rays, giving his eyes time to adjust while he packed his coat into the already overstuffed knapsack. Bending down to pick up his bag, he realized he could actually see the ground. Ancient cobblestones rested underneath his feet and appeared to compose most of the surrounding streets. His road seemed to slope downward ahead so he assumed he was somewhere on the mountainside of Old Waiz.

As he began exploring, he felt a breeze run across his skin. The air enveloping his body warmed him to the bone; it was exhilarating. When he looked around, he saw mostly forest. Northward, he located several rock faces, and he could understand why Corwin referred to the mountain as "treacherous in some parts." Toward the south he was unable to make out anything besides the green flowing down the mountainside in front of him.

He had never seen any place without snow and marveled at the blue sky above. *Color is so much cooler than white*, he smiled to himself. Joel was hoping to make out the towers where the bridge stood or maybe even the ocean, but there was little around him besides the station. In fact, the only other structures in sight were several roadside stands. Horses and carts lined the streets, and, to his surprise, everyone was talking.

As he started toward the far end of the road, passing by the market stands, people shouted out "Hello!" and "Good day, young man!" Joel stopped in his tracks and pointed to himself. *Are they talking to me?* "Uh, hi," he waved nervously.

First no snow, now talking in public. It didn't take a scholar to see that these people were different, just as Corwin had said. Not only were they clothed in bright, contrasting colors, but their countenances seemed to match their apparel. Each person held a broad smile, and many were laughing as if they had just heard the most hilarious joke in all of Waiz. They positively oozed knowledge of the secret of happiness. *And the bizarre thing is, these people are old—like the Black Coats.* Joel was puzzled; they seemed so much younger.

One even said, "Welcome to Waiz," and threw him a shiny yellow fruit as he walked past.

"Thank you, sir," he replied, and stuffed it into his pocket. "I might need this for later."

Sarah had tried to describe as much as she could remember about the city, although she had not been there since she was a small child. *I guess she forgot to mention this was "Happy land."* But he soon found the smiles contagious, and, even though he was now alone, his step seemed a little lighter. With no road signs around and no companions to direct him, Joel decided to follow the road.

Augustine bit her nails, hoping Corwin would take his time getting back. She wanted Joel to have plenty of time to get ahead of them, and she was not sure she felt like telling Corwin the exact truth.

When Sebastian had given her a pitiful look as Joel walked out the door, she had responded, "I did that for you. He's in some sort of trouble. We can't trust him. He'd just get in the way. Quit giving me that look!" She had avoided his eyes since then and had begun to second-guess her dismissal of Joel.

Corwin returned sooner than she had hoped and raised his eyebrow. "What happened to Joel?" he asked, while looking directly at her.

She decided to stand by her decision and cocked her head sharply. "He decided he would go on alone like he promised," she said matter-of-factly.

"Uh-huh," said Corwin, apparently unconvinced, glancing down at Sebastian, who raised his eyes to the corners and shrugged his shoulders. "That's too bad; an extra hand would have helped." Corwin sighed and then looked toward the exit. "Well, collect your things, Augustine."

She looked at him in confusion and then realized that he meant for her to push the wheelchair and to carry the bulk of the luggage. Her sour expression returned as she picked up all the bags. She hoped Joel would be far enough ahead by now that Corwin wouldn't see him and discover the truth—although she was pretty sure he had already discerned what had happened.

The soft, angelic sound of soprano voices rang overhead through the temple sanctuary. Though its surroundings were dark and snowy, the inside of the building held a special glow as the massive choir stood together blending their voices into melodious sounds.

Isabelle fidgeted. *After all these years, you would think this place could afford some new robes.* She scratched an itch close to her gray collar. Just then she caught a handsome brown-haired young man and several of his cronies trying to ring the organ pipes located high behind them with bits of paper she was sure were covered in saliva. She rolled her eyes, catching a glimpse of the stained-glass displayed on the chapel's ceiling.

A blast of cold air rushed past her, causing a long, shiny, blond strand to fall into her eyes. She squinted past the ivory pews toward the front doors. Though only candle flames lit the front of the hall, she was sure there was no one by the cathedral-inspired doorway. *Someone must have opened the door to the right of the loft,* she mused, as she brushed her hair back out of her face.

Isabelle fumbled through the pages of her song book. *Surely, only two more songs. I haven't even started Professor Louis's paper.* A sigh blew through her singing lips as she asked herself, *Why didn't I start that two days ago?* An all-too-familiar sarcastic reply rang in her head: "*His name has four letters.*" Whatever, she told the voice that had so rudely interrupted her thoughts. *Twenty references by tomorrow ... I'll be at the library all night,* she guessed, as she tried to refocus on the words of the song.

Isabelle hated feeling distracted, as her passion was singing. She pouted while thinking of how schoolwork and deadlines seemed to poison her social and extracurricular life, leaving little room for much else. *Well, okay, except for the boy with the four-letter name.* She smiled and felt her golden locket rise and fall on her chest as she sang. By the conclusion of this internal discussion, the song had ended. The normally murmuring group of singers had, to Isabelle's surprise, fallen completely silent.

Isabelle jerked her head up from her song book and then stood on her toes, craning her neck over the others to see what the silence was about. All heads seemed turned toward Ms. Harte, the music teacher/ student/apprentice. In fact, Ms. Harte had many jobs here, and Isabelle was not exactly sure what her official title was. Isabelle soon discovered the reason for the cold air she felt earlier. A shiver went up her spine as she saw the headmaster walk across the plush red carpet toward Ms. Harte.

She should have known someone official had entered, for no one was allowed to use the sanctuary side doors that passed by the sacred alcoves. There he strode in his long, imported silk robes. *Now that's what I'm talking about,* Isabelle noted with appreciation, even though her jaw tightened. The presence of the headmaster generally made her heart beat faster, yet seeing him in this setting seemed to have an even worse effect than usual.

He made a motion to Ms. Harte, who responded with a nod of her head. The boys nearby gestured an excited "yes," knowing they were about to be freed from practice, and Isabelle, with references to collect, could not help but share their sentiments.

Ms. Harte faced the choir with a flushed face and unsteady voice. "Everyone, that sounded lovely. Please keep practicing in your groups, as we will need to cut today's practice short. Thank you all for coming. You are dismissed."

As Isabelle waited for her section to move out, she eyed Ms. Harte curiously. She knew the woman was terrified at this unexpected visit from the headmaster. *And so she should be,* judged Isabelle as she looked around. There were well over seventy students in the tenor section, yet it was obvious to everyone that someone was missing. Though Isabelle wasn't certain, she highly suspected that Ms. Harte was somehow involved in this mysterious disappearance. *He really did it*—she paused to think about such a feat. Isabelle envied his freedom but not the pressure of being hunted by Templins.

The silence in the room lingered as Isabelle got in line to leave. She moved cautiously down the steps, catching the eye of the spitball champion. He shrugged his broad shoulders and winked at her when she communicated her uneasiness at seeing the headmaster. His reassurance calmed her spirit, and Isabelle began wondering which section of the library would be best for her reference search. She was almost to the bottom step when suddenly a firm hand gripped her shoulder.

"What? Ma'am?" Isabelle barely had time to respond before Ms. Harte had yanked her completely out of line.

"Isabelle, would you gather my music sheets, please?" Ms. Harte asked loudly before hastily whispering under her breath. "I've been asked to bring you along."

Isabelle stood there speechless, mortified at being singled out in front of her peers. She was sure the entire choir knew Ms. Harte was capable of collecting her music, as the sheets lay on one single podium.

She gathered the music hurriedly while trying to regain her composure. She handed the petite, middle-aged woman the music and whispered close to her ear, "Why me?"

Ms. Harte continued waving goodbye to students, and Isabelle thought she might not have heard. Ms. Harte eventually turned slightly toward Isabelle and nonchalantly raised her hand to her cheek for a brief moment. That was the only explanation Isabelle needed before her face began to burn with shame.

Isabelle stood there, absorbing the shock from having the old wound reopened, a wound she had desperately tried to keep closed. She lowered her head in defeat, knowing she had no other choice but to follow Ms. Harte and stand before the headmaster. She blinked furiously to fight off tears of embarrassment and gingerly touched the side of her face as if to stave off old memories.

Isabelle followed Ms. Harte out of the sanctuary, her memories continuing to flash, tormenting her with feelings of both hate and love. Ms. Harte and Isabelle soon stood in the presence of the headmaster. Isabelle's eyes were on the floor when he spoke.

"Ah, yes, Ms. Harte and Miss Isabelle. I need to ask you both a few questions."

CHAPTER 4

AFTER WALKING A little over half an hour, Joel pulled the apple out of his pocket. He had wanted to try it from the time he'd caught it, wondering if even the food tasted better in this place. He laughed after taking his first bite. "Of course, it tastes better."

He still hadn't made out anything past the forest around him. The road had turned to dirt after making his first turn off the station street, and, so far, he'd been the only person on the road. *I wonder if walking everywhere is normal here?*

Just then, the image of Augustine waving scornfully at him as she passed by in a taxi ran through his mind. "She's such a brat," he said to himself as he shifted the bag to his other shoulder. As he gazed onward, he noticed the road up ahead disappeared under water. *Hm, this will be interesting,* he thought as he looked down at his boots and long pants.

By the time he reached the flooded portion of the road, he heard a creek rushing next to him. The creek flowed parallel to the road and was poorly dammed, sending excess water over the dam and onto the road. The dirt and water from the road had mixed into a thick mud, making it difficult to decipher how deep the murky water was. On the banks, he saw large tracks in the mud where some sort of vehicle had passed through. He stared at the tracks for a few moments, puzzled at what could have made them.

Wet boots would be miserable. He was sure he had several more hours of walking left. As he bent down to remove his boots, he glanced down both directions of the road. Since he had not seen a soul in the last hour, he decided he might as well strip down before crossing.

Joel soon felt the sun beaming through the trees onto his pale skin. The water was a cool welcome from the hot, dusty road. His first step at the water's edge made a funny familiar sound when his foot squished into the mud. Joel grinned when he heard the same sound with his second step. Aware that no one was watching him, he could not resist pushing both feet up and down in rhythmic fashion as he passed through the water. He soon added his own beat-boxing sound effects.

During his rendition of "The Anthem of Differe," he was interrupted by a clanging sound. Joel turned to find a pack of horses coming down the road. He could tell by the way they moved that they were attached to something. His spirits rose at the thought of company. Perhaps he could even hitch a ride; then he immediately remembered his lack of clothing. *Great.*

Thankfully he wasn't nervous about crossing the water. *If the carriage can make it, I know I can.* He bolted across the water with shirt, pants, boots, and knapsack held high above his head. He thrust his stuff down quickly when he reached the other side and ran back to the water's edge. As he washed the excess mud off his feet and legs, he could now see that the beasts of burden he had thought were horses were actually two large oxen.

The vehicle they pulled was bizarre, as it appeared to be part-carriage and part-wagon. Directly behind the oxen was the closed portion of the vehicle, which resembled a carriage with a driver atop. Joel watched the driver bounce up and down as the skinny carriage wheels moved across the road. The portion dragging behind the carriage was a flatbed wagon. When the oxen reached the water the driver encouraged them to cross with a crack from his whip.

As Joel strode up the embankment he heard the driver call out, "Come on, boys, just a little water."

Joel began to dry off, hoping to at least get his pants on before the driver made it to the other side.

The oxen splashed their way through the water and stopped short of the embankment. "Blast!" the driver called out.

Joel peered down to see that the back wheels of the flat bed were snagged by something in the mud.

"Hey! You there, can you see what's snagged the wheel?" asked the driver, craning his neck to catch a glimpse of the back wheels.

Joel ran back down the bank with pants in hand. "No, sir, it's too hard to tell from here," Joel called back.

"Well, since you're, uh, already undressed, do you think you could lend a hand?" the man asked.

Joel gave the man a quick nod and threw his pants onto the bank by his bag.

The back portion of the wagon seemed to be caught on a log that had flowed onto the road. "It's a log! It's running the length of the wheels," Joel yelled to the driver.

"Do you think you can move it by yourself?"

"Yes, sir. Give me a minute."

"Not in a hurry, can't really go anywhere," the driver chuckled.

Joel bent down to see if he could lift the log in any way. The wheels had caused the log to become wedged between them and mud. This had created a suction effect, causing the log to be snugly trapped in the mud. *Okay, let's try shoving it sideways,* he thought in frustration, but there was still no movement. "Uh, it's pretty stuck. I think the air in the mud has created some sort of suction—"

"What?" the driver interrupted.

"Forget it," Joel muttered to himself. "Do you think you could back up the uh, this thing up?"

"It's called a *norrac,*" the driver called out. "And yes. Stand back now."

The driver tugged on the oxen and they slowly moved backwards.

"Stop! That's good!" Joel exclaimed when he saw the log move.

As Joel was reaching for the log, the passenger from the carriage peered out the window, "May I be of any help?" Corwin and Joel locked eyes for a brief moment.

"You've got to be kidding," Joel murmured while turning away, rethinking the task.

"Joel!"

"No, I got it," Joel said, still feeling Corwin's eyes on him. Joel heaved the log out from the under the wheel. "Might as well," he told himself sarcastically. "I'm already undressed, as the driver pointed out. Okay, you're all clear," Joel shouted to the driver.

"Ah!" The driver exclaimed, as the oxen strode out of the water.

Joel shielded his face from the mud and water as the norrac followed the oxen. He washed off quickly and met the driver at the top of the bank.

"Many thanks to you, young man," he said as he bent down to examine the back wheels.

"Don't mention it," Joel said while thinking, *really, please don't mention it. Especially to Augustine.*

By the time he was back by his knapsack, the driver told him thankfully no damage had been done. "Where are you headed? To the next kalona?" the driver asked.

"Uh, yeah, how far is it from here?" Joel asked.

"Oh, Adams is about another hour's walk—say, wouldn't you rather ride? I'm much obliged to you." He motioned to the carriage portion of the norrac.

At this point, Joel was close enough to the norrac to catch Corwin and Sebastian staring at him.

"Joel, the least we can do is offer you a ride," Corwin called out.

Joel stepped closer, holding his pants in front of him.

"We're headed to Adams, also, so it wouldn't be out of the way or anything," Sebastian piped in.

When he approached close enough to see inside the open-air window, he saw Augustine had her eyes fixed straight ahead.

"This your only luggage?"

Joel turned around to see the driver pointing to his knapsack. "Yes, I left in a hurry," he said emphatically. When he turned to face the window he caught Augie staring at him. She blushed as her eyes darted away. Joel ducked his head into the window then turned back to the driver. "You know, I appreciate the offer, but I think it's a little too crowded in there for my taste," he said while gesturing at the empty seat by Augustine. Judging by the twitch at the corner of her mouth, he knew she'd heard him.

"You sure? It's awfully warm out," the driver replied.

"I'll take my chances. I'd probably freeze to death in there." This time he had gotten the reaction he was digging for, a full facial expression of disdain. He looked right back at her, put his arms around himself, and shook as he let out a mocking "br-r-r-r" sound.

Looking astonished at his boldness, Augustine said, "You're more accustomed to colder temperatures, anyway."

"Yes, as well as extreme unkindness, unfortunately." He walked past the driver and said, "Thanks, but I'd definitely rather walk."

The driver, clearly puzzled by this whole scene, shook his head. "All right, thanks again, and here's a little something for your trouble. Should get you a fine meal in Adams."

"Yes, Joel, thank you very much," Corwin called out.

Joel nodded and began putting on his clothes.

As the norrac bounced down the road, Augustine clenched her fists until the whites in her knuckles showed.

"Augustine," Corwin called to her, concern in his tone.

"I have nothing to say," she stated matter-of-factly, as she continued to ball her fists. Corwin was about to open his mouth again when Augustine gushed out, "I'm glad he's gone, and I don't care what he thinks about me. He's in trouble, you know. I told you on the train how we met him. Something's wrong with him. Did you see how he ate and how thin he is? He is entirely rude and obviously hates me. He would make quite poor company. However, I did agree with him on one thing—a ride with him in here would, indeed, be too crowded." She stopped, gasping for a breath.

"I thought you had nothing to say," Sebastian smiled.

Augustine soon realized what a mouthful she had just uttered, and the entire cabin burst into laughter. "Right. You should know better than anyone that I always have something to say," she said, smiling back at him.

The sun shone through the open windows, and fresh air blew throughout the cabin as the norrac continued down the road. Augustine kept brushing loose wavy strands from her face.

After some silence, Sebastian spoke up. "Well, rude or not, I liked him." He shrugged at Augustine and then turned to a pensive Corwin. "What did you think of him, Corwin?"

"I am unsure ... as interesting as Joel may be, he's proved to be quite helpful since we encountered him. He warned you against going to the inquiry desk, brought you near the place we were supposed to meet, carried Sebastian's wheelchair with no hesitation, rescued your mother's bag, and has just now freed our norrac wheel in his skivvies." He chuckled and took a deep breath. "He didn't appear to have any intention of manipulating a ticket from me. He eventually kept his word to you, Augustine, and left our party. I almost feel indebted to the young man," he said as he drummed his fingers on the seat. "But, if help is to be returned, there will be an opportunity."

"Well, you got him to Waiz, which I'm sure he couldn't have done by himself," Augustine mused.

"I'm not sure I believe that, either. He's traveled quite a distance by himself."

"Is he from the temple?" she asked quietly.

"I did not ask him, dear, and the extreme unkindness he mentioned can be found in many places," Corwin replied.

Soon the norrac came to a halt as the group arrived in Adams. While Sebastian waited to get out, Augustine thought about Joel. *I bet Sebastian hopes we'll find him again.*

Sure enough, the driver didn't lie, Joel thought as he came upon the kalona called "Adams" an hour or so later. The dirt road turned to rocky, sandy ground. On the outskirts of Adams, old, wooden fences guarded the green acres that surrounded several stone houses. The homes were humble, simplistic abodes with thatched roofs and brick chimneys. A few flower boxes hung by the windows for color. Joel spotted a variety of farm animals among the houses, and parked outside the homes were empty cart wagons alongside farming tools.

The land was slightly sloped, and he soon found himself walking uphill towards a coarse stone wall. The wall ran the length of the congested group of buildings he saw above it. As Joel looked up at the kalona, his eyes caught the highest point in Adams. *There's one place I want stay clear of.* A steeple rose through the middle of the crowded buildings.

As he drew nearer, Joel acquired company. He moved down the road with a crowd clothed in khaki along with their animals. Joel entered Adams cautiously through the iron gate, hoping he'd avoid Augustine's norrac. *Good. No sign of it,* he thought as he watched the road turn to cobblestone. After walking through the gate, Joel found himself on a side street.

"This street just circles the kalona," said an older woman, as she smiled warmly at his lost expression. "If you turn up there, it will get you to the square faster. The chapel you're looking for is near the square."

Joel returned her smile and nodded politely, pretending to understand why she was giving him these directions.

The old buildings were quite decorated, in contrast to the houses. Most were Tudor style, with a few vehicles beside them. The crowd around him thickened, as well as the noises, as he strode down the street. Joel took in the sounds from the people, the animals, and the exchange of commerce.

As he turned up toward the center of Adams, just as the woman had instructed, he realized how small the kalona was. He almost immediately came upon the community square. The square was filled with dozens of shops on either side. A courtyard lined with an open-air market filled the middle of the square. The area was hardly bare, but not near as crowded as Differe.

The smiling faces of the vendors he was approaching were kind and old. The sellers knew their products and claimed each was their "specialty," from leather to spices. After politely refusing several of them, Joel found himself in a grassy area near the end of the courtyard. An old farming truck drove past him, and Joel breathed in the smell of fresh fish. *From New Waiz?* Ringing church bells distracted him, along with a group of children dressed in uniforms. He watched a group of boys drop their school bags and run onto the grassy spot where he was standing.

Joel broke out into a cold sweat and felt panicky. As he pulled his hood over his head, he jumped at a thud that landed at his feet.

"Hey! Over here! Send it back, please!"

Joel fought the urge to run and picked up the soccer ball. He carefully walked over to the small group of boys.

"Uh, here you go."

"Thanks," one said.

"You wanna play?" another chimed in.

"I don't want to upset your professors."

"Huh?"

"Isn't this part of your recess?" Joel asked.

"It's summer here, silly," one smiled.

"This," another pointed to his uniform, "is for some boring history class about the Majestic that our grandparents make us attend every summer."

"The Majestic?"

"Where are you from?" one asked, as they all looked at him incredulously.

"Far away."

They all nodded while looking over his clothes. Wanting to get away, Joel asked, "Can you tell me where a pub is?"

Joel sat surrounded by flowers on the green field at the edge of the kalona's park with a cold beverage in hand. Truckloads passing by full of harvested goods filled his eyesight. Life here seemed simple, but good. With his mind somewhat at ease, he leaned his back against a grand oak and rested.

Augustine had just settled her things onto the inn's dresser.

"How long do you think we will stay here, Augie?" Sebastian asked.

She smiled at him. "Only a little while. Is the room okay with you? Good thing we are used to sharing one, huh?"

"Yeah. Fine," he replied, then changed to a whisper, "Glad it's just you and me ... I don't think I'd get much sleep with Corwin's snoring."

She laughed and pointed to the adjoining tightly shut door. "He can't hear you."

"Oh," he smiled, then rolled over to the window. "Can you hardly believe it, Augie?" he asked as he took in the view.

"What? The green, the warmth, the commonness?" she called back from the closet.

He sighed, "No, that we're here." He breathed heavily, "We are finally here."

She nodded and then remembered he could not hear a nod. "Mm, yes, it's been a long time coming."

She folded the clothes and placed them in the drawer, then walked over to the window to kneel beside him. "Hey, you ready to get out of this chair?" He gave her a startled, confused look, so she quickly added, "I mean, do you want your braces on now?"

"Oh, yeah. That'd be good."

"Okay, I'll get them."

She rummaged through a couple of packs before saying, "Corwin must have them; let me check."

"I don't want to be a bother."

"It's no trouble," she said quietly as she knocked on his door. When there was no answer she knocked a bit more firmly. "Still no answer."

"Maybe he's snoring," Sebastian giggled.

The door creaked slightly when she cracked it open. She glanced around the room, yet Corwin was nowhere to be found. Her nerves that had just settled became riled up again. She saw Sebastian's bag and scanned the room as she walked over to get the braces. Bits of paper with drawings and encryptions were sprawled across his desk. An ink pen lay next to bits of mismatched paper. She also saw a long strip of thick leather thrown across the bed with his coat.

"Augie, did you find them?" Sebastian called out.

"Yes, I'm coming. Corwin's not in here…. I wonder where he could be?" she thought aloud as she shut the door.

"Here they are, good as new." She locked the chair as she knelt down to begin putting Sebastian's braces on his little legs. "How are you feeling? Do you like the warmth here?"

"I can't tell, but I definitely like the way it looks." She felt his little hands form around her face. "Augie, if we find Joel again, do you think you could try to like him for me?"

"Sebastian, you're still thinking about him. He's—he's—"

"—Been helpful, like Corwin said."

"Well, I really doubt we'll see him again."

"But if we do?" he implored with big eyes.

"If we do, I will. I'll treat him in the same manner with which he treats me. Does that satisfy?" He rolled his eyes as she pried his hands away.

Just then there was tap at the window. Both peered down and caught Corwin grinning as he threw rocks up at them. Sebastian smiled and waved down at him as Augustine opened the window.

"Hello! Ready to have a look around?" he called up.

"Well, at least have some dinner," Sebastian yelled back.

"Fair enough."

"Could you lend a hand?" Augustine gestured towards Sebastian.

"Oh. Yes," he said, as if he had forgotten. "I'll be up in a moment."

A minute later a younger looking and robust Corwin appeared, wearing linen in shades of white and khaki. "Ah, ready, Sebastian?"

"Almost. Could you take me to the bathroom?" he asked.

"I can take you," Augustine piped in.

Corwin waved his hand. "I don't mind in the least."

Once in the bathroom, Corwin bent down to help Sebastian with his trousers. "Wait," Sebastian grabbed his hand. "I don't have to go."

"Then what is it you must need to tell me?"

"Well," Sebastian lowered his voice. "I realized when we were unpacking that, well, I must've given Joel the map Dad gave us for the station, along with a few others."

Corwin raised his eyebrows. "Well, we aren't planning to go back to the station, and you won't go anywhere without me."

"Augustine is going to kill me."

Corwin laughed, but then stopped when he saw Sebastian's worried face. "With her words perhaps, but that's only if you let her. Even then you have the choice of what to do with her words." When Corwin realized these words brought no comfort, he added, "Don't worry, there's no need for her to know right now. And I think it's quite possible that we shall meet Joel again."

As Joel returned to the square, the steeple bells clanged again, and it seemed as if the whole town had disappeared. The bells were the only sound Joel heard besides the wind as he strolled up the street. The shops were closed, and, as if on cue, a downpour started. Joel quickly ducked under an awning. He leaned against the storefront door for a moment trying to decide if he should make a run for it. *But to where?* The rain was so thick he couldn't see much past the middle of the road. He turned around and faced the storefront window. He pressed his face up to the glass, but was careful not to touch it.

The shop seemed full of both groceries and nicknacks. An old piano sat at one side and canned goods were in the back. Enticing fresh goods were encased before him and at the checkout counter. Just as his mouth began watering at the baked goods in front of him, Joel was startled when he thought he heard a muffled cry. *What the?* Joel wondered, as he leaned back out towards the road. *Nothing.* He then leaned toward the side of the building and heard another cry. As he listened more intently, he could hear that the sound was coming from behind the building. The next time he was able to make out the word "Help!"

CHAPTER 5

WITHOUT A SECOND thought, Joel dropped his bag and dashed towards the cry. He found himself in an alley next to the storefront as he yelled, "Hello! Hello!"

"Help!" came another cry, and this time he instantly located it. The yell came from a large, bald headed man lying on the ground a few yards away.

"Hang on, I see you!" Joel ran through the rain as it pelted down on his body.

"Hello? Someone there?" the man cried when Joel arrived.

"Yes, sir. Are you—"

"Oh, good," the man interrupted. "Please, do you see a pair of spectacles lying about? They're a bright shade of red."

Joel scanned the area and easily spotted the brightly colored glasses. "Yes, sir. I've got them," he said as he reached down to wipe the gravel and mud off the frames.

"Oh, bravo! Thank you!" the man replied as he reached out in the opposite direction of where Joel was standing.

He must really need these. Joel reached over to put them into his hand. "Here! Here they are!" Joel yelled over the sound of the downpour.

"Oh, bless you! Ah, that's better," he said while squinting at Joel through the rain. "You're a young man. Not from here? I don't recognize you."

"No, sir," Joel said as he wiped his eyes. "Can I help you up, sir?"

"Oh? Well, yes."

Joel reached down to give him a hand. "Uh, sir, you seem to have hit your head." Joel gestured, while touching the back of his own head.

The man winced as he reached for the back of his head. He looked at his bloodstained hand. "Oh, well, hopefully, just a scratch," he said, giving Joel his other hand.

"Were you carrying those?" Joel had noticed several large crates sprawled out behind him.

"Yes, I hope they're not ruined. Mushrooms," he said directly. "They are heavier than you would think."

Joel nodded sympathetically.

"You've done quite enough already, but could you lend a hand, perhaps? I understand if you can't spare the time. My shop's just down the way," he motioned. "I could also provide you with a dry place to stay for a couple of hours."

Joel eyed the gray skies above and quickly bent down to pick up a box. "Lead the way."

As the man stacked Joel's arms full of trays, he asked, "So, what's your name?"

"Joel."

"Just 'Joel'?" the man yelled through the rain.

"Yes, sir," Joel replied, while avoiding his eyes.

"Are you just passing through, or do you mean to stay a while? This way," he said as he walked back towards the storefront.

"I, well, I mean to pass through, but well …"

"No funds?" the man speculated.

"Is it that obvious?" Joel smiled.

"Well, yes, and you have a bit of a lost look about you," the man joked. "But tell you what, I need some help this time of year with extra folks around for the summer. Interested? You can stay on as long or short as you like."

Joel hardly considered the offer before sputtering out, "Yes, sir. That is very kind." He felt dumbfounded at the man's willingness to take in a stranger with no last name, so he added, "I'd be honored to help you."

"Then I'll be glad to have you," replied the shop owner.

Once at the door, both put down the crates. Joel went to pick up his bag, and the owner unlocked the door. When Joel turned back towards the man, he had his hand stuck out.

"Name's Haskell Rutherford. Been in Waiz most of my life and have owned this fine establishment for over twenty years."

Joel nodded, giving him a firm, wet handshake. Haskell was just under Joel's height yet many pounds heavier. The rotund man was dressed in a loose white button-down and khaki shorts. A few freckles dotted his fair-skinned face, and though his head was shaven, Joel could see that the man was mostly bald.

"Let's leave these trays out here to dry out," the man told Joel.

"What can I do for you now, sir?" Joel asked once inside.

"How about dry off," the shop owner said as he looked disapprovingly at the water dripping on the floor from Joel's clothes. He went behind the counter and threw Joel a towel.

"Oh, sorry, sir." Joel tried to grab the ends of his shirt and ring it into the towel.

"No matter, mine are dripping, too. There's a mop in the back."

"I have a change of clothes," Joel pointed to his bag.

The shop owner cocked an eyebrow. "That all your belongings?"

Joel gritted his teeth, wondering how many more times he'd have to answer this question. "Yes, sir. I believe in traveling light."

"Yes, apparently. Go ahead and change. The bathroom is behind this counter and to the left."

"Your head," Joel let out.

"Oh, yes, I'll tend to it. You go and change."

Joel was about to turn left when Mr. Rutherford called out to him, "Joel! There's also some soap in the bathroom. Put it to good use."

In the bathroom, Joel peeled the wet clothes off his body and studied his appearance. He had not thought to bring a comb of any sort and he carefully ran his fingers through his hair before he grabbed the soap. A few minutes later he looked into the mirror at the finished product. He smiled his first real smile in days at the dry clothes, clean face, and hair. He took a deep breath and sighed, "Finally, something good." The combination of the sigh and smile seemed to relax his tense muscles. He put his hands on the sink and then noticed an oddly shaped colored rock was beside his head. The rock was suspended on a gold chain that hung on a jeweled peg. Joel reached up to touch the stone then quickly pulled his hand away, grabbed his bag, and headed back to the shop.

As Joel passed through the store, he walked behind the long counter that held an assortment of meats, pastas, and sandwiches underneath. Every wall was covered from floor to ceiling with shelves. The shelves by the piano held mostly books, the back shelves were stocked with canned goods, while the one behind the counter held spices and sugars. Antique furniture and objects were housed throughout the place. An old mirror decorated with postcards sat above the upright grand. Pots, lanterns, and old filming equipment hung from the ceiling.

"Go ahead, have a good look around," piped in the old man, who was bandaging his head. "I'm fine," he said, when Joel started towards him.

Joel nodded, "Thanks, I will." Joel walked to the center kiosk and studied its contents. He supposed it was just cheap merchandise, for there were buckets full of each item. He saw jingle bells, handcrafted wooden books, woven baskets, and even colored stones like the one he had seen on the jeweled peg.

"Sir, are these just souvenir-type trinkets?"

"Trinkets! Trinkets, trinkets? No!"

Upon hearing Mr. Rutherford's offended tone, Joel realized he'd said the wrong thing. "Oh, well, they're very nice. Your price is generous. I just figured for such a bargain ..." Joel could not think of more to say.

"Oh yes, I see," Mr. Rutherford relaxed. "Yes, most people don't have much faith in these sacred stones anymore," he sighed sadly. "So, I had to drop the price."

The shopkeeper walked over to the shelf near the piano. "Joel, you're from far away," he declared as he grabbed a book from the shelf. "Here, take this and read it. The history is glorious," he said, and Joel saw the old man's eyes begin to mist. "The old days so glorious," he said again as a far off expression crossed his face. "Here, read it, and then we will discuss those items," he commanded, shoving the book into Joel's hands and pointing to the kiosk.

"No, sir, I won't be doing any reading on this trip."

At first the man appeared puzzled at Joel's rejection, but soon smiled. "Ah, pleasure trip," he said while placing the book back on the shelf. "Ignorance can be bliss, and you won't need that knowledge to make sandwiches, stock shelves, and take out the garbage, eh?" he shrugged at Joel.

"Hardly," Joel grinned.

"Come, let's go over the menu, and I'll teach you how to use the daily system. You know, counting, stocking, filing, and such."

Joel finished up the day having convinced the shop owner that he was more than qualified for the position. Though thrilled to have a job, even proud, the reality of food and shelter weighed on Joel's mind. He had secretly hoped the shopkeeper might see his desperate state and offer him one of the shop's floors for the night. *But I guess that would be asking too much. After all, I am a stranger from "far away."*

Thankfully, he still had the money from the norrac driver. It would buy him two cheap dinners, but was not enough for a night's stay at the inn. *Food is more important.* He went back to the park located at the edge of the kalona. He sighed as he spotted an inn directly across the street.

The rain had moved out, and the sky was full of pink hues. There was just enough light left to lead him down a worn path.

Corwin sat on his window ledge puffing smoke from his pipe out into the moonlight. The time was late, and many stars were twinkling signals to one another. The town below was sleeping—*just as I should be.* He puffed on his pipe thoughtfully. He was able to see more than stars from his window. Hours earlier he had seen Joel walk down the park trail across the street. He had yet to return. "Why aren't you making your way to New Waiz?" he had wondered aloud when Joel had passed by.

Corwin was undecided in his answer. His suspicion was that money might be a factor, but he couldn't imagine that would stop Joel completely. He glanced back at the mass of tattered papers and musty books sprawled on his desk. All sat next to the single candle that flickered in the room. Corwin raised his hand to rub his eyes and took another draw from the pipe.

Waiz had been a pleasant stop among his travels for many years, yet the pressure surrounding this visit had caused Corwin to indulge in his old habit of smoking. The children in the next room were now his responsibility. As if on cue, his pocket watch began to chime in the new hour. He put his pipe down carefully and crept towards the adjoining door. He cracked it open slowly and grimaced when the door hinges squeaked. Augustine turned over just as he peeked in. Sebastian lay sleeping with a book rising and falling on his chest.

Corwin smiled as he closed the door. *Looks the same as the last hour.* He walked over to the window to grab his pipe again. When he had first seen them in the flesh at the station all the hairs on his neck had stood up. He supposed he was in awe of the responsibility he now carried. The bit of pressure from the strained relationship he held with their parents certainly didn't help matters.

He leaned his head against the frame, frustrated at being awake. *Is it stress, anxiety, fear?* "I don't believe it's the responsibility that feels heavy, but rather the weight of their faith being in me," he said aloud as if he were conversing with someone other than himself. "Should I be believed in?" he posed the question to himself.

He turned back towards the candlelight. The chair next to the desk caught his eye. The heavy strip of leather Augie had noted earlier lay carefully folded over the chair. Hope filled his heart upon seeing the object. The candle seemed to burst into flame and light the whole room at once. He laughed as he got up. "Of course, weighed down, weighed down," he hummed. He walked over and ran his hand gingerly over the leather. He then fell onto the bed and into a deep sleep.

Joel awoke colder than he would have thought he would be for such warm weather. He rubbed his hands together and quickly turned his wrist to catch the time. He quietly crept to crack open the slats on the small barn's window. When he was sure he saw no one, he descended the ladder and made his way back to Adams. Though displeased that his current accommodation was a goat barn, Joel almost skipped to the shop. He could not remember the last time he had been trusted with any kind of position, let alone a real job. Smiling from ear to ear, even the pessimistic voice admonishing him not to "screw up" seemed to have little effect on his demeanor. He took long strides as he walked, addressing each passerby with pride.

"Good morning," he cheered to the vendors who were setting up shop outside on the street. Usually the people yelled to him first, but the culture had already rubbed off on him.

"Hello!"

"Off to work?"

"Have a good day!"

The responses varied a little, but all were cheerful.

By the time he reached the shop, he was beaming. He swiftly pushed the door open and gushed, "Good morning, Mr. Rutherford."

"Ah, hello there, Joel," he said as he brought out a tray of sliced meat. "Ready to get to work?"

Joel nodded as he hung up his bag and slipped on an apron.

"All right, just as we discussed, yesterday the menu for today is ready to put out, and this is to prepare for tomorrow."

Joel prepared the menu with such ease that at one point Mr. Rutherford asked, "Done this before?"

Joel was unsure if this was a jab or a personal question.

"A few times."

"Well, I need to get a few things from upstairs. Carry on until I get back."

"Upstairs, sir?" Joel asked looking up from his cutting board.

"Oh yes, most shops have a rooftop for storage, gardening, or quietness," he said as he winked and walked away. Just before he went upstairs he hollered out, "Oh Joel, turn our sign to 'Open,' please."

A few hours later, Joel had performed Mr. Rutherford's description of his job as well or better than anyone who had ever worked in the shop. Between customers, Mr. Rutherford taught Joel how to take orders and work the cash register. Joel tackled each new task with enthusiasm, and felt satisfied when he realized Mr. Rutherford was quickly beginning to like and trust him.

When the day was done, Joel was still energized despite the growls from his stomach.

"I guess it's about that time," his boss let out when the clock chimed. "Oh my, Joel! I am so sorry. I failed to give you a break for lunch today." The old man, with spectacles perched on his nose, glanced up from counting money.

"Oh, that's okay. I was too busy to really notice." His stomach growled again.

"There, get a before dinner snack," he pointed to the trays underneath the counter.

"Thank you, sir, anything else I can do for you?"

"Absolutely not, see you tomorrow."

As he sat in the goat house enjoying his sandwich with a glass of fresh goat's milk, he thought about what a good day he had enjoyed. For the past twelve years of his life, good days had been few and far between. Maybe there would be no need to go to New Waiz.

Just as he was about to take his last gulp, the barn door swung open. He dashed for cover, but he was too late.

CHAPTER 6

BEFORE THE SHOP opened the next morning, Mr. Rutherford asked Joel to take a few crates to the rooftop. Joel hurried so enthusiastically to the bottom of the steps that he almost lost his balance. "Now I know why Mr. Rutherford fell. These are heavier than they look," he said to himself as he shifted the crate of produce to his other hip.

Joel pushed open the door that led to the rooftop and immediately felt sunbeams glaring down on him. As he looked to the top of the stairs, his eyes met the sky. He cracked the door behind him and carefully ascended the steep, wooden staircase. With each squeaky step, an excitement built in his heart. *Maybe I'll see the towers.* That had been one of the sights he'd longed to see since arriving in Waiz.

He stepped onto the patio rooftop, unable to see past the mushroom crates he held in his arms. He saw the drying trays by his feet. He kicked them apart and quickly got to work. Just as he began putting the mushrooms onto the drying crates, Joel heard a little bird singing above him. His eyes followed the tiny sparrow to the rooftop's ledge. When the bird landed, Joel slowly stood.

The mushrooms fell out of his hands at the same time his jaw dropped. It was as if the entire place was in perfect balance of color.

The blue from the sky drifted into vibrant, green rolling hills. The hills meshed into deeply wooded, hunter green forests, but the most glorious color of all was the shimmering emerald sea. White foam from the crashing waves danced around a great deal of moving objects. *Boats?* Joel had forgotten such objects existed on the seas. Though he could not tell the shape or size of the images, he was sure they were moving.

"Ha!" He put both hands on his head. "I knew it!"

"What's so funny?" Joel was surprised to find Mr. Rutherford standing beside him.

"Oh, I'm—I'm sorry, sir. I was just—I mean, the mushrooms, and a bird," he gestured with his hands.

"That's quite all right," the old man said, as he put a pudgy hand on Joel's shoulder. "Magnificent, isn't it?"

"Yes," was the only reply that came to Joel's mind.

As the two stood there, Mr. Rutherford began pointing out landmarks and explaining the surrounding areas. "Much of Waiz's commerce takes place down at the sea. Right there by the docks." He pointed to where Joel was looking. "The trucks you see coming up here mostly bear treasures from the Valtina Sea," he explained. "If you haven't seen her waters up close or breathed in her sea air, well, you should," he paused as his eyes lingered on the water. Eventually Mr. Rutherford turned and gestured to the new city in disapproval. "Otherwise, there are not many reasons to venture to New Waiz."

"Oh, I see," Joel said, trying to act as if he agreed.

Joel glanced at the deep forest of Old Waiz before following it to green, rolling hills and then onto a series of boxy buildings. Joel paid close attention as his eyes darted up from the buildings. He knew the Bridge of Miren divided the north and south, or in this case the Old and the New. Soon he found what he was looking for—there they stood. In comparison to the surrounding New Waiz buildings, Joel found the dense gray towers to be smaller in stature than he'd imagined. The Bridge of Miren extended east to west and was easily seen after discovering the towers. The Pallas River that ran south underneath the bridge was a rich, cool blue. He tried to follow the river through the city, but soon realized it was impossible to do so as the river was eclipsed from sight by buildings located past the bridge.

"Shame, really. Look at the beautiful Bridge of Miren, and then," Mr. Rutherford changed his tone, "All those unfit buildings." He shook his head in disgust. "Now, if you want to see something of real value, Joel, turn around."

Joel had to blink his eyes to pry his gaze away from New Waiz, but he obediently stepped forward and turned around. Expecting a less impressive sight, he unexpectedly let out a surprised, "Whoa." He saw several other kalonas surrounding Adams. He then realized that Adams, as well as the other kalonas, sat on the hillside of what he now saw was an enormous mountain. The green landscape was sparse past the kalonas, and most of the mountain was covered with stony rock faces. Joel whistled with amazement at the height of the mountain as his eyes rose to its peak, which appeared to be covered with snow.

"Are there any roads on the mountain?"

"Treacherous trails only."

"But how would you get to the—" Joel stopped short and quickly scanned the mountainside to avoid Mr. Rutherford's scrutinizing gaze. "The temple, or—" He tried to recall the name of something that would satisfy his boss's curiosity. He chided himself to remember. "The Majestic place."

"Ah, so you have heard of our dear 'Majestic.'" Joel noticed that the man's round face softened, and his mouth lingered on the word "Majestic." "It's no temple, but a meeting place, my friend, right before the land climbs. It's in the very first kalona of Old Waiz."

Joel felt a thickness fall into the air around them. He moved towards the crates of mushrooms to take his mind off the change in the atmosphere.

"Almost forgot why I was up here," he said as he bent down. "I only heard about the Majestic because I ran into a summer class of children. I rescued their soccer ball," he said nonchalantly over his shoulder.

"I'm sure they were much obliged. I have several books on the Majestic," Mr. Rutherford said, as if asking Joel a question. Just then, to Joel's relief, the bells rang downstairs, indicating that a customer had entered the shop. "Finish up here and be sure to bring down some fresh herbs. The farmers' wives are always wanting some."

"Yes, sir."

Joel wiped the sweat from his forehead, all the while hurrying to put the mushrooms out to dry. The sun beat down on his back as he thought about the two cities. He viewed the mountainside when he had thrown the crates toward the stairs. *I'm not looking for a meeting place.* As he plucked the herbs from their pots, he took in the towers again. New Waiz seemed more exciting to him, but the peace and simplicity in Old Waiz had also proved enticing. *And, I have a job here.* He had managed to get to this place but could not help still feeling lost. *Maybe I'll bump into Corwin again*—which was really more of a hope.

When Augustine saw her reflection in the storefront window, she brushed the pleats of her new dress. She then peered past her reflection and saw an assortment of culinary delights. She found herself licking her lips when the bells rang above her head as she opened the door to the shop. Delicious scents filled her senses as she looked around.

The fresh trays of lunch meals ran the length of the shop, under the long cashier's counter. A plethora of spices were shelved on the wall behind the counter, and the back wall held a diverse group of canned goods. Augustine walked to the back of the storefront display to examine the baked goods. Before she had time to look, she saw Sebastian and Corwin grinning at her from outside the shop. She laughed in surprise. They both motioned that they were hungry and pointed to the park. She nodded and gave them a thumbs-up.

As she turned back around, she casually observed the place. She caught a glimpse of several antique pieces over to her right. She moseyed over toward the old things, noting the bookshelf stuffed with books and the old boiling pots that loomed over her head. Still, she saw no one, so she naturally ventured toward the back of the shop. She soon whispered, "Lovely."

Just as her hand reached out to touch the old set of ivory keys, she heard a voice.

"That's not for sale, dear."

"Oh, yes, sir," she said as she quickly drew her hand away, clearly taken back by the man standing behind her. "I'm just here to pick up some lunch," she said as she raised her head in a mildly defensive sort of way.

"Well, you've come to the right place."

"Oh yes, I saw your things in the window. They look delicious." She gestured toward the front.

"I like to think so. Come, pick out a few things," he said kindly as he led her to the counter.

She carefully looked over the menu and cases in front of her. "Hmm, I think two roast beefs and two turkeys should be plenty for the three of us, don't you think? It's just me, my brother, and my—our—friend." She hesitated.

"Should be plenty, I'd think. I'll get that right out to you," he answered and grabbed a pen.

"Oh, and may I have several of these?" She pointed to some fruit bowls.

When her request was met with silence, Augustine looked at the bald head in front of her and wondered if the man had heard her.

"Sir?" she questioned, noting his distracted face.

"Oh yes, of course." He straightened his red frames then began writing down her order. "May I ask how you acquired such a beautiful ring?" he asked, not looking up from the order pad.

"Oh, this?" She looked down to examine the item herself. "From my mother."

He nodded then leaned across the counter. "You know, while I get this going, I'd be most obliged if you would look over that old thing." He motioned to the piano. "I figure, since it's just been sitting there, some of the keys may need to be checked. You do play, don't you?"

Augustine could hardly contain her excitement. "Yes, I do. I'd be happy to look over the keys for you," she gushed.

"Wonderful," he said, as he went away to place her order.

Mr. Rutherford met Joel on the stairs. "All finished?"

"Yes, sir."

"Good. I have an order for you. I'm going to grab a few things from up here. The customer will be over by the piano." He handed Joel the ticket order as he moved past him.

Joel ran to the kitchen to gather the paper carry out bags. He heard a few notes from the piano when he entered the front of the shop. He stood on his toes in order to see over the kiosks and get a view across the room. He soon spotted the back of a young woman, who was standing at the piano and shuffling sheet music. Her olive-colored skin was in contrast to the light blue dress she wore. Her long dark hair was loosely pulled back behind her ears. The short shift dress revealed her petite curvy figure. Joel found himself unable to tear his eyes away from the beautiful silhouette and waited for her to sit down so that he might catch a glimpse of her face. When she turned her ear towards the keys, her profile revealed someone familiar to him. *Augie,* he grunted in his head.

He trudged toward the counter to grab the sandwiches, thinking hard about whether or not to spit in one of them. *Which one would she eat, turkey or roast beef?* Joel decided against this act of retaliation when he remembered how much he liked Sebastian and Corwin. In his mind they deserved a fine lunch. Even so, his insides squirmed at the thought of having to hand the order to her. All his excitement about having a job had dissipated at seeing her, knowing she would think even less of him. He hated the way she saw him. Unlike her brother, who had chosen to accept and trust him, Augie had continually reminded Joel how unwelcome and untrustworthy he was.

The image of her in the blue dress was stamped in his mind as he bagged up her order. He tiptoed and peeked over the kiosks again while listening to a few more notes play. As he stared at her, he realized he had dubbed her a "double-take." The boys at the temple had come up with this term for certain girls. It simply meant that one glance was not enough, so a "double-take" would be in order to take the girl all in.

Irritated by this fact, Joel stated the obvious to himself. *The dress looks new. She's the most dangerous kind of brat—a rich one.* He huffed as he walked back behind the counter, still continuing to rant about her in his head. *Why do I care what she thinks?* he questioned himself. He soon gathered his pride, rang the counter bell, and yelled, "Order up!"

The notes stopped, and, just as Augie approached, Joel bent down to pick up the bag. He put the bag on the counter and stood up when he saw her hands grasp the bag. Before their eyes met, he saw that she looked as if she was about to say, "thank you." The words, however, never reached her mouth. She gasped at seeing him, then took in a sharp breath and held her head in a more erect position. Silence lingered for a moment as each eyed the other with a look of disdain. Joel finally broke the silence when he opened the cashier's drawer. "Got everything you need, ma'am?" he asked in a sarcastic tone.

She glared at him when she handed him the money. Surprisingly, she continued her silence. Joel purposely counted the money as slowly as possible before putting it in the drawer. He enjoyed watching Augie get antsy as he did this and decided to count her change the same way. Just as he was about to hand her the change, he looked to make sure Mr. Rutherford had not returned. He then held out a half-closed hand with a cocked eyebrow. "What? No tip?"

"Not on your shift," she snarled, as she yanked the money out of his grip.

Just before she swung the door open, Mr. Rutherford called out to her, "Miss! Miss! Did you find the piano to your liking?"

Joel noticed that the bowing in her back lessened, but that her hand remained on the door handle.

"Yes. It really is a nice old piece. Just probably needs to be played some."

"Well, I close my shop at dusk and clean it before I go home."

Augustine turned and waited for his point.

"Hearing a melody may put some pep in my cleaning, if you want to come by and tinker on the old thing."

Her stiffened shoulders softened and she smiled.

He then held out his hand. "I'm Haskell Rutherford."

She nodded and shook his hand. "Augustine. Thank you, sir, for the offer," she said hesitantly. "I'll have to ask my friend if it's all right with him. I'm not sure what our plans are for the evening." Joel recognized the tone of suspicion he had encountered before. "Thank you for the lunch," she said politely and walked out the door.

"Thank you," called out Mr. Rutherford.

Joel watched the shopkeeper begin to stroke his chin thoughtfully. "Sir, need anything from upstairs?"

"No," he replied as if he was pulled out of deep thought. "But we'll need to throw out the scraps in a half hour or so," he said, still seeming far off. "Beautiful girl, don't you think?"

"I like blonds," was the quick reply.

The office of Headmaster Dark was adorned with the finest furnishings Isabelle had ever seen on the temple grounds. Ivory pedestals supporting the sculpted heads of several predecessors towered throughout the room. A great multitude of dark oak bookshelves housing hundreds of books stood behind his desk. A glass case running along the top of the bookshelves displayed his many plaques and trophies. A crystal cabinet filled with an assortment of different colored liquors sat to the left, behind his desk. On his desk, a golden clock and glass timetable sat side by side. A stone book, as well as several real books, was tucked at the opposite corner next to a large compass. A small jewelry case, which Isabelle had always assumed was the home of the ruby ring he wore on his index finger, sat in the middle of the desk. His wing back chair was cloaked in plush, green velvet.

The velvet seating was plentiful about the large office, but Ms. Harte and Isabelle were not asked to sit down for their interrogation. The two dared not look at one another. As far back as Isabelle could remember she had been afraid of Professor Dark. He held an aura about him, much like his name, that seemed not only dark but also very powerful. Isabelle had not been in his office often, but she had felt completely terrified in his presence the previous times.

As far as she knew, Professor Dark had been headmaster of the Temple of Differe for the past thirty years. The way he looked reminded her of the different generals she had studied in Professor Louis's class. The man kept his black hair short, parted mostly to one side and slathered with product. His salt and pepper mustache and dark eyebrows, however, were full and bushy. The creases on his forehead and around his eyes indicated that the man was nearing his late fifties. Isabelle knew he was slightly less than six feet, but the man was well-proportioned and filled out his official school garb just fine. She found his size just large enough to be intimidating.

He was not one to cross, no matter the cost. Due to the headmaster's violent temper, Isabelle had found that lying proved to produce painful consequences. Her eyes remained on the floor when the headmaster sat down in his chair. He cleared his throat, yet it was not his voice she heard the next moment.

"Miss Isabelle, are you aware of the prestige this facility exemplifies? Who attended this school? What we teach here on the temple grounds? What an immense privilege acceptance is?"

With each harassing question her heart beat faster, and she could feel her pale skin grow red and heated.

"And, might I add, what an honor it is to be permitted to remain here? Here, among the elite." The head Templin, Hertz Marlis, grew louder with each breath as he paced in front of her. "As you well know, the temple makes very few exceptions for those with ... hmm ..." He snarled, his shoes now right next to her feet. "What shall I call them? Flaws ..."

As the headmaster's right hand man cooed those words quietly into her ear, Isabelle looked with disdain at him, noting, as always, his short and unattractive appearance. His evil smile housed a row of crooked teeth and underneath his robe, she could see his bony, unathletic frame.

Isabelle had watched Hertz, only a few years older than she, gain his place of authority by sucking up to professors, cheating on his tests, and tattling on every student that crossed him or the temple rules. Though most of the students considered him to be an overall imbecile, they also found him to be downright merciless after gaining such power.

Due to his age and the fact that she had known him before he received the assistantship, Isabelle generally found it hard to take Hertz seriously. She remembered an incident in the past, when he was substituting and he'd caught her passing a note. Taking full advantage of his prideful nature, she had convinced him that his lecture was so interesting she had needed another student to help her write it all down.

He's an idiot. But even though she knew his talents were lacking, her anxiety escalated as he danced with his self-important power in front of her. Isabelle clenched her jaw to keep her teeth from chattering.

Then Isabelle saw a gesture of mercy from the headmaster, as he waved his hand and gave Hertz a stern look. "That will do."

After some silence, the headmaster addressed her, "Miss Isabelle, do you know the answers to these questions, or do you need reminding?"

Take a deep breath, Bella, don't stammer, she told herself even though tears of fear were springing to her eyes. "Yes, sir. I am reminded everyday of your kindness in allowing me to stay at the temple. I am continually grateful to you for the opportunity."

He straightened and smiled. "I thought as much, my dear. I am glad you feel that way." He nodded to Hertz. "Unfortunately, some students do not share your sentiments about me or the temple. In fact, they defy the very principles the temple was founded upon. The ones we continue to teach here." He turned to look in her direction. "Do you know any such students, Miss Isabelle?" he asked softly.

"No, sir."

Just then Hertz slid something across his desk.

"These rebellious students sometimes become so deceived by their lofty ideas of freedom that they attempt to leave the premises." His tone was one of disapproval. "But you see, my dear, these students are delusional and lost. They impose danger on others and even to themselves," he said in a sickeningly sympathetic sort of way. "Dealing with these troubled souls is a great challenge. In the past, it has always been best for them to be kept here until they can untangle their thoughts with temple truths and learn how to manage themselves appropriately. This, of course, is for their own safety." When he had finished, his bushy eyebrows rose and he looked at her expectantly.

Assuming he wanted some sort of affirmation, she nodded slightly. "Yes, sir, I understand."

"Miss Isabelle, recently a young man escaped from the grounds long before it was time for him to leave." He motioned towards himself. "Miss Isabelle, come here, please."

She managed to have enough feeling left in her legs to move her feet across the floor. When she arrived on the opposite side of his desk, he leaned forward. "Are you familiar with Joel?"

Her temples began to throb as quickly as her heart was beating. "No, sir," she said, darting her eyes away from his and losing confidence with every heartbeat.

He raised his eyebrows and swept his hand across his desk. "Please, then perhaps explain this," he stated as he lifted an old, tattered photograph to her face.

Stammering was the only natural response at this point. "Well, y-y-yes, well yes, I do remember him," she said through chattering teeth.

"Obviously," he nodded condescendingly.

"But, headmaster, I only remember him from when I was very young. I am very young in this photo," she defended. She quickly regretted this statement as she watched him begin to lose his patience.

"Miss Isabelle," he hissed. "Do you know where you are in this picture?"

Nausea welled up in her senses. "Please, sir," she pleaded, dropping her head towards the floor. "I do not wish to remember that time in my life. I can assure you I have not spoken to Joel in several years."

He waved his hand again, and this time the gesture alarmed her.

"According to your friend Mr. Langston, you were seen with Joel the night before he left."

Just then the head Templin pulled in Holt Langston, the "spitball champion." At first, Isabelle was relieved to see her tall, handsome, broad-shouldered boyfriend of two years, yet when she tried to catch his eye, he seemed indignant. Confused, Isabelle caught herself on the headmaster's desk and then quickly removed her hand. *How could he have seen us?* Her mind raced as she glared at him.

Though she knew Holt loathed Joel, he had rarely expressed insecurity about her past with him. There really was no need, as Isabelle had not spoken to Joel in the last few years prior to the night he left. Joel had caught her by mere chance. *He must have been waiting for me outside the music room,* she had thought after their meeting.

"Mr. Langston?" the headmaster spoke.

"Yes, I saw them that night, and heard him beg her to go with him."

The shock of betrayal coursed through her veins and quickly turned to anger. Though she was powerless in the situation, she found some consolation by imagining Mr. Langston enduring a fair punishment, enforced by her, for tattling.

Before Isabelle could respond, Ms. Harte interjected, "That's impossible. Isabelle was having a singing lesson in my study that night. You had asked me to give her private lessons, Master Dark."

Headmaster Dark looked disapprovingly at the boy. "Can you prove that, Ms. Harte?"

"Of course, sir, I have my sign-in book from that evening. You will also find no record of Isabelle attending dinner. She's a very dedicated student." Ms. Harte did not sound the least bit afraid.

As the blood rushed from her head, Isabelle could not understand why in the world Ms. Harte would vouch for her. She had spoken as much to Ms. Harte as she had to Joel in the past few years. In fact, the last time they had spoken had been about Joel, and the conversation had been fairly heated.

The headmaster pushed, "Ms. Harte, are you saying Mr. Langston is lying? Isabelle, is this true?"

Isabelle's whole body began to shake in torment. *What should I do?*

"Best to tell the truth," he instructed. "As you have already displayed dishonesty," he continued, while holding up the photograph.

Isabelle looked at Ms. Harte and then at Holt, who thumped his hand on his muscular chest. She sighed softly and slowly shook her head no.

The headmaster let out a large breath of air, "Ah, good girl." He reached across the desk and patted her hand. "Good girl." He smiled, and she felt a tiny bit of reassurance.

The headmaster called for Hertz and walked over to Ms. Harte. "Tsk, tsk." Headmaster Dark shook his index finger in her face. "Yes, please take Ms. Harte to Moonstruck. She's familiar enough. I'll be down within the hour."

Isabelle noted that Ms. Harte did not even flinch when Hertz roughly grabbed her.

The headmaster put his hand on his head, "Sarah, when will you learn? I shall teach you again and again until you do." Then with a cold voice he ordered, "Take her."

CHAPTER 7

ISABELLE RETURNED HER eyes to the floor, unsure she had made the right decision. After she heard the door close, the professor took her arm and escorted her to a nearby chair.

"Here, child, do sit down."

As she sat down she made brief eye contact with Holt, whose hand remained on his chest. She could not tell if his eyes pleaded for forgiveness or aired disapproval. She sank deep into the chair, feeling weighty enough to fall through the middle.

After she sat down, the headmaster returned to his desk. He reached in his top drawer, removed a small key, and held it up. Just before a robed Templin grasped the key, the headmaster quickly clenched his hand into a fist. "Wait, no. Mr. Langston?"

Holt snapped to attention. "Yes, sir?"

The headmaster opened his hand, "The usual, please."

"Yes, sir, of course," answered Holt, taking the key straight over to the liquor cabinet.

What is going on here? How would Holt know …

"Miss Isabelle," the professor interrupted her thoughts. "I need you to give a detailed account of your interaction with Joel before he left. And don't be afraid, child, the truth is good."

"Well, sir, he only came to me, to ask me to go with him."

"Go where?"

"I don't know." She shook her head. "You see, I cut him off before he could tell me."

"Are you sure?" the headmaster pressed.

"You were standing there long enough for him to tell you," Holt accused as he sat the headmaster's glass on the desk.

Isabelle began to tremble.

"It's all right, dear; just try to remember," the headmaster coached, as he raised the glass to his mustache.

Isabelle put her head back against the chair and closed her eyes, trying to drown out all the emotions she was feeling. The first recollection of the memory that came to her mind was hearing Joel say he had waited nearly two hours outside the music room for her.

Ms. Harte was right. Isabelle had skipped dinner that night, but her reason for missing the meal was not really related to her beloved singing studies. She had felt confused and strangely lonely that day. So that evening she had hid in one of the few places of comfort for her on the entire grounds.

Ms. Harte had known Isabelle since she was a small girl. In fact, Ms. Harte had helped to foster Isabelle's love for music and singing. Long before her relationship with Ms. Harte cooled, Ms. Harte had presented Isabelle with a precious gift—the key to the music room. If anyone asked, she had a special assignment and was Ms. Harte's apprentice. Out of respect and care for Ms. Harte, Isabelle was cautious in using the key even after their relationship faded to purely a memory.

Isabelle remembered not feeling like dinner that night, her mind wrapped around her to-do list. Her stomach had been in knots, so as soon as the others were off to the cafeteria, she had trudged over to the music room. She had knocked quietly and even put her ear to the door. *I distinctly remember making sure no one saw me go in*, she remembered....

After clearing her mind and calming her worries with a few melodies, she had blown out the candles and peeked out the windows. She cracked the door and, when she saw no one in sight, quickly slipped out the key and locked the door shut. As she started down the darkened path back toward her hall, she began going over her to-do list in her head once again.

Then all of a sudden, she was startled by a figure that jumped in front of her.

Her yelp was met by a firmly pressed hand against her mouth.

"Isabelle, shh. It's Joel," he said, as he dragged her into a bit of light for her to see him.

"How'd you know I was here?" she asked after he released his hand, knowing full well that he knew she had a key to the music room.

"Easy. You're unhappy," he stated firmly.

"Uh, excuse me, I am not." She backed away from him though he still held a loose grip on her arm.

"Right. No dinner, and didn't I hear a little composing going on? Doesn't that equal distressed?"

This is a fine meeting. She sighed, trying to remember the last time she had spoken to him. It had been a least a year or more, and any serious discussions had been longer than that. *And here he is telling me how I feel,* she thought, while shunning any feelings that he might be right.

"I'm fine."

"Yeah, that sounds very convincing."

She watched his head bounce above hers, trying to keep a look out. He soon dug into his pocket and produced a familiar item. "Lose this?" he asked, as he held up a golden heart-shaped locket.

"Ah," she gasped. "Oh, my! Where did you—thank you," she stammered, as tears formed in her eyes.

He nodded and placed it in her hand.

She stuck the object in her pocket and sighed deeply, relaxing her body. She then looked up into the face she had known all her days at the temple and smiled. "Hi."

He smiled briefly and let go of her arm. "Hi. Lock your box." He gestured to her pocket.

Silence lingered for a minute before Joel whispered, "I wanted to tell you something."

Having heard this tone of his before, Isabelle put up her guard, yet gently touched Joel's arm. "Well, I don't want to hear it."

"Bella," he grabbed her hand. "Please. Just give me a minute, then you never have to talk to me again," he said, slowly rolling out the last part. He waited patiently for a response.

"Okay, all right." She shrugged in surrender.

As he pulled her farther into the shadow she playfully cut into the solemnity of the moment. "This is serious," she said with exaggerated shock in her voice.

"Listen to me," Joel whispered. "I'm leaving."

"Leaving? Where?" Her eyes widened in the darkness then she thought aloud. "Here? You're leaving here? How?"

He did not answer but responded with an offer. "Come with me." He then grabbed both of her hands. "Come on, Bella. We always wanted to get out of here. I—I have it all worked out. We could finally be free."

Her heart leapt at freedom, yet her mind screamed the opposite. "Joel, leave? No. No, I can't—I can't leave school and—and—"

"Holt?" Joel interjected. "He could care less about you. Why can't you see that? He doesn't even know where you are right now. I'd give up anything to get you free, and he wouldn't even—he didn't even look for your locket."

"Joel, stop. I can't. My family." She tried to pull away but contemplated the offer as he held her hands tighter.

"Come on, Bella. Isn't there any part of you that wants to go?"

Maybe. Her heart tugged at his words.

"To finally get away?" He took a breath and brought her hands to his chest. "To be with me."

That push was all her mind needed to overcome the feelings of her heart. She raised her head indignantly. "Joel, I told you. It's over. We can never be together. It's over. It's over."

He let her hands go, wounded by her rebuff. He burst out angrily, "You'd actually rather be here?"

I need an out, she thought quickly. "You're—you're crazy. You can't even take care of yourself." She shook her finger near his face. "You're just running from school because you can't do any of your studies yourself."

"What!"

She could feel his body temperature rise as he grabbed her shoulders. "You actually believe everybody else, don't you?" He gave her a slight shake. "You think—you think—"

She saw the pain on his face, unable to say the words. "If I say I think you're crazy, will it make you leave me alone?"

He looked back at her, stunned.

In the most serious tone she could muster, she dug the knife deeper. "Joel, I can't follow a lunatic."

He stood back, crushed by her insult. He let go of her, unable to speak. Before she knew what she was doing she closed her eyes, cowered, and covered her ears. She stood in that position less than a minute before screaming in her head, *What are you doing? You're not seven years old.* When she opened her eyes she realized Joel had vanished into the darkness. She reached in her pocket and clutched the locket for a moment. She remembered it took only twenty steps to make it back to the music room. There were no candles lit on the second visit, and there was no singing. Isabelle's quiet sobs were the only sounds coming from the room.

As Isabelle's mind left the memories of that night she opened her eyes. She was once again met with her present reality. She had just finished her account and had told the complete truth as commanded. Unfortunately, her obedience had not produced any feelings of release, but more shame and humiliation. She hung her head as she awaited her fate in front of the headmaster. The long pause was painful and exhausting.

"Thank you, Miss Isabelle. I believe you have told me a true account. I do not expect you will hear from Joel again; however, you are to report to me if you are contacted in any way or think of any place he might have gone. Do you understand?"

She nodded compliantly, thinking, *anything to get me out of here.*

He stirred his drink and took a sip. "You will also speak of this to no one. And, as always, I recommend you focus on your studies at this time. You have several papers due, correct?"

"Yes, sir." *Thanks for reminding me*, she thought, wondering how he knew such particulars.

The headmaster picked up the old photo again and dug into an old wound. "Joel was a dear companion to you at one time. Seems he longed for something more."

She brought her hand to her forehead, hoping she would not have to respond.

"Mr. Langston," the headmaster raised his glass towards him. "Congratulations on your joining the Templin training program. At this time I have a recommendation for you, also."

"Yes, sir." Holt took out a small writing pad.

"You are embarking on a course where distractions are unacceptable." He stood and moved towards the boy, putting a hand on his shoulder. "Your company should match that of your rank. Strong stand with the strong and weak sit with the weak." He gestured towards Isabelle. "Do not associate with Miss Isabelle in a romantic nature. She need not serve as a distraction or weakness. Do you understand?"

Isabelle held her breath when Holt presented his answer. "Of course, headmaster, I wish to be one of the strong. Like my father."

"Ah yes, a fine Templin."

The headmaster frowned when turning back to Isabelle and flicked his fingers at her. "Miss Isabelle, that is all. You are dismissed."

Rough Templin hands firmly removed her from the chair. Isabelle felt her heart break and burn at the same time. She had just told the truth for nothing. Remorse overtook her as she realized she had lost the ability to see her enemies. Joel had always known, as had Sarah.

"Take her away," the headmaster said in the same tone he had used to dismiss Ms. Harte.

While being dragged out and receiving no solace from Holt, she felt moved to do something. "Wait, sir," she called out.

"Yes, Miss Isabelle, what is it?" the headmaster said, clearly annoyed she was still there.

"What—what will you do to Ms. Harte?"

"Ah. I will remind her why she should tell the truth."

With newfound courage she pressed on. "May I be reminded, as well?"

He gave her a look of shock, as did the Templins.

"The weak sit with the weak," she shot out.

He seemed stunned for a few seconds. "Er, no, dear. You have told the truth. The lesson is only hers this time. Send Miss Isabelle out, please," he said looking to Holt.

Tears she had been holding back poured from her eyes as she was walked out of the headmaster's office. When back on the temple grounds, Holt was asked to continue escorting her. He kept his eyes straight ahead and marched her towards her dormitory.

When she stopped suddenly he responded by gripping her arm firmly. "Come along," he commanded.

She swung back from his grip and opened her mouth to speak.

"Stop! Don't think of talking to me," he said with the same meanness she had seen from other Templins.

She trembled as she closed her mouth, her arm now in a death grip. She reached her hand up to smooth a tear from her face.

His grip relaxed and he whispered, "I'm sorry, Isabelle. I have to be one of the strong—for my family." She turned her head away. "We're going different directions," his voice trailed off.

He led her quietly to the pathway of her hall and let her go at the foot of the first stepping-stone. He nodded, "Goodbye," and turned quickly before seeing her reaction. As he strode away, he muttered almost too softly for her to hear, "You're not as weak as you think you are."

As Joel gathered the meal scraps in the kitchen he thought through his meeting with Augustine and Sebastian. *How in the world did we all end up in the same station, on the same train, and now in the same kalona? What are they doing here?* He still wondered if Corwin was really some sort of spy, ready to give him up at any time. When he thought of Sebastian, though, there was something so genuine about the little boy that made Joel trust him completely. *How could he and Augie even be from the same family?*

Joel went outside to scrape the leftover meat scraps into the dumpster. He noticed a stray dog and decided to share the scraps. As he watched the dog devour the pieces of meat he thought to himself, *that actually doesn't look so bad.* A clicking sound coming down the sidewalk interrupted his thoughts. He took in a deep sigh and turned towards the dumpster. When he began to pour the rest of the contents into the trash he heard a "Psst!"

Joel's heart skipped a beat. He wondered if he should ignore the sound. "Psst... Joel!"

Since the "psst" knew his name he figured he should look around. He soon found Sebastian leaning against the wall of the building. He stood about four feet tall with braces on both on his legs and arms. He smiled at the little fellow, excited to see him standing and happy to see him in general.

Sebastian smiled back, "How's Adams treating you?"

"Fair enough. How was your lunch?"

"Um, pretty good, but I couldn't quite finish it. I don't really care for roast beef. I came down here to throw it away."

"Well, this is quite an inconvenient place to throw it away," Joel smiled as he realized Sebastian had to have passed several trash cans before finding his way to the dumpster.

"Joel, here take it." Sebastian held out the rest of the contents from his lunch.

"No, I couldn't. I'm really—I'm not that hungry."

"Then why did you give that dog such a jealous look?" It was Sebastian's turn to grin. "I promise this is better than the food in there," he said, pointing to the dumpster.

As if on cue, Joel's stomach growled. "Yeah, guess I better. Thanks."

Sebastian nodded as he handed Joel the bag. "Sure. How'd you get the job?"

Through mouthfuls of food, Joel explained his meeting with Mr. Rutherford.

"Do you like it?"

"Yeah, I actually do. I mean, I have to deal with a few difficult customers."

Sebastian chuckled, and Joel was sure he knew full well who he meant.

"Where are you staying?" Joel inquired.

"An inn just down the street. What about you?"

"Oh, an old barn." Sebastian raised his eyebrows. "I've gotta save up some money. Have you seen the bridge yet?" Joel asked, wanting to change the subject.

"No, we haven't ventured that far down."

Sebastian stood up straight, and Joel could not help asking, "Sebastian, how old are you?"

"How old do you reckon I am?" he said, while posing for Joel.

"I really have no idea." Joel stroked his chin playfully, as if considering a weighty issue.

"Well, when you have a guess, I'll let you know how close you are." The little boy then suddenly started to walk away. "Break's over, Joel," he said smirking. "I'll see you here tomorrow?"

"Um … yeah, sure. Tomorrow."

CHAPTER 8

THE FOLLOWING DAY, Augustine picked at the green grass while sitting upright on a picnic blanket. The sun shone pleasantly through the trees, warming her bare shoulders. She loved the feeling of the sun on her skin—it was so much more pleasant than being hidden underneath a layer of coats. And just as Corwin had said, she had fallen in love with the fashion of Waiz.

Corwin had taken her to the market the day after they arrived. Though on a tight budget with the little money her parents had offered her, Augustine had enjoyed searching through the soft, light clothing. Most things she had bought secondhand, but the vibrant colors dyed into the fabric made each item appear brand new. Most of the secondhand barrels had arrived from New Waiz, which greatly peaked her interest about the southern city. *Though I must say, I am quite comfortable in this simple place,* she thought to herself as she overlooked the quiet hillside.

She had rested well at the inn, discovered her way around the kalona, and even enjoyed the people recognizing her as she walked through the market. She felt as light as her clothes. Adams was old, as Differe was, but the atmosphere was quite different. Adams seemed to have so much more life in it.

Augustine looked over at Corwin as he lay on the other side of the blanket. His complexion, though similar to hers, was slightly darker. *Probably because he's gotten more sun.* Corwin's build was *large*—there was no other word for it. He was tall, thick, and muscular. The burly, nearly forty-something's best feature though, in Augustine's opinion, was his smile. His dark brown eyes lit up every time he displayed his straight row of pearly whites, which considerably resembled her own. She did think Corwin was handsome, but in a rough, outdoorsy sort of way.

He was propped up smoking his pipe and staring off into the distance. Though she didn't know him all that well, Augustine could not help but notice how pensive he had become since they arrived in Waiz. She tried not to let his demeanor bother her, in hopes that his thinking was helpful in some way.

As she started wrapping up the meal spread in front of her, Augustine's thoughts drifted to a certain redhead. She had been infuriated upon meeting Joel, just wondering why he might still be in Old Waiz. She felt sure he was headed to New Waiz and still held high suspicion that he was trying to follow Corwin. *Why else would he keep finding us?*

When Sebastian acted excited about the possibility of seeing him, Augustine reminded him that Joel was dangerous and a liar. She had decided not to tell Corwin about seeing him but had let it slip out to Sebastian. This was only because Sebastian had seen her disturbed look as she walked out of the store and insisted she tell him what happened. *That seemed to be the opposite of Corwin's problem,* she judged. At times, she was glad he didn't dig for information. Other times she found his lack of questioning irresponsible and wished he would push, as in Joel's case.

"Corwin, did you enjoy your lunch?" she asked, pulling him out of his trance.

"Yes, I did."

"Oh, good. How about your pipe?" She drew in an apprehensive breath, wondering if she had picked up the right tobacco for him.

"It's fine, dear."

She exhaled loudly in relief, "I'm glad." She twisted her ruby ring around her finger then started again. "Uh … yes … I'm glad." She stopped short, again deciding not to tell him about Joel, but she could read the concern on Corwin's face.

"Augustine, is something on your mind?"

"Oh, no. Nothing," she said softly, while avoiding his direct gaze.

"Okay," was his non intrusive response.

A minute slipped by before Augustine remembered what she had really wanted to ask him. "Well, actually I wondered, is it safe here? You know, can I trust these people?"

He rubbed his chin. "Well, that depends entirely on what you need to trust them with." She gave him a look that indicated his answer was most unsatisfying. He chuckled, while showing her his wonderful smile. "Augustine, trusting others often takes some faith … and most times, letting go of the past."

Augustine could not have been less interested in getting into anything deep, so she went straight to the point. "Well, the shopkeeper," she pointed towards the shop, "where I bought lunch, Mr. Rutherford is his name, caught me staring at his old piano while I was browsing in the store. He asked me to inspect it for him and even invited me to come back to play while he closes up the shop."

As she relayed the story, Corwin felt like he was watching Augustine dance as she swayed and moved her hands with enthusiasm. "And well, Corwin, he seemed pleasant enough. What is your opinion?"

Corwin sat up and looked down into her face. She was so beautiful and grew even more radiant with the excitement of getting to do something she so loved. "I think that would be an excellent idea and quite entertaining, for Mr. Rutherford adores music. He's even bound to dance." He winked.

"So, you know him then? He's okay then?" She hesitated still.

"More than okay."

She smiled at him, which made his heart leap. He turned his head sharply as unexpected tears came to his eyes.

Joel was just beginning to bring down the crates for the next morning when he heard a small knock on the front door. Mr. Rutherford had already turned the sign to "Closed" and locked the door. "Mr. Rutherford?" Joel called out, hardly able to see over the large load he was carrying. The knock came again, and Joel hurried to the counter. He made out Augustine's silhouette as he wiped his hands on his dusting apron. Joel looked around. *Where's Mr. Rutherford?*

Augustine knocked forcefully the third time while also yelling, "I see you! I know you can hear me!"

"Good grief," he muttered at her persistence.

He slowly moved towards the door and undid the lock. He slightly nudged the door open, just barely able to peer out. "Yes, may I help you?" he asked sarcastically, noticing now that Sebastian was leaning on his crutches behind her.

"No, *you* cannot. I'm here to help Mr. Rutherford. He asked me to—"

She was then interrupted by Mr. Rutherford himself. "Joel, who's there? Oh, wonderful! So glad you could come, Miss Augustine. Oh, and who's this?" he asked as he pushed the door open. "You brought an audience with you."

She pushed past Joel toward Mr. Rutherford. "Yes, sir, thank you for inviting me. Would it be all right if my brother, Sebastian, came in, also?" She motioned to the little boy.

"Of course. Come in, lad. I'm Haskell Rutherford," he said, as he stuck out his hand.

"This is Sebastian." Augustine gestured to both of them, much to Joel's irritation.

As if I didn't know.

Each stood there for a moment looking at the other. Finally Mr. Rutherford spoke up. "Joel, please finish bringing down the crates for the morning. You know where the piano is, dear. Sebastian, I'm glad to have you. Let me know if you want to do something besides listen. We can always use an extra hand around here."

Sebastian beamed at the stranger who was treating him so normally. *It's as if Mr. Rutherford is unaware of the braces on his legs.*

Sebastian nodded confidently. "Yes, sir. I can be quite helpful."

"Well now, can you read and count?"

Joel watched as Sebastian nodded.

"Very well then, let's set you up right here. You can help me tally the money for today and help with the budgeting of goods we need to order." Mr. Rutherford grabbed two stools. "Here, Sebastian, have a seat. And, of course, one for you," he said as he handed the other stool to Augustine.

"Thank you." She smiled and walked toward the piano.

Her fingers had been covered in dust when she played earlier, so when Augustine spotted a rag lying on the floor, she used it to dust off the keys. She was about to sit on the stool when she realized the shopkeeper had not offered her any music.

"Mr. Rutherford?" she called out, then walked back over to the counter where he and Sebastian were counting change. "Excuse me, sir, where is your sheet music?"

"Oh, I'm afraid I don't have any music," he said matter-of-factly, then went back to counting his money.

Funny, I'm almost positive I used some the other day, she thought to herself, but she did not dare argue with the generous round man. She looked down, unsure of what she should do.

"Something wrong, dear?" the shopkeeper asked looking at her through the red spectacles on the end of his nose.

"Well, I'm not sure what I should play."

The shopkeeper put down the money and came around the counter. Augustine felt his warm hand take hers and lead her back over to the old piano.

He put his hands on her shoulders and signaled for her to sit down on the stool. "Now then, tell me, were you self-taught or taught by masters of some sort?"

"I taught myself," Augustine said sharply, being too proud to say there had not been money for teachers.

"Ah, perfect. Then think back to discovering the notes without paper and don't think about all the practicalities." He set her fingers on the piano. "Close your eyes." Augustine obeyed. "Now just play," he coached.

With eyes closed she took a deep breath. "But this is impossible," she blinked.

"Only until you try. I am quite certain you have it in you," he added softly.

She groaned and opened her eyes.

The shopkeeper gingerly chided her, "Nope. Keep your eyes closed. Let's just say it's an added rule tonight." Her shoulders dropped. "There now, I didn't say it had to be perfect, just from inside. Not performance, nor memory, or sheet music. Play what's inside you." And with that, he left her.

Augustine had never felt so vulnerable, even with so few people around. *Play the music inside me. No wonder you and Corwin are friends.* She wondered what it meant to play from somewhere "inside you." She rolled her eyes and tinkered on a few notes.

As Joel stocked the shelves nearby, he noted her arched back through her yellow blouse and dubbed her completely prideful. He watched unnoticed as she took another deep breath and bumbled through a couple of notes. Joel found this entire scene incredibly amusing as he stocked the bins off to the side. He wondered what "it" Mr. Rutherford thought Augustine had in her. The girl may have been married to her sheet music, but just hearing her "try" proved she must be a magnificent player.

Self-taught? What a joke. Sarah had been his music professor, and, though the piano was not her specialty, she had taught several of the best at the temple. He knew master-trained when he heard the music. It was always stiff, cold, and full of the "practicality," what Sarah might have called "technique," that Mr. Rutherford had referred to.

As Augustine played on, Joel got lost in his thoughts. He was sure no one was missing him at the temple, as he had managed to ostracize himself from almost every student in the place before he left. He had thought of the temple as little as he could upon leaving, but since he had only just escaped several days ago, the place was still on his mind. The temple grounds had been the only surroundings he had known for the past twelve years. Now he found himself comparing everything in Waiz to the Temple of Differe.

He had been surprised and grateful at Sebastian's quick acceptance by Mr. Rutherford. He glanced over at the counter. Sebastian was counting money with his new boss and clearly glowing at having been given a job despite his handicap. Joel smiled, thinking that in many ways he and Sebastian were similar and that he knew how Sebastian probably felt in that moment.

Just then Augustine started into one of Differe's patriotic songs from obvious memory.

Gag me. "I've finished restocking, sir. Can I help in some other way?"

"Yes, maybe so. Do you happen to know the name of this song?" he asked.

"Yes, sir, it's 'The March of Differe,'" Joel answered without thinking.

"Oh, is that right?" Mr. Rutherford paused. "Augustine! What is that pepping tune you're playing?"

The music stopped. "My eyes are closed, I promise, but sorry, I did cheat. It's from memory. It's 'The March of Differe.'"

Mr. Rutherford nodded his head toward Joel, who made a small bow. "Ah, I didn't think I recognized it. Well, I suppose that's where the three of you are from, correct?" he asked, but not in a prying sort of way. When none of them responded, Mr. Rutherford raised his eyebrows. "Well, in any case, you do know the song." He motioned for them to all move towards the piano. Augustine sat waiting with her hands in her lap.

"Miss Augustine, can you play with singers accompanying you?"

She nodded, "Yes, of course."

"Are you able to sing and play yourself?"

"No," she answered quickly as if not sure where the conversation was going.

"Well, I love historical facts and stories, as Joel well knows. I'd very much like to hear your 'March of Differe' with the words. Marches from history always tell a story," he said as he set up a recording machine. "Is it okay if I record this tale? I'm rather fond of collecting patriotic ballads."

Augustine blushed slightly and then nodded. "Sure, but I can't sing and play."

"Oh yes, I think I have a solution for that. Joel here is an excellent singer. I've heard him on the rooftop."

Joel felt his face turn the color of his hair. *How'd he hear me?* He only occasionally sang a phase or hummed a tune when he was up there, and he was always certain he was alone.

Sebastian covered his mouth to keep from laughing, and Augustine grinned as she asked, "Do you know the words?"

"I'd prefer not to sing with her, sir."

"But you do know the words then? Could you write them down?"

Joel did not respond right away and ran his fingers through his flaming hair. "Well, I know two versions to the march."

Mr. Rutherford looked curious and excited. "Well, I don't think I can stand not to hear them right now—how about a bonus? I'll give you a bonus and Miss Augustine a free lunch tomorrow for the recording."

Joel had just heard an offer he could not refuse. He swallowed his pride and smiled. "Deal."

Mr. Rutherford was delighted. Sebastian purposely avoided Joel's eyes to keep from laughing; however, Joel managed to elbow him in the ribcage as he moved toward Augustine.

"Can you play it in F Major?" he asked in an arrogant tone while looking down at her.

"No, I only know it in a lower arrangement," she responded coolly.

He smiled, took her hands, and moved them up the keys. He bent close to her ear. "Liar," he whispered.

She quickly moved them down. "Lower only."

Thankfully Joel's tactic to get her in his key worked. "Okay, version one first."

Joel belted out the march with great talent and Augustine played flawlessly. Sebastian's jaw dropped as they finished. Augustine looked up at Joel, a furious look on her face.

"Nice job," he told her smugly.

"Oh, that was glorious. Now for version two!" Mr. Rutherford rang out.

Joel bent down and moved Augustine's hands again. "Sure you don't want to try F Major?" he asked softly.

She looked confused, but kept her hands in place this time. "Fine," she muttered.

"Ahem, I wrote this version myself," Joel stated.

Augustine rolled her eyes as Mr. Rutherford said, "Splendid."

Augustine played a simple introduction and then Joel began his masterpiece. He sang the first line in the most irritating, high-pitched voice he could muster. Augustine startled at his voice but kept playing.

As each line was sung, the mood lightened and each individual, except for the singer, began to double over in laughter. As Joel finished the last line, Augustine removed her hands from the keys and held her stomach as she laughed. She even looked up in Joel's face. He smiled back at her and made a small bow.

She let out a clap with her hands and shouted, "Encore!"

His smile faded momentarily and then he stated in a professional tone, "No, that's all for tonight. I have to rest my instrument." He motioned to his throat. "You'll have to come back tomorrow night for more."

The crew was still laughing when they left the shop. Mr. Rutherford broke in with a serious tone as he locked up. "Joel, will you see that they get home?"

"Yes, sir, of course," he nodded, the smile still on his face.

"See you in the morning, and Miss Augustine, don't forget to come by for your free lunch."

She waved, "Yes, sir, goodnight."

The three of them walked down the dark streets of Adams.

"'They dress of all black and wholesome speech lack.' How did you come up with all those lines?" Augustine asked, chuckling.

Joel shrugged in the darkness. "Just came to me."

"Do you mean you didn't make that up until tonight?" Sebastian asked.

"Well, I'd made up about half of it. All you have to do is start thinking of words that rhyme, and it fits together," Joel stated nonchalantly.

Augustine stopped and looked at him perplexed. "Hmpf" was all she said.

"You're a good piano player," Joel said, deciding to compliment Augustine while he appeared to be in her favor. He expected her to say in her grown-up tone, "Why thank you, I learned from the best masters." Instead she just shrugged as he had. This odd response puzzled Joel.

"Yes, she is excellent," piped in Sebastian.

"Here's our stop," said Augustine back to her brisk tone.

Joel stopped as she opened the door for Sebastian. "Goodnight. Don't forget to come by tomorrow for your free lunch." Joel waved.

"Yes, goodnight." Augustine turned sharply to pick up Sebastian.

"Augustine, do you need some help?" he called out after her. She shook her head "no" without turning around. He sighed and walked toward the lonely park path.

Augustine plopped Sebastian down at the top of the stairs and helped him to their door. After she unlocked it, Sebastian pushed past her toward Corwin's room. He was knocking on the man's door when Augustine picked up a note on the desk.

"Corwin! Hello? We're back!" Sebastian called out as he knocked.

"Sebastian, here's a note. I don't think Corwin will be eating dinner with us," she said nervously as she opened the envelope.

All of a sudden a thump hit the window, and she jumped. "Sebastian, quick! Get away from the window." She quickly blew out the candles on the desk. The thuds soon sounded like pellets hitting the window.

"Augie, it's rocks. Maybe it's Corwin," Sebastian whispered, now crouching and squeaking across the floor toward her.

She held her breath, aggravated that she could not see Corwin's note in the dark. She moved toward Sebastian, and both watched the window.

CHAPTER 9

THREE MINUTES PASSED before the rocks stopped. Augustine pressed a finger to her lips as she slowly rose and inched her way against the wall toward the window. She saw no one below. "I think they're gone, and it wasn't Corwin," she said, feeling worried. Sebastian stood and lit the candles again. She went back over to the desk.

A small knock hit their door as she grabbed Corwin's letter. A familiar voice accompanied the second knock. "Sebastian, Augustine? You there?" came Joel's muffled voice from the other side of the door.

Before Augustine could stop him, Sebastian opened the door. "Yes, we're here," he replied, smiling brightly.

"Was, was that you throwing rocks at the window?" asked Augustine, barely able to contain her fury.

"Yeah, why didn't you look down? I was making sure you made it up to the top. It didn't look like Corwin was here." He motioned next door.

"He's not, we were so sc—"

"Just how did you know he was staying next to us? And how'd you figure he wasn't here?" Augustine hissed, as she interrupted her brother.

Joel's answer sounded truthful but puzzled, as if he didn't know where her hostility was coming from. "I've seen Corwin sitting on his window ledge at night. Tonight, his room wasn't lit, so I assumed he wasn't here. And when your light went out suddenly," Joel shrugged.

He appeared to be honestly following Mr. Rutherford's orders and seeing them home. Augustine told herself that Joel figured if they weren't safe and Mr. Rutherford heard about it, he would lose his bonus. *He's sure I'd tell Mr. Rutherford if he had not seen us home properly.*

"Well, we're fine, and I'm not inviting you in," Augustine said stiffly.

"Yes, I can see that," he said, almost apologetically.

Sebastian broke in between them and shook Corwin's note in Augustine's face. "Look at this." Then he turned to Joel and tugged on his shirt. "Come on, I want to show you something."

"Show him what?"

Sebastian rolled his eyes. "Just read your note," he said, as he dragged Joel over to the bed.

Joel had yet to see Sebastian stand his ground with his sister and he liked the feistiness he saw.

"You scared her to death," Sebastian whispered, motioning to the window.

"That would explain why your light went out. Sorry. Where's Corwin?"

"I don't know, but I'm getting hungry for dinner. You?"

"Always hungry. Is someone looking for you?" Joel asked.

Sebastian did not answer right away. "When you're in a place where you know no one, wouldn't you find it scary if someone pelted your window with rocks?"

Joel took a minute to think it over. "Yeah. I guess so. Um, you wanted to show me something?" he asked.

"What are you both whispering about? Joel, you—you can't stay here!" Augustine shouted.

"Yes, here it is." Sebastian dug into a bag full of books and drew one out for Joel. "Look, my—" Sebastian eyed Augustine to see if she was listening. "I got this as a present. Look! See, it's a songbook from the Temple of Differe. It has all the songs they sing there."

Joel tried to act excited for the little boy. "Wow, what a nice, er, gift," he said, inspecting the pages.

"Some of it's quite boring."

"Sebastian!" Augustine scolded.

"But some of it's also quite nice."

"But mostly boring," Joel agreed as he closed it shut.

"So, you know it, do you?" Augustine asked.

"Well, I'm ready for dinner, anyone else?" Joel asked, completely avoiding her question.

"Yes, me!" Sebastian rang out.

"Thank you, Joel, for checking on us, but we must see you out now. We've had enough excitement—"

Suddenly they all heard it—a loud clatter from Corwin's room.

Joel bent down toward the floor to see under the adjoining room's door. When he saw no light come on after the second clatter, he instinctively put a finger to his lips. Augustine drew Sebastian back against the bed and watched silently as Joel tiptoed over to the door to Corwin's room. Sebastian looked up at Augustine and mouthed, "the note." Augustine shrugged. Joel picked up Sebastian's crutch as he neared Corwin's door. Then it dawned on him that he might be able to see if Corwin's balcony doors were open. He rushed to the opposite wall near the window as the sound of things crashing in Corwin's room continued.

Joel plastered himself against the wall and slid over enough to see that Corwin's balcony doors were propped open. He pointed and whispered, "His doors are open." Joel ran back over to the desk closest to Corwin's door and pushed it sideways to pin the door shut.

Augustine held Sebastian with her hand over his chest. "What are you doing? What are you going to do?" she asked, her face white with fear.

Joel was not sure what had gotten into him, but he felt Mr. Rutherford had given him some sort of strange responsibility for these two. His mind kept reminding him that his frame was slim and that a crutch would not be of much help against the clanging culprit.

"I'm keeping you safe. If I'm not back in five minutes I want you to run into the park. There's a goat house—a barn—halfway in toward the farm. Wait for me there. Do you understand?"

"You'll not tell me what to do," Augustine stiffened.

Irritated, Joel ignored her and looked down at Sebastian. "Do you know where it is?"

Sebastian nodded.

"But why can't we just go there now? Why do you have to go in the room?" Augustine pleaded.

"Good thinking." Joel nodded at her. "Once I get in the room, go ahead and make a run for it, but keep to the left side of the walkway. It's less lit. Okay," he ran his fingers through his hair. "Get your stuff. What do you need to take?" he asked.

They all scrambled to gather a few things, and Augustine nodded when she was ready. Joel grabbed a poker from the fireplace rack and gave Sebastian his crutches. He motioned for them to head for the door.

"Wait! Joel, Corwin's balcony's fake, I mean, it's just for looks."

Joel shook his head at Augustine in confusion.

"It's narrow," she whispered. "There's no room on it, that's why you've seen him sitting on his window ledge."

Joel nodded that he understood and hurried them out the door. It only took him a few seconds to cross the floor and slide the window open. He flung himself over the window ledge and onto the inn's siding.

Joel stood still on the siding for a moment, and let his eyes adjust to the darkness outside. He waited to make sure Augustine and Sebastian made it safely to the path. He saw Augustine, with Sebastian on her back, run into the shadows toward the left as he had urged. Joel smiled as he saw Sebastian raise his small fist toward him before they faded into the darkness.

Joel took a deep breath, grasped the fire poker tightly, then leapt onto the ledge of Corwin's balcony. He saw feathers from Corwin's bedding fluttering out the doorway as he crossed over onto the balcony's narrow platform. When he heard the unknown intruder trying to pry open the room's adjacent door, he mumbled, "No you don't," and stepped into the room. He was unseen and quickly ducked near the side of the bed. He saw the intruder was a man draped in a cloak. His insides churned. *A Templin?* Hate rose in him as he inched toward the end of the bed. The man paused, catching his breath then walked toward the balcony. Joel rose, but before he could lift the poker the man swung his fist into Joel's stomach.

Joel fell down, dropping the poker with a loud clang. With his other hand the man pulled out a long sword that glistened in the moonlight.

"What do you want?" Joel asked, holding his stomach, astonished at the sword.

"The papers. Where are the papers?" the voice said frantically. "The maps!" When Joel did not respond the man kicked him in the mouth, knocking Joel face first to the floor again.

"I don't know," Joel replied, as he wiped fresh blood from his lips.

"Oh, yeah. What's this?" Joel received another blow to his face as the man ripped Sebastian's maps out of Joel's back pocket.

The man stopped to examine the maps, giving Joel just the opportunity he needed. Joel grasped the poker and jumped to his feet. The man thrust his sword forward while hurriedly forcing the maps into his cloak.

"Oh, you want a sword fight, do you?" he mocked Joel while smirking at the poker. He swung, and Joel jumped back, barely avoiding the blow. At the next swing, the man's sword met Joel's poker. Had Joel not had two hands on the object it would have flung out of his hands.

The blow was so hard Joel saw sparks fly into the room.

Suddenly the man drew his sword back and began to step away. His eyes widened as if he was seeing a ghost. A soft glow beamed into the room, casting shadows throughout the place. Joel could not determine the light's source but watched it surround them, unveiling the man's face. He was a younger man with great scars marring one side of his face.

"Don't! Please, don't hurt me," the man whimpered, dropping his sword tip down.

Joel looked behind himself, unsure if the man was talking to him. When he faced forward again, Joel thrust the poker out, gaining confidence in the mysterious light. "Give me back the maps."

"Please, please, they'll kill me. I must take them. Have mercy on me." The man sprung toward the balcony.

Joel got to the ledge just in time to see the man jump onto the old siding of the inn. He was down the gutter pipeline in a matter of seconds. *He's had lots of practice with this.* He watched the man run swiftly in the opposite direction of the park and toward New Waiz. The street lamp revealed his cloak was a deep green and kept most of the man, even his head, completely covered. If Joel hadn't seen the scar on the man's face, he would have had no way to identify him other than the green cloak.

Joel was completely baffled by the turn of events. *So much for a safe walk home*, he thought, as he surveyed Corwin's room. The entire room had been completely turned upside down. Drawers were pulled loose and turned over, the mattress had been stripped, and feathers were scattered about the room.

Joel remembered that Corwin had carried at least one personal bag, and that bag was missing. He saw only blank scraps of paper and pencils on the floor by the desk. "Did Corwin know someone was coming?" he wondered aloud. He carefully checked the bathroom and closet for anything important, but saw nothing. Either Corwin had his valuables with him, or the Green Cloak now had them in his possession.

He carefully climbed back over to the siblings' room. Augustine and Sebastian had taken two soft bags with a few items. Joel grabbed one of the larger, hard leather bags and stuffed it full of clothes, Sebastian's books, and Augustine's girly things. Just before he cracked the door to leave, he noticed a small, pink bag under the bed.

Augustine's body had responded with serious flight instinct. She had run the entire way to the goat house with Sebastian on her back. She breathed heavily and neither said a word until they approached the old barn.

"This is it," Sebastian whispered in her ear.

She sniffed when she got inside, and, to her surprise, the place was clean and full of iceboxes holding fresh milk and cheese. There were two lit lanterns in the middle of the barn on a small, round table.

"Let's hide up there," she said while pointing to the hayloft and grabbing a lantern. After climbing the ladder, she found Joel's "bed" and thrust their bags close by. She hoisted Sebastian up the ladder, and both fell back in the hay for a few minutes.

"Augustine, what did the note say?" Sebastian asked emphatically.

"Oh, dear, yes. Here, it's in my pocket." She fished it out quickly and read it to them:

> Dear children, I hope you enjoyed your time with Mr. Rutherford. He's been a trusted friend of mine for many years.
>
> Yesterday I discovered I was missing several items needed for our journey to New Waiz. I need to retrieve these items as soon as possible.
>
> Forgive me, Augustine, for not saying goodbye and leaving this in a letter. I had to catch the train. I would have taken you both with me, but this trip would have been too difficult for Sebastian to travel.
>
> You are not to worry. I will return in five days, on the eve of the twelfth. I have left some money under the bed for your meals. The board is paid until the fifteenth. If you should have any difficulties, let Mr. Rutherford know, as he is aware of my journey.
>
> You should explore the Old Waiz Museum while I am away. Also, you will see Joel soon enough. I think it would be best to stick together.
>
> Corwin

She folded the letter on her lap.

"Augie, did you get the money?"

She gasped, "No, I was in such a hurry that I didn't even think to find it. Oh, dear." She ran her fingers through her hair and quickly caught them in a tangled knot.

"At least you brought your brush." Sebastian smiled, trying to ease his sister's mind. "Maybe Joel got the money."

"That's just what I'm afraid of," she replied, still fidgeting with her hair.

Joel's heart was thumping with adrenaline as he hurried to the barn. Every few steps he would go off the path and wait a few seconds to ensure he was not being followed. By the time he reached the goat house, he felt safe and entered with a little confidence.

"Augustine? Sebastian?" he called softly.

"We're up here," came Sebastian's reply.

"Oh," said Joel, wondering how he got up there. "Um, do you want all your stuff up there? I tried to bring as much as I could."

"Will we have to stay *here*?" Augustine asked, looking over the ladder.

"Unless you have a better idea. I wouldn't recommend going back to the inn tonight," Joel muttered, unsure of how excited he was to share his quarters with these two.

"Is—is the ... what happened in Corwin's room? What all did you bring? Well, do you mind?" Augustine motioned down at her skirt as she shakily stepped over the ladder.

"I'll send it up if you like."

"No, I'll come down and look through it. Um, please." She motioned with her hand for him to turn around.

He thought she was being ridiculous, but obliged her all the same. When he turned around he was facing the large icebox. "Would you both like some milk and cheese?"

"Yes, I'm hungry," called out Sebastian.

"Is it from those goats outside. I mean, would it be stealing?" piped in Augustine.

"Probably, but I'm pretty sure we're already trespassing."

Joel did not mention that the owner of the barn had caught him red-handed his second night there. The man had taken pity on him and told Joel he could have as much milk as he wanted, as long as Joel personally milked the goats himself.

"Nothing in life is completely free," the man had told him.

So we're just stealing cheese.

Augustine sighed, "Well perhaps we can find the farmer and pay him back later."

"Is that two yeses?" Joel asked.

"Yes," both chimed in.

Though Augustine indicated all things were accounted for, Joel noted she was frantically searching for something as he brought the lantern over to her.

"Did I miss something?"

"Well, I was looking for—oh my! Never mind. Is there any water in here? Any rags?" she asked, while looking around.

"Yes, there's a pump right outside. What is it?" he asked, noting her worried face.

"Your face needs tending to. Go on up there. I can get the water. I'll use this." She found a clean sock in her bag.

Minutes later all were in the loft with a milk and cheese picnic.

"Here, let me take care of that," she gestured with the cloth.

"I can't see my face, and I'm starving. Let's eat first." He brushed the cloth away, but quickly added, "But thanks for doing that."

"Here's some crackers, these are mine," he gestured to Augustine.

She looked at him curiously. "You are quite—" She paused, as if to catch herself.

Joel waited, bracing himself, then finally interjected, "Yes?"

"Well, interesting."

"With your vocabulary, 'interesting' is the best you could come up with?" he questioned.

"Sorry to disappoint." She stopped short, taking in a mouthful of food. Both Sebastian and Joel chuckled.

"I'll tell you what she really thinks. You are a vocal genius, prodigy of songwriting and singing, your culinary talent is exquisite, and you're the most resourceful young man we've met in a long, long time," stated Sebastian while imitating Augustine's posture and hand gestures.

He swiftly dodged the cracker aimed for his head.

"All right, your stomach is full," Augustine said as she held up the sock and moved towards Joel. "I'll do it," she said as she brushed his hand away, "but I expect a full account of what happened after we left."

"Well, there was someone in Corwin's room."

"Could you see who it was?" she asked, while gently brushing the dried blood off his face.

Joel shook his head. "The room was completely dark. But, well, just let me finish. I got into the room without being seen and watched the guy rummage through the desk and drawers."

Joel took a swallow. "He was looking for something."

"That's what it sounded like, all right," Sebastian butted in.

"I thought he was headed out, and I had the poker from the other room. Just when I was about to grab his legs he spotted me, and, well, I took a few blows, obviously." Joel pointed to his face and stomach.

Augustine shook her head in dismay.

"He had a sword."

Their eyes widened at him.

"And he knew how to use it."

Joel recapped how the poker got knocked from his hand.

"Did you talk to him, ask him what he was looking for?" Augustine asked.

"Yeah, papers. He said something about papers and maps."

"What happened next?" asked Sebastian, on the edge of his seat.

"Oh, well," Joel scratched his head, still wondering about the next part. "I got the poker back in my hands. The guy swung once and missed. The next hit we clashed and … I don't know what happened. He—he—I don't know—he was afraid of me. He dropped his sword and asked me not to hurt him."

"You're making this up?" Augustine interjected, moving away from him.

"No, I'm not. There was a bunch of light, and that was the only time I got a glimpse of his face. It was scarred badly on one side."

"And then," Sebastian encouraged.

Joel smiled at him. "Well, then he got away."

"Where was he going? Did he say?" Augustine asked.

"No, our conversation was pretty short. He ran in the direction of New Waiz. He wore a green cloak, looked like something official."

The other two looked just as confused as Joel.

"He just got scared and jumped off the balcony? I suppose he didn't even get what he was looking for," Augustine mused, dabbing Joel's face with something slimy.

"I doubt it. Ugh, what is that?"

"Hold still," she commanded.

"Well, none of Corwin's stuff was in the room, but whoever the Green Cloak is working for sounds dangerous," said Joel thoughtfully.

"Why would you say that?" she asked as she looked into Joel's hazel eyes.

"The man said they'd kill him if he didn't take, um, if he didn't find what he was looking for," Joel said carefully, leaving out the fact that he did get away with several maps.

"Well, Corwin's left for several days, and I'm sure he didn't leave anything important lying about, thank goodness. So, the Green Cloaks, whoever they are, shouldn't have any documents from us."

Joel's stomach ached from being hit, but that wasn't the only reason. He also felt sick knowing that the Green Cloak had snatched the maps before he escaped, and yet, he wasn't ready to frighten Augustine.

"Is Corwin coming back?" Joel asked.

"Of course, he's only gone until the twelfth."

Much to Joel's surprise, she handed him the note. *Someone's trust meter just went up,* he thought as he skimmed the letter. "Hm, well, it's getting late, and I have to go to work tomorrow. About time for bed."

Augustine looked at him in shock. "You mean, we'll just sleep up here?"

"You have the whole barn. You can sleep wherever you want." Joel watched her fidget in response.

"Is it safe? Have you been staying here?"

"It's safer than the inn tonight," he said and watched her shake a little in response. "It's fine," he added, trying to reassure her; then he realized she had been fidgeting since she washed his face.

"Augie, are you cold?" He reached out for her hand. "Good grief," he said as he touched her icy fingers. "Why didn't you say something? Where's your red coat?"

She sighed and shook her head. "It's not here. I—"

"Shoot, I forgot to check the closets," Joel sputtered.

"No, it's not there. I sold it so I could buy some lighter things for us." She lowered her head a bit.

Sebastian shrugged his shoulders, indicating to Joel that he didn't know why his sister was ashamed, especially in front of someone whose belongings fit into a single knapsack.

Joel walked over to his stash of goods. When he came back, Augustine barely looked up at him as he cleared his throat. He peered down at her with an odd expression.

"What?" she asked defensively.

"I think you're a lot more 'interesting' than me." He tossed his coat down to her and turned before seeing her reaction. "Night."

All was quiet for a few minutes.

"Joel, what should we do?" came Sebastian's voice.

"Sebastian, what's wrong? Can I help you?" Augustine let out.

"Joel?" came his voice again.

"What do you mean 'what should we do?'" Joel responded.

"I mean, what should we do while Corwin's gone?"

"Oh. Well, I think you should hang out at the shop with me and Mr. Rutherford, and how about we go to the museum on Saturday? We're only open a half-day." Joel was surprised when his suggestion was met with silence. "Um, sound good, Sebastian?"

"Yes. Uh, are we going to tell Mr. Rutherford about tonight?"

"I don't know." Joel paused, "Oh, and Augustine?"

"Yes?" she called out in the darkness.

"The money is in your pink bag."

CHAPTER 10

AFTER HOLT WALKED her back to Thymes Hall, Isabelle cried, but only for a few minutes. She soon swept the deep wounds into the pit of her heart and to the back of her mind.

You've got a paper due tomorrow. Snap out of it, she told herself. *Maybe a broken heart will be inspirational,* she thought ruefully as she wiped the last tear from her eye. She thrust her remaining energy into the paper for the rest of the evening. While giving it the final proofread she muttered, "For how wretched I feel, this is not nearly good enough."

Just before dawn, Isabelle put on her heaviest overcoat and made her way through the early morning blizzard. As she rushed through the cold wind, she felt half-dazed from a sleepless night. To her advantage, a heavy snow was falling, so none of the Templins saw her make for the covered path to the music room. As she paced down the path, her heart pounded in fear that Sarah would throw her back out into the cold. *Will she be able to forgive me?* was the fearful question that resounded in her mind.

Through the night, visions of Sarah had run through her head. Some were of her forgiving Isabelle and freely welcoming her back into the music room. The others were more like nightmares. Isabelle was sure the "lesson" Headmaster Dark had intended for Sarah was much like the many she and Joel had received.

"Beating the body to break the mind," she heard his voice saying in her head.

Holt had once asked her if she hated the headmaster.

"No. I'm too terrified of him to hate him," was Isabelle's response.

Much to her chagrin, she had also thought of Holt throughout the night. *Now, "hate" may be in order there.* However, she had nevertheless envisioned the handsome young man taking her back into his strong arms.

Isabelle's mind was flooded with memories as she approached the classroom. The memories ran as far back as her first day here.

Our pasts ... maybe she'll remember the past and be able to forgive me, Isabelle hoped as she nervously fumbled with her key. She gently pushed the door open.

"Ms. Harte," she called out softly into the darkened room. "Are you here?"

She quickly lit a small candle on the professor's desk and made her way to the upper room that held Sarah's quarters. Isabelle glanced at the floor beneath the apartment door.

Looks dark in there, too, she thought, swallowing a lump in her throat. "Ms. Harte, are you in there?" she whispered as she knocked gently. "It's Isabelle. Please, if you're there, please, I'm sorry." Tears choked her voice, but she pushed through to continue, softly lamenting, "So very, very sorry, for everything."

She hung her head and retreated back down the steps to the classroom.

Though the room was regularly heated to keep the instruments in good condition, Isabelle had still known to bring her large coat. The room was naturally cool and seemed even colder when it was silent. She glanced around the room, eyeing the instruments one by one, knowing full well the only instrument she had ever mastered was her own voice.

Each music maker seemed to be looking back at her in contempt for betraying their master.

"She'll be here soon. I know she will," she said out loud to these silent companions. She slid to the floor next to a pile of blankets and waited.

During the hours that passed, Isabelle rehearsed her apology over and over in her mind.

I must say what I am sorry for. I need to make a list. She hurried to find a pen and piece of paper. *I'm not leaving anything out.* She wrote, "I'm sorry for …" and number one on the paper. *Betraying you and Joel. That should definitely be first.* She sighed heavily with regret. "It was only to keep Holt…. No, don't put that. The 'why' is not important." She quickly scratched out his name. *I just need to list the actions, not the excuses. I refuse to blame anyone but myself.*

An hour past breakfast, she had managed to write three full pages of offenses.

What could be keeping her? She looked at the door, a shadow of fear beginning to creep into her mind. *Why would he keep her down there so long?* She began to worry as she waited and eventually grew weary of looking at her list of sins. Soon the bell rang, alerting her that her paper was due.

She had desperately wanted to skip class, but felt she had no choice but to attend since she had a paper to turn in. Faking sickness would be no use. *Everyone knows by now I had a meeting with the headmaster.*

That being the case, she was unsure how to prepare herself for her entry into the class. She was certain her regular seat had been moved in all of her classes. *Yes, the Templin groupies will have seen to that.* She decided to arrive a few minutes early, hoping to draw the least amount of attention towards herself as possible.

When she walked in, just a few students were already sitting in class. As she approached Professor Louis's desk, she saw his gray head bowed over a stack of notes.

Without looking up, he made a motion with his hand. "Just put your paper there in the box with the others." He finally looked up and straightened his glasses when he noticed the student had not moved away from his desk. "Yes, Isabelle? Can't seem to part with your paper today?"

"Oh no, sir, I'm very glad to be rid of it." His teasing actually caused her to smile.

She lowered her voice when she spoke the second time. "I was just wondering if my seat assignment had changed."

He looked around to see why she might be lowering her tone, then whispered playfully, "No, not since yesterday."

Since she had not expected this answer, she stood there for a moment before being able to respond. "Oh, okay. Thanks."

He nodded and then went back to his stack of papers.

As she walked over to her seat, she was certain that Professor Louis knew her well enough to know that she would not ask such a question for no reason.

Maybe he doesn't know what happened with Holt. Ugh. The thought of sitting next to Holt made her feel nauseated. She shakily pulled out her history book and tried to focus on the words of the chapter they were supposed to be reading. When the bell rang again, Isabelle held her breath when she heard a group of rambunctious young men burst through the door.

"Just in time, as usual. Papers here." Professor Louis wrinkled his brow in disapproval. "Mr. Langston, now that you are in league with the Templins I will expect you to be on time, as well as your assignments. Do you not agree that Professor Dark would expect the same behavior from one of those representing him?"

There were a few snickers in the class, and, though Isabelle tried to look straight ahead, she could not help but want to see his reaction.

Holt stood tall and smoothed his official robe. "Yes, I will. I mean, yes, he would. I will get here more promptly," he said in a serious tone.

"And a bit more quietly, I hope," the professor commented.

"Yes, sir."

"Good. Well, to celebrate your new title, I've moved your seat assignment to the back right corner." Holt looked puzzled for a moment then Professor Louis continued, "You can keep a better watch from there."

It seemed Holt understood and moved quickly to the back.

"Uh, Mr. Langston, aren't you forgetting something?"

Holt turned back red-faced. "Sir?"

"Your paper, please," said Professor Louis as he held out his hand.

Isabelle watched as Holt's thug buddies covered their mouths to keep from laughing. She had relaxed a bit by this point; however, she noted that Holt's seat was positioned on the exact opposite side from hers.

He knows. She studied Professor Louis's timeworn face. He was famous for giving unruly students a difficult time, but this scene felt different to her. Whether it was purposeful or not, the event felt like a small victory.

There, I've won the first battle. First class done.

After class, Isabelle would have normally walked with Holt and his followers to their next class. Today, however, she stayed in Professor Louis's class until it was almost empty. She got up from her desk, unaware of how slowly she moved and how slumped her shoulders looked as she passed by the professor.

"Isabelle, as always I look forward to seeing your work," he stated.

"Sir, forgive me if it isn't my best. I did spend hours on it, but—" She bit her lip.

"It will do, I'm sure."

Feeling his compassion, she looked up with watery eyes. "Do we have music class today?"

He looked away towards his desk again. "No. I'm afraid it's been cancelled for a few days."

She nodded in understanding.

"Hurry now," he pushed. "You will need a new seat assignment for the rest of your classes."

Hours later Isabelle thought, *he wasn't lying.* She had been shuffled to the back of every classroom except for his. The other professors had been less kind and absolutely less discreet about the change. As Isabelle sat in the back, she realized that the position greatly changed her perspective and that she could indeed see everything that went on.

Before his promotion, Holt would have passed notes during each class just to annoy those around him. He enjoyed creating disruptions in class immensely, especially at the expense of another student. Isabelle had always excused his actions, explaining that Holt simply had a different sense of humor than she did. Thankfully, she had never been the recipient of any of his jokes. He had kept her too close to prey upon. She had sat by Holt in every class, every study hall, and at every meal. Everywhere she went, he was by her side.

It had been that way for at least two years. She had rather hated him the first few years she had known him, as she had found his verbal abuse of others extremely unattractive. He had been merciless to Joel. In fact, any time Isabelle recalled a scene between the two of them, her mouth twitched and insides revolted. Each had a deep hatred for the other, and Isabelle was the cause.

When things were at their lowest between the two boys, Isabelle decided to make a choice. When Holt begged her to choose him over Joel, her reply was not a giddy "yes." What Joel never knew was that she had looked at Holt sternly and said, "If I do, will you leave Joel alone? Will you just stay away from him?"

Holt had promised to do so, but only if Isabelle did the same. "It's me and no one else." So Isabelle had made a deal, one she did not realize would cost her so dearly, for now Holt was all she had.

Most were so afraid of being the victim of one of the brawny teenager's pranks that hardly anyone had befriended Isabelle after she partnered with him. Though she had been his girl for over two years, contrary to Holt's thinking, he did not know her as Joel did. Joel and she were put together their first year at the temple. No one knew her as he did; no one else knew all her secrets.

Although Isabelle handled the gossip and stares in her classes with quiet shame, she skipped lunch all the same. She decided she was not ready to face the entire school cafeteria. *Besides, I'm not hungry, anyway. Guilt must take away one's appetite.* At this point she could not get Sarah out of her mind.

After lunch Isabelle ran up to one of the school custodians when she noticed the woman locking up the music room.

Out of breath, she gasped for a second then spoke, "Excuse me, Miss, but is Ms. Harte in her office?"

"Yes, ma'am. I did see a light on in there." She winked at her as she pushed the door back open for her.

Isabelle found her behavior a little odd but said, "Well, thank you."

Isabelle's insides began to turn at the thought of seeing Sarah. *Will she forgive me?* she questioned herself again. She glanced around and then, with a sense of helplessness, she muttered, "I don't have anyone else."

She took out her key to lock herself inside. She quickly ran to the cabinets behind Sarah's desk and unlocked the one that held all the first aid items. She grabbed the case of bandages and ran up the stairs toward the professor's apartment. She was surprised to see darkness under the doorway again, yet knocked anyway.

"Sarah," she called softly. When there was no answer, she knocked more firmly. "Sarah, it's," she paused, "It's Bella. I've brought some bandages. Please open the door. I'm so sorry. Please forgive me." She struggled through more tears and waited again for an answer.

"Isabelle, she's not here," said a male voice.

Though twenty-four hours prior the voice would have been a comfort, Holt's voice caused a chill to run up her spine. Even though the meanness she had heard in his voice the day before had subsided, she nodded silently, too afraid to speak. *What's he doing here?* she wondered as he unlatched the door. She bowed her head, purposely avoiding any eye contact.

"She's still at Moonstruck, so you don't need that." He motioned to the first aid box.

She nodded silently again and moved down the steps towards the opening where he was standing.

"Did the maid unlock the cabinet for you?" he asked suspiciously.

She bit her tongue, not sure what to say. She did not want to get another innocent person in trouble.

"Isabelle, do you see this badge, or do I need to remind you again that I'm now in the temple league? Did she open the cabinet for you?" he asked impatiently.

Fearing he would take her key, she lied and nodded her head yes, while thinking, *I told the truth and was burned. I suppose I'll try lying again.*

"Silly woman," he scoffed. "I told her only to let you inside."

She looked up at him in surprise.

"Yes, that's right. Put that up." He pointed to the box and thrust her his key.

For someone who promised not to "associate" with me, he sure is doing a lot of talking. She locked the cabinet door desperately hoping the maid would not be in any trouble on account of her lie. When she turned around, he cocked his head at her and held out his hand. *He must want something … What does he want?* She walked over and put the key in his hand.

It was then that he appeared to notice her puzzled expression. "You may speak," he said condescendingly.

"What do you want?" she asked softly, in almost a whisper.

"You missed lunch and your first afternoon class."

"Report me then," she sighed in exhaustion.

"I can, you know," he said indignantly.

She stepped towards him and boldly traced his badge with her finger. "Yes, I know."

The frigid winds from outside hollered around the building's exterior as the two stood there in silence.

Holt finally let out a deep sigh. "I don't want—" He stopped in mid-sentence and walked away from her over to the wall. He stopped in front of the largest portrait that hung in the room. "I do want to be a Templin—make my father proud."

Isabelle watched him clumsily smooth his robes as he spoke. She both understood yet disagreed with his desire to win the affection of someone who had seemed to care so little about him. All of a sudden, though Holt stood straight and tall, he appeared small in front of her. She had seen him this way before; this familiar persona always formed in front of his father. Isabelle knew deep down that Holt's verbal accusations had been learned well from the one he most wanted to please.

Despite the anger and resentment she felt towards him for being betrayed, his demeanor moved her to compassion. "You will."

He turned back towards her voice.

"You will make him proud," she nodded in approval.

"I don't want to report you," he swallowed hard. "I didn't *want* to report you."

"But you did." She felt her anger rising up again.

"I had to! I—I—" He stammered and wiped his lip. "He'd assigned me to Joel; it was part of my job. I'm sorry you were involved. Really, Izzy, I'm sorry."

Isabelle looked at him in disbelief and then shot him a suspicious glance. "Why would the headmaster assign you to someone like Joel? Someone with whom you had such obvious conflict?"

"He knew I'd turn him in. He was my initiation pass to get into the junior league."

She nodded sadly. She had not only been betrayed, but also used by him for personal gain.

"Do you plan on missing the rest of your classes today?" he asked, as he resumed his authoritative tone.

"I do," she said quietly, but with perhaps enough defiance to get her put in Moonstruck with Sarah.

She watched him march back over to the door to make sure it was locked tightly.

"Why have you been waiting for her? I've seen you perched outside, and you asked all the professors about music class."

"Why, Mr. Langston, are you not following Master Dark's recommendation about speaking with weaklings? You'd best follow his counsel." Isabelle was surprised at her own coolness.

"Yes, I have thought about that," he said calmly, *too calmly*, thought Isabelle.

When he walked towards her again, she backed away.

"I'm not going to hurt you," he said as he moved closer.

"No, you've already done that," she murmured as she looked away from him.

Her fear of him grew with his every step, for she knew he could do whatever he liked in his new official robe.

"Ms. Harte broke the rules. She needed to be disciplined."

"You learn quickly, don't you? Congratulations, you already sound just like a Templin," she said sarcastically, while giving him a small clap of applause.

He sighed, "Don't mock me. She needed to learn her lesson."

"Yes, I'm all too familiar with the lessons learned at Moonstruck," she hissed, amazed at her confidence towards him.

"Watch your mouth, or you'll end up there again. What's wrong with you? You've never talked to me, or about Master Dark, this way," he threatened, as he came closer.

She clenched her jaw to force herself to keep her mouth shut.

"Don't disagree with the temple system, Isabelle. It's what makes things work, make sense, keeps things surviving."

She rolled her eyes and shook her head at him.

"I believe in it, and I'm certainly not the outcast here," he looked down at her. "The whole temple heard about your little chat with Joel the Moonie—"

"Thanks to you, I'm sure." Isabelle stiffened as she cut him off and walked to the other side of the room.

She could tell by his exasperated sigh that he was shocked by her behavior. She had always quietly submitted to his every whim and opinion. *A regular doormat.*

"Well, I had to tell them something," he said. She noted how defensive he sounded.

"And just what did you tell them?" she called from across the room and then continued in anger, "That I cheated on you with a crazy person? That I'm weak? And ..." Her angry tears quickly exposed her hurting heart. "Whatever," she whispered, and waved her hand at him in surrender.

Isabelle hated conflict, and the tension in the room felt beyond uncomfortable to her. Holt did not move a muscle until she collected herself and continued.

"What do you want?" she asked again, then to ease the tension she smiled wryly and added, "I'm sure you have more important things to do than catch a student missing class. Although, I could help you find one who spoke very disrespectfully to a Templin official."

He smiled slightly back at her, which helped to decrease the strain they both were feeling.

She gazed across the room at him and said in a more serious tone, "I am sorry. I do understand the system, I just don't like it. I understand. I understand about your family, I mean, wanting to make your father proud and everything." Her eyes shone brightly with tears again as she shrugged her shoulders. "I can't fit into that system. I was never going to. You don't call me Moonie, but I lived in Moonstruck too, you know."

She saw his broad chest rise and fall heavily before he spoke. "Well, yes, I was hoping to work out an arrangement," he said with a hard swallow, as he moved toward her again.

She eyed him with curiosity, and a small bit of hope bounced back into her heart. *He betrayed you, remember that,* she reminded herself.

"I missed you in class today," he said slowly.

She felt confused for a moment and then remembered Professor Hesper had announced last week she would be giving a pop quiz.

"I'll bet you did. How many questions didn't you know?" she asked in an embittered tone.

"Stop. Let me finish. Listen, I—I—"

Isabelle softened for a second as he stammered.

"Yes, I needed help," he admitted. "But—but—I—I—" He took a step nearer.

She was barely breathing as his lips neared her face.

"I need you."

She sharply drew her eyes away from his. "No, you don't." She shook her head. "I gave you all I had, and apparently that wasn't enough. You're a Templin now. You don't need anybody."

"What are you saying?" He looked at her, astonished.

"I'm saying whatever plan you're conjuring up isn't going to work. The 'system' you mentioned earlier won't allow it."

He grimaced, "Are you saying this because I gave you up to Master Dark?"

Just as she was about to respond, the clocked chimed in the new hour. "Ms. Harte isn't back yet," Isabelle pointed out.

His response was cold. "I don't know why you're here. She lied. And you know she helped Joel escape."

Isabelle nodded, "Probably, but how many times have you been beaten for lying to help someone else? She didn't deserve it." She pleaded with him, "I have to wait for her."

He shook his head in disapproval as he towered over her.

She leaned her head on his chest in weariness from their tense conversation. Out of habit, he gently began stroking her hair. As his fingers ran deep into the strands, they soon found the soft skin of her neck. Eventually his hand rested there and drew her petite frame closer into his chest. A few moments passed before his fingertips discovered something. To determine his find, Holt pressed the discovery deep into her skin.

"Ouch!" she pulled away. "What are you doing?" she asked while rubbing her neck.

All emotion and color had left his face. "Where did he find it?"

Though her nerves were shot, panic revived itself and rushed through her veins. "What? What are you talking about?" she asked shakily.

"What's around your neck?" he glared at her.

She swallowed hard, "It's not what you think. You don't understand."

He thrust her away to the floor. "Still, after all these years, after *me*, you'd choose him? A lunatic?" he shouted angrily.

"No! Please, it's not what you think!" She tried to reason with him.

"Oh yeah, then who gave that to you?"

She sat on the floor in silence, and his eyes widened in understanding.

"He gave it to you that night—the night he left." He spit on the floor near her. "Of all the conniving, ungrateful ... you little wench."

When he lifted his hand, she shielded herself and cried out, "Why can't you see that I chose you? I didn't go! I stayed here. I didn't go with him." She began to sob.

He put his hand down then grabbed the front of her robes.

"Go where? Where, Isabelle?" he asked forcefully. He slightly softened his grip when he felt her trembling.

"Isabelle, Ms. Harte won't talk. That's why she's still there. They're going to kill her. Izzy, you can save her. Where is he?" he pleaded.

Her heart was in turmoil. *I can't let them kill her, not because of me. I'm sorry, Joel. So sorry about many things.*

She closed her eyes then sputtered out in defeat, "Waiz. He went to the city of Waiz in the Southern Region."

He released her robes and then brushed off his hands. He stood quickly when a loud knock pounded on the door. The door soon unlocked and revealed Hertz Marlis.

The head Templin peered at Isabelle on the floor, and then quickly raised his eyes to Holt. "Did you get it?" he asked.

"Yes, sir. Waiz, in the south country."

"Good, very good. The headmaster will be very pleased." Hertz walked over and knelt by Isabelle. "Did Isabelle give the information willingly?" he asked viciously, always ready, Isabelle knew, to hand out a beating.

"Yes, sir. Very respectfully. She's just emotional."

"Oh, do I sense compassion for her emotions, Mr. Langston?" Hertz scoffed.

"No, sir. Isabelle, collect yourself. You may return to your hall, and you will attend dinner," Holt ordered.

Isabelle shakily walked toward the doorway and nodded in obedience as she passed by him.

After sunset, the thought of Sarah being beaten to death began to haunt her. She sighed when she heard the dinner bell. Even though she had skipped breakfast and lunch, she still did not feel the least bit hungry.

When the smells from the cafeteria filled her senses, she kept her eyes away from the table where she and Holt usually sat. Her shattered heart felt raw. She felt on the verge of tears at the very thought of seeing him.

"Ms. Radford, has my seating changed?" she asked, as she looked into the red face of the largest woman at the temple.

"Hm, probably, let me see. I heard about your discussion with Professor Dark," she smirked, as she thumbed through the student list.

Yes, as I'm sure the rest of the school has by now.

Ms. Radford stopped on Isabelle's name and raised her eyebrows. "Well, you're not being sent back to Moonstruck this time, but you do get your friend's old place in the back of the kitchen," the woman said as she jerked her thumb behind her head. "You know where it is?"

"Yes, ma'am," Isabelle said, feeling her humiliation grow.

A cup of water, loaf of stale bread, knife, and some indescribable goo sat at her small table.

"Oh Joel, I'm so sorry," she whispered, as several tears fell.

She turned her face from the kitchen to hide from the staff's judging eyes. She put her head in her hand and lifted the cup of water to her mouth. The water felt good on her parched lips. She closed her eyes as the water seeped into her body. Just as she was about to put the cup down, she saw something.

She ran her fingers over a carving that was the only comfort in this desolate place. There, as plain as day, was her name, "Isabelle," carved deep into the wood. She smiled as a fiery courage rose within her. She turned and looked straight in the eyes of those around her. *I'm getting out of here.*

CHAPTER 11

EACH TIME CORWIN blew into the cold air, he saw his breath in front of his bearded face. He loathed being back in the miserable city of Differe. He had concluded years ago that, much like the city itself, its inhabitants also lacked both warmth and passion. As he strode down the sidewalk in silence, he felt the feeling in his fingertips disappear. He thrust his hands in his pocket.

"Almost there," he muttered under his breath as he neared the oldest section of the city.

The Differe Library was a major landmark in the city. It was shaded by ancient, snow-covered trees and occupied a large portion of land in its prime, downtown location. The building had experienced its fair share of renovations as, unlike most of Differe's buildings, it was made of wood.

The steps creaked under his weight as Corwin approached the porch. He pried the heavy oak door open just wide enough to push himself inside. As was the custom, he quickly removed his hat and nodded politely to the librarian.

The lady was slamming open book covers, loudly stamping the inside flaps, then smacking the hard covers back down.

Doesn't appear she's in the right line of work. Corwin eyed her, a bit amused.

She must have noticed his gaze, for she soon looked him over through the reading glasses perched on her long, thin nose.

"Help needed?" she asked flatly while tossing a book onto a stack on the floor.

I know better than to ask this old biddy for help. He shook his head. "No, thanks. You look rather busy, anyway."

The library was small in size and only housed a few hundred books. Five or six desks were located near the door, as the library had a "no check-out" policy. Bookshelves lined every inch of wall space with a few freestanding rows of shelves in the back of the room. In keeping with the tradition of the city, most of the books were near the same age as the library.

Years ago, when Corwin had asked about the fact that there were no new acquisitions to the library's volumes, the response he had received was less than satisfying. "The contents of these books have built the standards of our society for hundreds of years. New ones could not surpass the enlightened minds of the founding writers of this city. So you see, 'new' writings are simply not needed."

So much for being able to have creative ideas.

For the few years he had lived in the city, everyday Corwin had debated the subject of free thinking with the Differians. Each argument had been to no avail and had been met with no resolution for change. After enduring the torment of idle, traditional thinking, Corwin had finally moved back to Waiz. The children had been the only factor that had kept him in the city for as long as he'd stayed, yet even that relationship had been strained. After one long, drawn-out argument with the children's mother, he had moved back to Waiz.

Much to her pleasure, he realized, reminiscing about his doomed relationship as he studied the old book bindings....

He remembered seeing Sylvia in the house, waiting by the door and dangling his bag. "You should get back to where you belong," she had muttered sharply.

"Yeah, and just where is that?"

"In Waiz." Just then Augustine, just a small girl at the time, had walked through the doorway, so she quickly continued with, "Yet, unfortunately for you, that wretched, make-believe place doesn't exist." The hotheaded blonde motioned Augustine over to her. "Wherever it is you're going, you'll be needing this," she hissed, as she flung the bag at him. "Augustine, bid Uncle Corwin goodnight and goodbye."

He could still envision Augustine's bewildered face as she watched her mother and him have such a public, heated exchange.

"Mother, may I wait with him until his taxi arrives?" she asked.

Before Sylvia could say "no," a soft male voice from outside the room said, "Yes, dear, that will be fine. Sylvia, Sebastian needs you upstairs."

Sylvia immediately left the room, seeming to forget about Corwin and Augustine altogether.

Corwin took Augustine's little hand and led her out onto the porch. "Little Augustine, you can't stay out here very long. It's too cold for you in those night clothes," he said, as he picked her up and put her in his coat.

She wrinkled her nose when her smooth face pressed against his prickly beard. "Yes, I know, but I thought you might like some company. I don't like being by myself all the time."

"I know, dear," he mused. "But you do have Sebastian."

"Yes, but he can't really play. Well, not really, anyway."

All of a sudden, in very dramatic fashion, Augustine took his tan face in her small hands. "Are you going away, Uncle Corwin? Are you leaving me?"

"Yes, dear. It's time to let you—well—everyone, become a family in this house. You see, I make too many. I'm just in the way."

Tears began to form in her eyes. "Is that why mother is mad at you, because there is not enough room?"

He sighed, knowing Sylvia was angry about many things. "She's just ready for me to go."

"Well, where are you going, and who'll teach me?"

"I'm going back to where I was born. I'll be more comfortable there. It's not as cold as Differe," he smiled, trying to make light of the situation. "But I promise to keep sending you books. You'll do well on your own."

Her tears fell more freely then. "But I'll be alone."

"Maybe I could send you a piano, too. Over the years music has proved to be a great companion to many." Relief flooded over him as he watched her face light up.

"Really, Uncle Corwin? A real piano?"

"I'll see to it the moment I get home."

"I will like that." Contented, she leaned her head on his chest and then let out a small sigh.

"What is it?" he patted her small back.

"I'll still miss you," she said, as she ran her small fingers through his beard.

Tears then crept to the corners of his own eyes, and he wrapped her tighter while thinking, *Not as much as I will miss you.*

"Can I visit you?"

"I'm not sure. Sebastian would miss you so much."

Her dark curls bounced as she sadly nodded in agreement.

The lights from the taxi soon illuminated the street.

"Okay, back inside now. Goodnight."

He gently put her down and walked towards the paved walkway with a heavy heart. He did not turn around when he heard the house door open behind him.

When he opened the passenger door of the taxi, the driver pointed toward the house. "Sir!"

Corwin turned and saw Augustine running towards him with her bare feet in the snow.

"Augustine, you must go back inside. I have to go!"

She thrust herself into his arms and kissed him. "I love you!" She fell on him and let out between sobs, "Promise me—promise me you'll come get me if I need you."

By this time her mother was outside on the porch and yelling, "Augustine Bennett, get back here this minute! Young ladies do not run barefoot in the snow!"

Augustine wiped her eyes before leaving Corwin's arms. She took in a sharp breath and it was as if Corwin felt her turn into stone. She pushed away from him and stuck out her hand.

"Aug—Augustine," he stammered, as he shook her hand.

"Goodnight, sir," she said firmly as she turned to march up the walk.

"Augustine!" he called after her, yet she did not turn around. "Augustine! Augustine! I promise!"

As the vehicle sped down the street, Corwin hoped she had heard him.

"Find what you're looking for?" came an intruding voice.

"Uh, yes." To appease the nosy librarian, Corwin quickly grabbed a book from the shelf in front of him.

"The temple interest you?" she noted looking at the book.

He glanced at the title. "Well, I do enjoy a little history now and then."

The library was hardly crowded, so Corwin easily found a free desk near the right wall. He flipped open the front cover of the book. He was sure Joel had come from the temple, yet was puzzled at how Joel could have known so much about Waiz. *There was no way Waiz was acknowledged as anything besides fictional,* he reasoned.

The Government of Differe had always made excuses for the lack of change and progress the city had experienced over the years; however, Corwin was convinced the primary reason was fear. Fear had kept the city silent and more importantly, fear had kept certain people in power. Joel had either encountered someone from Waiz or had traveled to the train station in pure faith. *Well, either way, faith would have been needed, remarkable faith.*

Joel held Augustine's small mirror in front of his face. "You think Mr. Rutherford will notice?"

"Yes," they both answered matter-of-factly.

He sighed, as he looked over his cut, bruised face. "Then we tell him, or we make something up. I can't really think of a reason to lie to him, especially since he knows Corwin isn't around," he said decidedly.

"Maybe you should leave out the part where the Green Cloak went psycho," Augustine cautioned.

"Maybe he won't ask specifics when he sees this." Joel pointed to his face. "Okay, I have to go to work now. Why don't you two go with me, so you won't be here alone when the farmer comes," he said, hoping he could coerce Augustine to leave.

"Well, is there a shower at the shop or a place to wash up, at least?" she asked, now holding the mirror before her own face.

"Yeah, but," he paused, "I'm not sure it'll help."

Sebastian laughed as Augustine glared back at Joel.

"I meant my face," he said, while winking at Sebastian.

She dropped her hands to her hips and breathed her girlish sigh of disapproval again. "Whatever. Is all our stuff safe up here?"

"Probably so, but take the money just in case," he suggested.

Soon the three of them were headed to the square in Adams. The chorus of "good mornings" was still foreign to them as they passed through the marketplace. Joel enjoyed responding because he made Augie cringe each time he shouted. About halfway through the square, scrumptious smells filled their senses, and all three heads drifted toward the direction of the square's bakery.

"Oh, look! Cream-filled pastries!" Augustine exclaimed in delight.

Joel glanced over at the bakery and shrugged. He walked a few steps before noticing Augie and Sebastian had both stopped. He also noted that they both appeared to be salivating.

"You mean you've never had one before? What do you eat at holiday breakfast?" He knew the answer before the latter question came out of his mouth. He watched as the two hung their heads for a minute. "Well, what are you waiting for? Go get one!" He pointed at Augie's money bag.

"No—No, I couldn't use his money for that. I want to make sure I have enough," she stammered.

"You have enough—I saw it. He said to go to the museum and eat and all that. He wants you to have a good time while he's gone," Joel encouraged.

"No, I really shouldn't. Sebastian, get back here!" she called out as he hobbled over to the bakery counter.

"Augustine," Joel looked at her seriously. "You may have been poor in Differe, but you're in Waiz now with a purse full of cash. Get a pastry. Besides, don't forget you have a free lunch today."

She nodded, "Yes, you're—" then stopped short.

"Right? Were you about to say I was right?" he teased her.

She brushed him out of her face as she approached the place. "Three pastries, please. The cream-filled ones there, with the sugar sprinkled on top." She pointed to them as she instructed the smiling baker.

Joel turned to look at the big clock hanging in the square. "Let's get it to go; Mr. Rutherford won't mind if we eat there. After all, he can appreciate it being your first pastry."

All three hurried down to Mr. Rutherford's shop with the warm goodness in a paper bag.

"Good morning, Mr. Rutherford. I brought some guests with me," Joel rang out as he opened the door.

"Ah, I assume Miss Augustine and Mr. Sebastian. I'm just finishing up in here," he called from the washroom.

"Is it all right if we eat breakfast at the counter? It's the first pastry of their lives."

"How monumental!" he remarked. "Yes, that's fine."

Over the next few minutes delighted moaning and chewing were the only sounds heard in the store.

"Well, you are a quiet bunch," said Mr. Rutherford as he emerged from the back hallway.

"I've never had something so sweet and tasty in my life!" Sebastian exclaimed.

"Well said. Augustine, enjoying yours?" he asked.

Joel glanced at her and saw that the olive-skinned beauty was eating her pastry in the slowest manner possible, taking tiny bites and closing her eyes as she chewed.

"I bet this is what the king eats," she mused absentmindedly in response to the man's question. A second later she sat forward with a start, noticing that all heads had turned toward her. "I mean, someone in royalty—or rich. I'd imagine they eat things like this," she said, avoiding their eyes.

"You believe in kings, Augustine?" Mr. Rutherford asked.

She furiously shook her head no, as if to convince him otherwise.

"Oh well, I have several books on kings and such. I'd be happy to—oh, my!" Mr. Rutherford exclaimed, having finally looked directly at Joel. "What happened to your face?"

The three exchanged glances, but soon all eyes rested on Joel.

"Well, I followed these two home, and someone was in Corwin's room. He got a few licks at me," Joel said. He stuffed the last bite of pastry into his mouth while he watched Mr. Rutherford's reaction.

"You went in after him? You went into Corwin's room? That was both brave and foolish. I told you to watch after these two, not jeopardize their safety."

136

"They're here, aren't they?" Joel answered defensively, then took a deep breath. "I'm sorry, sir. I did make sure they'd left the building before I went into the room."

"Well, you're no good to them dead."

"You think he meant to kill me?" Joel asked in shock.

"No, he would've done that. What did he want from Corwin's room?"

"I didn't exactly get the chance to ask," Joel lied.

"Yes, I see," Mr. Rutherford said while studying Joel's face. "Well, who wants to recount the story? I assume there's more to tell." He raised his eyebrows at the three of them.

Sebastian piped up before Augustine could open her mouth. "Well, Joel followed us back to the inn, just as you asked. He waited downstairs until we got inside. Augie told him not to come upstairs."

Augustine opened her mouth and drew back in defense, but Sebastian cut her off. "Then we heard someone in Corwin's room and turned out our light. Joel noticed this and came up the stairs. Well, first he threw rocks at our window, and that's really why we blew out our light."

Mr. Rutherford nodded while attempting to follow Sebastian's account of the story.

"Anyway, once Joel was in our room, things started crashing in Corwin's room next to us. We knew it wasn't Corwin because he left us a note," the youngster paused to take a breath, "Joel made sure we got out safely, then met us down in Forest Park."

"Were you able to get a look at the intruder?" Mr. Rutherford asked Joel.

"Yes. It was a man, a young man. I was only able to see a little of his face. It had big scars across his cheeks."

Mr. Rutherford looked puzzled. "Why was that all you could see of him? Too dark?"

"No, sir. He wore a long green cloak. His face was under the hood." Joel's hand was perched over his head as he explained this.

"A green cloak? Are you sure? Any emblems on it?"

Joel cast him a bit of an exasperated look. "I don't know."

Mr. Rutherford looked even more confused than before, and all became quiet.

A sniff from Augustine broke their silence.

"Augustine, dear, are you all right?"

Without looking up she asked in a shaky voice, "Is there a place I can wash up? My hands are sticky."

"Yes, of course. Joel, please show her to the washroom."

Joel's stomach formed a knot at his words. He wondered if it was from eating the pastry so fast or from having to lead Augie, who looked about to cry, to the washroom.

"Sure, um, yeah. Just leave that. I'll get it," he told her, as she started gathering her trash from breakfast.

Mr. Rutherford, Joel, and Sebastian looked at each other dumb-founded and fumbled over what to say or do.

"Here's some new soap." Mr. Rutherford handed it over to Joel and shrugged at him.

Joel led Augustine in silence down the hallway. When they approached the washroom, Joel quickly opened the door for her.

"Here's the shower. I'll just put the soap here by the sink. Um, the blue one is my towel, if you want to use it. I'll see if we have another one. Um, need anything else?" He brushed past her, feeling completely uncomfortable.

"Yes," she said, and her tone of voice forced him to look at her.

He relaxed when he saw no trace of tears on her face.

"Keep an eye on Sebastian for me."

"Yeah, he'll be fine."

Her blue eyes shot him a look that let him know she was deadly serious.

"I will." When she did not move a muscle in response, Joel knew he would have to do better. "I won't let him out of my sight." She still did not budge, so he tried again. "I will, I promise. Always."

As he walked away, he blew out a huge sigh. Taking care of her felt like an enormous weight. *One I didn't ask for.* His frown slowly turned upward. *But beats being alone.*

"Everything okay?" asked Mr. Rutherford, seeming to sense Joel's uneasiness.

"Yes, sir. Where would you like me to start this morning?"

"Well, I've cleaned up the breakfast mess," he smiled and put his hand on his round middle. "Joel, I was just telling Sebastian that I'm going down to the midpoint to pick up some fresh produce today. It's between the two cities, in the neutral section, and some shipments don't come until the evening. That means I'll be gone until tomorrow. Typically, I close up the shop."

"Shall we go with you?" Joel asked excitedly.

"No, it's really a one man job." Mr. Rutherford stopped and sighed. "I don't like the idea of leaving you three considering your entanglement last night, but I seriously doubt the Green Cloak will venture back here. I'd think Adams is the safest place for the three of you to be until Corwin returns."

"Do you know where he is, sir?"

Mr. Rutherford shook his head. "Corwin comes and goes as he pleases. He seldom tells me where he's going."

"Well then, what did he tell you?" Sebastian asked.

"That he'd be gone until the twelfth and that all you needed to know would be put into a letter. He simply asked me to make sure you got home safely last night. I told him about hiring you." He turned to Joel. "He seemed to trust you greatly. He must have been right about you," he said while pointing to Joel's face.

Mr. Rutherford grabbed some riding gloves and sacks. "Joel, I'm leaving you in charge of the shop today. Close at dusk, as usual."

"But, sir?"

"No, you can do it. I've never seen anyone learn so quickly. Start by putting out the fresh goods from the rooftop."

Joel felt confused as he watched the shopkeeper scurry around the shop.

"Joel, Corwin is a very old friend of mine. I'm leaving Sebastian and Augustine in your care."

"She doesn't want to be in my care," Joel scowled.

"Become a better caretaker, and she will."

"That's it? Become a better caretaker?"

"I'm a shopkeeper, Joel, not a relationship specialist," he answered as he headed out the door.

"Sir, what time shall I come in tomorrow?"

"We're off tomorrow. Maybe try out the museum." He smiled back at Joel.

"But," Joel began, but was Mr. Rutherford cut him off again.

"See you, Sebastian. Of course, tell Augustine to play. Joel, be sure to lock up and throw out the scraps."

And just like that he was gone.

That was weird. Perplexed, he shrugged his shoulders, and Sebastian nodded in agreement.

Joel, though befuddled, was eager to show his little companion the rooftop. "Well, at least I've moved up in status. We don't have to eat at the dumpster today."

"You mean you don't need my other half of roast beef?" Sebastian smiled.

"No thanks, but in addition to your free lunch, I'd like to offer you the best view in all Adams," he said in an official tone.

"Very good. Any chance of me seeing it before lunch?"

"Yes, that's where I need to get started. It's up a few stairs. You aren't against me helping you get there?" Joel asked.

"Do I have a choice?" Sebastian joked, as if brushing off Joel's pity.

"Not really," Joel responded playfully.

"All right, then. Onward."

Sebastian clutched his hands around Joel's neck and rode in piggyback fashion up the stairs.

"Okay, here we are." He put Sebastian down and helped the little boy place his crutches.

"Whoa," Sebastian let out. "Amazing!" he gasped as he took in the towers and the sea.

"Look all around," Joel encouraged.

Sebastian slowly hopped a full circle.

"What do you think?" Joel asked, completely thrilled to see his little friend so impressed.

"It's magnificent."

"Well, thank you. I'm in charge of keeping it tidy," Joel grinned.

"Oh, yes, the rooftop is nice enough, but I was referring to the view."

Joel smiled again as he began gathering the produce for the day.

Sebastian pointed toward the sea and asked, "South?"

"Yes, towards the sea is south—New Waiz. The mountains are north. And then, see the bridge there, anything to either side is east or west."

"The bridge is strategically placed, then."

"Oh, yeah," Joel answered. "In fact, that's the way to spot Waiz."

Joel stood, and both looked down between the two towers at the Bridge of Miren.

"I think it's the only way across the Pallas River. There may be a few more places to cross near the bottom of New Waiz, but that's the only way, that I know about, that is that far up the river," Joel said.

"It's interesting that the bridge is horizontal, east to west. I thought it'd be north to south and connect the two cities. What does the word *miren* mean?"

"'Peace,' I think. That makes sense, anyway."

"Why?" Sebastian inquired.

"Well, the city of Waiz originally started up here on the mountainside. It's aged well, but is definitely old and a bit rustic in some places. See the kalonas behind us?" Joel motioned. "Anyways, as the city grew I think some of the younger population moved south into the valley. Eventually the city pretty much split in half, with the older generations north and the younger south. And, as it happens among families and differing ages, arguments about how to run things started." Joel stopped his lecture and started washing the produce.

"And?" Sebastian implored to get him going again.

"Oh, and the city, though still called 'Waiz,' divided, with the Bridge of Miren serving as the boundary line between the old and new regions. There's a neutral section just up from the bridge that you heard Mr. Rutherford mention."

"Uh, so just to be clear, the Bridge of *Miren* means 'peace' but didn't necessarily bring resolution?"

Joel laughed and shook his head at Sebastian's question.

"Thirty." Joel focused on his face. "I think you're going on thirty years old."

"Eeh! Wrong."

"Are you sure?" Joel eyed Sebastian teasingly.

"I have no reason to lie to you."

"Okay, then, is Augustine really your sister?"

Sebastian's eyes widened at Joel launching into something serious. "Well, yes, she is," Sebastian rolled out slowly. "Can't you tell by how overprotective she is?" he groaned.

Joel nodded.

"And you, you're from the temple?"

Joel should have expected a serious question in return and figured it was only fair to answer. "Yes, unfortunately." He rolled his eyes, trying to keep up his playful demeanor despite the serious questions.

"I figured so, since you seem to know so much about the city, and well, everything," Sebastian answered.

"Well, I only learned some of that information in class. The professors actually said this place was only a legend. It is amazing, though; I can't wait to get down there. What about you?"

"It looks nice, but I like the slow pace of the kalonas. Although last night kind of changed my mind."

"Yeah," Joel replied, while stacking the crates.

"Does your family know you're here, Joel?" Sebastian asked, as Joel's expression hardened.

"I seriously doubt it."

"Oh, I didn't know if you were really supposed to meet them here."

"Ha! As I recall, I claimed you as family."

"I have no objection."

Hours after Corwin had left the library, a dark figure entered and gave the librarian a knowing look.

She shuddered upon seeing him. "Only one unusual. He left his books on the far table there. Searched through mostly history books."

The man walked heavily across the floor and roughly thumbed through the books. "These are all history? Is that the only commonality between them?"

"Aye, yes," she called out. "Though the man seemed to study the pictures more so than read the pages."

The Templin official carefully flipped through the books and aligned the pages with pictures. After a few moments, he snatched them up.

"These will need to go to the headmaster."

"As you say," she bowed slightly to the man.

"You will keep me informed," he commanded. Just before he reached for the door handle, he turned back toward her with a look of curiosity on his face. "Differian?"

"Excuse me?"

"The man, was he Differian? Dressed in black, dressed warmly?"

She shrugged, unsure.

"Madame, did he appear cold?"

"His skin was dark, and … yes, I remember now. He was cold. He didn't wear any gloves."

Corwin sat alone along the front window of the cafe. He sipped on hot coffee as he watched the Templin leave the library. His eyebrows rose as the Templin passed by the window.

Well, it appears we enjoy researching the same books. He saw the three books he had read earlier clutched in the man's hands. Corwin patted the breast pocket of his brown overcoat.

The quick sketches he had copied of the pictures would be enough to help him and the others get what they needed. He'd hoped to explore a few of the places he had researched, but knew better than to visit the temple. For one thing, he was certain he wouldn't be allowed, and for another, he was sure he would be followed after he left. He did not want to risk leading anyone to Joel. The young man was now free. *Well, free from Differe, anyway.*

He felt certain Joel was with Augustine and Sebastian today. *Their all getting out of Differe together had not been mere chance,* he mused. It seemed too much of a coincidence that Joel and Augustine had met. *Joel had broken free from the one place she had always longed to be.*

The temple grounds were impressive, exquisite even. From what he had read, at one time the place had been warm, lush, green, and overflowing with colorful gardens. The school buildings were ornate and fashioned with more flair than any of the government buildings he had seen downtown. *Of course, maybe even then the architects knew the temple would overshadow the government at some point.* He took another sip from his mug.

The expansion of the campus was not broad, but not small, either. Each building was connected with covered pathways. Only a few buildings that had been added over the years, such as the infirmary, were disconnected from the campus. The temple chapel sat front and center on the property. It was the focal point and the most elaborately designed of all the buildings.

Corwin had only seen the outside of the temple chapel. When the sun set or rose, the whole building became aglow. Even with all its beauty, Corwin could not help but feel a bit like Joel toward the temple. He sighed as he realized there was not much more he could do here and that the drawings would have to do. *I suppose I'll surprise the three and return a few days early.*

Isabelle breathed hot air onto a nearby window as she sat and wished she were with Joel. *Free.* The word had a bitter taste on her tongue. She cursed herself numerous times for missing her chance. After dinner she had returned to her room, in which she had paced back and forth. The hot stares and cold snickers from the other girls, which she was used to from time to time, had struck a nerve this evening. Holt and his behavior had alienated her before, but at least she'd had him.

Now, she was an outcast like Joel, and completely alone. *And for what?* she thought, disgusted with herself. *Nothing. Absolutely nothing.* Her mind was still made up. *If Joel can do it, I can do it.* She found herself grimacing every so often, realizing a key player in her escape had yet to return to the temple grounds.

The lights remained dark in the music room as she passed by, so Isabelle strode to her next place of refuge. With most tests completed for the week, the library was sparse. She browsed through a few aisles before stopping in the history section. Well aware that two junior Templin officers were watching her, she was careful to act nonchalant as she overlooked the book titles. She eventually picked up one that was sitting on a floating cart.

"Isabelle, finding what you need?"

Startled that the Templin knew her name, Isabelle fumbled and dropped the book. "Yes, thank you," she replied as she bent down to pick it up.

"Have you turned in your paper?"

"Yes, today." She felt the Templin's eyes drill into her head as he grabbed the book from her.

"Foreign history? Pleasure reading?"

Her eyes floated to the ground as he placed the book on the shelf.

"There are no fairy tales in here," he snickered. "If you fancy studying something that may be useful to you, there are several books on honesty," he snarled.

She felt her whole body shrink back in humiliation. As she hurried to move toward the opposite aisle, she bumped straight into someone.

"Ah, Isabelle, find the book for your next assignment?" came Professor Louis's voice as he caught her arm.

Though embarrassed at having run into the professor, she shook her head curiously and hoped to catch his thought pattern.

"Do you have a recommendation, Professor?"

"Well, it's on foreign policies. Of course, exposing their faults and Differe's virtues," he stated, and Isabelle thought she saw him roll his hazel eyes.

"Yes, of course," she said in response, unsure of the game she was playing.

He thumbed down the row of books. "You know in Facilis, south of Differe, before any man can take political office, he must return to the place of his birth and regain all his documents." He cleared his throat. "It seems their culture places great importance on the candidate's past. I suppose they think these individuals, as well as the city itself, will find something of extreme value in their past—hopefully, something that will greatly benefit the future of the city," he said, still running his hand over the books. "The man has to retrieve every scrap of paper that has his name on it: birth certificate, tax forms, even school records. Perilous are many of these journeys." He pulled a book from the shelf. "Ah, here. Is this the one you were looking at earlier?"

Isabelle nodded.

146

"This should do fine. Pick a foreign policy out of here to discuss."

"And which side shall I choose to defend, Differe or the—"

"Always Differe here, Isabelle," he interrupted while looking in the direction of the Templins. He then lowered his voice. "You know, many times when the men returned to their hometowns, a family member had been put under house arrest. This serious gesture acted as a ransom for Facilis, ensuring that the individual would return with the entire list of proper documents. So, you see, in returning to his past, the man gains freedom for both himself and another," he said as he smiled amusingly at her.

Isabelle nodded, somewhat understanding, yet she did not fully comprehend why Professor Louis was so willing to help her.

She studied the book until the library closed. As she lay in bed that night, she wondered how she would manage to sneak down to Moonstruck. For some reason, she was sure there must be something there she needed to find.

CHAPTER 12

AFTER JOEL DREW in a deep breath at the bottom of the stairs, his head jerked toward an intoxicating scent. He looked down at Sebastian in his arms, who motioned toward the washroom.

"Must've been some nice soap," Joel quipped.

Sebastian giggled. "Now what are we doing?" he asked.

"We?" Joel asked.

"Well, I figured I could help you. I don't have anything else to do," Sebastian suggested.

"Okay, we'll start in the kitchen. This way."

Joel carried him to the back of the shop. The small kitchen's centerpiece was a lengthy old island made of wood. The surface of the island had been well used, complete with burn marks and scratches etched into the wood. Joel grabbed one of the stools from around the island and moved it next to the sink, which was deep, with a hand pump. The stove itself was moderate in size, holding a double oven as well as a stovetop with eyes and a griddle.

While still toting his little friend, Joel grabbed two copper pots that were hanging on a pegboard above the stovetop. Joel eventually plopped Sebastian down onto the stool he put near the sink. Joel strode towards the ancient humming icebox that sat in the corner of the room and returned with an armful of fresh produce, meats, and bread.

"Is that all for today?" Sebastian asked in surprise.

"Mostly. Well, I guess it is, since we're closed tomorrow." Joel scratched his head and counted through the stacks. "I was thinking of making a few things for us to take back to the barn. You know, to have for tomorrow."

Augustine had bought Joel's pastry, but he did not expect any further charity from her.

"Here, you wash these, and I'll get them ready." Joel pointed to the sink and then to the chopping block on the island.

Joel sliced, diced, sautéed, and prepared the food for the day. He barely skimmed the actual menu recipes. Soon the smell of his concoctions overpowered Augustine's freshly showered scent.

"Where did you learn how to do all this?" Augustine asked as she entered, looking impressed.

"The temple," he said flatly, deciding there was no reason to hide the real answer at this point. "The *only* good thing I learned there," he added emphatically, sensing Augustine's immediate interest in the subject.

"Can you make pastries?" Sebastian asked hopefully.

Joel couldn't help chuckling when he looked up at their eager faces. "No baking. Just cooking."

Augustine recognized the tone in Joel's voice and asked her next question carefully. "Do they have fine things like pastries to eat there? What was the food like?" She desperately wanted information about the most prestigious facility in all Differe, and hoped that by asking a few lighter questions Joel might offer her some answers.

Joel answered curtly. "Yeah, some people ate pastries."

When she realized he was not going to say anything else, she gently prodded again. "Cooking is taught at the temple? And, it's taught to males?"

"Hardly. I taught myself," Joel answered, while not taking his eyes off the food.

"Oh. So there isn't a class for boys—I mean 'males'?"

"The only thing allowed in a temple class is an old, boring book," Joel replied, obviously irritated at her questions.

She eyed his colorful masterpieces. "But you must have spent some time in a kitchen there."

"There. These are ready to go out front," he said as moved away from her and ignored her last statement. "Anyone want to volunteer for a taste test?"

Sebastian raised his arm up as far as he could reach. "Me! Pick me!"

Joel jokingly looked over his sandy blond head. "No takers. What a shame," he said, as he shoved a sample morsel into his mouth.

"Hello!" Sebastian banged a crutch on the island.

"Oh, there is someone! Here."

After he had satisfied Sebastian he turned to Augustine. "Want one?"

"No thanks. I'm still full from the pastry." Joel acted a bit rebuffed so she quickly added, "But I want to reserve that one and that one for my free lunch, please."

"Very well," he said, as he made her a goofy bow.

As Augustine helped carry the trays to the front, she noticed that someone was missing. "Where's Mr. Rutherford?"

"He had to go pick up some goods at the midpoint. It was kind of weird." Joel shook his head at her. "He was just like, 'I have to pick up something and by the way we're closed tomorrow.' He told us to go to the museum. Anyways, he left me in charge of the shop today while he's gone."

"That is strange," Augustine agreed.

As she closed the glass case over the food trays, she eyed Joel's silhouette. She noticed a few extra pounds had been added to his physique. She knew something was not right about his knowing how to cook yet, at the same time, being so thin when they met him. There had to be an explanation, but he was not giving one.

Normally Isabelle would have had little difficulty figuring a reason to be out after hours. Her voice had been her ticket out of Moonstruck, and that talent had allowed her to bend the rules on numerous occasions. As long as she explained that her actions were for the betterment of the temple ceremony that week, rarely would a Templin question her behavior. Since Ms. Harte was missing and no ceremony practices had taken place, she was not sure this tactic would work tonight.

I don't really care. If I get caught and beaten, well, at least I deserve it. Her face continued to flush with deep shame anytime she thought of Joel or Sarah. They had each been nothing else but kind to her.

Isabelle waited until the rustling of blankets stopped and all she heard was the deep breathing of the girls in her room. She quickly threw off her covers and bolted from the bed fully dressed. She grabbed the history book just in case, thinking, *maybe this would be a good excuse.* She took no flashlight, hoping to stay fully hidden. The darkness was a small matter; she could probably find the place blindfolded.

Though accepted to the temple, Isabelle, because of her grandfather's wealth, and Joel, because of … well she wasn't sure, both had been confined to Moonstruck for several years before being brought onto the school grounds. One had to pass through the boundary gate of the courtyard to get to their first residence.

Moonstruck was not a secret at the temple. It had been created when the school was built. At first the place simply posed as a location for disciplining unruly students. It resembled a dilapidated old house from the front. Isabelle and Joel had seldom been on the top floor of the house. In fact, Isabelle could not even remember them having ever used the front door. The back door was adjoined to a gray stone staircase that led to the "dungeon," as Isabelle and Joel had referred to it in later years.

Underneath the first floor of the house was a full basement, completely underground and concealed from the outside. Few knew the basement actually existed. It was comprised of one large room that held a schoolroom, bunk bed, and an enclosed washroom. Its walls were bleak, and there was no color in the place except for the black wrought iron bars that outlined the schoolroom. It was as if she and Joel had been placed in a cage to study, hence the name "dungeon." Inside the floor to ceiling bars was a plain schoolroom housing only a few wooden desks and a chalkboard. The lockers in the dungeon had acted as closets for Joel and Isabelle during their time there. The wall right outside the dungeon's wrought iron gate had a built-in bunk bed for each of them.

Ms. Harte, or "Sarah" as they had called her in private, brought their meals in everyday from the cafeteria. Sarah was their only professor there and in charge of all their studies. She had met them their first day on the grounds.

Odd as may have seemed to someone else, Joel and she had arrived at the temple within hours of one another. For this reason, Isabelle had assumed their being put at Moonstruck was perfectly normal for first year students. She was not bothered by the situation, as she didn't know any differently. Joel, on the hand, had been more intuitive. She could still remember their first meeting.

Her very first day at the temple, she and her grandfather had been brought into the headmaster's private study. She had watched as the headmaster humbly treated her grandfather like a superior. He assured the old man Isabelle would be well cared for and thanked him immensely for his generous donation to the school. The headmaster then gently patted Isabelle on the head.

"Dear child, have you thanked your grandfather for this exceptional opportunity?"

She immediately turned to the graybeard standing next to her. "Thank you, Grandfather. I am very grateful."

He nodded, yet barely glanced at her. He turned toward Professor Dark and stated gruffly, "You will do well to remember our agreement."

After her grandfather put on his top hat and gloves, he walked toward the door and called out behind him, "Be obedient, Isabelle. Farewell."

And just like that, he was rid of me, Isabelle recalled, as she moved along the boundary gate with great caution. She frowned as she remembered the next moment.

"Ms. Harte, help Isabelle collect her bags."

A young, rosy-cheeked Sarah smiled brightly at Isabelle as she walked forward. "Her room assignment, sir?" Sarah asked, while gathering a few bags in her hands.

Professor Dark did not answer right away. He was focused on a small redhead walking up the lane. "Yes, I have a very special place for Miss Isabelle, but she'll need to wait in the common area until I can find a suitable companion for her. Please take her there."

Isabelle waited for an hour before Professor Dark emerged from his study and into the common area.

"Ready, Isabelle?"

She nodded calmly, trying to hide her excitement.

Professor Dark had led her, purposely, she was now sure, through the woods to Moonstruck rather than walking her across the grounds. When they arrived at Moonstruck, she was shocked to discover such a broken down old house. Even at five years old, Isabelle knew the temple had been established long ago, but this house looked like it was about to fall apart. She quietly concealed her shock and kept right behind the headmaster. He took her through the front door, and she saw a plethora of old tools, such as chains, old workbenches, and spikes. She was relieved when they walked past this room and into the back of the house. Professor Dark lit a torch and led her down the staircase.

At the bottom of the stairs, she first saw Ms. Harte's warm face and then noticed the schoolroom. "This? This is where I will go to school?"

"Yes, all this is yours," the headmaster said, acting as if he was giving her a castle.

When she looked up and smiled at him, he forced himself to look back at her. He winced before turning away, which she had seen others do many times before.

"All right, Isabelle, this is Ms. Harte, whom you've already met. She will see that you get all your studies and meals. I will be down to check on you from time to time. Your Grandfather gave excellent advice. Be an obedient little girl, and good things will follow you."

He turned to leave and stopped short. "Oh, Isabelle, I almost forgot. Over there under the bunk is Joel. He will be staying with you down here."

He then exited up the stairs, and Ms. Harte began to busy herself with Isabelle's bags.

Before walking around the basement, Isabelle slowly strode over to the bunk beds and sank to her knees. She was surprised to see a little redheaded boy staring back at her, and neither spoke for a moment.

"He's gone," Isabelle said. "You can come out." She gestured with her hand.

Joel refused her hand and quickly scrambled out from under the bed to look toward the door.

"Really, he's gone. I'm Isabelle," she said, smiling at him.

Joel stuck out his bottom lip for a minute, acting as if he was trying to figure out something.

"Your name is Joel," Isabelle continued.

He finally looked into her eyes and nodded.

"Which bed do you want?" she asked as she pointed in their direction.

He moved towards the bed on the bottom bunk and sat on it in silence. In fact, Joel did not talk until the next day....

All these thoughts ran together in Isabelle's head as she moved through the boundary gate toward Moonstruck. The snowy path was dark but open enough for her to follow. She had sneaked down unnoticed several times to see Joel before he was let out of Moonstruck, so she was not terribly anxious about being caught. Just the same, though, she covered her light hair with the dark hood of her cloak for a little extra camouflage and kept her ears open for any sound.

She was about to pass the front of the old house when all of a sudden she spotted a light glowing on the inside. The sound of muffled voices followed the glow, and, just as the front door opened, Isabelle ducked off the trail into deeply wooded darkness.

"Well, that was a worthless effort," she heard Hertz Marlis snarl.

"But at least some justice was done."

Isabelle was surprised to see Holt holding the light and locking the door.

"What were you hoping to find out?" Holt questioned, his tone respectful.

Hertz gave Holt an incredulous look. "Crazy Moonie's whereabouts. Do you honestly think Professor Dark, the headmaster of the temple, is going to just let him slip away?"

Holt did not respond for a moment. "Well, being that he is Crazy Moonie, why would the headmaster even bother with him?"

The head Templin turned sharply to face Holt and stopped him dead in his tracks. "What! Not bother? You imbecile, it has nothing to do with Joel!" he yelled, throwing his hands up, clearly communicating that he was flabbergasted by Holt's question. "Don't you see? You're in league with the temple guard now. We," Hertz pointed to his badge, "are everywhere. No one gets away, no one defies us. It is strictly on principle that he must be brought back here and punished."

And to ensure the headmaster's reputation stays above reproach, Isabelle thought, relishing the opportunity to eavesdrop on the two.

Isabelle watched Holt nod humbly under the heat of Hertz's lecture.

"Yes, of course." Holt seemed hesitant to continue the conversation. "Guards are stationed everywhere. But in Waiz, too? It isn't even a real place."

"If he's there, we will find him," Hertz said in a deadly serious tone.

"You don't believe there is such a place?" Holt asked slowly.

Isabelle saw Hertz grin, yet he kept silent in the dim light.

"Do you?"

When Hertz did not answer Holt for the second time, Isabelle feared what Hertz might know.

"Templin Marlis, is there a city of Waiz?" Holt asked again as the two made for the path.

"There are many places south and warm. The guards stationed in those areas are aware Joel escaped, and more were sent out today with maps from the ancient days. I promise you, even if he is in a fairyland, he'll be caught." Their voices got fainter as they walked away from Isabelle.

Isabelle shuddered under her robe. She wondered if Joel was safe. Was he hiding in Waiz? Did he even know he was in danger? She stayed in the brush until the area was completely quiet. She was almost certain Ms. Harte had been taken back to her room, as guards were typically stationed on the first floor when a "temple matter" was being "pursued." She questioned whether to turn back or not. Then she decided, *I didn't come all this way this late to turn around.* Professor Louis had clearly indicated she would find something she needed here.

Because the front door had just been locked, she automatically started toward the back of the house. She slipped her way down the icy path as she dashed to the back door. When the last slip landed her on her backside, she almost laughed out loud in spite of herself. She searched for any light beneath the door and then carefully pressed her ear against it. Once she was sure the place was empty, she fumbled in the dark to find the door opener.

The door posts had limestone lions on either side, and the one on the right could nod his head. Isabelle had to work her fist through the packed snow before she caught a glimpse of the lion's head. She reached up with both hands and jerked his head forward. When she heard the door locks loosen, she swiftly pushed open the door. She grabbed the unlit torch hanging next to the door, but chose to feel her way down the stairs.

Isabelle was surprised at how she felt once she entered the basement. Usually even the thought of this place brought on a wave of nausea, as she was forced to relive her past all over again. Over the years, though, she had learned to resolve *the past is past* when these thoughts would creep up. Just as she had expected, the room was dark and quiet.

Isabelle pulled a box of matches from her pocket and lit the torch. She lit a few others and began her search. Memory lane tumbled into her mind as she looked around the place. The schoolroom, separated from the rest of the room by its iron bars, had been such a haven and then, once the truth was discovered, a real prison. She walked into the schoolroom and saw that her and Joel's desks still sat in the same spots as years ago. As she drew closer to the front of the blackboard, she noticed Sarah's desk was covered in piles of dust. In fact, she was disgusted to find that the filthy substance marked the whole room. She soon smiled as she recalled the desks looked exactly the same way as when she and Joel had had flour fights.

One day Sarah had brought them small sacks of flour to use for a science project on gravity. When Isabelle had rushed forward in excitement, the bottom of her bag ripped. She was not sure who grabbed the first handful, but soon flour was all over each of them and the room. After that day, Sarah would occasionally surprise the two by bringing them socks full of flour. Isabelle pursed her lips as she remembered it was Joel who usually won the flour fights that followed.

She bent down to look at the contents in Sarah's desk. *Nothing. Completely empty.* The dusty student desks also appeared not to have been touched in ages, yet she still made out her first roommate's name carved into his desk as she moved towards the lockers, which appeared to be untouched, as well. She gazed through the iron bars, finding that the bunk had been removed, and that an enormous open filing system now lined the whole wall. "Bingo! What are those?" she wondered, as she marched forward in curiosity.

The wooden frame housing all the mysterious documents was aligned to the wall. The frame resembled a floor to ceiling cubby unit.

Each cubby was a little over a foot high as well as a foot wide and stuffed with files. The letters on each cubbyhole indicated the files were in some sort of order. She was hesitant to grab one, suspecting the wall might be attached to an alarm sensor. The files were leather binders of some sort. There were hundreds, yet only three-fourths of the case housed these particular files.

She moved toward the far end of the frame, discovering a bunch of very old parchment scrolls that lay in that area. As she moved the light slowly over its contents, she discovered that a large section of scrolls appeared to be missing. She sighed. "So, that's why they're really after you." She wondered if Sarah knew. She could not imagine her giving him something that might put him in such jeopardy.

She shook her head as she wondered aloud, "You just had to steal them. Ugh, but why? You hardly took anything with you."

She knew this for a fact, as she had seen most of Joel's belongings floating around the school. This was not too unusual, as over the years most of Joel's things had been stolen or taken from him by boys like Holt. However, she had seen nearly all his clothes, books, and even gifts from his father everywhere on the grounds the past few days.

"He would've only taken something he thought he would need, right?" she questioned aloud.

Though he tended to be fairly responsible, she had also seen him act quite recklessly in situations past. Most of the time he acted that way merely to infuriate the Templins.

"Good grief, Joel," she chided, then tried to move closer to the scrolls, but felt her shoe stick to the floor instead. She twisted her feet and felt something sticky on the bottom of her shoes. *What now?* She lifted her foot.

She noted the damp floor had caused the bottom of her shoes to become moist. *What is this white stuff?* The water and "dust" appeared to have mixed into a sticky concoction. She paused, puzzled for a moment, then rushed back into the schoolroom.

"That's not dust on the desk—it's flour!" she exclaimed. *Someone's been down here, not a Templin, though. Someone wanted this place to look like it hadn't been touched. Professor Louis? Sarah?* She put her fingers on the desk, then the floor, and then the lockers. *Flour, it's all flour. Why?*

She started problem solving aloud. "It's supposed to look untouched because ..." she stopped briefly, "because they're hiding something?"

She decided to look in the lockers first. Joel's was empty, as were the two next to it. She was feeling disappointed by the time she finally cracked open her own. To her amazement, there lay a leather binder and two rolls of parchment. She gasped. *Which one should I grab first?* She jumped at the clock chiming in the early morning hour. Her time was growing short. The temple servants would begin working around the property in a few hours. *The binder.* She grabbed it.

The front was plain, displaying only the temple's emblem on the cover. The binder was stuffed full of papers. She opened to the first page, which held her picture and acceptance letter. *What is this? My school file?* She thumbed through the massive pile of documents. She longed to sit and study the pages one at a time, but her attention was drawn to a flaming red tab.

She quickly flipped to the tab and first found the picture Professor Dark had held in front of her during her interrogation. It was attached to a stapled group of papers. The cover page had the words "*Operation Flight*" written on it. The next sheet listed basic details about the operation.

"Fugitive: Joel From Moonstruck; Location: South, possibly Waiz. Witnesses: Sarah Harte, Holt Langston, Isabelle Chanton. Plan of Action: Question the witnesses, Dispatch appropriate officers, Utilize bait if necessary. Dispatched Officers: Private Mason, Templin Shaelip. Bait: Isabelle Chanton."

She felt the blood leave her face when she saw her name in the big, bold letters.

"Oh, no!" she cried. "They're going to use me as bait to get him to come back here—to catch him."

Her heart sank, but she tried to think differently. *No, he won't come back. He won't fall for that.* Even after the words ran through her mind, her heart was still not convinced. It pounded as she closed the binder. *I've got to warn him! I've got to get to Waiz before the Templins do. I've got to find his file.* She ran to the wall and then suddenly heard a loud thud above her. She darted to blow out the torches and whispered frantically, "Smoke, get out quick."

She heard voices and quickly crammed herself into her old locker.

CHAPTER 13

A FEW MINUTES after Augustine had turned the sign to "Open," several of the shop's regulars entered for their daily purchases. Over the next few hours she witnessed Joel's interactions with the inhabitants of Old Waiz from behind the counter. His freckled face greeted each customer with a friendly word and he even seemed to know a little about each one, despite only having worked in the shop a few days. She marveled as he confidently asked questions like, "Do you want the usual?" or, "Were you able to find the part you need in order to repair your norrac?"

It almost appeared to Augustine that Joel was really from Waiz. This thought led her to believe he must have been somewhat of an outcast in Differe. She had judged from her previous observations that Joel's main pleasure came from being right or from being rather difficult. As she watched him laugh and smile with the customers, he convinced her otherwise. She felt her heart begin to trust that he was genuine.

Almost, she thought, as the image of him running down the hall at their first meeting flashed through her mind. *And, why would anyone run away from the temple?* she had asked herself a dozen times, yet had only developed two answers. *He was either kicked out or in big trouble for something.* While she continued thinking over her suspicions, she watched him help an elderly lady with her bag.

For the first time since the shop had opened that morning, Joel caught her blue eyes staring at him. He was distracted briefly then turned back toward the woman he was helping.

"Now, we're getting in new produce from the midpoint, so be sure to come back. Oh, but remember, we'll be closed tomorrow."

"Ah, that time already. What do you plan to do on your day off?" the woman inquired as she glanced behind the counter at Augustine and winked.

"Well, the museum has been recommended to us several times now, so I think we'll check it out."

The lady frowned in disapproval. "Yes, you all should go, but don't miss the sunshine. I'd recommend not just reading about the old places but going exploring."

"Sounds great. Uh, how would we go about finding those places?"

"There are a few maps at the museum, but, even so, I said 'exploring' because it'll still take some effort to find them."

"Well, we'll definitely look into it. Thanks, Mrs. Hutch."

"Goodbye, dear." Before she walked out the door, she turned back to Augustine. "You are so beautiful in that color—matches your eyes."

"Oh, it's just a secondhand dress," Augustine responded, totally taken aback.

"Beautiful just the same." The woman smiled at her again before she lifted the door handle.

Even though an hour later it was just the three of them inside the shop, Joel remained hard at work. Augustine and Sebastian followed his lead and also found little things to do for Mr. Rutherford while he was away. Augustine had not realized how much time had passed until Joel went to flip the sign.

"Your free lunch is ready," he called out from the door.

She looked with amazement at the tray he had just plopped on the counter.

"Isn't this what you wanted?" Joel murmured as he approached.

"Yes. Yes, it is. Um, thank you."

Though her head was still raised in high indignation, Joel was glad that the girl had at least thanked him.

"Can you carry this tray?"

She looked puzzled but nodded. She watched curiously as the two boys exchanged grins.

Sebastian jumped onto Joel's back while the redhead grabbed a jug of water and a few cups.

Joel then walked over to the door and said, "Come on, we're eating up here." He fled up the stairs and quickly put everything down so he could grab the tray from Augustine once she reached the top.

She had followed obediently and once she was at the top asked breathlessly, "Is this the roof?"

Joel fought the urge to chastise her for asking such a dumb question and simply nodded as he took the tray from her.

"Oh wow, a rooftop garden. So this is where you get all your food for the day? I wondered where it all came from," she said as she knelt down by the plants.

The two boys were already digging into their lunch by the time she moved to the table.

"A tasty *and* free lunch," she said, as she grabbed her plate.

Sebastian burped about this time, and the two boys chuckled together.

"Sebastian! I mean, look at both of you," Augustine chided.

"What?" Joel asked with a mouthful of food.

"No wonder we have to eat up here, removed from the rest of the city. No manners! Either of you."

Joel shook his head at her as he chewed. He stood up in front of her.

He swallowed. "That's it, Augie. You're finally looking the right direction."

"What do you mean?"

He pulled her arm gently toward the roof's ledge. "Look up! Look around you." As she did, he let go of her arm.

Augustine didn't speak for a long time. When she finally turned around, she sputtered toward Sebastian, "Have—have you seen it already?"

He nodded, giddy at her reaction. "While you were in the shower."

Joel continued standing close by her.

"I've never seen anything like it in all my life," she said, shaking her head without taking her eyes off New Waiz. "No snow."

"Do you see the towers?" Joel pointed, and she squinted in the towers' direction.

"Yes! And I see the Bridge of Miren. There doesn't seem to be much on the east side of the bridge. They look completely different than the surrounding buildings, almost Differian."

"You're right." Joel nodded at her observation.

"I didn't think they would be that old. When did New Waiz form?"

Joel shrugged. "I'll bet we'll find out at the museum tomorrow."

"You're coming too, then?"

Did she not hear me talking to Ms. Hutch? "Yes, Mr. Rutherford told me to look out for you two."

"I don't need looking after," she said sharply.

Sebastian looked embarrassed, and Joel grimaced, bet he's a little ashamed of us getting into another petty argument. He interjected, "Did you see the mountainside, Augustine?"

Her gaze drifted towards the other side of the roof. "I don't think I've ever seen a mountain uncovered. It's brilliant." She walked forward to see more. "Wow, there must be a dozen or more kalonas up here."

"Maybe we can visit a few tomorrow," Joel said as he sat back down to eat.

She looked back and shot Joel a stern look.

"Really, Augie? That's the way you feel? Fine. After lunch you're free to leave. I'm not holding you hostage or anything," Joel snapped at her.

"Maybe I will," she threatened.

"You will, but he won't. He promised Mr. Rutherford he'd help with the bookkeeping at closing." The flame of Joel's fiery temper was beginning to match his hair color.

"I did promise," Sebastian squeaked out.

"Listen, Joel, I don't need your—"

"Help?" he interrupted. "Yeah, I know, Augie. I don't think I mentioned *helping* you tomorrow." *Looking after is entirely different.* But she was being so irrational he dared not share his opinion.

"No, I was going to say I don't need looking after."

"Whatever," Joel said, beginning to think maybe he should share his definition of those words.

"Stop!" Sebastian's yell surprised both of them. "Get over yourselves. Corwin said to stick together, and that's what we'll do until he gets back."

Both looked at him and then slowly nodded in unison. Augustine then quietly settled into her chair, and Joel poured her a cup of water.

Like the night before, Augustine played the piano while the others closed up the shop. She had brought a few music books from her bag this time, so she played with much more confidence. She was surprised to find that Joel was able to whistle along with most of the old classics she played.

The view at lunch had helped the three make the decision to stay and dine at the store on leftovers. As they sat on the rooftop again, each marveled at the sunset. It was the most beautiful evening sky Augustine had ever seen. Down by the ocean a glorious sun was sparkling across the water and shading the scant clouds in vivid pink and purple hues. As the large moon began to look down upon them, the blue sky in Old

Waiz began to deepen in color. With stomachs full and each surrounded by beauty, all sighed in contentment as they walked in the dark back to the old goat house.

Augustine smiled as she watched Joel hoist Sebastian up the ladder to the hayloft. *I'd have never found this hiding spot.* She also knew what a difficult time she'd had on her own trying to get Sebastian up the ladder. Perhaps Joel really was useful, just as Corwin and Sebastian had argued. He handed her his coat again. *Perhaps I do need looking after.*

"Hurry up, now. Good heavens! Get out of my way!" Isabelle heard the headmaster cry.

"Sorry, Delano, I'm a bit hazy at this hour," said a yawning voice that she recognized as Professor Louis's.

"Do you smell smoke?" asked the headmaster as he sniffed in suspicion.

"No, I smell a musty, old, unused basement."

"Light another torch for me," the headmaster commanded impatiently.

Through the slit in the door Isabelle saw Professor Louis light her freshly extinguished torch. She noted that he handed the headmaster his own torch and kept hers.

"Here, take mine. This one's a bit weak."

The two took their torches to the cubbies.

"See! Tsk!" the headmaster spat loudly. "Missing!"

"Yes, missing scrolls about a legendary place. What a tragedy," Professor Louis commented unsympathetically.

"For heaven's sake, Emerson! Be serious. Those scrolls are hundreds of years old, and you know that truth is found in the old things," the headmaster said as he shook a scroll in front of Professor Louis's face. "Of course Waiz exists, or what's left of it. The most frustrating part about Joel taking these scrolls is they each contain different information. I don't even know what he has! Maps? Writings from *The Book of Order?* Some of these were from Theodore Waiz's journal."

Professor Louis stood back and stroked his chin while he watched the headmaster begin to rummage through the files.

"Well? What are you doing?" Professor Dark asked sharply when he realized his colleague seemed aloof. "Come. Help me look for Joel's file."

"Delano, if he took the Waiz scrolls, do you honestly think he left his file?"

"He couldn't have gotten to the file. Only Tower faculty have access to these. Even Ms. Harte couldn't have pulled his file without the Templins being alerted."

Professor Louis shot him a look of doubt before the headmaster turned back toward the files. He had not moved an inch by the time the headmaster gave up his search.

"Blast!" the headmaster yelled as he smacked his cane again the wooden frame. "How! I want to know how this happened!"

"Delano, don't give yourself a heart attack. You almost sound nervous."

Isabelle had never seen Professor Louis in such rare satirical form.

"Well, his family is bound to—" Professor Dark sighed, then wearily continued, "We must find him."

"And just how do you propose to do that?"

"What I have already done. Dispatch the Templins to the south, or to Waiz, really. And if that plan proves futile then I will use a more persuasive method—bait."

"And just like that you think he will turn up?" Professor Louis asked with skepticism in his voice.

"No, I do not," the headmaster shook his head. "But I do think his 'voices' will manifest soon enough. His own mental weaknesses will give him up," he said with his finger raised confidently. "What? You think it an ill-fit plan?" he barked in the other professor's face.

"No, probably not," Professor Louis shook his head. "No, I think you're just overlooking one very important matter. What will you do with him once you catch him?"

Professor Dark's face then produced a sinister grin. "Oh, I have that planned out."

When Augustine stirred from her slumber the next morning, she noticed that Sebastian was perched over by the window. She rubbed her eyes and murmured, "What are you doing?"

"Shhh!"

She was quickly alarmed and scrambled to her hands and knees.

When she crawled over to him, he whispered, "Look!"

Augustine saw Joel through the window slat and soon realized a herd full of goats was not his only companion.

"Who's that?" Augustine asked as she squinted and observed a man holding a large staff and a bucket of feed.

"I think it's the farmer," the little boy replied.

The man's sun-kissed skin was clothed in khaki much like Corwin's, though much older and more worn out. Joel also held a bucket and shook it over the ground as he called out to the goats. They seemed to be gathering the herd for something.

"Got 'em?" the farmer yelled to Joel.

"Just about! The gate's open," he called back as he moved toward the far end of the field.

All the goats followed Joel as the farmer gently prodded them from behind. Sebastian and Augustine paused and looked at one another in amazement.

"How does he know so many people here?" she questioned aloud.

The gate was soon closed, and the two made their way back up to the barn.

Augustine and Sebastian waited by the window in hopes of making out some of their conversation.

"The bells ring in everything. Dern annoying after a while," the farmer complained. "On any account, you best come or make yourself scarce tomorrow," he advised.

"I'll take the latter. I'm much better at that."

The farmer smiled and nodded at Joel's reply. They both stopped at the fence for a moment.

"Got enough milk for today? Had to move the herd early."

"Yes, sir. I got up early this morning."

The farmer nodded. Augustine wondered if he had noticed several more cleaned pails than usual earlier that morning and if he had asked Joel about them. Though she and Sebastian could no longer see the two, they were able to hear them through the old wood.

"This here's a big stack," the farmer mused and the two heard him rattle the buckets.

"I can get them," Joel replied quickly.

"Nah, I'll help you. I've got to grab a few jugs to take to the house."

Augustine and Sebastian held their breaths as Joel and the farmer entered the barn.

The farmer cast a good look around before he shelved the buckets and headed toward the icebox. Joel glanced up, relieved to see no trace of the brother and sister he was charged with protecting.

"Sure you don't want to come up to the house?" the farmer offered.

"Only if you need help. Otherwise, I need to head out," Joel answered.

"No, I can manage." The man waved his hand as he placed a few of jugs into his belted pack. "All right, then. See you later."

All three waited a few minutes before moving.

"Psst. Hey!" Joel yelled. "You two awake?"

"Yep!"

Joel soon saw Sebastian's grimy, smiling face looking down at him. The little boy was caked with dirt and hay, which moved Joel to inspect his own dirty hands.

"Breakfast?" Sebastian called down.

"You're filthy!" Augustine exclaimed.

Joel didn't see Augustine, so he was not exactly sure if she was talking to him or Sebastian.

"Who cares?" Sebastian spat back.

"Your food does. You don't want to eat with those hands."

Joel heard the rustling of hay and saw Augustine's shiny face peer over the loft at him.

"You look clean," she said in a way that sounded more like an accusation than an observation.

"Already showered."

"Before you worked with the goats?" she asked as she wrinkled her nose.

Joel was confused for a moment then realized they must have been watching him through the window slats.

"They're not that dirty," he replied as he hid his hands behind his back.

"They live outside," she remarked hastily.

"And you're living in a barn."

"Exactly," she agreed, then laughed. "Is there a place Sebastian can wash up?"

"You sound like my mother. I'm hungry," Sebastian complained.

Joel watched Augustine's smile fade as she went silent at Sebastian's comment. Feeling some invisible tension, he quickly offered, "Uh, Sebastian, I gotta wash my hands. Why don't you come and at least do that? Augustine can fix our breakfast. By the time we get back, it'll be ready to eat."

Sebastian sighed and muttered an exasperated, "Okay."

Joel climbed up the ladder and grabbed the little boy.

Augustine sponged herself off and dressed quickly. She wasn't sure where they would end up today so she chose a pair of shorts, casual shirt, and shoes that could withstand various kinds of terrain. She gathered Sebastian's things into a bag and stood trying to decide whether to bring his braces or just to push him in the wheelchair.

She carefully set out the milk glasses, cheese, and crackers, then neatly spread the cheese onto several crackers and filled the milk glasses. As a special treat, she had saved a few bites of pastry and divided it onto everyone's napkin. Once she was finished, she realized she had almost forgotten to check her face in the mirror.

She ran out to the pump and wondered where the shower was. The boys were nowhere to be found. She washed her face first and debated brushing her teeth. She ran back into the barn, dabbed her face dry, and then ran a comb loosely through her hair. As she was about to climb up the ladder for her makeup bag, she heard the other two approaching.

Joel's plan had worked perfectly. It had only taken one good splash to get Sebastian much cleaner than he had planned.

"I know you did that on purpose," Sebastian stated, clearly annoyed at Joel's tactic.

"Yeah, worked pretty good, don't you think?"

Sebastian laughed and was back to his good-natured self. Joel was surprised to see Augustine out of a dress when they walked back inside. He found her so unpredictable. Her breakfast resembled a small feast compared to what he had eaten in the past few days. Since he would be spending the whole day with the dark-haired pianist, he decided to simply say, "Thanks."

"How long has he known about your being here?" Augustine nodded towards the buckets.

With a mouthful of food Joel shrugged, "For most of the time."

"What do you know about him?"

"He's got a lot of kids and lives up in a house behind those hills." Joel jerked his head back in the direction of the house.

"Why don't his kids help him farm?" Sebastian asked.

"I'm not sure. I think they help at the house, making milk and cheese. He's mentioned something about them being in class and some being in New Waiz. I don't really know."

Joel did not mention that the farmer asked him regularly if he wanted to stay at the house or at least come eat. He was pretty sure the farmer was the only one who knew he was staying in the barn. At their first meeting, the farmer had given him the choice to come to the house or keep himself scarce. Joel had not found any kids trying to catch a glimpse of him since that night, so he supposed he was indeed doing a good job of making himself scarce.

Joel explained to the siblings that the farmer had caught him the night after they arrived in Waiz. He had scared him half to death with a pitchfork. When the farmer found that Joel was harmless, he had asked if he could work. Joel was willing to do anything to keep a place to stay.

"So, the farmer worked a deal with me. If I helped him with the herd, I could have a free place to stay."

"So you trust him?" Augustine asked.

"Don't know him well enough. The deal we made was just for me, so I wasn't sure I should say anything about you two. But, hey, at least we have access to all this fine milk and cheese."

"He brings it to you?" she asked, astonished at the man's generosity.

"Yeah. Sometimes I go to the milking pins and help."

"You know how to milk a goat?" Augustine gave him an incredulous look and added, "Is there anything you don't know how to do?"

He looked amused but didn't answer right away allowing the opportunity for a suppressed memory to surface. In disparaging fashion the headmaster had once asked and answered this same question in Joel's presence.

His emotions must have shown on his face, because Sebastian soon exclaimed, "It's okay, Joel. No one's perfect."

Joel began to clean up breakfast about the time Augustine asked if Sebastian had brushed his teeth.

"I ate breakfast."

"That doesn't count. Come on, you missed last night."

Joel had noticed, that even without water, Augie had brushed her teeth every morning and night. *A bit obsessive, really.*

After the three finished preparing for the day, they headed toward the Old Waiz Museum. Sebastian had only found himself alone with Joel a few times, yet he had not gotten up enough nerve to ask Joel for the maps Sebastian's father had given him. He had thought about asking for them at the shower, but had quickly forgotten once the water fight ensued. He wasn't too worried about the maps, figuring they were safe with Joel, though he would hate for Augustine to find out he had them. Although she didn't seem to loathe him as much as when they first met, she had made it apparent that she still did not trust him. He also feared her reaction due to her overall low tolerance for, well, most people.

It had always been just the two of them for the most part. Their parents worked in a factory most days, so Augustine had been his caretaker for as long as he could remember. Thankfully, she was not as overprotective as his mother and tended to know his limits better than his mother. Every now and then, on holidays, other family members would participate in a meal, but never friends. Uncle Corwin, which Sebastian had never called him, was their favorite relative. The man had left Differe before Sebastian was old enough to remember him. Their mother had forbid them to call him "uncle" and Sebastian was still unclear as to why she loathed the man so much. Corwin always remembered to send gifts for their birthdays and Christmas. Sebastian figured that the man was quite eccentric because the gifts he'd sent were always exotic. One birthday he received a red fedora with peacock feathers attached to one side. His mother had promptly disposed of the gift, stating, "The hat's palette is too colorful for a place like Differe."

His mother had always been a strict follower of Differian culture, whereas his father always seemed amused by Corwin's gifts. Typically Corwin's packages incorporated both a fun item and something educational. Most of his and Augustine's library was comprised of the books Corwin had sent them over the years. Corwin had even given Sebastian his very first reader book. As far as Sebastian was concerned, the book was the greatest gift he had ever received.

Apparently, before Corwin had left Differe, he had tutored Augustine. Though she had rarely mentioned it, Sebastian knew her time with Corwin had been very special to her since their parents had little time for her after he was born. By the time Corwin left Differe, Augustine had gained enough basic knowledge to be able to teach herself to read and write. In turn, she taught Sebastian.

Though the temple had never been an option, he felt he was just as learned as any student there. He and Augustine had read most of the great literary works, studied all of Differian history, written reports, and had even completed standardized testing at the Education Department of Differe. He was proud of all they had accomplished on their own, but he still sensed Augustine was ashamed.

He knew she felt abandoned by Corwin and that allowing him back into her life had been particularly uncomfortable for her. All that to say, having an adult who was not only present but also peculiar was very exciting to him. And, on top of that, having another boy who considered him a friend was beyond a dream to Sebastian.

He was having the time of his life in this place. He knew Joel was much smarter than he was letting on. He hoped, just as Joel had helped and taught them a few things, that they might be able to offer him something in return. He pondered all these things as Joel pushed him down the path to the museum.

"Joel, when you were walking up the hill with the farmer, he told you to be scarce or come to something. What did he mean?"

Joel shook his head in playful disapproval. "Tsk, tsk. Eavesdropping." Joel looked over at Augustine, who had started blushing. "Both of you, huh? Guess you'll never know what the farmer said," he teased.

"Oh, come on. Please," Sebastian begged.

Joel made a zipper motion over his mouth.

"I'll pay for you to get into the museum."

Joel's jaw dropped. Sebastian could tell he was surprised at Augustine's bribery. "Wow, inquiring minds indeed," he said, clearly enjoying the power his secret had over them.

Just then the bells rang overhead.

"Chapel," Joel announced, gesturing toward the direction of the bells.

As Sebastian turned his head toward the sounds, he wondered if Joel was just stating a fact or answering his question.

CHAPTER 14

ISABELLE FELT THE safest place for her file to remain was down in Moonstruck. She barely made it back to her room before the morning crew began working. She tried to sleep for the few hours left in the night, but her mind was ransacked with questions and speculations as to what "Operation Flight" could mean for Joel. He was being hunted, and, knowing him, he probably didn't even have a clue. It was not that he was careless. *He was just too laid back for his own good.*

Isabelle had always pushed him to be more calculated and wary, with hardly any lasting effects. The two had started at the temple together and had always planned to finish the same way. Her first night in Moonstruck she had snuggled under her covers, completely enthralled to have been selected to attend the "finest" establishment in her whole country. Joel lay below her and had continued in his sulky silence.

Isabelle had rarely seen her parents since that day. Most of the staff frowned upon parental contact, as it was insinuated that parental influence would only intrude on the temple's teaching. It was as if parents turned their children over to the temple to be raised and indoctrinated by its ideals and politics. Now, a much older Isabelle spit on the ground as she thought about it. *Joel would spit if he was here.*

She remembered her mother being ecstatic when her grandfather had brought over her acceptance letter. Her mother placed a money jar in the middle of the kitchen that day and added every spare dime she could to ensure Isabelle would have a new outfit for her first day of school. "Then the school will provide robes, of course," her mother explained, as she had attended the temple herself. Apparently those were "the good ol' days" in her mom's eyes.

Every time her mother spoke of the temple, she lit up. "There's a library full of books, rooms full of learning, professors who know everything, and such glorious music. Your voice will fit right in. The choir actually performs in the temple chapel. You'll get to sing in the most beautiful building in all Differe."

Her enthusiasm about the place had been contagious to Isabelle as a small girl. She was puzzled when her father had not shared her mother's sentiments. In fact, though he, too, had attended the temple, she had rarely heard him say a word about it. Upon her leaving, he had kissed her and said, "I hope you will enjoy yourself, dear. You have made your mother very happy." She had sung, studied, and above all stayed, only for that very reason; she hated the thought of making her mother "unhappy."

Still occupied with her thoughts of home, Isabelle strode towards the music room and fiddled with the door handle. "Locked," she whispered, then reached for the key in her pocket.

"Still no music class, Isabelle," she heard Hertz Marlis say behind her in an annoyed tone.

When she turned toward him, she saw Holt by his side, making Hertz look like a midget. "And when should I expect classes to resume?" she asked softly.

"Speak up, Isabelle!" Hertz said.

Had she not felt the need to stay in line in order to protect Joel, she would have cocked her head and shouted her question again. She instead remained silent.

"Do you have short-term memory problems, Isabelle?" he smirked, revealing both rows of crooked teeth.

Isabelle braced herself knowing Hertz would decidedly use her silence as an opportunity to ridicule her. Classes were changing, and she knew he could draw a crowd. "No sir, I—"

"No, I think you do," he interrupted her, appearing very pleased to see a small group of students approaching.

He immediately motioned to the surrounding students to encircle them. The students obeyed the tiny master, understanding this was his most desired way of teaching.

"If I remember correctly, music class hasn't been held all week, yet I see you here, day after day. Feeling guilty, Isabelle?"

She hung her head, knowing there was no use trying to argue with him. She had watched Joel receive this type of treatment time after time, and in some ways that gave her comfort while Hertz continued his "lesson."

"And why hasn't class been resumed?" he asked her flippantly, while adding emphasis on the word "resumed," indicating that he had heard her earlier question just fine. "Where has Ms. Harte been?" he cried out loudly as he looked around at the circle of students. "Isabelle, unlike you, I have spoken loud and clear. Where has Ms. Harte been?"

She felt his pointy nose pressing against her skin as he spoke forcefully into her ear. "Moonstruck," she murmured.

"Oh, good. You do remember something. Since she's still employed, I assume she's not crazy, as the name 'Moonstruck' suggests. I wonder then—I wonder why she was taken to Moonstruck—to be beaten."

His pauses were agonizing, and he soon began circling her like a wild animal about to pounce on its prey.

"But you know why, don't you, Isabelle? Enlighten us," he mocked her.

When she remained silent, his rage ignited. "Enlighten us!" he screamed in her face.

178

For some reason Isabelle could not give him the robotic answer he wanted; her remorse was too great. "She did nothing wrong," she answered just loudly enough for all those around to hear.

She did not have time to brace herself for his blow, but was able to catch herself before she fell on her face. Near the ground, she caught a glimpse of Holt's boots. His sturdy iron legs did not move an inch.

"She lied! Ms. Harte lied to the headmaster, just as you have now."

"But her motives were to protect me," Isabelle said as she spit fresh blood out from the side of her mouth.

"What is going on here?" came a familiar voice.

"Just making an example of what happens to those who lie, sir. In fact, Isabelle was just arguing that 'motives'," Hertz gestured with his fingers, "should make lying legal on our grounds."

"I see," Professor Louis said as the slender young woman stood to her feet. "Isabelle," he sighed, "ethics paper discussing the subject of honesty and the temple's policy on fabrications due tomorrow morning."

"But, sir, tomorrow morning is chapel," she said as she wiped her lip.

"Well, next time you'll think better than to disrespect Head Templin Marlis."

Isabelle restrained herself from striking Hertz's smug face.

"Mr. Langston, you will oversee Isabelle to ensure she completes this assignment. Templin Marlis has more important matters that demand his time," Professor Louis said as he towered over the three of them.

She watched both Templins nod in agreement with the old professor.

"Fair enough," Hertz said, then he jabbed Holt with his bony elbow. "Hope you learn something. Babysit this one, and let me know if she gives you any trouble." He then turned to the circle of students. "There's nothing left to see here. Don't you have class or something? Move out of my way." Hertz roughly brushed them aside as he walked off.

When Holt, Isabelle, and the professor stood alone, Professor Louis gestured to Holt, "Take her to have that looked at."

"Professor, I'm fine, and I'll get the paper done. Templin Langston probably has more important tasks he's assigned to."

Professor Louis sneered slightly. "No, *Junior* Templin Langston does not. He will do as I say—paper in the morning."

Before he began to walk off, Holt started to grab Isabelle's arm. "Langston, watch yourself. You're only to report to me if Isabelle rebels against her assignment," the professor ordered him. "You are *not* to use any physical measures in correcting her. Do you understand?" he said in a highly authoritative tone.

"Yes, sir."

"Good. Enough blood has been spilled in this matter."

Neither looked at the other when the professor finally walked off.

Holt eventually gestured toward the infirmary. "Well, come on, then."

When Isabelle did not move right away, he went to grab her arm again. She was ready this time and drew back, much to his astonishment.

"No physical measures."

Her tone was so sharp it surprised even herself. She looked at him full in the face as she touched her swollen lip with her fingers. She hoped he could feel the disdain she had for him and what he was doing. His countenance became bewildered, registering his confusion about how to get her to comply without touching her.

She glanced down the covered path just in time to see Professor Louis enter the history center. *He just saved me*, she thought, then immediately frowned. *He also just punished me, but I'll follow through for him.*

Isabelle pulled out a small compact mirror and stuck her tongue out to free some of the dried blood from her chin. There was a small gash in her lip that probably needed a good cleaning. She envisioned the infirmary and soon shuddered, thinking, *they'll want to scrub my whole face.*

She then turned again to the music room and told herself, *no, it's time to change. Maybe if I start with the outside, the inside will catch up.*

She drew courage as she glanced at the room's door and thought of the two people that had always loved and seen her for who she was.

"Okay, I'm ready."

She and Holt marched to the infirmary in silence.

The infirmary was one of the larger buildings that had been added onto the grounds. It operated much like a small hospital, employing many specialized doctors and nurses. It housed outpatient clinics, a surgery center, inpatient beds, and a behavioral medicine unit.

Nurse Polma ran the place like a tight ship. The building was quite plain in accordance with her belief that "those of us in medicine and science have no need for elaborate architecture to prove our importance. We have been, and will always be, needed." Nurse Polma had told Isabelle this on more than one occasion, as well as pronouncing a similar belief: "Plus, we are inside all day, so it really makes no matter what our building looks like. Our appreciation of art is found in the human body."

Isabelle had been there plenty of times. Medicine had been handed out like candy to students at one time. It had become so unregulated that if one needed a good night's sleep or a night awake for a project, acquiring a drug was easy to come by, for a small fee, of course. Nothing here was free. Eventually the infirmary staff had caught on to the abuse and had become very good at distinguishing the sick from the hustlers. So at this point, most who ventured to the building were genuinely in need of something. Due to this fact, the place was very unpleasant to visit.

In her early years, she had thought all students visited the infirmary on a weekly basis, just as she and Joel had. Her belief was far from the truth and was exposed even as she watched Holt head uncertainly in the direction of the surgery center.

"This way," Isabelle motioned.

She knew the building inside and out, much like the back of her hand. She had zero good memories of this place, and her stomach churned with anxiety on most visits. With courage and change on her mind however, today the visit did not seem so bad.

Isabelle opened the door to the small outpatient clinic. She walked through the waiting room to the sliding glass window at the front desk. The inside of the place was grossly outdated and completely uninviting. The seating and decor consisted of wooden benches and one ugly painting. The rest of the room was bare.

"Isabelle, what a surprise! Oh dear, look at you," the receptionist said, as she gave Isabelle a look of pity and handed her a clipboard. "The last thing you need is another scar on that side. Here, fill this out, and we'll get that stitched up shortly."

Isabelle smiled weakly and nodded.

"Oh," the woman exclaimed when she noticed Holt standing behind her. "Is this the boyfriend you told me about?"

"Er, well—" Isabelle stammered.

"Isabelle just turned into a beauty once you came along. She said she had to look her best for the most handsome student at the temple. Why, she even told me that you're one of the great Langstons," the woman gushed.

"This is actually just a junior Templin helping me get this taken care of," Isabelle said through clenched teeth.

"Oh. Well, my mistake. I just thought you two were inseparable."

Isabelle turned from the desk to fill out the paperwork, her eyes still wide in annoyance.

"I also heard about your little redheaded friend. Such a shame."

A few days ago, Isabelle would have turned around and said, "He's not my friend," but today she had to bite her lip to keep from saying, "It's not a shame. I wish I was with him."

The woman continued before Isabelle could answer, "He was such a troubled young man. I suspect he won't last out there."

Please shut up, lady.

"We need to get this done," she heard Holt say next to her.

As soon as Isabelle completed updating her information, she was called back. Holt stood when she did, and she cast him a pleading look.

"Must you come back? It's not like you're going to—I mean, I don't need you to hold my hand or anything."

He paused and sat back down.

"Thanks," she mumbled under her breath.

She was taken to a small exam room that held a table, chair, sink, and counter full of medical goodies. She was surprised to find that Dr. Pryderi walked in behind her, as she was used to waiting hours in these tiny rooms. She had known him since her first week here. At first, she had been deathly afraid of him, not having ever met a dark complexioned person. She presumed he was a foreigner to Differe but knew little about his background.

"Hello, Isabelle. Any updates I need to know about?" he asked, as his dark brown eyes scanned her face.

"No, sir," she said, as she gestured toward her clipboard. He took it from her and turned to wash his hands.

"Well, I hear you got into a little tussle with the Templins."

"Head Templin Marlis hit me, if that's what you mean."

She spoke more freely with the doctor, knowing that sewing up students from faculty blows rather than true accidents deeply irritated the middle-aged man.

"Well, if it was a Templin," he paused to turn on his light and start examining her lip, "I'm supposed to say you deserved it." The two stared at one another in silence for a moment. "But I was raised to believe that young ladies, or rather anyone seen as weaker than others, are not to be taken advantage of." Dr. Pryderi put down the light and sighed, "Just a few stitches."

As he prepared his supplies, Isabelle was surprised there was no nurse around.

"May I ask what provoked the Templin to hit you?" Dr. Pryderi asked.

"I—I told the truth, or I expressed what I felt the truth was."

"Ah, feelings or rather one's own interpretation of them. They don't like that. I must say, you sound a bit like your old friend today. If I had a bonus for every time I sewed him up for speaking 'his' truth—well, I'd be retired," he chuckled, which actually caused Isabelle to smile.

"Yeah, he wasn't afraid to fight."

"Maybe," the doctor said as he threaded the needle. "But I think he was a bit more courageous than that. He wasn't afraid to fight, but he was even more unafraid to say what he *felt* was right. He decided shortly after he got here not to believe something just because it was 'temple policy'."

"You know, I haven't talked to him in a while, but this week, since he's been gone, I've really missed him," Isabelle said sadly.

"Can't say I won't miss him myself."

"May I have something to clean my face?" she ventured, as she watched his dark hands prepare the supplies.

Dr. Pryderi turned and gave her a perplexed look. "Well, I'm going to clean the wound," he said, then a light bulb expression appeared on his face. "Oh, Isabelle, only the nurses make you clean your whole face. It's really not necessary."

"It is today, Dr. Pryderi," she said emphatically.

"What do you mean?"

"I don't want to risk any infection," she answered, as she narrowed her eyes.

"Really, it'll be fine," he said while giving her shoulder a reassuring squeeze.

Isabelle put her pale-skinned hand onto his dark colored arm to let him know she was serious. "The Templins have humiliated me by insisting on their truth. I have obliged them over and over, and they have still made me an outcast. I'm sitting in the kitchen for my meals." She watched the doctor's eyes widen in surprise. "Today I was hit in the face for speaking what I felt; they have abused me long enough. I'm even being monitored to do my homework. Holt's been assigned to watch me write a ridiculous assignment on honesty," she blurted out in frustration.

The doctor shook his head, and she knew he was well acquainted with what kind of student she was.

"I'm missing chapel in the morning. I'm—I'm an outcast." She had not meant to spill her guts to the doctor but found great release in doing so.

He laughed gently, "Sounds like someone we know."

"Yes, yes it does. I'm ready to become myself—whoever that is," she sighed.

"And your first plan of action is to wash your face?" he questioned.

"Yes, sir. I know it sounds backwards, but I'm starting with the outside. They've made me an outcast and want the truth, so I'm going to give it to them."

"Isabelle, are you sure you want more attention?" he asked. "Please fully think through the repercussions of this action."

She instantly thought of Joel. *If he finds out about the change, would they tell him something awful? Would he know if this change is for good?* Isabelle determined she would somehow get a message to him.

"Someone should take his place, Dr. Pryderi."

"In the name of honor, then," he replied.

Yes, as well as out of contempt for the Templins, she thought, as she nodded.

He wet a cloth in warm water and said, "All right, unveil, my lady."

Isabelle hopped off the table and peered courageously into the mirror. She took a deep breath as she reached into the basin of warm water. The damp cloth felt soothing on her cool skin.

"Careful," Dr. Pryderi called out as she neared the cut. Once she had rubbed around her face a few times he interjected, "How about I finish the rest?"

"Yes, sir," she sighed heavily as she backed away from the mirror.

He sewed her lip in a matter of minutes and obviously did most of the talking during the procedure.

"Joel wasn't ever meant to be here in my opinion." He noted her look of curiosity and continued, "The cure he needed was way beyond conventional medicine, though the pride in this place would not dare admit that." He backed away from her to inspect his work. "If there's

185

one thing this place hates, it's something they can't control. There, all finished." He turned away to wash his hands.

"But what about me, Dr. Pryderi, am I supposed to be here? Do I belong here?"

"That voice of yours—my, that's proof enough you belong here," he said as his freshly wet hands clasped hers. "Besides, where else would you go?"

She looked down and smiled, "Some place warm."

She was about to jump down from the table again, but he held his finger up.

"Here, before you face the world, take a look."

Isabelle was not sure she wanted to look at her unveiled face; however, she did want to check the stitches in her mouth. She held the mirror far away and turned her head from left to right.

"Nice job. Compliments the rest of my face well." She tried to laugh, but she knew Dr. Pryderi could not help but hear the sadness in her voice.

"You don't have to leave like this." He paused by the door with the clipboard in hand.

"No, it's fine. I—I just haven't seen myself in a while. It'll take a little time to get used to again. This is me, and I intend to—" she lost her voice as tears crept into her eyes.

The doctor sympathetically handed her a tissue. "You don't have to be brave for him, Isabelle. Joel never did care whether you looked like Isabelle from Moonstruck or Isabelle the soprano soloist while he was here. He certainly doesn't now."

"What if I didn't have my voice, doctor?"

"What are you asking me, Isabelle?"

"My voice, if I couldn't sing. Could you say that I belonged here?"

Caught off guard, he shook his head. "Well, I suppose your grandfather has endowed you to belong here, too."

"I've often wondered if he knew about my being in Moonstruck. If I couldn't sing I'd still be locked up in that place because of this disgraceful scar on my face."

"Isabelle, I'm worried they may put you back there if you don't put this back on." He stopped and gestured toward the miracle powder.

"No, they won't. I'm quite valuable." She let the words slip out before she thought about what she was saying to him. "I mean, unvalued. They won't waste their time on me."

"Please, Isabelle, you're sure?"

"Yes, I want no risk of infection."

Dr. Pryderi opened the door and led her out. "We're all finished here, then."

She nodded and replied confidently, "Yes, we are."

Isabelle expected a greater reaction from Holt, but all he gave her was a grimace and then a confused look.

"To the library, then?" She brushed past and walked just fast enough to be a pace or two ahead of him.

A few students were gathered around an open fire as they crossed the grounds to the library.

"Holt, oh, Holt!" cooed a female voice in their direction.

Eris Brunell flipped her silky brunette hair as she strutted over to Holt and Isabelle. She clutched his arm and whined, "I've missed you. Where were you during our classes today?"

What is this? Unbelievable! She saw the most deceitful, unkind girl in the whole school latching onto the arm of her former beau.

"Templin business, Eris. I'll be busy until tomorrow morning."

"All night?" Eris's curvy figure was right in front him. "With what? With *her*?"

For some reason, Eris had just seemed to notice Holt had been following Isabelle. Isabelle turned to face her, and the reaction she got this time was beyond dramatic.

"Oh—my—gosh! What happened to your face?"

"Templin Marlis gave her a good one," yelled a kid from the fire.

"Yes, I heard, but look!" she pointed. "He didn't give her that hideous scar on her cheek. I've never seen it before." Eris approached Isabelle and leaned towards her face. "You've been hiding it. Haven't you?" she accused Isabelle and then spoke loudly enough for all to hear, "It's all true then. You did come from Moonstruck."

The crowd around the fire let out gasps and whispers.

"Bet you miss ol' Moonie," Eris said coyly, as she patted Holt's hand. "See what you would've missed?" she mocked Isabelle as she looked up at his handsome face.

Isabelle diverted her eyes toward the clock tower. *Come on, Holt. I've gotta get this started if we want any sleep tonight.*

"Well, do you really have to stay with her all night?" she heard Eris fuss to Holt.

"She has an assignment, and I need to make sure she completes it," he responded.

"She's smarter than she looks. Isabelle will finish her work quickly." Eris cocked her head in Isabelle's direction. "Do you hear me, Isabelle? I have plans with Holt tonight. Understand what that means?"

Isabelle did not flinch at the girl's threats, but wanted to vomit when she saw Eris cup Holt's face in her hands.

"I'll see you later." As Eris brushed past Isabelle, she lobbed a parting shot. "By the way, I knew a deformed girl like you shouldn't have such a pretty locket."

"It was you?" Isabelle was almost unable to contain her fury.

Eris shrugged as she walked off. "I don't have the slightest idea of what you're talking about."

A young man in his twenties with extensive scars on his own face stood in the corner of a dark room. Andi searched the large table that contained the Order of New Waiz for familiar faces. Each person held documents in their hands and was scrutinizing the words on every page. The rough, wooden, rectangular table held more than a dozen men, both young and old. The headquarters of the New Order was housed in a cave and not well lit. It was nearly impossible for the young man to make out the faces of the New Order.

Soon the man at the head of the table stood before the group.

"Order. Has everyone had time to read the minutes?"

Andi instantly recognized the voice of Emil Marcell, the leader of the New Waiz Order. Heads from around the table nodded in response to Marcell's question.

"Right, then. An apprentice," the man gestured then for Andi to come forward, "has acquired some valuable items."

Andi kept his green hood over his dark locks as he approached the table.

"The papers, please," the man instructed.

Andi reached under his cloak and handed Joel's and Sebastian's maps to the head of the Order.

"Have you inspected these?" asked someone to Andi's left.

"No, sir, I was only instructed to retrieve them," Andi lied.

"Good man," Marcell said, as he took the papers from his hand. "That will be all for now."

Andi turned away. He had difficulty suppressing his disappointment at not being invited to stay for the meeting.

"Oh, Andropolis?" he heard Marcell call out before he reached the door handle. "You have done well. Don't go far."

Andropolis didn't go far; in fact, he only went a few feet above them. While preparing for the meeting, a member of the New Order had carelessly left open the trap door that led to the storage room above the meeting area. He was not able to see much as he peeked through the wooden cracks where the floor had aged, but he was able to hear plenty.

Andi knew several new members were being added to the New Order at this meeting, and he hoped Marcell would elaborate on the evening's business more than he usually did.

"How came the apprentice upon these documents?" was the first question Andi heard.

"Gracious!" another exclaimed, "The parchment used for this one is from the ancient days."

"He was doing a routine assignment," Marcell stated. "The Order has apprentices (*might as well say 'spies.'*) at each port and train stop. If any individual seems well, suspicious—"

"Or rich," another member interrupted.

"Or very learned," piped in another.

"Powerful," another suggested.

"Yes, thank you," Marcell acknowledged their input respectfully. "In any case, an apprentice is to follow this individual and search their belongings. If any remarkable object is found, even if it is the person himself, the apprentice is to confiscate the property or have the individual brought here for proper inspection. It's a simple way of keeping the peace, really," Marcell surmised.

"So, who was this taken from?" asked a gruff voice.

"A name that will be most familiar; however, we haven't heard it in a long time ... Corwin Audrey Atticus."

Silence lingered in the air until Andi heard the gruff voice speak again, "Aye, we haven't heard that name in a long time."

"And who is this man?" Andi was glad for the new member's question.

"He is a native," Marcell started again. "Born and raised here. In his younger years he was known for traveling abroad quite a bit. He often brought back many interesting items."

"Compromising, you mean," the gruff voice said.

"Yes. Many of his items would have compromised this organization. He actually left Waiz for a brief number of years and then returned and he has been strangely quiet ever since."

"What sort of items did he collect? Is he dangerous?" asked another new member.

"Oh, all sorts of rubbish about the Majestic, but mostly political propaganda items," Marcell stated in disdain.

"No," argued the gruff voice, "There were dangerous items, too. Things that could have brought down this institution."

"All right, then, what about these items?" Marcell asked and then paused. Andi suspected that the middle-aged man was putting on his reading glasses.

"There are only three. This first one appears to be a sketch of a railroad station. I see platforms and, oh, yes, it says it right here, 'Crossroads Train Station.'"

"That's in Differe," a member called out.

"Ah, very good, then. We know he's been traveling from Differe. Here, I will pass this on to you for further inspection. Doubt there's anything valuable there," Andi heard Marcell say.

There was another pause, and Andi figured that map number two was being unraveled.

"This one appears to be a sketch of Waiz itself. It only has a few basic landmarks listed, but it's quite old. Doesn't seem too harmful. This last one here is ... let's see." Andi heard Marcell draw in a sharp breath and his voice hardened. "A caychura. That's it again! He's looking for a caychura."

Andi heard Marcell slap the paper on the table.

"What's a *caychura*?" someone asked.

"Are you certain these are Corwin's? He knows the train station, and he knows Waiz. Are these not meant for someone else? Did Andropolis say if he was traveling alone?" the gruff voice questioned.

"Good intuition, my old friend. No, Corwin's not alone these days. He has two children with him, and interestingly enough, one is disabled."

The head of the New Order rolled out an exasperated sigh before answering the other question. "A caychura is a place that holds the power or presence of the great Majestic."

Andi was sure Marcell paused again to roll his eyes before speaking. "The Old Waiz citizens have searched for these places for a number of years in hopes of finding comfort, peace, answers, and, of course, different forms of healing."

"Do they exist?"

Most of the New Order broke out into laughter at the newcomer's question.

"About as much as the so-called Majestic does," Marcell answered. *Bet he's grinning.*

"Well, what is to be done?" the gruff voice questioned again.

"Well, Corwin can't go far without his map to his fictitious place. With the map in our possession he won't spread any dangerous nonsense about the Majestic to the Old Order. We need Old Waiz as weak and hopeless as possible for the next council meeting. We shall continue to keep a watch on him. Yes, I think that would be best at this time, particularly on the little handicapped fellow," Marcell said slowly.

The men around the table all expressed their agreement.

"Well, I do not think there is anything else to discuss in this matter. We will dispatch someone to take the assignment after the meeting is finished."

Andi's dark hand fumbled around the one map he had kept. He did not dare tell the New Order the maps had not been Corwin's or that, in fact, the man was actually gone. Corwin had left no trace of himself in his room. Andi surmised that the redheaded kid was nearly the age of the girl. He had recognized him instantly in Corwin's room, as the kid had been with the other three the day they arrived in Waiz.

The redhead had definitely surprised him by jumping into the room, but he found his boldness even more astonishing. The teenage kid had been completely unafraid of him. There had been just enough light in the room to expose the maps in his back pocket. The expression on the redhead's face let Andi know their contents were valuable.

Andi's face blushed for the hundredth time as he thought of running away from a kid who was probably several years younger than him. He had decided, mostly to make himself feel better, that the redhead had somehow put him under a spell. That's why he had run out of the room like a scared little mouse. "Yeah, just keep telling yourself that," he heard a voice in his head say.

When their weapons had met, something had shifted in the room. The "kid" was gone, and Andropolis had seen someone else. He had always experienced horrible sleep, encountering dream after dream during the night, and his meeting with the redhead had only encouraged this struggle. Since their confrontation, the scene from that moment had been more frequent and somewhat relentless in his sleepless mind. So whatever it was that had happened in the room that night scared him. For that reason, Andi thought it best to keep one map just in case someone was now after him.

The map also gave him a sense of power. He thought he held something the New Order found valuable, but grew less confident after hearing Marcell dismiss the other two maps. He had, of course, examined the document, and it, too, was more or less a sketch. This one appeared to be more in-depth than the others, which was why he chose it. This map included the floor plans and grounds of some location centered by a big chapel. After studying the sketch further, he concluded the place was a school, and a prestigious one at that. He was confident the school and the kid were linked somehow.

His thoughts were interrupted upon hearing his name.

"Andropolis? You think he is ready for such a task?"

"Yes," the head of the New Order declared. "I have seen his desire to be part of the New Order. He longs to honor his family, his father. I can't think of a finer way to pay tribute than by him making his mark at the meeting between the New and Old Waiz Councils. He has been in training and shall be delighted at the opportunity for promotion."

Delighted was far from what Andropolis felt as he heard these words, for he knew the truth of them. He had just been promoted from apprentice to assassin.

CHAPTER 15

THE OLD WAIZ Museum was located in the northern part of the kalona, up toward the mountains. The three visitors inspected the building as they approached. It certainly was not new, but not quite as old as the buildings around the square. The structure was encased in the same heavy block siding as the rest of the buildings in Adams, and Joel guessed the architect had designed it to blend in with the others.

"Have you been to a museum before, Joel?" Sebastian glanced back at him.

"I don't think so, but if a museum is just a place filled with history and old stuff then I guess the train station could count."

Sebastian nodded. "That's true."

"Okay, last chance for a free ticket," Augustine said as she flipped some money in his face.

"I already told you the answer," he smirked.

"You did not," she argued.

"I did too, when the bells rang."

Augustine stared back at him in disbelief, so he stopped and put his hand on his hip.

"Come on now, think. What do most towns do on Sunday?"

"Chapel? The farmer asked you to come to chapel?" Augustine asked in surprise.

"Bingo! Yeah, apparently it's a big deal here. Everything closes down in the square."

Augustine became pensive for a moment. "So, do we need to go tomorrow? I don't want to get into any trouble."

"She means, she wants to follow the rules," Sebastian piped in.

"You can go if you want. Not me," Joel said adamantly.

"I'm staying with Joel, then," Sebastian said as he crossed his arms.

"You'll stay with me," Augustine commanded.

Joel watched Sebastian display pouty lips in his sister's direction before suddenly turning wide-eyed. Joel shifted his gaze to follow Sebastian's gawking stare.

"Tour of the museum today?" inquired a thick foreign accent.

Joel was shocked to find the voice belonged to the large woman from the Old Waiz Station. All three stood still and gaped in amazement at the woman's sizeable presence.

"Yes," Augustine sputtered out.

The woman furrowed her eyebrows at Augustine in disapproval, so Joel quickly interjected, "Yes, *ma'am*. Thank you. Where do we start?"

She nodded politely at him then motioned with her hand. "Come in, children. This way." The woman continued as she led them inside, "You three are not from here, I assume. There are very few children your age in Old Waiz anymore. Most children only come here in the summer to attend summer school or to work the farms with their elderly family members."

Her accent required Joel to listen intently. He wondered if the other two were having difficulty understanding what she was saying. He also wondered when the rest of the world would 'fess up and quit calling him a child.

"Okay, you will need to sign in here. Hmm … Corwin's lot, yes?"

Augustine, following Joel's example, answered, "Yes, ma'am."

"All right, here's the roster. Just sign by your names."

The woman handed the clipboard to Joel first.

"I'm just 'Joel,'" he said hesitantly, assuming Corwin had not put down a last name for him.

"Ah, yes, sign here." She pointed to a single name.

After the other two signed in, the woman smiled. "Okay, we have Joel, Sebastian, and Augustine. I am Madame Charlotta Bontecou," she said while placing her hand over her heart. "I've been in Old Waiz for many years and run the museum. This museum is strictly about the history of our city, meaning you won't find much in here about New Waiz." All three noted the hint of disdain she added to the words *New Waiz*. "If you wish to know about that place, you will have to go there yourself. All right, Corwin paid for a private tour, so let's begin."

Joel fought the urge to groan, wondering if this lady would be speaking the entire time. *Thanks a lot, Corwin*, Joel thought sarcastically, but soon realized the situation was not all that bad, as it was at least entertaining to watch the lady move.

"The museum was erected after the city divided. The people of Old Waiz felt it was important to represent from where the city as a whole had truly evolved. Of course, the people also hoped the museum could educate the younger generations, many of which have moved to New Waiz."

Joel opened his mouth to ask a question, but Madame Bontecou's quickly raised hand silenced him. "There will be time for questions after the tour."

The first hallway the group entered was lined with old photos and portraits.

"Let's begin here," Madame Bontecou said as she pointed to the first photo.

Augustine looked down the long hallway of pictures then to Joel. He knew she was also curious as to how long the tour was going to take.

"Here is Theodore Waiz, founder of the city."

Joel studied the painting closely, having not known that Waiz had been someone's last name.

"He discovered our mountains while exploring regions in the south. Mr. Waiz found not only a mountain, but also a kalona. The peculiar thing about Mr. Waiz's discovery was that, though there were several established places such as a mill, chapel, and school already located in the kalona, there were no inhabitants. He even found several abandoned plowed fields, as well as many orchards that had been left to run wild. It was as if the kalona had been tried and then vacated. Whenever we refer to his first discoveries, we call them parts of the 'old' old city. Let's move on."

She strode to the next picture. It was actually an older photo rather than a painting.

"Here's the first farm in Old Waiz. Farming was the original industry of Waiz. It provided food for the people and animals. It was good for the ground, and good for trading or exporting, though exporting beyond our borders was and still is quite rare. All right, next."

The three marveled at the enormous crop production shown in the photo before they went to their next stop.

The next picture was also a photo; it showed a group of men and women.

"Ah, these are the kalona's first leaders. Mr. Waiz led the town for some time, but then felt a group of councilmen and women should be formed to create a more balanced form of leadership. This is one of the first councils of Waiz. At present, there is still a council for Old Waiz and also one for New Waiz. They are only comprised of men now."

Joel thought he heard a hint of bitterness in her voice as she made the latter remark.

"Look at how happy they look," Augustine noted. "Just like the people in Adams."

"All right, lastly and most importantly, here's a picture of the oldest place in Waiz. It's the Marcell House. I'm sure you've heard the bells ring from our chapel. This meeting place began the tradition of bell ringing. It has three bells in its tower, though they're seldom used now. The building was used for any sort of gathering—a feast, wedding, recreation, commerce, government, and worship. It had many uses, but has been closed for many years due to preservation purposes. Any questions before we move on?"

No one said a word, though Joel had many questions in his mind, and he suspected Augustine and Sebastian did, too.

They moved from the hall into a room that was full of objects encased in glass.

"This room is full of historical artifacts that are precious and revered by the people of Old Waiz." She led them to the first glass case. "This is a rare stone in our city, mined from one of our mountains. It is from a caychura."

All three watched her with enormous curiosity as she all but whispered the last word. They waited in expectation for the woman to explain the stone's significance.

"Beautiful, yes?"

The three nodded in unison as they gazed upon the stone, which, in fact, resembled three stones. The center of the stone was the most defined in shape. It was a small, jagged circle that sparkled like a diamond, yet also had colorful ruby-red threads weaving through its inside. A layer of transparent gold, encrusted with crystals, surrounded the rest of the stone.

Much to their dismay, Madame Bontecou turned to the next case.

"This is *The Book of Order* which is still used by our council in Old Waiz and at all the dual meetings with New Waiz."

As they continued their tour Joel began to understand why Mr. Rutherford so enjoyed explaining the city's history. The museum was evidence that local history was incredibly important to the people of Waiz.

"Over here is a *teneh*," Madam Bontecou said, as she pointed to what they all had presumed was an old basket. "This was used to give the Majestic a place in a person's abundance. You will see what I mean in a moment." She said the word "Majestic" with the same reverence every other Old Waiz native had since they arrived there.

Joel thought back to the picture of the crops. *Abundance, no kidding. They'd have plenty to give the Majestic, or whatever.*

A leather strip lay in the case closest to the exit.

"Just as every object in this room came from a caychura, so did this strip of leather. I cannot tell you what it is, as its name is unknown. Though I can assure you there has been much debate about it."

"Corwin has one," Augustine whispered to the two of them.

Interesting. He studied the object more closely.

Madame Bontecou soon interrupted his thoughts. "Some believe it was a weapon, but I find that highly unlikely, as the need to fight by physical measures was, and is, unnecessary in Waiz." She smiled, and her eyes danced over the room in delight. "It's now time for you to find out more about our dear Majestic. The next room tells this story and is our most beloved place in the museum." She let out a small laugh and then said, "Meaning, this is the highlight."

Joel could not argue with her. He had been waiting to discover what "the Majestic" was. They followed the enormous figure in front of them and left the artifact room, as she directed them into a hallway that led to a set of closed double doors.

Madame opened the doors and bade them to enter.

The first thing Joel noticed was the sound of dozens of tinkling chimes and ringing bells. *For the sake of some cheesy heavenly ambiance,* he figured, unimpressed.

A circular skylight had been crafted into the ceiling, and beams of light shone into the room. The light shimmered on the silver bells and stained glass chimes that hung throughout the room. Madame had shut the doors they entered through, so that the only light shining inside was from the skylight. The three saw dozens of baskets, or *tenehs*, filled with produce and other goods. The tenehs ranged in size and lay on the floor at the foot of something underneath the skylight. The rest of the room was quite dark, so the three moved toward the center of the place.

All walked forward to find that the baskets had been left under and around a large, blue, stone table. The slick, round tabletop was a foot thick. The table's edge had been hollowed out into a deep groove that was filled with running water. Joel could not figure out how the water was moving, as he saw no place for the water to flow in or out. In the middle of the table stood a vertically erected rock. Joel guessed it was about three feet tall and two feet wide. The stone held blackened inscriptions that appeared to have been burned into the rock.

This is it? A rock? Joel offered to pick Sebastian up to give him a better view, but the little boy motioned he could see the rock just fine.

"This is our Majestic."

The group stared at her in astonishment and disappointment.

"Theodore Waiz came here looking for a greater good and a greater purpose to his life. And what did he find? He found a whole city waiting for him—an empty city sat waiting for a new people and a new leader. You see, he found his purpose in Old Waiz. When he came here, he was miles away from his home and his family, yet here was this place. How was he to know that this was his land? How was he to determine whether it had truly been built for his destiny? You must understand that many before him feared the land was cursed and that its people had left in defeat. Did Theodore believe the land was cursed and leave? No, he believed this was his land! That this place had been prepared for *him* and was waiting for *him* to take ownership. So why did he think this? How was he so sure of himself?"

The three stood there with their mouths open, baited by her every word.

"He had an encounter with the Majestic. The Majestic is the king of all the lands in every direction. He possesses it all." She spread her gigantic arms open wide. "Though most of the explorers who came here were skeptical of a king owning these lands, Theodore knew there was a reason why the legend of a king existing had not died out. He searched out the land before taking it and found a *caychura*." Each noted her whispery tone again. "There are very few in our land that have been experienced and most are hidden. Caychuras are the secret places of the Majestic. He does not live there, but a caychura is like a portal or connection to his presence," the woman tried to explain.

In his mind, Joel began to agree with the skeptics, thinking, *sounds like no one has actually seen this thing to know if it really exists.*

"As I said, Theodore first discovered our mountains, then the kalona. A few weeks after his arrival, he came to a cave on the mountainside and went in to explore. It was there that he met the king, His Majesty, our Majestic."

King, Majesty, Majestic. How many names does this thing have? Joel looked at his companions, who also seemed puzzled.

"The Majestic told Theodore that he had, indeed, prepared this land for him. The Majestic said, 'Take the land, and do good to all who will dwell here.' Theodore hurried to bring his family to Waiz, and, of course, others followed. After Theodore moved to Waiz, he continued to seek out caychuras. His searches led him all over the land as the king seldom appeared in the same place at the same time. When Theodore would meet with the Majestic, he was given all sorts of instructions, and each instruction was also backed by a consequence if one should choose to disobey the king's orders. An example would be the principle of the giving of abundance: Share your abundance, and the land will be blessed in return. *The Book of Order* was also drawn up during these times, as well as the idea for a council. Now, before you join the other skeptics, let me assure you that Theodore was not the only one to hear from the Majestic. Many other people in the kalona, including children, were visited from time to time. The Majestic seemed to have no set agenda." Madame Bontecou stopped there and moved back toward the doors.

"Instructions" sounds like a fancy way of saying "rules, rules, rules." He was ready for the tour to end.

Madame Bontecou continued. "As the town grew and the older generations who had encountered the Majestic died out, the people became busy. Busy with work and busy with progress. And soon, seeing became believing. If one did not see or hear the Majestic himself, he did not believe anymore." She sighed. "There became little time to search for caychuras, so chapel was established. Chapel still meets every week in Old Waiz, and we use it as an opportunity to pay homage to the Majestic."

Augustine eyed Joel, and he glared back at her, indicating that he was still not going to chapel the next day.

The woman then pointed back to the table. "That stone came from Theodore's line and is the last written record we have of the Majestic speaking to all of Waiz. As you can see, many here continue to believe in the Majestic and give to him," she said as she pointed to the tenehs.

Joel searched the baskets for milk and cheese, curious if their farmer believed in this Majestic thing.

"In most of our kalonas, people continue to pray to the Majestic, and the councilmen still consider themselves the Majestic's sacred ambassadors. All of us hope for the old times of unity to return, which leads us to our next room," she said as she exited back through the double doors.

Their next stop was a room housing a replica of the Bridge of Miren, which was surrounded by a few photographs.

"So," Madame Bontecou began as she pointed to the blue water under the replica, "here you have the Pallas River, which starts at the top of the mountains and flows all the way out to the Valtina Sea. If you look at this map here, you can see that the river widens as it flows down the mountain. Although most of Old Waiz rests on the West side of the river, Pallas can be easily crossed in most parts of Old Waiz."

The three followed the river on the replica with their eyes and waited for Madame Bontecou to continue.

"The city of Waiz originally started up here on the hillside of this mountain. Kalonas were comprised of mostly families back then and soon were spread out all around the area. The group of kalonas soon became known as the city of Waiz, and the council was formed shortly after the city was established. Over the course of time, foreigners from outside our city, such as yourselves, began to spill into the region."

Joel felt the citizens of Waiz had not exactly treated them as foreigners, yet he had recognized they certainly made a habit of pointing out the fact they were "not from here." Though none had said so, he surmised that foreigners might have helped cause the split between the two cities. He focused on the woman's words to see if his suspicions were correct.

"Each individual, of course, brought his own ideas and habits from his homeland. Many of these outsiders moved into the valley, believing better commerce would be found closer to the sea. Many of the young people who were living in what is now Old Waiz soon saw the success of the foreigners and began to argue with the council about moving the location of the city. Of course, the council continued to see the great value of farming and was unmoved by the young people's persuasion."

Sebastian straightened in his wheelchair and whispered to Joel, "Maybe now we'll know the real reason why the Bridge of Miren was built."

"With progress on their minds, many of the younger generations left this area of Waiz and built down by the lower part of the river and the sea. This area grew at a fast rate, as the buildings you see there," she pointed by the towers, "seemed to go up just as quickly as Waiz's overall exporting and importing capabilities. The Old Waiz Council continues to keep a strong watch on this area's business policies even to this day."

Joel noted the contempt the woman expressed towards the "younger generations." *So ... younger generations and foreigners ... great, I fit both of those.*

"As Waiz natives realized their kalonas, farms, forests, and, most importantly, traditions were being infringed upon by this new territory, they aroused the council to meet with the younger generations in the valley. Rumors had spread that leaders had risen among the people in the valley and a new council had evolved. The rumors were found to be true, and the city then divided." She sounded regretful, as if she viewed the Old Waiz residents as the martyrs in the situation.

"The two sides came to an agreement that the councils would meet quarterly in hopes of maintaining the peace between the Old and, now, the New Waiz. The Bridge of Miren was established by both sides during this time and is the dividing line of our cities. *Miren* means peace, but the bridge has not brought it," she finished sadly.

"Thankfully, the ties of family, the younger visiting the older, have remained and helped to keep the peace at this time. Many of the younger generations have forgotten or do not know these old stories you have learned here today. We, the people of Old Waiz, long for the days of old, with the Majestic reigning over us again. New Waiz, well, they care only for themselves and for progress."

Each looked at the replica, a bit exhausted from all the information. Their lecturer led them down a final hallway, which was also lined with photos of farmland and buildings.

"Farming continues to be our main industry here—" Madame Bontecou and the group were suddenly interrupted by loud voices echoing down the hallway. "Ah, here's summer school."

How has this place not died out? Joel pondered whether or not that was what had happened to the abandoned city Theodore had found.

"All right, we are finished. Come; here are a few flyers about Waiz. Oh, and I promised to answer questions. You have questions, yes?"

Augustine cocked her head while Joel searched to find a map.

"Why are women not allowed on the council anymore?" she inquired.

"That is a good question for which I have no answer, but I suppose women have just gotten busy doing other things."

Sebastian asked, "Are the crops still as big as they were in those first pictures we saw?"

"The crop produce depends on the rain that year."

"What does the rock say?" Joel asked.

"Excuse me?" the woman turned toward him.

"The last word from the Majestic—on the rock back in there—what's inscribed on it?"

"Ah, it has many messages, and each person seems to interpret them differently. The pamphlet you have there has the last message written on the inside. You can read it and decide for yourself."

Joel nodded, and Madame Bontecou smoothed the pleats on her dress.

"Are those all your questions?"

"Those artifacts from the caychura that we saw, how long ago were they found?" Joel asked, then continued before their tour guide had time to answer. "Is there any power or, I mean 'connection,' left in them?"

"It was long ago, before the Bridge of Miren, but after the move to New Waiz. I would say a hundred years or so. There is no connection, but we consider them sacred, just as well."

"Thank you for the tour, ma'am," Joel said. The three left the museum quickly and, after purchasing a few popsicles, went to sit in the shade to reflect on the tour.

"What was that woman saying about caychuras? I mean, what's so special about them?" Augustine asked.

When Joel just sucked on his popsicle and did not answer right away, she stared directly into his face to get his attention.

"Come on, apparently you know a lot about this place."

"Saying he's smart?" Sebastian cut in.

Her mouth did not budge.

"Well, I figured we'd go explore the older kalonas and look for one this afternoon."

Augustine's mouth dropped open at Joel's suggestion.

"Whatever. Don't act so surprised, Miss Dressed-in-Exploring-Clothes."

"Fine. As long as it's safe, but I suppose a piggyback will be in order for you," she said in a softer tone toward Sebastian. "I'm not sure your wheelchair or braces will comply with the terrain."

His face saddened at her comment, and he looked away from them as he responded. "Why don't you two go? I can just stay here."

"Yes, that's exactly what we should do," Joel let out sarcastically. "Augustine and I have just been waiting for time to be alone together." Joel leaned down near the little boy and gave him a nudge. "I'm much stronger than I look."

"You're sure?" Sebastian grinned back at him.

"I wouldn't have it any other way," Joel smiled as he unhooked Sebastian from the wheelchair.

Augustine's heart warmed as she saw the boy she hardly knew extend such great compassion towards her younger brother. This Joel character had led them to Corwin and was now leading them around Waiz. He had fed, bathed, and protected them without asking for anything in return. *Maybe he's expecting Corwin to pay him when he gets back.* Her heart was not convinced. *He hasn't asked a dime of me, and he saw all that money Corwin left.*

She picked up Sebastian's bag and watched Joel skip around with the little boy on his back. *Is this Joel as good as he seems?* She could hardly fathom someone wanting to leave the beauty of the temple, as well as the bright future one would have after going to school there. *Something went terribly wrong there*, she thought, remembering the ragged, angry young man that had eaten across from her on the train the first night they met. *He must have been an amazing student. He seems to know everything about everything … a bit annoying.* Seeing her brother smile as he rode on Joel's back quickly derailed her negative thoughts about him. *This Joel is giving my brother joy.*

Joel acted surprised when Augustine called his name. "Joel?"

"Yeah? Come on; we've got to get going before the sun goes down."

"Right," was all she said.

Joel decided to follow the road that led to the nearest mountain and the older kalonas. Truth be told, like Theodore, he, too, had heard the rumors about a king. Sarah had always believed the king was real, but she was never quite able to convince Joel or Isabelle he existed. As he took in every word Madame Bontecou spoke and after he saw the objects from the caychura, his faith had slowly increased; however, he had been more than disappointed when he saw the burnt rock. *Perhaps my faith has heightened because I'm so desperate for this thing to exist,* he reasoned, as he felt Sebastian bounce on his back. He was a light load, and Joel could not help but wonder if a caychura could help his little friend. *Is that why he's here? Does Corwin know about these?* If Joel were able to determine that caychuras were, in fact, real, he would be in hot pursuit of one after today.

"Well, how do you suppose we find one of these caychuras?" Sebastian asked, as if reading his thoughts.

"To be honest, I really don't know. I can't imagine they're easy to find, considering none have been found in years."

"Wait, what?" Augustine questioned as she stopped in the middle of the road.

"Weren't you listening to Madam Bontecou?" Joel teased her.

"Yes," she replied in annoyance, then continued. "But how do we know if these caychuras even exist?"

"I don't know, but I wasn't even sure Waiz existed until I got here," Joel shrugged.

While Joel and Sebastian marched on ahead, Augustine remained stopped in the middle of the road. Joel looked back at her and was amused by her perplexed expression.

"Great," she muttered, "Now I know what you're doing. Going purely on faith. My favorite thing to do."

"Come on, Augustine!" Sebastian hollered back at her. "I'm sure we'll find something interesting."

"Well, where are we going? How do you know where you're going?" she asked breathlessly as she ran up to meet them again.

Joel pulled the museum pamphlet from his shirt pocket and removed its map. "I wanted to go up to these other kalonas. The ones near the mountains are older."

"Oh, sounds great," Augustine said cynically. "And then we'll just walk up to someone and say, 'Excuse me, have you seen a caychura around here?'"

Joel buffered her skepticism with little patience. "Augustine, would you like to sit around Adams the rest of the day? I'm pretty sure we've seen the whole place. It's my day off, and I want to look around Old Waiz. Here, let's," he paused, then pointed to an object on the map, "go to the old meeting place—the Marcell House. It's one of the oldest landmarks in the city."

"How do you know that?" she asked.

This time both shot her amused glances.

"Umm … you really weren't listening, were you?" Joel grinned.

"It says it right there on the paper, Augie," Sebastian pointed.

"Oh," she paused, sounding a bit embarrassed at her persistence, "I guess you *do* know where you're going. Sorry. Let's go," she said, brushing past them.

Joel let her go on a few steps before starting again. He whispered back to Sebastian, "Did I just hear the word 'sorry' come out of her mouth?"

"Shhh. Not so loud, or you may never hear it again."

Joel spotted a walking trail that separated from the main road about half a mile from Adams. Since the trail was also on the map and appeared to be a shortcut, the three veered off the main road. Though the cool, wooded trail was a nice change from the hot, dusty road, it had not been well maintained. Low branches hung across the trail and forest debris cluttered the path.

"Well, this obviously isn't a popular route," Augustine stated, while pushing branches out of her face.

"Apparently," Joel replied, as he and Sebastian ducked under a large spider-web.

The trail was nearing the mountains and it soon became a steady uphill climb. After half an hour, Joel stopped to catch his breath.

"What's wrong?" Augustine asked.

"Nothing, just think it might be time for a break. Anyone opposed?"

Augustine sunk to her knees as Joel put Sebastian down on the ground.

"Ah-h-h," Joel sighed as he bent over to stretch out his back.

"Well, do you think we're getting close?" Augustine asked.

"Oh, definitely closer," Joel smirked, and she rolled her eyes at him.

"Here," he said as he threw the pamphlet at her.

"Ouch!"

"That did not hurt!" Sebastian said emphatically.

She quickly unrolled the paper. "Well, the Marcell House is pretty far from Adams. We'll only have a short time to see it before we'll have to turn back. I really don't want to walk this in the dark."

"Agreed. Hey, is the writing on the rock in that?" Joel asked as he propped himself up against a tree.

She looked over the pages of the pamphlet and then said, "Yeah, it's weird, though. Completely open to interpretation, just like Madam Bontecou said."

"So, you were listening a little?"

"Yes, as a matter fact. I can read the message, if you're interested."

"I want to hear it," Sebastian said eagerly.

"Okay. 'The message inscribed on the rock was chiseled into the stone by fire. It is not clear if Theodore Waiz did this himself or if the Majestic burned this inscription into the rock.' That's interesting," Augustine mused, then continued reading. "'The inscription states, *Follow The Book of Order, and maintain the old ways. Good will come to you, your land, and your family. You will find Me in abundance and tradition, for both are sacred.*'"

Joel opened his eyes and thought aloud without meaning to. "That's it? 'Follow the rules'?"

"What? You could do better?"

The voice was unfamiliar and its tone was demanding. Joel bolted upright and saw a man with a long white beard bounding down the trail toward them.

"Well?" he growled as he glared at Joel.

"No, sir. I—I suppose not," Joel cowered.

"*You* suppose correctly. Cocky New Waiz brat." The man muttered the latter statement under his breath, just loud enough for the three of them to hear.

"I'm sorry, sir, for the offense. Uh, it's just my ignorance. I'm actually a stranger to Waiz."

"Ah, that does explain your foolish comment. Find what you're looking for here?"

Joel shied away from answering too quickly, unsure of what the man was asking.

"Oh, come now, everyone who comes to Waiz is looking for something, usually for their benefit. Take! That's all you outsiders do!" He pointed his aged, bony finger at Joel in accusation and began to stroke his beard. "Or have you and your friends come to help us—to help 'better us' here in Old Waiz? *That* has worked well." His voice dripped sarcasm. "*Your* ideas split our city in half."

The three Differians watched his eyes narrow in hatred. Silently they stood in shock at their first encounter with an unkind and angry Waizen.

Joel eventually found his voice again. "Sir, we've just come from the museum and hope to learn more about the history of Old Waiz. That's why we're traveling this trail. We've not even been to New Waiz." Joel hoped his latter remark would help to soothe the old man's anger.

"Been with Madam Bontecou?"

All nodded in reply.

"Well, you still have much to learn. Headed to the Marcell House, I presume?" he questioned, with only the smallest change in his gruff demeanor.

"Yes, yes, *sir,* I mean. That's right," Augustine answered.

"Well, you're close. It's a chapel now, right on the outskirts of the kalona. This trail will run you into the main road, and it will be straight ahead. Not that exciting, though—it'll probably be disappointing to a lot like you," he sighed in contempt, as he studied Sebastian's small frame. "And what's wrong with you?"

Joel grabbed Augustine's shoulder to keep her calm.

"My legs don't work like they should," Sebastian shrugged at the man.

"Yes, I guess not. Suppose the warmer weather is helping you?" the man eyed him suspiciously.

"Yes, sir," Sebastian nodded politely.

"Figures. Takers! Takers, takers, takers," he muttered, as if really saying, "Tsk, tsk, tsk," at them as he barreled down the trail toward Adams.

"Uh, friendly fellow," Joel kidded after the man was out of sight.

"Yes, maybe we'll have the pleasure of running into him *again* on the way back," Augustine replied, as she helped hoist Sebastian onto Joel's back.

"Do you think the others from the older kalonas will be like that? Do you think we should turn back?" Sebastian asked as he wrapped his arms around Joel's neck.

"Heck, no!" Joel shook his head. "We'll just remind them to 'do good,' just like the Majestic told Theodore. Bet they can't argue with that."

Sure enough, the trail dead-ended into the main road after a few more miles. Straight ahead stood the square of the kalona. It was smaller than Adams and obviously much older. There were fewer outlying homes, and the only buildings on the square were the chapel and one other. The suspicions Joel had pondered at the museum regarding Old Waiz seemed to be confirmed by this place. It resembled an old, dying town.

"Well, I can't fault the man for being honest. This is disappointing," Joel admitted as they entered the chapel. Its four walls were bare, and nothing stood at the front of the room. There were only several rows of wooden pews placed on a cement slab.

"Nothing seems majestic about this place," Augustine surmised. "Well, let's at least see if we can get some food to take back with us."

The other building on the square was a county store. It had a very limited amount of goods, and everything inside, according to the owner, was "local." Though the store owner was not rude, each somehow felt unwelcome in the little shop. *Maybe it's because we like Mr. Rutherford so much*, thought Joel as he pictured the bald man smiling at the three of them.

After they walked out, Augustine glanced sideways at Joel for a moment. "You've got a gift with people. Appeasing Madam Bontecou, calming down that nasty old man," she paused. "It's like you have some magic power. I wish I knew how to gain favor like that, but ..." Her voice trailed off, and Joel didn't answer.

With daylight beginning to fade, the group decided to head back down the trail. They stopped further down from their previous rest area to have a small dinner.

As they munched on their food, Augustine commented, "Hey, I was thinking back to what Madame Bontecou said. Weren't there bells in the old meeting place, the Marcell House?"

Joel could have kicked himself when he thought about her question. "Ugh, yes."

She quickly pulled out the map to look it over again. "This doesn't make any sense. I think that old man lied to us. The chapel couldn't have been the Marcell House," she said, as she handed Joel the map.

The feeling of being hoodwinked settled on all of them as Joel studied the map.

He soon sighed in frustration. "All that way ... I can't believe this! I shouldn't have trusted him."

"It's okay, Joel. I had fun getting out of Adams. I bet Corwin knows where the house is; he can take us there." Sebastian patted Joel's back.

"Yes, you're right," Joel said, though still clearly upset.

"I had a good time, too. It was great to get in a long walk," Augustine nodded at Joel.

None said much after this. Once they got back to the main road in Adams, Sebastian suggested Augustine and Joel add more lines to Joel's version of the "March of Differe." They obliged him, laughing and singing until they reached the barn. By this time darkness had fallen, and all were worn out from the day.

After Joel laid the sleeping Sebastian onto a bed of hay, he noted that Augustine had not come up the ladder yet. He climbed back down and saw a glass of milk on the table next to the lantern. When Augustine turned from the icebox with another glass in her hand, she gestured to Joel that the glass on the table was for him. He nodded his thanks as she sat down across from him. Both sat in silence for a moment as they sipped their milk.

At his last gulp, Joel smacked his lips in contentment. "Aw ... that's good stuff," he said.

"Definitely better fresh like this," she agreed.

"Corwin should be back in the next day or two," he started.

"Yes, I'll be so glad to see him. We have a lot to catch him up on," she smiled.

Joel nodded, "Yeah, I guess you'll be glad to get out of this place." He gestured at their surroundings.

Her mouth twitched at his remark. "I'm not too good for this place, although, a toilet inside would be nice," she answered with a small laugh. "I'll miss this," she said as she held up her glass. "Sebastian will miss being with you."

"He's ... I don't know what he is," he finished in obvious admiration.

"He—he keeps asking if you'll stay with us when Corwin comes back."

"Hm ... you done?" was all Joel said, as he reached for her glass.

She stared at his face through the glow of the lantern, and he finally stopped to look back at her, recognizing she wanted his attention.

"I want you to know that I won't forget what you did for my brother today."

214

Joel shrugged, appreciating how hard it must be for her guarded little self to say something like that to him.

"Don't say it was nothing," she said firmly.

"Wasn't going to."

Joel held the light by the ladder when Augustine started climbing. She suddenly stopped and gazed down toward him. He looked into her big blue eyes again and waited for her to say what he hoped she would tell him.

"It's okay if you decide to stay with us."

Though he did not find her offer extreme in terms of fairness—after all, he had let them stay with him—he did marvel at the fact she had finally let down a wall. Thanks to Sebastian, the fiery girl who had just tumbled over the top of the ladder had finally found him worthy, worthy of her trust.

CHAPTER 16

ISABELLE TRUDGED TO the library with Holt by her side. She could hardly contain her anger at Eris's threat. *I hope it takes all night to finish this paper, just to spite her.* She took off her coat and placed it on the table that would host her for the evening. After removing her scarf, she walked over to the ethics section of the library. Though she just had to write a paper, Isabelle had found that all the professors, especially Professor Louis, were always impressed by references. As she searched for a book on truth and honesty, Isabelle hardly noticed the two Templins that marched past her in pursuit of Holt.

Though her mind was fixed on using the traditional, mundane methods for completing her paper, she kept feeling a nudge to walk over and explore the foreign policy section. *Professor Louis could appreciate a different perspective,* she thought, half-believing herself, as she tiptoed over to the section. Isabelle could not quite figure out how the books were categorized and was soon wiping the dust from the signs that were posted on the shelves. The sign that read "Discovering Truth" hung on one of the middle shelves, and Isabelle turned her head sideways to read the book titles. *Finding Truth within Yourself* sounded promising, and she quickly grabbed the book from the shelf.

The anger she was still holding towards Hertz, Eris, and Holt made her feel a bit brash and maybe even courageous. "I'm going to write what I want," she whispered to herself, then immediately realized she had heard Joel say these same words to her before. *My grades have always mattered more to me than doing what I really felt was right.* She shook her head in disgust at this revelation. *What do I feel? What do I really even think?* Suddenly she shuddered, thinking, *this place has brainwashed me.*

With the book clutched in her hand, she confidently approached her table, which was surrounded by three junior Templins.

"What happened to you?" asked one of the young officers.

His voice was apparently a little too loud, as the librarian nearby replied with a "Shhhhh!"

Isabelle, well aware of the visible scar the Templin was referring to, fixed her eyes on Holt and sat down in silence. The Templin who had spoken to her leaned forward to grab her arm, but his hand was swiftly caught by Holt's.

"She has work to do. A special assignment from Professor Louis," he spoke sternly to the Templin.

"So, are you saying she shouldn't have to respond to me?" he huffed in Holt's face.

Holt looked at Isabelle and said, "Answer quickly so you can begin your paper."

Isabelle pursed her lips then began. "I've had it since I was a child. It used to be darker, deeper, and much, much bigger. The infirmary works small miracles here." She hoped they caught her hint of sarcasm. "Or, if you are referring to this," she pointed to her lip, "then my answer would be that I was hit for telling the truth."

She opened the book and searched through the table of contents. "Hopefully this will give me some tips, so I can avoid such a dreadful scene again," she said, as she lifted the book and hid her face behind its cover.

"I think your girlfriend's gone mad," the same Templin who had spoken to her said to Holt.

The other Templin made a slashing sound as he drew his finger across his jaw line. He then smacked Holt on the shoulder and laughed out loud, much to the nearby librarian's exasperation. "Sorry," the Templin whispered towards the librarian, then turned back to Holt. "Definitely tainted, unless you want to admit you gave her that one." The speaker slowly grinned as he pointed in Holt's face. "Wait, didn't I see you with Eris last night? Are you double dipping, then?"

"I'm with neither," Holt said in defense.

"Oh yes, I forget, trying to live up to your father and all that. Your lovers are work and duty. How noble," the young man scoffed as he threw Holt a set of keys. "Suppose you can close this place down then?" he said, continuing to mock Holt.

"I will see to it," Holt nodded.

Isabelle watched them leave with great disdain. Her eyes met Holt's for a brief moment before he abruptly looked away. She knew he felt what she did. Though obviously apart, both were living in difficult seasons. The two were experiencing misery in their own ways, but unlike before, were unable to lean on one another. This situation put them back on common ground, yet the tension status and duty brought kept any comfort or encouragement they once had offered to each other silent.

After an hour or so of her thumbing through the book, he spoke quietly as not to disturb the library. "Is that from the foreign section?"

She nodded at him. "I thought it might give me a few extra points to write the paper from a different viewpoint."

"A foreign one?" He sounded doubtful.

"I had to pick something interesting to keep me awake," she said in self-defense, as she rubbed her eyes.

A few minutes later she felt like poking at him. "I'm not going to leave, if you have something else to do. Eris is probably waiting for you."

"Maybe she is," he shrugged.

Frustrated she did not get more of a reaction out of him, she turned back to the book and her outline. An hour later she had her outline and reference notes.

"I'm finished with this," she pointed to the book. "I can write this back in the common room. I promise I'll finish it. You don't have to watch me," she pleaded with him.

"You are my assignment, and I have to stay to lock up the library, anyway," he said matter-of-factly.

The hours slowly crept by as Isabelle wrote and Holt wandered around the library. Eventually the staff went home, which left only the two of them inside. Each of their bodies cried for sleep, tempted by the quiet in the place. The few dim lights that remained on did not help in this struggle. As long as Isabelle's hand moved in strokes across the page she stayed alert. Any stopping caused her eyelids to droop and her head to fall. It was not until she was halfway through reading over her first draft that she noticed Holt was breathing heavily with his eyes closed in the chair across the table from her. She eyed him with great displeasure, but soon said to herself, *at least he didn't take my music room key.*

She returned her eyes to her paper to make corrections. After she completed her final draft, she was sure Holt was in deep sleep. She sat across from him with her hand propped under her chin as she wondered what she should do. *I could leave him here.* She was certain sleeping on the job was punishable. When she scooted her chair back, she eyed the set of keys dangling from his hand. *Now that would be pretty dramatic.* She smirked while envisioning him trying to explain to Hertz how his keys had disappeared. *No, he'd know it was me and make my life even more miserable.* She gathered her papers and pencils, careful not to make a sound. *Leaving may just be the best option.* She sighed as she silently put on her coat and scarf.

She soon stood beside him and stopped to study him while he slept soundly. *I hate you, but you are still so handsome,* she realized, as she watched his thick chest rise and fall peacefully. He looked older to her. He seemed to have matured somehow in just a matter of weeks. He had moved past the arrogant boy and into a Templin official. "I'm sure your father is pleased with you, but your momma would not be proud of how you betrayed me," she whispered over him and then headed for the door.

She braced herself for the harsh cold as she nervously opened the door. Isabelle knew being out after hours without a Templin escort was dangerous enough, but being alone the night before chapel caused her anxiety to escalate. *If I'm caught by myself I'll be in even more trouble.* She raced across the lighted path and into the dark shadows near the courtyard fence.

She was inching carefully towards her hall when all of a sudden she saw two images emerge from behind the courtyard gate. Isabelle froze and pressed herself hard against the fence, hoping to blend in with the dark shadows that surrounded her. The two images were moving toward her, and she soon heard their voices.

"Good heavens! You are overreacting, Master Dark."

Isabelle recognized the speaker as Professor Louis.

"Her file was stolen, or at least went missing after the meeting, and now she is missing from her hall. How am I overreacting?" she heard the headmaster snap back at him.

"Who told you she was missing this evening?" Professor Louis asked loudly as he had fallen a few steps behind the headmaster.

"Eris Brunell."

Isabelle seethed under her hood upon hearing the girl's name.

"Gracious, that girl—Blast! Stop!" Professor Louis yelled as he grabbed the headmaster's shoulder, but his actions were to no avail. "You are becoming paranoid over a small boy, one who is completely harmless, I might add. He has no power," he said breathlessly, having to jog to keep at the headmaster's pace. "So, he's gone," Professor Louis let out as he sped up and rounded in front of the headmaster. "You know as well as I do that he's probably dead. That would make retrieving most anyone impossible."

The headmaster finally stopped and rubbed his head in frustration.

"Eris Brunell is Mr. Langston's new love interest," Professor Louis continued.

"Well, the girl was not lying. The housekeeper had not seen Isabelle, either," the headmaster countered.

"Perhaps, but I'm doubtful that Eris told the whole truth."

Isabelle's heart pounded furiously when she realized that they were talking about her. Here she was in the shadows without Holt. *If they find me, it will look like I am running away.* She started backtracking toward the library. She kept flush against the fence and moved as speedily as the need to be quiet would allow. She was able to hear a few more words before she was completely out of earshot.

"Oh, please, Emerson. I am aware who has the power here, but this is about principle. No one escapes here; they are released."

"Principles? And are you sure finances have no matter in this?"

Isabelle thought Professor Louis's question sounded more like an accusation.

"Yes," she heard the headmaster hiss back at him. "In fact, in both of these matters much is on the line."

"You haven't told Joel's father, have you?"

Isabelle stopped to hear the headmaster's answer, but she instead heard nothing.

"That's what I thought," Professor Louis said to the headmaster's silence.

Just when Isabelle thought the headmaster had calmed down, he let out an angry growl and then barked, "Where *is* Templin Langston?"

Isabelle saw a Templin on the far corner of the courtyard step forward and shout softly, "He is closing up the library tonight, headmaster."

They're everywhere! She wondered how she had not been caught yet.

While the three discussed Langston's whereabouts, Isabelle made a mad dash toward the library. She ran just outside the lit path to remain hidden.

"Come on," she heard the headmaster yell behind her.

Oh no, she thought, as she viewed the lighted and clearly visible library doorway. *How will I get in without being seen?* She saw the two heading for the path to the library and panicked. She knew the headmaster was ready to have a reason to punish her or use her as "bait."

She ran anxiously to the back of the library building, aware that the headmaster was closer with his every step.

When Isabelle reached the back of the building, through pitch black she easily spotted a light shining through a small window. She began to beat on the window hard enough to wake Holt but lightly enough to not be heard by the headmaster. After a few moments Isabelle peered through the window and was vaguely able to make out Holt, who still appeared to be fast asleep. She pounded harder in a desperate attempt to wake him. She finally resorted to breaking the window and turned to scour the ground for a hard object. A lump went into her throat when she heard footsteps coming from around the side of the building.

"A banging! There's some banging back here!" she heard the headmaster cry.

Isabelle stood frozen in fear and then thought to do something she had not done in a number of years. "Just let me get in," she cried out to some unseen presence for help. *Run!* her mind screamed. She swiftly picked up her feet to head in the opposite direction of the headmaster's voice.

When she reached the front, she waited cautiously for a brief second and then decided to make for the doorway. She squinted once she was back in the light, but quickly eyed the library's door handle. She slammed the door behind her and ran to the table, turning lights back on as she zoomed through the place. She shook Holt just as she heard the front door begin to open again.

Holt stirred, and she kicked him hard from underneath the table after she sat down.

"What?" he started.

But she interrupted him in a loud, robotic voice, "I am finished with my assignment and ready to go back to my hall."

He looked at her as if she had gone mad.

"Oh," Isabelle cooed as she looked past Holt in feigned surprise. "Headmaster," she bowed her head towards him.

A look of terror came over Holt's face, and he quickly stood in honor of the headmaster. "Sir," he bowed his head.

"What is the meaning of this?" the headmaster spoke sharply.

"Oh yes, I had forgotten," Professor Louis waved his hand then gave an explanation, "I gave Isabelle a special assignment after an incident today—a paper on finding honesty and truth. Mr. Langston was to oversee her to ensure she completed the assignment. It's due in ... well, a few hours," he said, as he glanced down at his watch.

The headmaster looked at Professor Louis in furious disbelief. "You're just now remembering this?"

"Uh, yes."

Isabelle caught the amused tone in the professor's voice.

In his continued fury, the headmaster turned to Isabelle and spoke sternly. "Is the paper in your bag?"

"Yes, sir, right here," she said as she pulled it out.

"No, I shall look it over after Professor Louis approves it," the headmaster replied as he motioned for her to put it away.

Isabelle watched the headmaster's eyes linger on her and then move to Holt's chair, which was covered with his unbuttoned coat.

"Isabelle, you're fully dressed. Have you been outside?" he asked suspiciously, but before she could answer he continued, "Langston, have you been awake? Miss Isabelle, has Mr. Langston been awake these last few hours? I hope I need not remind you that you just completed writing a paper on honesty and truth," he reprimanded her harshly.

Isabelle looked across the table at Holt. *My, how the tables have turned.* She paused before she answered, imagining herself holding a glowing, tangible power in her hands over Holt's head. She did not particularly want to save Holt's rear end, but having the opportunity to lie to the headmaster was a far more enticing option. She also needed Holt as an alibi since the headmaster had been hunting her minutes earlier.

"Headmaster, Mr. Langston told me I had to be finished and in my coat by two-thirty."

The headmaster looked at Holt in satisfaction. "Good job keeping charge, Langston; however, I stand by my counsel for you to keep your association with Miss Isabelle strictly professional."

Holt nodded, "Yes, sir, of course."

The headmaster sighed wearily and motioned to Professor Louis. "All right, let's go. Lock up, Langston."

"Yes, good night. See you in the morning, Isabelle," Professor Louis waved and followed behind the headmaster.

Holt put on his coat and cloak in silence then led Isabelle to the library's front door. He pulled out his keys and then turned to face her. "How long was I asleep?" he asked nervously.

"Only the last two and a half hours," she said matter-of-factly before pushing past him to open the door.

"Why did you come back?" he called out as he moved swiftly between her and the door.

She pulled on her hood and did not answer.

"How could—why did you lie to the headmaster—for me?" he sputtered out in a whisper.

She smiled to herself then said, half-smirking, "To make my momma proud."

The next morning Isabelle barely woke in time to get showered before going to see Professor Louis. She was surprised to see he was not dressed for chapel and appeared to have no intention of attending. She came dressed in her robes just in case she was dismissed early. With all the warnings and bizarre clues he had given her, she had anticipated his response to her attempt at a more emotional paper.

"Ah, good morning," he said brightly when he saw her approaching.

"Good morning, sir," she replied politely as she handed him the paper.

Professor Louis looked over the paper while Isabelle sat by the window and waited for him to dismiss her. A few minutes into his read, she heard him make an "ahem" noise. She turned toward him as he removed his spectacles and shook his head.

"Isabelle, I'm torn. This is fine writing, one of your better papers." He paused.

"Thank you, sir."

"Yes, well, the writing may be outstanding, but your content is not."

"I'm sorry, sir?" she asked, wondering what he could mean.

"Isabelle, the content of this paper contradicts what the temple teaches. You wrote in this about discovering truth through experiences and by the examples of heroic people. But, my dear, the truth, is well ... the real truth is found in what the temple teaches you is truth. Truth is learned through the temple's education, and, by truth being learned this way, it is kept."

"So, you're saying that all truth is only found in books, and furthermore, that all truth can only be found on these grounds? Are you saying the uneducated live in complete ignorance?" she asked.

Professor Louis raised his eyebrows, and she wondered if her defensive tone had overstepped her bounds.

"I'm sorry, sir. I didn't mean to contradict *you*," she stated. *I only intended to contradict the temple.*

"Well, in any case, this is completely unacceptable due to content, but I will give you a second chance. A reference from the ethics section would be more appropriate for this subject."

She looked down in disappointment and heard him say she was dismissed. "Professor Louis, with all due respect, you didn't answer my questions."

"Isabelle, I do not have to answer questions that accuse my knowledge on a subject. However, I will say this: you belong to this temple and so do I. I am to teach what the establishment has requested. It is how I show honor to my authority. So, I will say that the temple doctrine states that all truth rests here, and that is what I teach. But," he lowered his voice, "that does not mean my personal beliefs always hold the same ideas as those of the temple's doctrine. Understood?" he asked firmly.

She was a bit puzzled but was slowly catching on to his words.

"Hopefully you understand, then, why this is unacceptable. I will need another one by tomorrow morning," he said, as he threw her paper into the trash can.

Isabelle had no response. She watched him begin to busy himself with other papers on his desk.

When he noticed she had not moved, he flicked his wrist toward her and said, "That will be all."

Her shoulders drooped as she headed for the door. She felt completely defeated by the only one she thought might understand. *He's just like the others. He—*

Her thought was interrupted by his voice. "Oh, Isabelle? Don't forget that the headmaster wanted to see your paper."

CHAPTER 17

SEBASTIAN AWOKE JUST in time to see Joel disappear down the ladder. When Sebastian didn't hear the barn door open, he scooted to the edge of the loft. He decided to spy on his friend and kept his head down low in the hay. When he peered over the edge, Joel was glancing right in his direction. Sebastian held his breath, but Joel did not seem to notice him.

Sebastian watched with curiosity as Joel moved a loose board from the wall that held all the shelves for the milking equipment. He saw Joel grab his knapsack from behind the board. First, Joel pulled out a pair of old, worn boots. He rummaged through the bag for a few moments and then found a pair of pants. A large scroll slipped from one of the pant legs when he attempted to shake the fabric out of its wrinkled state. Sebastian saw three smaller documents slide out from the scroll. *My maps!* Joel shot a sharp glance towards the loft and then quickly stuffed the scroll and knapsack back into their hiding place. Joel then wandered under the loft to change clothes. *And to get ready for the milking, I bet.*

The little boy always enjoyed helping others, but he especially wanted to help Joel. Sebastian had not been able to thank Joel for carrying him all over Old Waiz the day before, and besides that, he just really liked being with him. *He makes me laugh*, Sebastian thought, as he spotted Joel's red hair directly beneath him. Sebastian began dropping strands of hay on Joel's head until he finally turned around to see who the culprit was. Sebastian held a finger to his lips to indicate that Augustine was still asleep.

Joel gestured, "Do you want me to come get you?"

Sebastian nodded an eager yes.

Both nearly held their breath until they reached the outside of the barn.

"Thanks," Sebastian exclaimed cheerfully.

"Good morning, and don't thank me yet. I'm putting you to work." Joel smiled, knowing that was truly the desire of Sebastian's heart.

"What about the farmer?" Sebastian whispered nervously.

"He won't be coming around today. It's that whole chapel deal I told you about. He told me just to get what I wanted and that he'd be out later or not at all," Joel said as he grabbed some rope.

"How do you know which ones to milk, then?" Sebastian asked.

"We should be able to tell who's ready, but I'm pretty sure the farmer left the ones that needed to be milked in this pen. We just need two, though—one for me and one for you. I thought we'd go old fashioned today, just buckets and hands."

Sebastian studied his hands; he was thankful that they worked better than his legs.

Joel carried him, two buckets and some rope toward the pen. He sat Sebastian down on a small stool and then hooked the ropes to each goat and tied them to the fence post. He picked up the stool with the little boy sitting on top of it and parked it next to a goat.

"Have you ever done this before?" Joel asked.

"No. I can assure you," Sebastian replied.

"All right. Well, she knows what you need to do, so she shouldn't give you much trouble," Joel said while stroking the goat's neck. "The bucket goes here, of course, and you pretty much just tug."

After a few tries, Sebastian was on a roll, and Joel started on his goat.

"Hey, Joel," Sebastian called out from below the goat.

"Hm? You doing okay?" Joel called back.

"Yes, of course. I just wanted to tell you I had a good time yesterday. I couldn't have gone without you," Sebastian admitted.

Joel blew off the compliment by saying, "I definitely want to go out again."

"Yeah, me, too." Sebastian decided it was time to think of a way to bring up the scroll he had seen in Joel's knapsack. "Sure was a good thing you had that map yesterday."

"Mm-hm," Joel replied.

"Hey, you know, I just remembered you have the map my dad drew of Crossroads Station," Sebastian said. He tried to act nonchalant about the topic, although he had to catch himself from saying "maps."

"Yeah, guess we don't need that anymore," Joel said. Sebastian could see the perspiration start to build on Joel's forehead.

"Um ... Augustine doesn't know you have that or the others. There were a few other maps with that one. She'd kill me if she knew you had them."

"Pretty sure she wouldn't kill you, just get really mad at me. She's good at that," Joel reassured him.

"Well, if you could sneak them back to me, um ..."

When Joel stood up, he looked over the goats and saw Sebastian's nervous face. "Sebastian, it's okay to ask me for something that belongs to you."

Joel watched the little boy's stiff shoulders relax.

"I didn't want to offend you. I heard Augustine last night ... she wants you to stay with us, and you know I do," he said earnestly.

"You weren't asleep? You little faker," Joel playfully scolded him and continued, "And seriously, let's clarify, Augustine didn't say she wanted me to stay; she was giving me *permission* to stay."

"Well it might help not to make her mad, so maybe you could get those maps back to me."

Joel acted as if he did not hear Sebastian.

"Joel?" Sebastian asked politely and was again met with total silence.

"Joel?" Sebastian asked more forcefully, and Joel soon plopped his stool next to Sebastian's.

"Yeah, there's a small problem there."

Sebastian waited for Joel to explain.

Joel gritted his teeth and looked away from him. He let out a short sigh and turned back to look Sebastian in the eyes. "When the guy in the green cloak hit me, he also emptied my pockets. He took yours and my maps. I don't have them anymore."

Both kept looking at the other, but neither said a word. By this time, they had finished milking their goats, and Joel untied the ropes from the fence.

As Sebastian watched Joel lead the goats slowly to a neighboring pen, he felt a wave of betrayal wash over him. He had seen Joel with three maps this morning! *He's lying to me. Why would he lie to me? I won't tell Augustine! Why doesn't he trust me? Why is he stealing from me?*

All these questions and more ran wild in his head but came with no answers. He so wanted Joel to be his friend. He wanted to trust him, yet he seemed just like Augustine. *Doesn't trust anyone,* Sebastian scowled as he looked down at his pail full of milk. He was deeply saddened, and his excitement about helping his friend today was gone.

Joel walked over to him. "Wow, you got a full pail on your first try! You're an expert," Joel complimented Sebastian lightheartedly, then turned a bit more serious. "Listen, you think we can keep the missing maps our secret for now?"

"Are you going to tell Corwin?"

When Joel did not answer right away, Sebastian pressed him. "Why didn't you mention the maps that night or tell Mr. Rutherford?"

"If you'll remember, I wasn't supposed to have those maps in the first place. I didn't think it would sound very good to Augustine, or Mr. Rutherford, or to you for that matter."

Sebastian still felt sure Joel was lying, but decided not to push him anymore.

"Ready to take these up?" Joel smiled at him, acting as if nothing was wrong.

"Yes," Sebastian frowned back at him. "You know, I am excellent at keeping secrets," Sebastian said as he raised his chin towards Joel.

"Yes, I believe that," Joel said as he picked him up.

When they returned to the barn, Augustine greeted them. "Good Morning!" Joel noted that she was not flustered or frightened at having awakened to find both of them missing.

"Augustine, I want to go to chapel today," Sebastian announced. The two others expressed their surprise, for it was not a request but a demand.

"Well, okay. Do you know what time we should be there? Oh, and what we should wear?"

Joel sighed, confused at Sebastian's interest in the place. "The blue dress should be fine and whatever goes with that," Joel said as he motioned to Sebastian.

"Yes, we can go, but let's wash up first. We need to hurry, so *no* fussing." She was surprised when her little brother only nodded. "Can you manage breakfast?" Augustine asked Joel.

"Probably more like a snack," he replied.

"Fine. We'll wash up quickly—I mean, if that's all right? You—you don't plan to go, do you?" she asked.

Joel saw the look of apprehension on her face but kept his resolve. "I'll get you there, but I'm not attending," he said stiffly.

Joel was thankful the two knew very little about chapel, or he was sure Augie would scold him for not going. He planned to make himself scarce today just as the farmer had recommended. He wanted to search for a caychura again or at least try to find the Marcell House. He supposed he would now have to wait on the other two. As he fixed breakfast he thought about his conversation with Sebastian. Joel had not wanted to tell Corwin about the Green Cloak, but he was sure the intruder had wanted something of Corwin's. In Joel's mind, the Green Cloak finding him with the maps had just been plain lucky for the scarred faced man.

Augustine carefully helped Sebastian get ready, even though they were in a hurry. "What have you been up to this morning?"

"I helped Joel milk the goats."

"Wow, that was a first. How did you fare?" she smiled at him.

"I managed to get a whole bucket with hardly any help."

"Impressive," she said as she started to dry him off.

"Yes, that's what Joel said," he added.

"So, why this sudden interest in chapel today, might I ask?"

"Well, we've never been before, which was usually because I couldn't get out in the cold or because the poor weren't allowed that day. All that has changed here; so I thought we should try it," Sebastian shrugged at her.

"Oh, I figured Madame Bontecou had lured you with her fine speech yesterday," she winked at him.

"It was interesting," he laughed, as he pulled on his shirt.

"I wish Joel would go," she said, shocking even herself.

Sebastian shot her a look of disbelief.

"Well, I assume he's been quite a bit, and you know I don't enjoy doing new things by myself."

"You won't be by yourself," Sebastian said defensively.

"No, of course not. Sorry," she tenderly touched his arm. "I just meant it would be nice to have someone who knew what to do inside. That's all."

He brushed his hair while she brushed her teeth.

"Well, I bet he'll go looking for one of those crazy caychura things again."

Augie sensed the irritation in his voice. "Sebastian, did you not have a good time exploring yesterday?"

"It was boring. Let's just stay around here today," he answered.

"Well, all right," she paused in confusion. "We can just ask Joel—"

"He can do what he wants," Sebastian interrupted her.

Augustine then knelt down beside him. "Sebastian, is there something you wish to tell me? I promise it will stay between us."

She watched him avoid her gaze, as he answered with a firm "No."

"Are you sure? Nothing between you and Joel I need to know about?" she questioned further.

Sebastian shrugged and in continued irritation responded, "No, maybe I just need a break from him."

Augustine was completely taken aback by her brother's behavior, but decided maybe a break really was what he needed. She did not push him anymore on the subject, as she well knew the toxic effect negative emotions had on the little boy's body.

"Well then, we'll take a break today, just me and you."

"Maybe Corwin, too, if he gets back early," replied Sebastian.

Augustine nodded in response, seriously hoping that Corwin would arrive.

As they headed back towards the barn, he tugged at her sleeve and whined, "I also don't want to stay here tonight. Can we go somewhere with a bed?"

Augustine was alarmed at his behavior and was unsure how to respond. She dared not reprimand his dreadful attitude, fearing that irritating him further would immediately compromise his fragile condition. She did not want to face a swift decline in his health without Corwin.

"Our bags are pretty much packed. Maybe the chapel would have a place for us. Let's at least take our things," he pleaded.

"Sebastian, I don't know," Augustine said, trying to sound calm in spite of the apprehension she felt.

"I don't want to leave my stuff here," he demanded.

"Okay, yes, we'll take it with us. Probably not everything, but most of it," she said. Her nervousness was hard to control as she tried to soothe his heated emotions.

They entered the barn and found Joel's snack he had fixed for the two of them.

"Here. Go ahead and eat, and I'll get the bags," she said to Sebastian.

Joel cast her a puzzled look, and she tried to communicate by showing him a confused shrug.

"Joel, can you help me grab a few things?"

"Uh, sure." Joel watched as she quickly stuffed Sebastian's and her things into two bags.

She suddenly whispered to him, "Did anything happen between you two while you were milking the goats?"

Joel shrugged and shook his head. "No."

Out of respect for her brother and fearing a fatal breathing episode, Augustine said nothing of the emotions she was sensing from him. Joel was obviously confused as to why she was packing up their bags but helped her get them down just the same.

"Thank you. We'll get the rest later," she said while grabbing her snack and glass of milk.

"Are you not coming back here tonight?" he asked slowly.

"Well, uh, we're not sure. If we can find a *bed* in safety we may try that tonight."

She turned to take the bags from his hands, "But, Joel, thank you for letting us stay with you."

Joel felt a slight sense of rejection but was mindful of Augustine's offer from the night before. He wondered if a bed would be offered to him, as well. He nodded at her but still did not quite understand what was happening.

"Ready?" she looked at Sebastian.

"Ready," he nodded.

"Can I help you walk to chapel?" Joel asked when he realized they were about to leave.

"Sure. That would be great," Augustine said with surprising kindness in her voice.

Joel noted that the silence on the trail was strange for their group, particularly for Sebastian.

"Anything we should know about chapel?" Augustine asked, finally breaking the silence.

"No. Just follow everyone else. If they sit down, sit. If they stand up, stand and sing, then sit down and then stand and sing. And so on. You get the point."

She nodded and said, "Sounds robotic."

"That and boring," Joel replied.

"Will you look for a caychura again today?" she asked.

"I was hoping to, but I can wait until chapel is over for you two," he offered.

"Well, I think we may stay around here today," she said and looked away as if avoiding his look of surprise.

"Sebastian, you up for another adventure today?" Joel asked playfully.

"No, I don't want to go. *You* should go on alone. I don't think I believe in caychuras. Come find us if you locate one."

Joel was stunned at his little friend's harsh answer and almost stopped pushing him.

They reached the edge of the clearing, and the chapel bells began to chime.

"Just in time," Joel announced.

Augustine stopped and reached for the bag he was carrying. "Well, thank you. I think we can manage from here."

"So, I'll see you later," he said, realizing he sounded like he was asking if he would.

His eyes met Augustine's, and he noted their sadness, as well as even remorse. "Corwin should be back soon, and well, I think we can manage on our own today," she said, taking the wheelchair handles from him.

Is this the end? He wondered if Augustine was revoking her invitation.

"So, I won't see you later," he muttered as anger flooded his face quickly hiding any signs of hurt he may be feeling.

"No, not today," she said softly.

Did Sebastian tell her about the maps? What's this all about?

"Perhaps we'll see you at the shop sometime," she shrugged.

"Maybe. Now that I have less responsibility I may head to New Waiz," he quipped, and she knew he meant it as a barb.

"Thank you so much," she raised her hand as if to touch him, but then let it fall away. "Thank you for everything."

"If you feel you need compensation for your *responsibility*, I'm sure Corwin will oblige you," Sebastian said haughtily, causing Augustine to cringe.

Joel was used to seeing haughtiness from Augustine, but he was not sure how to react with it coming from Sebastian. It was as if they had changed personalities over the course of an hour.

What is wrong with him? The young fellow had not acted a bit angry towards him while they were milking, not even about the maps. *Besides, it's not my fault really. And I was protecting them from being killed. This is ridiculous.* He was so angry he could barely muster a response.

"No, I—money," he sputtered and then gained control. "I guess this is goodbye, then."

Augustine nodded through gritted teeth.

"Farewell," Sebastian called out from the wheelchair without turning around.

Augustine mouthed, "Thank you," in silence.

Joel shrugged and raised his hand in farewell as he began walking in the opposite direction. Thoughts about the past few days ran through his mind. He had wanted to search for a caychura, but could not shake off the emotions he felt from the seemingly ended relationship with the brother and sister. He was reminded how losing people seemed to be his fate. Every relationship became entangled, began to fail, and then finally ended.

He thought of Isabelle and wondered if she had thought of him. *Has she even noticed I'm gone?* He remembered being so furious when he had caught Holt giving Eris Isabelle's locket that he thought he might go out of his mind. Isabelle had hidden the family heirloom away in a lock box, as it was one of the very few things of value her family owned. Her grandfather had given it to her after she had received her temple acceptance letter. Joel thought that retrieving the locket, as he had several times before, would be enough to win Isabelle over. *To win her away from him,* he thought, as he pictured Holt in his mind. He knew deep down Holt cared for her in his own way, but he was such a fathead. Joel had always felt that he himself did not deserve Isabelle, and that is why, above all else, he had hated seeing her with Holt. Holt thought he deserved her. *He used his father's name to get everything he wanted.* He had observed Holt's entitlement persona on numerous occasions. There was no denying Langston was a powerful name, but in Joel's mind it did not change the fact that Holt was still a fathead.

He closed his eyes and thought of her beautiful face, her silky blond hair, and her voice. Her voice was the most beautiful sound he had ever heard. In his times of trouble, she had sung to him. Her voice had been the only thing that had comforted him in their many years at Moonstruck.

To his surprise, Augustine standing in her blue dress flashed through his mind as he reminisced. Something had changed in her since she had come to Adams; he supposed in some ways they had all changed.

The bells began to chime overhead, and the doors of the chapel soon opened. The crowd came out, and he quickly spotted the siblings. Sebastian hobbled out while Augustine followed behind him carrying a few items. Joel wondered where the wheelchair was and craned his neck from his place on the ground to look around them. He soon located the chair and its carrier. "Guess it all worked out for them," he said bitterly, as he watched Corwin walk a few feet behind them with the wheelchair under his arm.

Jealousy entered his heart as he watched them smile and laugh in the square. He spat and stood to his feet. *The responsibility Corwin entrusted to me is now done.* He had the museum map and all afternoon. He did not care what Sebastian had said. This place did not just happen by chance. If there were any caychuras left he would find them, and the sooner the better because Adams was becoming too small for the three of them, and the New City was beckoning.

When Professor Louis reminded Isabelle that the headmaster wanted to read her paper, she understood his response, although she still could not decide if he really agreed with her content or not. As she walked back to the library, she remembered it would be locked until after chapel. She sat on the cold stone steps and tried to think of a more traditional way to write her paper. *No wonder it was my best writing; I actually enjoyed it. Traditional* methods had always translated into "boring" to her.

"Need a key?" someone asked, interrupting her thoughts.

She looked up and was surprised to see Holt standing in front of her.

"Yes, in fact. You were right. Foreign policy didn't go over so well," she said in disgust.

"Doing another?" he cocked his head at her.

"Yes, due tomorrow morning," she sighed.

"The library isn't supposed to open until this afternoon."

"Yes, I know." She looked pleadingly at him.

He grinned. "Come on."

A few moments later she had found her book.

"Just give me a few minutes, and I'll have what I need," she said, as she looked around for Holt.

"Take your time. I'm still on assignment to ensure you get it done," he called out from the other side of the room.

Just as she had said, in a matter of minutes Isabelle had copied all she needed for her second paper. "All right, all done. Thanks," she said as she approached him.

Holt looked at his watch and smiled, "You're seriously the smartest student I know."

She noted his tone had been all but professional today. "You don't have to do me any favors for saving your cloak last night, especially flattery," she protested.

"I know, but I'd told you that several times before," he said, tenderness in his voice.

Isabelle softened at his words, and soon their eyes met.

"Do you enjoy your work?" she asked as she folded her pages of notes.

"Not like I thought I would," Holt replied, and Isabelle moved closer to him.

"Do you enjoy your father's approval?"

When his lips did not budge, Isabelle gave him a sympathetic smile. There was a long pause before either spoke again.

"Right. Well, I need to get this finished for the both of us."

Holt nodded and got his keys ready.

He started to follow her back towards Thymes Hall, but she turned to him and held her hand up. "No really, I can do this alone."

He made a motion to continue by her side, but suddenly turned to walk off in the opposite direction.

As she watched him walk away, slightly satisfied that he had obeyed her request, she thought of the night before. How had she not been caught or seen with the Templin guards everywhere? And why on earth had she called out to something in the darkness?

She had done that very thing much in her childhood and many times in Moonstruck. When things were bad or scary, she found herself calling out for help. And, she could rarely think of a time when something did not happen in response. It was bizarre, and she had not spoken of it to anyone besides Joel. He didn't think it was strange and, since it made her feel better, had encouraged her to do it. *Maybe I am crazy ... maybe they were right to put me in Moonstruck.*

CHAPTER 18

MUCH TO HIS dismay, when Joel tried to make his way back toward the Marcell House, the main road was blocked. When he asked a couple walking toward Forest Park about it, they said it was in honor of *The Book of Order.*

"It's for rest. All the main roads are blocked, and most of the shops are closed on the day of chapel. This is done in order to encourage those in Old Waiz to participate in the principle of rest."

I'm sure New Waiz is still alive today. He looked down at the empty square. He thought about trying to trek through the woods to the Marcell House, but was afraid the darkness would find him before he could get back to the barn.

Near the end of the afternoon, he trudged back to the barn, defeated by *The Book of Order.* He was cautious to make sure no one was around before he slid open the barn door.

"I was hoping I'd catch you before I left," said a familiar female voice as he closed the door.

He turned around to find Augustine stuffing the rest of her and Sebastian's belongings into a luggage bag.

"I brought you something. I thought you might be hungry," she said as she gestured next to the large, glowing lantern seated on the table.

Though he expected to see cheese and milk, he was pleasantly surprised to find three sausage kabobs wrapped in paper next to a buttered roll. There was also a small jug of water Joel figured she must have pumped for him from outside. The aroma of the food soon reached his senses, and his body begged him to eat.

"It's from lunch, but I figured you wouldn't mind it being a little cool," she said, looking at him apprehensively.

"No, it's great," he assured her as he moved toward the table. He wanted to ask her about Corwin being back and where they were staying, but he refrained while thinking, *what's the point? I won't be seeing them anymore.* He ate in silence as she finished packing. As he bit into his second kabob, Augustine joined him at the table.

"Good?" she asked while trying to peek at his face from around the large lamp.

"Fine," he muttered through a bite.

"Did you explore today? Did you—did you find anything?"

He shook his head no. "Roads were blocked," he said through a mouthful of food, then took a gulp of water.

"Oh, right, rest principle and all. You were right, I was more bored in chapel than I was at the museum." She smiled at him then reached into her pocket and slid something across the table. "Here's a little dessert from Corwin. He had hoped to see you, but … he's keeping Sebastian."

Little traitor. He glanced at the packaging on the chocolate she had just given him.

"Corwin's been in Differe!" he declared in surprise.

"He hasn't said where he went, and I haven't had a chance to ask him," Augustine shrugged.

"It wasn't a question, Augie. I've seen these before," he pointed to the chocolate. "They're from downtown Differe, *and* it's the only place you can get them—not exported." *Did Corwin want me to know that he had been in Differe?* "Augustine, did he tell you to give this to me?"

She nodded, "Yes, he said it was a very small thanks from him."

She moved the lamp from the center of the table, so she could get a clearer look at him. "Joel, I know I told you that you could stay—"

Joel did not give her the opportunity to finish. "Really you don't have to explain. I get it. Corwin's back, and you don't need me to carry your little brother everywhere anymore."

Augustine deflected the anger in his voice with her own harsh words. "I didn't need you in the first place."

"Oh yeah, really? Well, next time I'll let you save yourself and your brother from a mad man," he spat out sharply.

"He would have left eventually. You just had to jump into the room to prove you're some sort of hero," she accused.

"*Eventually* he would've come into your room, and well, I guess I should have just left you to find that out!" he yelled at her.

"Well, at least *then* I would have a story that is more believable than yours. What really happened in that room?" she asked, while slightly raising the decibel level of her voice.

He stood up and glared at her. "Get out. I don't care what you think. And contrary to what you said, you *are* too good for this place. I should've left you at the inn."

"I'm going!" she rose with the bag in her hand. She moved toward him fiercely and shouted, "But first, what happened this morning? What did you do to Sebastian?"

"I don't know! Ask him!" he yelled back at her while wondering how things had gotten so heated.

"I have!" she screamed as she dropped the bag. "He won't say a word, but only that he wants you to be on your way. Tell me what happened," she commanded.

She was shaking with rage. Joel scoffed and shook his finger in her face. "He has you wrapped around his little finger, doesn't he? Do you ever think of yourself, Augie?"

Before he could move, she slapped his cheek. She drew back and Joel felt an expression of hate cross his face.

"There you are, Augie. I was wondering where you'd been," he said sarcastically.

She stepped back and buried her face in her hands, and Joel could see the shock on her face at what she had done. He watched her shrink to the ground in sobs.

"Please, Joel. He's all I have and he's—he's so frail. I can't lose him. I will be a failure, but worst of all I'll be all alone."

"Join the club," he replied unsympathetically, as he grabbed her bag and threw it by the barn door. "Get out."

When she didn't move, Joel walked over and grabbed her arm.

"Please, Joel," she pleaded with him, and he saw that her other hand held the little pink bag stuffed with cash. He clenched his jaw in annoyance, infuriated by her gesture.

"Augustine," he said firmly, "I can honestly say I don't know what has gotten into him. He did ask me about something I borrowed from him this morning. That's I all can remember."

In her mind's eye Augustine saw her mother slapping her father's face, just as she had just done to Joel. She felt shame flow over her as she looked at him. She knew he was telling the truth; somehow, she had learned to judge his truthfulness by his eyes. Even so, she decided to press him. "Borrowed or stole?" She knew the answer when he did not respond.

"Well, where is it then? Let's clean up this mess," she sighed as she wiped away her tears.

He ignored her and went over to climb the ladder.

"Please, Joel. Please," she called out after him. "Where is it? We can fix this."

"No, we can't," he said under his breath. "It's with the Green Cloak, but I'm sure you don't believe that, either." And with that, he toppled over the ladder into the loft.

The next morning Isabelle promptly turned her paper in to Professor Louis. Holt was with her to witness that his duty had been fulfilled. Isabelle was pleased when Professor Louis gave her a passing mark.

"Isabelle, the headmaster is very interested in seeing you learned your lesson in this matter. He has requested you and Mr. Langston present this paper to him at nine o'clock this morning. You obviously have permission to skip my class, which is also at that time." He marked the paper then handed it back to her.

"Sir, will you be going with us?" she asked nervously.

The professor shot her a small smile and said, "No, dear, for as I just said, I have a class to teach. My passing mark should indicate my judgment on the paper."

As usual, she lingered around his desk until he looked up and said, "That will be all, Isabelle." The two students were about to leave his classroom when all of the sudden Professor Louis called out after Holt. "Mr. Langston, as I recall, you have a meeting with the headmaster just prior to nine o'clock. Is that correct?"

"Yes, sir," Holt nodded.

"I would hurry if I were you," he encouraged him.

"Isabelle, you may wait in the headmaster's lobby until you are called back."

Both headed to the headmaster's building in silence. Isabelle's heart pounded as her spirit filled with dread. *Weren't we just here?* she thought as they entered the door to the lobby. The two soon sat across from one another in the middle of the room on plush emerald velvet couches.

The headmaster's lobby mostly mimicked his office. A monstrous crystal chandelier hung under a hand-painted dome ceiling. The room was windowless and walled in by dark wooden panels. There was a large fireplace encased by a wrought iron grate. The iron reminded Isabelle of Moonstruck, and she had always hated looking at it. The floors were covered by a thick hand-stitched rug with golden threads that shined as they reflected the chandelier's light.

Holt's and Isabelle's couches and a few silk covered chairs were placed throughout the room. Considering that the temple still belonged to the city of Differe, which placed little value on inside decor, it was surprising to find the building's exterior had an interior to match. Holt was quickly called into the headmaster's study while Isabelle was left to anxiously wait her turn. While flipping and thumbing through her paper, she tried to prepare for any questions the headmaster might ask her. *This time I'll play the part of the typical Differian robot, just like everyone else at this school.*

Head Templin Hertz Marlis was bringing the headmaster a drink when Holt walked into the room.

"Well, good to see you are on time. Have a seat," the dark-haired Templin commanded.

Holt sat uneasily in the same green chair he had seen Isabelle sit in the last time he was here. He was sure Isabelle had not told on him for falling asleep, but he had no idea why he was sitting in the headmaster's study.

"Well, I suppose you are wondering why you are here?"

Holt hesitated. He nodded at the headmaster as he watched his jewelry-adorned fingers grab his glass.

"Tell him, Templin Marlis," the headmaster instructed before sipping his drink.

"Well I have bad news for *you,* Langston," Hertz smirked as he flashed his dark eyes at Holt. "Your father has become aware that you failed your first assignment."

Holt felt his blood pressure drop as Hertz continued, "Yes, he knows all you had to do was watch two deranged students from Moonstruck.

In fact, he was furious to learn you let one escape, and was practically repulsed to find out you were actually in love with the other."

Hertz watched with an expression of great pleasure as shame clouded Holt's face. Holt turned his head towards the floor as his spirit filled with grief.

The somber moment passed when Holt suddenly heard the headmaster and Hertz sputter into laughter. Holt watched in disbelief as Hertz held his stomach, gasping for breath.

"He—he thought I was serious," Hertz let out between bellows of laughter. "You—you should see your face." Hertz sat down into a corner chair and continued to snicker.

The headmaster was less demonstrative, but had certainly let out a few sharp chuckles. "Relax, Mr. Langston. Your father is a much too busy man to be bothered by the affairs of a junior Templin, even if you are his son."

Holt felt the color return to his face, and his breathing return to normal.

"Mr. Langston, I assume you are aware that Templin officers, as well as the Differian Army, are in pursuit of Joel?"

Holt nodded as he wiped away beads of sweat from underneath the brown locks that lay on his forehead.

"The temple has reason to believe Joel's whereabouts will be located in the next several days."

"So soon?" Hertz interrupted from the corner.

"Yes. The Templins have a significant lead," the headmaster said in his direction. He turned back towards Holt. "Mr. Langston, due to your past relationship with Miss Isabelle, I have a few questions I need you to answer."

Holt put his hands into the pockets of his robe so he would not fidget. "Yes, sir, I understand."

"Good. Is there any reason to believe Miss Isabelle has or will contact Joel?" the headmaster asked, pulling at one of his dark, bushy eyebrows.

"I don't think that would be possible without your knowing it, sir," Holt replied respectfully.

The headmaster smiled coldly. "You are right about that. How about Isabelle trying to escape? Would you find that likely?"

"Hardly attainable," interjected Hertz.

"Yes, but perhaps desirable," the headmaster mused, as he put his glass down. He leaned forward and clasped his hands. "Mr. Langston, at this point in time would you suspect Isabelle desires to leave the temple?"

Holt thought about the events that had transpired in the past few weeks. Isabelle had been betrayed, assaulted, and rejected. She was now alone and scarred in more ways than one.

"Yes, sir … but even though I think she may desire to escape, she is also deeply loyal to her mother, who she knows would wish her to stay here."

The headmaster's raised eyebrows were followed by a curt nod. "I believe both of those statements are correct; nonetheless it is imperative the Templin guard ensure Isabelle stays here. What I am about to tell you is confidential to all but the Templin guard. Do you understand?"

"Yes, sir."

"Where is the file?" the headmaster asked, as his hand fluttered in the air towards Hertz.

"Sir, remember we lost—" Hertz began.

He was sharply interrupted by the headmaster. "Oh, drat. Yes, I remember," he said. "Well, the plain and simple version of our plan is that Miss Isabelle will act as the prime bait needed to entice Joel to return here. We intend to keep her here at all costs, as we will need her penmanship skills momentarily."

Holt's brown eyes gave the headmaster a puzzled look.

"We'll be using her to correspond with Joel. The content of her letters must appear authentic and be in her own handwriting. She will be writing of her hardships here, the dangers of her returning to Moonstruck, and even perhaps of her love for him, if that's necessary."

Holt was surprised at the tension he felt at the latter part of the headmaster's statement, particularly at the word *love*. Though the headmaster had explained *Operation Flight*, Holt was still unsure of his responsibility in the task.

"Headmaster Dark, how am I to be involved, as you have wisely suggested I disassociate with Miss Isabelle?"

"Thank you for reminding me about what I have said, Mr. Langston," he replied tersely, and Holt quickly realized he had said the wrong thing.

"I'm sorry, sir. Please tell me. What is my duty in this matter?"

"That's the attitude, Mr. Langston," the headmaster replied. "Yes, it's true that you made the unfortunate choice of romancing such a commoner, but I think that may be used to our advantage. Is there any chance you could rekindle that relationship? In the name of duty, and, of course, clearly under false pretenses?"

Holt realized what the headmaster was really asking him was would he be reason enough for Isabelle to want to remain at the temple school.

The headmaster soon seemed to sense his hesitation and explained his request further. "You see, Mr. Langston, I could just lock her up in Moonstruck. That would be the easiest solution. But as you know, I am really not one for using such harsh measures, particularly on the weaker sex."

Holt saw straight through the headmaster's false piety. *If her grandfather found out she was locked up there again, you would lose a large funding source.* "Sir, though she desires it, I firmly believe in our Templin security. She cannot escape."

"Langston, you are right, but somehow Joel escaped. Whether it was an inside job, luck, or some divine intervention, he got free. I will use all measures necessary to ensure it does not happen again. Do you understand?"

Holt knew the headmaster realized he had not answered his original question and was not surprised when asked again.

"Right, so then a rekindling, perhaps?" the headmaster wiggled his fingers playfully.

Holt slowly shook his head no. He did not want to say all his reasons, but his betrayal was probably enough for her not to return to him. He also knew Isabelle was too smart to fall for such a game. She knew the difference between real and fake love.

"No, not even for duty's sake?"

Holt shook his head at the headmaster again.

"Well, why ever not?" he sighed aloud then seemed to remember the events from the night before. "Oh yes, Miss Eris, I forgot. Female jealousy runs deep. Hmm …" the headmaster mused, and Holt was relieved at not having to answer him. "We must think of something else, then."

"Yes, we don't need another one to get away. Poor Daddy would be most unhappy," mocked Hertz as he sat up and walked over to Holt.

"It takes more than one Templin, a *junior Templin* at that who was still in training, to let one boy escape," Holt defended, feeling his anger rising.

"Hertz is right; I will deeply regret informing your father of this mishap," the headmaster frowned sympathetically at Holt. "Unless, well …" The headmaster showed Holt a wry smile. "Unless you have another idea regarding Miss Isabelle's containment."

As the two peered at him, Holt thought of the "idea" the headmaster was looking for. "She has a family heirloom that was given to her by her grandfather. It's the only one of his that her family owns." Holt knew it was low, but he could not risk receiving his father's disapproval.

"Yes, go on," the headmaster encouraged.

"I believe it's the last—well, the only thing of real value her family has left. It's a locket, and it is the only piece of wealth her family owns."

"Perfect," Templin Marlis pronounced.

"Well done, Mr. Langston," the headmaster said as he raised his glass towards him.

Holt was relieved at their praise, but quickly realized what he had just done. "Sir, if I am to continue to watch over Miss Isabelle, I believe—well, if I'm at all able to coerce her into a false romantic relationship, I will need to win her trust again."

"Meaning you do not wish us to tell her that taking the locket was your idea?"

Holt did not feel he needed to answer the headmaster's question.

"Fair enough, but in any case, you will get to witness it. Time to bring her in. Go and fetch her."

Isabelle failed to attend the rest of her classes after her meeting with the headmaster. She found sanctuary in the common room of her hall. The music room had still been locked when she passed by, and she decided since all the other girls were in class, the room would be quiet and empty.

Professor Dark had been more than persuasive when she first balked at writing the letter. Even when he had taken the last thing of value she owned, stating it was simply a "safety deposit," she had refused him. She even risked being thrown into Moonstruck, but he had then threatened to keep Ms. Harte there longer.

At one point he had asked Holt to leave the room. When the headmaster threatened to expel Holt for his failed assignment, Isabelle fell into defeat. She wrote a letter that sounded most unlike her and only hoped Joel would be able to decipher the temple's plot. She had faced the headmaster, his wrath, his punishments, and his threats. Her fear of him was subsiding into a strong hate. *He is an evil, evil man, "dark" just like his name,* she judged in her head as she shuddered in the quiet room.

There were four halls in all on the temple grounds. The age range varied among the buildings, and these residences were divided by sex and then into alphabetical order. Each building occupied its own corner lot inside the boundary gate and housed several hundred students. Though most of the buildings were covered in snow, each one was uniquely crafted. The clearly displayed masculine and feminine designs easily helped one determine which hall belonged to which sex.

Edson Hall, located in the corner nearest to the infirmary, resembled an enormous mountain lodge encased by earthy, jagged rocks and large wooden beams. Its common room was the largest of all the halls, housing an abundance of taxidermy. The focal point of the room was a gigantic white bear, a species that all in Differe were most familiar with. Langston Hall, the other male residence, was located nearest to Moonstruck. Its architecture resembled a mighty fortress encased by smooth, glistening, dark-colored pebbles. The hall's most unique feature was its clock tower. The tower, which chimed in each new hour, offered the most spectacular views of the grounds.

Owen Hall was located on the corner below Edson Hall. The place was similar to an old plantation mansion. Its deep red brick and massive white columns comprised the outside of the female dorm. The hall had an exquisite wraparound porch that went mostly unused, as it lay blanketed in snow for most of the year.

Isabelle's hall, or Thymes Hall, occupied the corner across from Langston Hall. The residence's exterior was built of large white stone blocks inlaid with mosaic tiles. The rainbow of pastel colors that flowed across the face of the building, as well as the bottom half of the rest of the structure, was barely visible under the snowy ice. In Isabelle's opinion, Thymes held the best common room. The front of the hall as well as the length of the hall were shaped into an arc. The common room was built outside of the arc and attached by a short hallway.

The common room and its glass domed ceiling resembled a princess's tower. It was called the "sunroom" and was located just past the foyer and to the left of the building. When Isabelle's mother had attended, she said the ceiling had been covered by cascading ivy and wildflowers. The room held two arched windows that ran all the way from the glass ceiling to the neutral-colored tiled floor. Each was draped by dense peach velvet curtains. There was a white brick fireplace on the far wall and the room was filled with sage green and soft yellow furniture covered with fabric in a floral design. Sterling silver serving pieces had been placed in prominent places throughout the room.

Isabelle sat alone on one of the wooden window benches. With her room becoming less inviting, Isabelle had sought sanctuary in the sunroom since Sarah had been gone. She had little privacy in her room now, as each of the other girls stared at her when she got in and out of bed. Some watched in silence, while others sneered at her scarred face.

As she looked at her reflection in the window, she knew she was worth more than the face she saw looking back at her would suggest. Still, even at this new revelation, Isabelle could not help reminding herself of the temple's standards of physical beauty. *Please, does it always have to be in my face—literally?* She was still determined to leave but desperately needed Sarah's help, which would require Isabelle patching things up with her. Which would be no small task, she knew.

A deep pain ran through her heart when she thought of seeing Sarah again, but she felt an even deeper one when she thought of Joel and the letter she had just written. *Ugh.* It made her feel sick to her stomach. At that moment, she wished her pain was tangible, like an old weathered coat that she could just sling off and instead put on something of beauty and true warmth.

A man bringing suitcases into the foyer soon distracted her. *Oh yeah, a bunch of new robots coming in today.* She turned back toward the window and ran her fingers through her long golden hair, pondering the rejection she had experienced since Professor Dark had interrogated her the day after Joel left. "This must be how he felt," she said softly to herself.

A small giggle was heard over her shoulder, and Isabelle turned to see a little curly-haired girl staring back at her. "Oh, don't mind her, that's just crazy Izzy," said an older student to the new arrival.

Isabelle decided to ignore them and turned back to the window. She sighed softly and pressed her hand against the window. It was frigid to her touch, and she saw that the snow continued to fall. She blinked back tears of regret and jealousy, while imagining Joel enjoying the sunshine in the city of Waiz. *Surely he made it, or he would have been caught by this time.* Sarah had told them both about the city during their days at Moonstruck.

Isabelle leaned her head against the windowsill and tried not to think. In the place between being awake and asleep, the haunting memory replayed itself over and over in Isabelle's mind. Though Joel was only the age of nine, he was mature far beyond his years. He was compassionately brushing her face with his hand.

"You are pretty, Bella; don't listen to them," he pleaded with her. "They can't see you. I can, I can see you. I think, I think you're beautiful," Joel blurted out into her face.

"Really? How can I believe you?" Isabelle forced out through a sob.

Joel bit his lip and then his face lit up with a "eureka" expression. He dropped his hand from her cheek and bent down and kissed her in the same spot where her scar was.

She gasped at him in shock.

"*See,* you are that pretty to me, and worth kissing."

She smiled a little, and he bent to kiss her again. This time her smile was wider, and he went back for a third time.

She drew back and giggled, "Okay, I believe you."

"Good." He quickly grabbed her hand and pulled her in the direction of their quarters. "Come on, let's get back to Moonstruck. Sarah will be worried about us, and besides, I have a great story to tell you ..."

Isabelle soon awakened to a body peering over her. She was startled at first, but then saw it was the same little girl who had arrived that afternoon. The little girl stared at Isabelle for a moment before raising a tissue toward her face. Isabelle touched her wet cheeks in surprise and then nodded her thanks.

The little girl gave her a small smile and whispered, "You don't look crazy to me."

Taken aback, Isabelle did not know whether to laugh or cry in response.

"Come on, Jill," the older girl called out after her, and the little girl soon skipped off.

Isabelle turned back to the window in a daze. Darkness had fallen, yet suddenly a light rose up behind her. Isabelle looked at the reflection in the glass window and saw Sarah standing behind her with a large glowing candle in her hand. *She looks like an angel.* She hung her head in shame. She could not turn to face her as she thought of how she had betrayed Joel and her, and all for nothing. Tears filled Isabelle's eyes, and she began to heave out heavy sobs. She was barely able to force out a faint, "I'm sorry."

"Shush," came the reply.

It was only when Isabelle saw Sarah's outstretched hand reaching toward her that could she look up. "Forgive me," Isabelle uttered breathlessly as she took her hand.

"Yes, I have."

CHAPTER 19

JOEL WENT BACK to work the next day and was very glad not to see the siblings and their guide as he dashed through the square. He and Mr. Rutherford started the day's work by unloading the shipment from New Waiz.

"Anything else interesting happen while I was gone?" the shopkeeper asked, as he and Joel opened the back of cart.

"Not much. We did go to the museum. It was interesting," Joel shrugged.

"Ah, yes, Madame Bontecou has done a nice job with that place. So, I assume you understand why this isn't just a trinket now?" he asked, pulling a chain from around his neck.

Joel saw a crystal stone dangling on the chain just like the ones he had seen his first day in Adams. He raised his eyebrows and asked, "Is that a real Majestic stone? Is it from a caychura?"

"Good, you did pay attention on the tour. Yes and no," he paused, as Joel took the chain from his hand. "Yes, this one, as well as the ones in the shop, is a Majestic stone. I suppose, though, they're really more imitation, or, well, I like to say 'a representation,' representing beauty, power, and unity. But, alas, they're, unfortunately, not from a caychura."

"Have ever you found a caychura?" Joel asked as he handed the blue stone back to him.

"Well," Mr. Rutherford started. He wiped the sweat from his balding head. "Sadly, no."

Joel expected him to continue, but the man turned to hand him a crate and asked, "Did you travel to the higher country to explore the historical landmarks?"

Joel told him the story of the three going up the trail and meeting the strange old man.

The shopkeeper nodded at the end of his tale. "The Old Order is still powerful here. Those in the *Old* Old Order hold great disdain against New Waiz and outsiders."

"With all due respect, sir, how does Old Waiz survive?"

"What?" Mr. Rutherford asked, and he seemed puzzled for a moment. "Oh, you mean since we're all old, how does the city not die out? Well, there's a special fountain we all drink from," he said with a funny grin, which let Joel know he was joking. "No, oddly enough, after a time, many of those from New Waiz return to their roots and come back here."

"Are you such a person?" Joel asked curiously.

"Let's just say I do know my way around the New City," the man said, winking at Joel.

Just as Joel was about to ask him another question, Mr. Rutherford stood up and said, "Well, let's bring in the last of it."

As they lifted the load, Joel could not refrain from asking his questions. "Mr. Rutherford, you offered me a book on the history of this city. I may have been a fool not to take it at the time, but honestly, I'd rather hear more about the city from your own experiences."

"You are foolish, but that's only due to your lack of experience, which you will make up for as you age." Mr. Rutherford chuckled as he opened the door to the shop. "What is it you wish to know, Joel?"

"There is a New Order in New Waiz. Right?"

"That's correct. We'll need to take these last two crates to the rooftop," he instructed. Both glanced out the window and saw a heavy rain beginning to fall. "Oh my, I think we're going to get wet."

Joel, still eager for answers, barely heard the man's observation. "Does the New Order," Joel paused to grab the crate, "Do they have officers ... that wear green cloaks?"

Joel's question was met with silence, as the shopkeeper was halfway up the stairs and appeared not to have heard him.

Once at the top, the two scurried about through the downpour. Once the crates were unloaded and the tarps secured, both headed back down the stairs, soaked from head to toe. They dried off then sat at the counter as they waited for the rain move out.

"This scenario seems familiar," Joel mused lightheartedly.

"Yes, it does," Mr. Rutherford smiled back at Joel. "Thankfully, today I had you to help from the beginning. The rains will start coming more frequently in the next few weeks."

"Why is that?" Joel asked.

"The cool season begins very soon." Mr. Rutherford noted the alarmed expression on Joel's face. "Yes, it's warmer here, Joel, but we also have seasons. Don't fret, though. As you may have noticed I didn't say 'cold,' just 'cool.'"

"Interesting, like coat-weather cold?" Joel wondered aloud.

"A green cloak might suffice," he said, as he shoved a steaming cup of tea toward Joel.

Joel laughed at him in surprise. "You did hear me?"

"Yes, I did. There are two Orders, and if I recall correctly, some of the officers wear cloaks of some sort."

"Why didn't you say anything the day I told you what happened at the inn?"

"Joel, I make it my priority not to meddle in the affairs of either Order. And well, your friend Corwin has been entangled with both."

"He's not my friend," Joel said immediately.

"Then how did you become acquainted with him, may I ask?"

"He was in my train compartment; that's all," Joel said, as he looked into his cup.

"Sebastian seems to be quite keen on you."

Joel glanced back up at him but said nothing.

"I suppose we'll see those two later. Are you still looking after them?" Mr. Rutherford asked, sounding surprised they had not come with Joel today.

"No, sir. Corwin's back."

"Hmm … that was faster than I expected." He took a sip from his cup. "Well, about the Green Cloaks, they typically shadow outsiders or outlaws arriving in Waiz. Although *outlaw* seems too harsh a word for Corwin."

"You mean, they follow them? Why? The Order? Which one?" Joel asked eagerly.

"It's really hard to tell. It would seem more likely to be the Old, as you saw how some react to outsiders, but the New also holds an interest in foreigners."

"Why?"

"Gracious, you are full of questions!" the man exclaimed.

"Sorry, sir. Is there something I could be doing for you?" Joel asked, while feeling a bit embarrassed.

"No, no, it's fine." There was a long pause between the two, then the shopkeeper finally answered Joel's question. "I think the Old Order wants to ensure the principles of Old Waiz are preserved."

Joel nodded in agreement.

"I believe the New Order wants power, and any outsider who holds some or who they think would take some is of great interest to them."

"I have no power," Joel thought aloud.

"As I recall, the Green Cloak was not after *you*."

"Oh, right," Joel said. *But he sure wanted those maps, and he acted like I had something—and that something scared him.*

The sunlight soon distracted him from their conversation. It peaked through the clouds and lit up the crystal stones hanging on the kiosk across from him. Both turned toward the dazzling prisms.

"Joel, take one."

"Sir, I couldn't … thank you, though," Joel replied, completely taken aback by the offer.

"Sure you can. I sense your curiosity about them, and though I still believe you are a foolish young person, you, unlike many your age, don't require something tangible in order for it to be real," he said, as he walked over to the stones.

Joel shot him a confused look.

"What I mean to say, is that you, young man, have great faith."

The shopkeeper stood before the kiosk and searched through the rack of stones. He eventually picked a red stone that held lines of wildly displaced gold inside its core. Mr. Rutherford held the chain out to Joel. The sunlight continued to flood into the store, and Joel noted the stone somehow reflected purple and pink hues in its light.

"How did you know that's the color I would've picked?" Joel asked, as he took the chain.

"Because, *I* am a very *wise* old man."

Joel didn't see Corwin or the others for the rest of the week. The shopkeeper seemed surprised and commented on the subject a few times but did not press Joel for information. Joel wondered if they had ventured on to New Waiz. His curiosity regarding Corwin had increased dramatically after hearing about his being some sort of outlaw. *In fact, his approval rating went up in my mind.* He supposed a Green Cloak looking for papers and maps was a small bother to Corwin. *I bet he's been hunted many times.* He remembered how Corwin had handled the security guard at Crossroads Station.

Toward the end of the week, Joel had given up on seeing him again. Mr. Rutherford had just popped open the cash register to tally up the sales for the day when a small knock was heard on the locked door.

Joel was kneeling in the back, but was surprised when he heard Mr. Rutherford exclaim, "Augustine! Dear, how have you been? I've missed you and your playing. Did you come to play this evening? Oh, hello there, Sebastian."

"Yes, sir, if that's okay with you. Corwin is away for the evening," Joel heard Augustine say.

"Yes, please come in. Joel's in the back corner there. Joel! Augustine and Sebastian are here," the man called to him.

The only reason Joel called back was to be polite to his boss. "Yes, sir!"

"Well, you know he's a hard worker," Mr. Rutherford stated, and Joel was glad the man let him be. "Augustine, the piano is all yours. Sebastian, I just opened the drawer if you want to help."

"Mr. Rutherford, would you mind if I glanced at your paper first?" Joel heard Augustine ask.

"Today's news? Yes, it's right here on the counter. I was just about to throw it out." Joel heard Mr. Rutherford grab the paper.

"Thank you," Augustine said politely.

"Something you're looking for?" the shopkeeper asked as she fished through the paper.

"Well, yes, I was hoping to see an article about the upcoming council meeting."

Joel stopped stocking to hear more.

"Oh, here, dear. Turn it around. The article is on the front page."

"Oh, thank you. I must have overlooked it."

Joel could hear a hint of embarrassment in her voice.

"What does it say about it, Augie?" Sebastian asked.

"Well, it says just what Madame Bontecou said. The councils meet every quarter on the Bridge of Miren, and the meeting is open to the public. It says here that the Orders each bring a list of topics to discuss. The topics are not to be disclosed prior to the meeting. I can't imagine that being a great idea," she mused thoughtfully.

"Well, the councilmen are quite good at thinking on their feet," Mr. Rutherford assured her.

"Corwin is planning to take us," Sebastian said, excitement in his voice.

"Is he now? Seeing men argue, how delightful," Mr. Rutherford said lightheartedly. "You will enjoy seeing the river and the towers. Sebastian, here's a pencil. Let's start with yesterday's receipts."

Joel heard Augustine head toward the piano and ducked around the corner. She warmed up her fingers by playing a few simple songs. He realized her playing had become less regimented and more beautiful since her first night at the shop.

As Augie played and Joel stocked the shelves, he grew lost in thought. He knew Augustine was probably aware he was deliberately trying to avoid them. *But, my goodness, isn't that what she asked for from the beginning?* He was glad for her interest in the council meeting, though. He also hoped to attend. He wanted to find that Green Cloak.

As he headed to the next row, the piano music suddenly began to change. Augie seemed to be playing something from memory; however, it did not sound stiff, *but ... alive ... connected.* He felt mesmerized by the sound. He peeked around the corner and saw a look of confidence about her he had not seen before. He marveled at the radiance she was exuding as she played. He stood there for a moment just staring before he realized he knew the melody. "What song is this?" he whispered to himself.

The song was eerily familiar. But why did it frighten him so much? He felt his insides begin to quake. He sank to his knees, starting to feel weak. His body was soon affected. His insides began to churn, and he trembled all over.

"Stop," he told himself forcefully. "Stop this!" he said, trying to control his shaking body. "Stop this, Joel! Come on, stop," he breathed through chattering teeth. "You're not in Differe anymore. You're free. You are ... you're free."

He felt a cold sweat break out onto his forehead; then heard a voice whisper, "Free? *You* are *not* free. *You* will never be free. Changing cities does not make you free, Moonie. Remember ... Remember ..."

"Go away," Joel hissed.

The voice responded stronger and louder, "No! Remember who you are!"

Joel's heart pounded and his breath became short and heavy. "No," Joel whispered as he gasped for air. "Please, leave me alone. No, I don't want to remember. No more memories replaying."

The snake-like coil he felt wrap around his neck indicated to him that the voice would not be showing him any mercy. He felt his eyes go dark as he hit the floor, passed out cold.

There Joel stood, about the age of eleven, on a makeshift stage that he, Bella, and Sarah had created during their time at Moonstruck. Isabelle sat before him giggling and beautiful with her gleaming blond hair as Joel acted out her favorite book. He made every character come to life by using different voices and props. One of his greatest pleasures in Moonstruck was making Isabelle smile. Sarah's eyes seemed to laugh more than her actual mouth and she always shouted, "Bravo!" at the end of each of his reenactments. Bella and Sarah clapped their hands in applause as Joel finished.

"Come on, Joel, one more," Bella had always pleaded, and he always obliged.

This night, however, as Joel prepared to perform his encore, suddenly a door slammed above them. All smiles faded as Sarah hurried them to their desks and began pretending she was teaching about the temple's nighttime rituals. Each tried to ignore the heavy footsteps heard coming down the stone steps. As they sat nervously in their seats, Joel sweetly reached over and gave Bella's hand a small squeeze.

Soon Professor Dark entered the room with two Templins. Sarah fought the urge to shudder as he walked toward the classroom. He floated across the room in his long, flowing robes, resembling a ghostly, dark figure. The two turned to look at him when they heard his footsteps close by.

"Well, hello there, children. You seem to be enjoying your studies. Hello, Ms. Harte."

"Professor," Ms. Harte responded politely.

Joel on the other hand, shot him a look of contempt, fuming that his eleven-year-old self was just called a "child."

The headmaster strode over close to Isabelle's desk, and Joel's blood began to boil. "Dear me, is that Isabelle?" he asked, clearly amused at his acting as if he did not know. The man rubbed his black mustache and smacked his lips. "My, how you've grown," he said as he bent down and tilted her chin up with his hand. He studied her face carefully. "Hmm ... lovely. She's ready," he nodded to the Templins. "Isabelle, it is time for you to come live on the temple grounds. Isn't that what you've always wanted?"

Isabelle nodded quickly.

"Good, I shall be very glad to see you there. You'll need to say goodbye to Joel now," the headmaster instructed coldly.

Isabelle seemed alarmed at his instruction and immediately pleaded with him. "Sir, may Joel please come with me?"

"No, Miss Isabelle, I am not inviting Joel today. You need to make this decision for yourself." The man looked at her face as if he sensed her hesitation. "What? Do you want to stay here? A beautiful girl like you," he paused looking around in disgust, "in this dungeon? Or would you rather be up singing in the glorious chapel?"

Isabelle turned to Joel then back to Professor Dark. She started to cry, and Joel somehow knew the tears were because of the choice she had to make between either leaving her best friend or remaining in Moonstruck forever.

Professor Dark raised his eyebrows impatiently. "I don't have time for this." He waved his hands at the Templins and said, "Take her."

The two young men rushed forward to grab Isabelle in a brutal fashion.

She began to scream, "Wait! No, wait! Let me say goodbye! *Please*! Let me say goodbye!"

When Joel could not stand for it any longer, he rushed out of his desk toward the stairs. He threw Professor Dark onto the stone steps and yelled in his face, "Let her go! Leave us alone!"

Professor Dark smacked Joel with his cane, knocking the breath out of him as he landed flat on his back.

"Joel," began the headmaster as he leered over him. "She is ready. Would you keep her from her dream? Do you care nothing for this girl?" He pointed to Isabelle's tear-stained face. "If you truly care for her, you will let her go."

Joel sat up in time to slip his fingers across Isabelle's. Hot tears ran down his cheeks as he watched them drag her away, leaving him alone with Sarah.

Isabelle sneaked down to see Joel for several years after she had moved to the temple grounds. During these visits, "story time" soon turned into time spent planning their escape. On occasion they would get caught meeting together, and both were punished severely. Isabelle was given extra schoolwork and stripped of her vocal privileges for the week, whereas Joel was beaten by the Templins. The last time they were caught, Isabelle was forced to watch Joel's beating. She told him afterward she could no longer come to see him. He begged her to reconsider, but she said the risks were too great.

Joel's dream seemed to shift scenes to several years later, when Joel eventually convinced Professor Dark to let him out of Moonstruck. By then, little did he know how much things had changed for Isabelle. As soon as he completed his transition training, he rushed to find her. There had seldom been a day since they had been apart that he had not thought of her. He ran to the chapel, knowing he would find her somewhere around music. She had told him during some of their secret meetings that she loved singing with the choir there. When he did not find her in the chapel, he headed toward Sarah's music class.

His breath was taken away when he walked in the room and saw Isabelle's long blond hair cascading over her shoulders. He stood in the doorway for a few moments to see if she would notice him. Eventually she shifted her gaze toward him, and he smiled brightly as he lifted his hand to wave at her. She paused and, with her eyes still on him, cocked her head at his wave. He watched in shock as she then lifted her chin and turned away as if to ignore his presence.

His countenance fell as he absorbed the emotional blow. He stood in the doorway with his confidence now crumbled into pieces. His jaw fell open then clenched back in anger when he saw a large young man stroking her hair and smirking at him.

Before Joel could turn to leave, the young man yelled toward him and pointed, "Hey, look! They let out a lunatic from Moonstruck this week."

Isabelle turned around sharply and squeezed the young man's arm fiercely.

"I heard you're a good storyteller," the young man teased. Suddenly he yelled "Ouch!" as Isabelle pinched him. He yanked her hand away.

"Yeah, so what if I am?" Joel decided he'd play along with the large boy.

"Well, let's hear one, crazy!" the young man challenged him.

Joel's face turned hot. "I'm not crazy …"

"Or," the young man said viciously, "all you in Langston can hear him scream them out in his sleep tonight. I'll give you a preview." The young man started toward Joel, but crouched into a huddle just before he reached him. He wrapped his arms around himself as he let out high-pitched shrieks. "Please! Stop! Please, leave me alone!"

The class burst into laughter, and Joel turned to leave, feeling completely horrified. He quickly felt something grip the back of his collar.

"Wait, I wanted a good story," the young man laughed from behind him. "What's your name?"

Joel responded with silence.

"Oh, don't have one? Need me to make up one for you? Let's see … 'Reject,' 'Crazy' … nah, too common," he mused while stroking his chin. "Hmm … how about something that reminds you of where you came from? Yes, that'd be good…. Uh, got it! 'Moonie.'" He looked at Joel in satisfaction. "Moonie from Moonstruck."

Thus began his life on the temple grounds. His greatest fear still remained: *Am I really crazy?*

As Joel lay unconscious and reliving scenes from his past, Augustine, unaware that he had passed out, finished her piece. She wondered if Joel had known the song and decided to walk over to him. She found him completely blacked out on the floor. He was slightly shaking with his face contorted. She rushed forward to him but was not sure she should touch him.

"Joel, are you all right?" she cried then screamed, "Mr. Rutherford!"

"Yes! What is it?" he rushed over to her voice.

"It's Joel; he seems to be having some sort of seizure or something."

The shopkeeper saw his young worker curled a ball on the floor. Joel moaned when Augustine shook him and screamed when Mr. Rutherford tried to sit him upright. Augustine was so frightened by his scream that she jumped back into the shelf behind her.

"I'm sorry," she cried as she scrambled to grab the goods she had knocked onto the floor.

"Augustine, stop." Mr. Rutherford grabbed her hands. "Don't worry. Run get a cool cloth."

She ran to the kitchen as fast as her legs would carry her. As she searched for a cloth, she began to cry out of fear. "Stop that! Stop that crying. Everything will be fine." She heard her mother's voice as she wiped away her tears. When she returned, Joel seemed to be coming out of whatever was happening to him, and his body seemed less rigid and more limp.

"Augustine, I must fetch the doctor. You must stay here. Can you handle that?" Mr. Rutherford asked hurriedly.

"Oh, I'm not sure, I—"

"Augustine," Mr. Rutherford interrupted her, "you are Sebastian's caregiver. You can do this."

She nodded toward him. "Yes, go, but please hurry." He patted the back of her head then left.

Augustine bent down over Joel to try and wipe his forehead. She was alarmed when she heard Sebastian yell her name.

"Augustine!"

"Yes, what is it?" she called back to him.

The second yell she recognized as a call for help. "I'm coming. I'm coming with the water."

"Augustine! Just come get me!" he cried out.

She knew he must be very upset about Joel, and his little body was reacting. She ran to grab him and then rushed him to the kitchen for water.

"Here, drink this." She shoved a cup of water into his hand. "It's all right. He's going to be fine and so are you," she said, trying to speak in the calmest voice she could muster.

All of the sudden the two heard a clatter in the next room.

"Joel must be trying to move around in all that stuff I knocked down," she said.

She hoisted Sebastian onto her hip and dodged back into the room. She looked to where Joel had lain and saw he was gone. She saw him closing the front door as he slung his bag over his shoulder. She rushed toward the door, and their eyes met for a brief second. She noted his eyes were red and puffy like hers. By the time she reached the door, she only caught a glimpse of him running down the street into the darkness.

CHAPTER 20

JOEL RAN DOWN the main road and didn't stop. Twenty minutes passed, but his plans to leave for New Waiz in the morning had changed. Thankfully, he had already packed up his belongings from the barn. He knew he couldn't outrun the voices but maybe he could exhaust them. Typically, if he could fix his mind on something else, they eventually tired of screaming at him.

The road was pitch black, steeper than he had imagined, and completely quiet. After he got a cramp in his side, he was forced to slow his pace. When he stopped to catch his breath, he realized his head was silent. *Lost them.* He wiped the sweat off his face and put down his bag.

Augustine's face flashed through his mind during most of his run. *She thinks you're crazy now,* his mind screamed, replaying the scene that had just exposed him. "Well, she can join the club. It's quite a large one and actually pretty elite—she'd like that part," he retorted to himself, then sighed heavily. "I'm surprised I could hide it this long. Just made it easier for me to move on." He picked up his bag again.

No chance of hitching a ride this late. Better get going if I'm going to get any rest tonight. He didn't dare stop to sleep here, as it was not nearly far away enough from where he had been found. He would get as far away from the voices as he could, even if he had to walk all the way to New Waiz tonight.

Joel wondered if Augustine would tell Corwin or Mr. Rutherford about the way he left. He also wondered what had happened to Sebastian. Joel had started coming out of his "fit" by the time Augustine rushed to get the little boy, and he knew something was wrong by the way he yelled. Joel could only imagine what he looked like on the floor and he cringed, knowing he probably had screamed. *That's what started it all.*

Soon after Joel's mother died, the voices had begun. Though just three years old, Joel vividly recalled his first encounter with the screaming tormentors. "No, I'm done with that. I'm not going there." Joel whacked the side of his head with his fist and his father's face came into focus.

"Of course, Joel, I've already thought of that. Look here." He watched his father pull a photograph out of Joel's half-packed suitcase. "See, here's the one of you, me, and momma. We won't seem so far away; even Momma will be close. She would be so—so happy to know you're going to a place that will help you have sweet dreams."

"How about funny dreams, Daddy?" Joel saw the five-year-old version of himself search the man's face.

"Well, anything's possible." His father tousled his red hair.

"Can I talk to you while I'm at school?"

His father frowned, "Well, they—the teachers—have asked that we not talk for a little while."

Tears formed in young Joel's eyes. "Daddy, I'll miss you!"

His father's eyes also misted, and he reached down to embrace him. "I will miss you, too, but I want you to know, Joel, I love you and would do anything to help you. So, we won't be able to talk or see each other, but it's just for a little while. I bet the headmaster will let us write letters, and we can both keep a journal. You can write down everything you want to tell me, and I'll do the same. How's that? How does that sound?" The man rubbed his back as he held him.

Joel nodded. "Good, Daddy."

A scamper across the road distracted Joel from reliving several other similar conversations he'd had with his father before being sent to the temple for treatment. Joel froze as he watched the doe take a drink from a nearby stream. He wondered if she was hurt, then realized she hadn't been dragging a broken limb across the road, but her small fawn. He watched the creature wobble toward the water and whispered, "Where's your dad?"

"I can't write my son?" His father's voice echoed in his head, pulling him into another memory.

"We prefer not to have any outside influences at first. It is for Joel's protection. At present, we do not know the source of his misfortune." The headmaster eyed his father suspiciously as the word "source" escaped his lips.

His father's flushed face turned to Joel. "You see? We will get to write to one another—in time."

Joel pestered the headmaster about contacting his father every time he saw him until one day the man stated abruptly, "We don't need him interfering with your progress, Joel. Your father may very well be part of your problem. Do you understand, Joel? You do not want to get worse now, do you?"

Twelve years later and zero letters. He gazed up at the moon and was reminded of a place he hated that had a similar name. Suddenly the doe splashed through the stream, causing him to jump.

"Sh! It's okay. You're having a dream. Wake up!" He heard Isabelle's voice.

"It's not a dream! Get off of my bed!" Joel had ripped the little blonde's hand off his mouth.

He experienced deep shame as he recalled covering his ears and rocking back and forth in front of the little girl. He felt her tremble as he whispered, "Stop, stop," over and over again. When he finally stopped, he was surprised to find her still sitting on his bed.

"Have they stopped?" she asked softly.

He shook his head no and began to cry. He then realized what she had just asked him. "Do you hear them, too?" He looked into her blue eyes.

"Sometimes. They say mean words. They *are* mean."

He nodded in response as she handed him a tissue from the pocket of her nightgown. "What do you do when you hear them?" He let out a hiccup.

"Well," she looked away shyly. "I say nice things."

Joel shot her a bewildered look. She wrinkled her nose as she let out a small giggle and bounded toward his pillow.

"Here, lie down," she said, and Joel obeyed. "Whenever they say a mean thing, I say a nice thing. So here, I'll say some nice things, and then you can try if you want. You have nice red hair. I have pretty blond hair. I am smart, and you are smart. Sarah is nice. This pillow is soft. Snowballs are fun to throw. Boogers are gross—"

"That's not nice," Joel interrupted.

"Yes, but it's funny." Both immediately giggled.

"Do you want to try?"

"No, you keep going."

"Hmm ... food is yummy. Fingers can wiggle. Singing is fun. Oh, I love to sing! Want me to sing you a song?" Isabelle asked excitedly.

"Yes," Joel responded eagerly. She sang to him that night for the first time.

Joel sucked in a breath of deep night air. "Gosh, I miss her voice."

Beyond her voice being the most beautiful at the temple, Joel had found it to be the most comforting sound he had ever known. After she had finished singing that first night, they lay side by side in silence.

"My mom used to sing that to me," Joel finally let out.

"Mine, too."

"Isabelle?"

"Yes?"

"Will you promise not to tell anyone I have nightmares?"

She grabbed his small hand with hers. "I promise."

She had sung to him every night they were in Moonstruck. Once she was taken away, rarely had he been able to sleep through the night. "Yeah, that promise lasted six years. Then Holt got a hold of you. Idiot," Joel spat out loud. The fawn raised its head at him in curiosity. "Yep, she moved from one prison to another." He never understood why his best friend hadn't been able to discern reality.

Their tutor, Sarah Harte, had taken great risk in telling them stories about a city named Waiz in that classroom. Joel was hazy on most of the details but often remembered the statement, "Waiz is a place where you are free to be whoever you want." As lightening lit the sky, he realized his real battle with the temple the last few years was traceable to all his knowledge about this place where he was now standing. A deeper desire to be free, even if he was to be crazy when he was free, had grown in him. The longer Joel stood there with the deer, the more he pondered whether or not Sarah had been right about him. *I made it here. Maybe I am exceptional.*

He reached up to scratch an itch on the back of his neck, then moved his fingers to the black stud in his ear as he continued thinking of the long years without hearing from his father....

The same week he was released from Moonstruck, Joel had his fifteenth birthday and his father was coming to visit. Joel sat in the lobby of the headmaster's building as he watched his father approach. He stood up once his father recognized him.

"Son!" he heard his father exclaim joyfully. The man reached out for him, but Joel backed away. His father quickly put his hand down and stood awkwardly in the doorway of the lobby, clearly unsure of what to do next. Joel saw he had a package in his hand, and eventually the man broke the silence with a "Happy Birthday."

Joel ran his fingers through his hair, feeling his anger rise. "Nice of you to come. What's it been, ten years?"

"Gosh, has it been that long?" his father asked. His voice was timid, and he had certainly aged, with his hair now showing flecks of gray and his face displaying a few crow's feet.

"Yes, it has been that long," Joel said sharply.

"Well, how—how've you been here?" his father asked.

"Like you care," Joel answered, as he looked away from him.

"Yes I do, or I wouldn't have asked. I wouldn't have come, for that matter."

"If you cared, you would've come a long time ago," Joel barked, still looking away from him.

"I—Joel, I told you I wanted what was best for you. I couldn't interfere."

"Couldn't, or wouldn't?" Joel shot him an angry look.

"Here's a present," his father offered.

"Great," Joel said sarcastically, as he took the package from his father's hand.

"Have you gotten the other packages I've sent?" his father asked.

"Yes," Joel muttered.

"Have you had what you've needed?"

Joel sensed the sincerity in his voice. "Yes."

"Do you want me to leave?"

Joel looked his father in the eyes and shook his head. "No."

His father looked relieved and motioned for them to sit down in the nearby chairs. "Here, open it."

Joel tore through the paper and found two small items in the box.

"Here, that one's from me," his father pointed and smiled. It was a pocket-sized book of southern cities and maps. "Your teacher, Ms. Harte, recommended it. She said you enjoyed maps and things."

Joel gave him a small smile as he thought about what Sarah's real motives were. "She knows me well. Thanks," Joel said politely.

The other item was in a tiny, wooden box. "That's from your mother."

Joel jerked his head up in surprise.

"She wanted you to have it on your fifteenth birthday."

He opened the box and saw a single ruby earring. "There's only one," Joel said in surprise.

"Yes, she only ever had the one, that I know of. There was some story or something that went with it. I'm sorry, all I have is the earring, but I did remember her saying she wanted you to have it on your fifteenth birthday."

Joel sat there with the tiny earring in his hand and thought it was the oddest gift he had ever received. "Was it her favorite or something?" Joel asked.

"I don't think so. She just said, 'Make sure Joel gets this by fifteen.'"

"Is this why you're here? To fulfill her dying wish?"

His father's sheepish expression gave Joel his answer. Strangely, the young man did not feel rebuffed; instead, he was glad his father had made the effort on behalf of his mother.

"How'd you get them to let you see me?"

"I had to do a little threatening," his father said playfully, and the two smirked at one another. "Joel," his father stated more seriously. "Are you okay? Are they treating you well?"

Even though his father asked, Joel wondered if he really wanted to hear the answer. "It's been okay," was his brief reply.

"Are they feeding you?" his father asked, eyeing his thin appearance.

"I eat in the kitchen."

"What does that mean, son?"

"It means—it means I'm a complete outcast." Joel quickly searched the area for any visible Templins and lowered his voice. "Dad, will you please take me with you? Will you please take me out of here?"

His father was alarmed by his request. "Why, son? What's going on?"

"Dad, they've had me and another girl locked in a basement for the past ten years. They just let me out this week. They're crazy here. They beat you if you disagree with them." Joel went on for several minutes as his father lovingly listened and nodded.

After he was finished, his father sighed then said, "Joel, it isn't really all that bad, is it?"

"What! Didn't you hear what I just told you?"

Joel's father responded to his outburst with a look of apprehension. "But, Joel, why would every other student want to stay here? I'm sure it can't be as bad as you're saying."

"Dad! Aren't you listening to me?" Joel cried out in exasperation.

"Joel, the headmaster told me you might try to twist my arm into letting you out of here by telling me some sort of wild tale." His father shook his head at him in disapproval.

"You—you think I'm making this up?" Joel sputtered out in disbelief.

"I know you are," his father replied gently yet firmly. "The headmaster gave me a tour of the place before I came to see you today. There's no such place as Moonstruck. Joel, he showed me your room, your seat in the cafeteria, we went over *all* of the grounds."

Furious, Joel stood up and groaned in frustration. In his rage, he picked up his chair and threw it against the wall. "Wait," he froze. "How do you know it's called Moonstruck?"

"Everything all right?" asked a Templin who seemed to appear out of nowhere.

Joel lunged toward the official and was soon bombarded by several more officers.

"So sorry you have to see this," Joel heard the headmaster's voice as he gave Joel one of Nurse Polma's injections. "He's actually been doing quite well."

His father was nowhere to be found when he awoke, but the presents he received had been stashed securely into his pocket.

"Stay with your mom," Joel instructed the fawn just before it dodged into the woods.

Andropolis drew back his bow and took his aim. When he was sure of his target, he released the arrow. The arrow struck the bull's-eye before he even had time to drop his bow. "Nice one, Andi," he said aloud to himself for about the twelfth time. He wasn't interested in wasting any more arrows and decided this was his last practice shot.

He picked up a few stray arrows as he approached the bull's-eye. *You can't miss tomorrow.* Andi was confident he was a good shot, perhaps even a great one, but he knew no man was perfect. He had been pleasantly surprised at not having encountered any foul dreams concerning his assignment. He knew the New Order would cover for him as long as he followed through. Because of this fact, his fears were few. His nerves, on the other hand, were many. *But I am determined to do my duty and then become part of the Order,* he thought, as he placed the last arrow in his quiver.

Being a part of the New Order would clear his family's name. "Completing this assignment will make it right," he told himself, though the statement did not quite convince him. He waited until late into the evening before climbing the East Tower of New Waiz.

CHAPTER 21

A S JOEL THOUGHT over the events of his past, hate seethed through him—hate for the temple, hate for the headmaster, and the deepest hate reserved for his father, who put him there.

So, I guess my voices are here in Waiz, too. He felt horribly disappointed. *At least I'm free to have them. No one can tell me they're not real anymore. No one can throw me away in a basement.*

This thought was met with one of the voices again. "You're free from the basement, but you're all alone with only a small bit of cash to your name. There's not much you can do without anyone."

"Shut up. I don't want to think anymore," Joel said aloud to the voice in the darkness.

The slope in the road was beginning to level out, and Joel hoped this meant he was getting close to New Waiz. The temperature had significantly dropped in Old Waiz this week, so he could not help but notice the dramatic increase in the temperature and humidity the further he went. Eventually the change became too much for him, and he stopped to strip off his sweat-soaked clothes.

Much better. He felt his skin breathe through the short-sleeved gray cotton shirt. He cast a glance down the road as he pulled on his khaki

278

shorts. He was delighted to see a light twinkling far above the tree line. *New Waiz? I must be close.*

As the road flattened, Joel heard a rushing sound nearby that he suspected was the Pallas River. A few yards later he realized he was passing through what resembled a kalona. By this time, it was late into the night, and the neighborhood lay quiet. Torches and lanterns hung outside the homes, which helped to light his way. The houses sat on small lots and were much closer to one another in comparison to Old Waiz. He made out their stucco finish through the dim light. He looked up again for the light he had seen above the tree line but saw nothing.

The road continued for several more miles until Joel came to a fork. To his right, the dirt road led into what looked like another kalona. To his left, the road turned downward and into cobblestone. Since he heard the river on the left side, he decided to take the cobblestone road. As Joel descended down the road, he was able to make out the top of the towers. He saw that the east one, across the river, was in the exact spot where he had seen the twinkling light earlier. Joel paused, wondering if he should head in their direction. He soon figured he would see them tomorrow, as he planned to attend the council meeting.

Why not? Should be interesting. Then he remembered the other three would be attending, also. *Well, maybe not.*

Before the cobblestone road met the downtown area, it split into a number of different directions in front of several buildings like the ones on Adams' square. Joel chose the best lit direction and wandered onward. When he approached the center of the city, he was mesmerized by the electric lights aglow on the outside of the buildings. The buildings themselves were impressive in size but not in structure.

Just mostly rectangular. There were about seven of them and each was identical to the others. Each building was tall in height and metallic in finish with numerous shiny glass windows. He followed the faint sound of music coming up the street as he neared the first building and soon began passing people on the street. They didn't speak to him like the people in Old Waiz, but were not at all silent like the people in

Differe. The ones coming out of the tall buildings were mostly young men dressed in fine suits and holding leather cases. Joel noted that these business folk were walking in pairs and chatting loudly to one another, particularly about how late it was.

"Had to get everything done, so I can make the meeting tomorrow," he heard one say.

"Yeah, I hear ya. Wouldn't want to miss it, though."

It seemed the next day held a great deal of excitement for these people, as almost every couple that passed him said something about the council meeting. *Must be a pretty big deal.*

Joel kept following the music and discovered more people; however, these young people had a different appearance. Their dress was not at all business-like and they were wearing the vibrant colors he had seen in the Waiz train station.

Wonder why Madam Bontecou wears New Waiz clothes? Flashing lights soon accompanied the music he heard enticing him to a corner street.

The whole street was full of people, and each was either dancing, laughing, or singing. All the storefronts were lit with flashing, multicolored lights while white twinkling lights dangled above the crowd. A piano and stringed instruments blared from a stage in the middle of the street. The sea of colorful people happily singing and dancing was *beautiful.* As odd a word as it was for him to think, it was the only one that came to mind. He paused to take the place in and wondered how long this party went on.

They're as happy as the people in Old Waiz. He glanced at his watch. It was near three in the morning, and he could not help but just look up and smile at this young crowd. *Carefree, wild, but mostly free.*

His thoughts were interrupted by bump from someone behind him. "Oh, sorry, man. Kinda hard to move around in such a tight crowd," said a young man about his age as he readjusted the grey plaid fedora on his head.

Curious, Joel waved his hand and called out to him, "It's okay. Is it like this every night, or is this a holiday or something?"

"Not from around here, aye?"

Joel nodded as he watched the young man grab a pint of beer from a nearby seller. The young man was at least half a foot shorter than Joel and several pounds lighter. His straight light-brown hair reached near his chin and he wore blue pants with a white v-neck shirt. Joel followed a silver chain down the young man's chest. Its anchor was a circular pendent displaying a foreign inscription.

"Yeah, me, neither. From the north," he said, while jerking his head in that direction. "Weather's so much better here, nice and warm," he remarked, while throwing the hand that held his pint up in the air above Joel's head.

Joel moved to dodge the liquid that spilled from the mug.

"Oops, sorry again. Anyway, ran away from home a few years ago and never looked back. Been hanging out in Old Waiz?" he eyed Joel's clothes as he took a sip.

"Yeah, had to make some cash before I could get down here."

"Understand. Here, this one's on me." He grabbed another pint and handed it to Joel.

"So, it's like this every night?" Joel asked before he brought the foamy drink to his lips.

"Oh, yeah. It's alive down here every night. The New City, the people here, they know how to live life, you know?"

Joel was not sure he did know and shrugged in response.

"Like celebrate, you know, they *stop* every night just to celebrate being alive. Look, they've got music, food, dancing, and, of course, booze," he said as he hit his pint against Joel's.

Joel nodded hesitantly, somewhat understanding what he meant. He turned back towards the music and was mesmerized by the crowd.

"You'll notice it's a classy sort of celebrating, with piano music, the violins. I mean, look, all the ladies there," the young man pointed to a group of young women serving wine. "If you'll notice, their goods are completely covered up."

Joel searched over other young women in the crowd and saw that each was dressed quite modestly.

"They're free to party, but keep their self-respect, see."

Joel grinned in response to the young man's smirk.

"And see, look at me," the young man pointed to himself. "I'm free to celebrate with this classy crowd and their classic music," he joked.

Joel furrowed his eyebrows at him, wondering what he was really trying to say.

"Not drunk, mate," he said seriously to Joel as he put a hand on his shoulder. "No such thing as a classy drunk. Not to say that I'm not feeling good," the young man laughed, and Joel knew both of his statements were true. "But see, look out there, no sloshing around. Folks know their limit. That's not to say in a few more hours you may see a different sight, but who'll remember that," the young man shrugged lightheartedly.

"I've never seen anything like it," Joel said.

"Well, you just gonna stand there or are you comin'?" the young lad gestured forward.

Joel followed his new friend deep into the crowd. When they were closest to the band, he felt his new buddy put his arm around him to pull him close.

"Hey! I forgot to tell you something!" he yelled into Joel's ear. "There are several streets like this one, but well, some of the ones down from here.... Well, just stay on this one!"

"What's on the others? I wanted to see the sunrise on the Valtina!" Joel yelled back at him as he covered his ear that was nearest to the stage.

"Just don't go! We call it 'the bottoms' for obvious reasons! It's not safe! Besides, why would you want to leave here?"

Joel watched him throw his hands up in the air and grab the girl closest to him. He laughed at him then continued to mosey through the crowd.

He saw each storefront was selling bread, sausage, cheese, and wine. Their glowing signs were the perfect backdrop to the scene. He took in a deep breath and smelled something sweet and rich. He passed by a stand of pastries. *Augustine would love that. Ugh. Why am I still thinking about her?* he wondered as he strode past dozens of young girls. The vibrant colors they wore made their faces shine with radiance. All of his senses were tempted on this street.

As he neared the edge, he peered down the next road and saw there were about three more dancing streets, just as the young man had said. He walked past the streets in awe. *This is completely crazy.* Eventually Joel caught a salty aroma in the air and hoped it was from the Valtina Sea. He wondered if he could make it to the beach before sunrise. Sarah had always told him that sunrise was the best time to see the Valtina, and he intended to make his first visit one of his best.

As he ventured into the outskirts of downtown, the road lights grew dim and the streets became quiet again. He thought he might be coming upon another kalona, but instead saw rows of cheap, darkened buildings. The barred windows and plentiful graffiti slapped on their walls made Joel wonder if he was in the bottoms. He was relieved when he saw a sign directing him towards the Valtina.

When he started towards the sign, he saw an older lady pushing a cart down the street in front of him. She was hunched over with a scarf tied around her head and Joel realized he would eventually have to pass by her.

How odd to see an older lady here ... and what's she doing at this time of night? He pondered whether or not he'd be able to avoid her. When he realized they were headed towards the same sign, he gritted his teeth and started forward.

She turned to greet him just when he was about to pass her. "Oh, hi, sonny. You're out late. Care to help an old lady?" Her old, cackling voice made Joel's skin crawl.

"Uh, no, ma'am. I'm kind of in a hurry," he let out as he looked over her dirty face and hands.

"Oh now, it won't take long. Can't you just help me push this to the end of the street? Look, just to that tree there," the woman pleaded as she pointed towards the tree.

283

Joel looked down the street and then back to the woman. He knew she really could use his help.

"Please, show me a little pity. I'm clearly overwhelmed," she said as she gestured to her small frame and then to the large cart.

"Sure," Joel finally sighed.

"Care for anything to eat?" she cackled again as she pulled out an apple.

Joel was immediately reminded of the tale *Snow White* and quickly declined her offer.

"Well, okay, then, almost there. I can't thank you enough, dearie."

Just as Joel was about to park the cart, two hands grabbed him from behind and threw him to the ground.

"Well, well, what do we have here?" A middle-aged man with a dirty face showed Joel a toothless smile.

"Get off of me!" Joel yelled.

"Take it easy," came another male voice from around the cart. "Get his knapsack," the voice commanded the woman.

"What do you want?" Joel shouted as he pushed against his attacker.

"Depends entirely on what you got," replied the toothless man.

"Not from around here, huh?" said another man, dark and middle-aged. "Cat got your tongue? You're as pale as a ghost. Must've been in Old Waiz a little too long. Only someone from there would have been stupid enough to walk in these parts alone," the dark-haired man sneered as he walked over to Joel. He was wearing an old dirty black cloak that reminded Joel of the Templins.

"Let me go!" Joel shouted again as he struggled.

"Not so fast," the toothless man said as he pinned him down harder.

"He's got some dark jewel in his ear," yelled the woman.

"Let's see here," the dark-haired man said as he knelt down next to Joel. "Nah, it's just a black plastic bead."

"Boys wearing jewelry," the woman scoffed as she poured all of Joel's possessions out into the street.

"Ho! What's going on here?" came a voice Joel couldn't see.

"Trouble?" said still another.

Joel craned his neck to see the small crowd forming.

"Oh, Watchmen, come on! Just having a little fun with a newcomer," the dark-haired man complained.

"Dispersing belongings? That's a little too much fun, I think."

"Kendrew," the toothless man began.

"Quit your whining, Rufus, and get out of here, the three of you, before I change my mind."

The toothless man gruffly released Joel, and the three of them soon disappeared into the darkness.

"Here," said a man in his mid-twenties, handing Joel his bag.

"Thanks," Joel replied, and started stuffing his things back into the knapsack.

"You just learned one of the most important rules in New Waiz. Everyone travels in pairs, especially at night," the one called Kendrew said, as he nodded towards the other young man on his left.

Joel sighed, then shrugged in frustration. "I don't know anyone, and well, I just wanted to see the sunrise."

"On the Valtina, I assume? It's a sight to behold. Come on, that's on our way."

Joel gathered his bag. *Guess I can trust these two since they just rescued me.*

"First night down?" the other man asked.

Joel nodded and then remembered a nod couldn't be heard in the dark. "Er, yes."

"We're part of the security group here in New Waiz. Our particular guard is called 'the Watchmen.' Those hoodlums back there are pretty much harmless, but even so, make a friend fast."

"Are you both on duty?" Joel asked.

"Sort of," Kendrew began. "In the bottoms you're always on duty. But honestly, with the council meeting tomorrow, all guards are put on watch, even if not on the clock."

"So, it's a pretty big deal, huh?" Joel asked, breathing hard as he hurried to keep their pace.

"Yes, definitely. It's kind of patriotic, you know, each city being represented and coming together in so-called unity."

Joel thought there was a hint of sarcasm in the other Watchman's voice.

"Tensions are growing thick, so either way, the meeting should be interesting. Here's the sea. Listen," Kendrew instructed.

All paused, and Joel could hear waves crashing into the shoreline.

"You'll be safe over there. After the sun's up, feel free to roam around. There'll be a crowd and Watchmen everywhere due to the meeting," Kendrew directed.

Joel gave them his thanks then climbed over the stone wall that was separating the street from the sandy beach. He could not see the water, so he sat in the sand under a tree. With only a few hours of darkness left, he leaned his head up against the tree as the sound of the waves put him into a deep sleep....

Nurse Polma shook her head at Dr. Pryderi as he stuck a long needle into Joel's arm, which had been tied down. "These mind games are accomplishing nothing," he snapped.

"Don't look at me, it wasn't my suggestion."

"No, yours is to drain our supply of Obtun. I'm already giving the boy enough to tranquilize a small elephant. This," the doctor pointed to Joel's secured limbs, "this is the true madness."

The nurse's eyes flickered when she noticed Joel was waking up. She jerked Dr. Pryderi to the side. "And what would you have? Him back with his father, the perpetrator?" she whispered.

"That is precisely what I recommended years ago. We have tried, Trinity," the doctor sighed. "We can't cure him."

"The headmaster knows this?"

The doctor nodded.

"Then why?"

"The reason doesn't matter. The boy needs to be with his kin, not locked up. If he's crazy what's the harm in letting him be so?"

"But he'd have to be sent to Trompe with the rest of Differe's unstable. Right?"

The doctor didn't answer.

Nurse Polma eyed Joel curiously and then grabbed the doctor's shoulder. "I am director of this facility. I will not have a subordinate keep secrets behind my back."

"Really, and why is that? In the best interest of the patient? Or to be in control of him?"

"This is—this is," she struggled for words. "Why? Tell me why the headmaster hasn't sent him to Trompe Asylum?"

Dr. Pryderi pried her hands off of him and walked back over to Joel. "Wake up, Joel. Those fools are done trying to instill truth in you." The man patted his face.

"What fools?" Joel's eyes fluttered.

"Nurse Polma, you may be the director but I am still the doctor." He watched her stiffen. "Joel remains here at the doctor's recommendation."

"But you just said he should be with his—"

"I am under oath not to breach confidentiality of care. Good night."

Her eyes followed him to the door until Joel moaned. She bent down to free his legs and arms. "Witless foreigner."

Deep in his subconscious Joel had just received a great revelation. The temple had failed to cure him but wouldn't admit it. In fact, the headmaster would've had to break numerous Differian laws in choosing not to send him to Trompe Asylum. "I will find you," he heard the headmaster say. *Oh no, they're after me.*

CHAPTER 22

JOEL AWOKE AT first light. It would have been impossible not to. The sun's rays were unguarded and blazing. Squinting, he rubbed his eyes as he sat up against the tree. The morning light was broken into pure golden beams that struck everything in their path. The water reflected shimmering orange hues of the golden light back into the sky. It was so bright Joel could not distinguish the white caps from the waves crashing onto the shore. He felt exhausted as he watched the boats coming into the port on his right. He had dreamed something significant last night but couldn't remember the details. He rubbed his chest. *I feel like I was fighting all night.*

Joel removed his shoes and dug his feet into the sand. He grabbed a brown bag out of his knapsack and ate his breakfast. As he ate sitting amidst such beauty, he realized it was one of the few meals he had eaten alone in Waiz. "Here I am, in the one of the most beautiful places in the world," Joel sighed.

A different voice than his own finished his thought. "And you are all alone."

The light was just beginning to sneak up the mountainside when Augustine went to wake her brother.

"Sebastian," Augustine shook him. "Wake up. It's time to get up."

"It's so early," he moaned.

"I know, but it's a long ride to New Waiz. You still want to go, right?"

He hesitated for a moment then sat up. "Yes, all right, I can't wait to see it."

She smiled and handed him a pair of clean clothes.

As he was changing his shirt he asked, "Do you think Joel made it to New Waiz?"

"I'm not sure that's where he went," she replied shortly, surprised he would even ask about him.

"I know he didn't go back to the barn."

"How do you know that?" she asked curiously as she handed him a hairbrush.

"Because I heard Corwin tell you he wasn't there. Why did Corwin go looking for him?" Sebastian demanded as he ran the brush through his blond hair.

"Because," she hesitated. She debated what to tell him and finally settled on the truth. *Sebastian would spot a lie, anyway.* "Because I asked him to. Joel wasn't right last night, Sebastian. He needed looking after."

"And you find yourself qualified to do so?"

Augustine was astounded at the meanness she heard in his accusation. "Listen, I don't know what happened between the two of you that has made you so upset, but despite his faults, and there are plenty, he took care of us while Corwin was gone."

Sebastian stared at her in silence.

"He was sick or something. But no, I am not qualified, and quite frankly, he freaked me out last night. That's why I sent Corwin and did not volunteer myself," Augustine sighed, as she pulled his socks on.

"Like Corwin would let you chase after him in the dark." Sebastian rolled his green eyes at her.

"He did the other night," she shot back at him more sharply than she intended.

"Oh?" Sebastian looked at her wide-eyed.

"Yes," she said, as she forced a shoe onto his foot. "I was the one who got the rest of our things."

Sebastian looked at her in shock but not disbelief. "What did you ask him?"

"A few things, but I got no answers," she said in a frustrated tone. "Anything you want to tell me?" she asked, as she batted her big, blue eyes at him.

"Nope," he assured her.

"All right. Well, then let's get your teeth brushed, and we'll be ready."

The water turned a magnificent shade of florescent turquoise as the sun rose. To Joel's left was a large harbor; he estimated it was housing over a hundred boats. As he watched the docks, he observed that the number of people emptying out of their boats increased every half hour. *This council thing really is a big deal.* The meeting was set for mid-morning, and though he didn't want to miss it, he figured he had time to explore one of the docks.

Joel pushed his way past the people who were headed towards the shore as he dodged the bait buckets, coolers, and fishing gear strewn about the dock. Sailboats of varying colors were anchored toward the end of the dock, whereas most of the smaller wooden boats were tied nearer to the shore. He was away from the crowd by the time he reached the end of the dock and turned to look back at the two cities.

New Waiz was much broader than Joel had expected, with most of the west side full of the houses he had seen the night before. He realized the area was like a kalona, but more residential. The houses had rooftops in a variety of terra cotta shades. Just west of the river he saw the downtown, the industry area that Mr. Rutherford and Professor Louis had mentioned. There was hardly anything on the east side of river, even up towards Old Waiz. He made out some of the kalonas in Old Waiz, and just as the museum map had showed, the Old City ended at the base of the rocky mountain cliffs.

Thankfully, Joel found the bottoms' streets much friendlier this morning. Just as Kendrew had said, there were plenty of Watchmen out directing the masses. He easily navigated his way back toward the towers, noticing that the "dancing streets" were empty this morning and littered with trash. As he approached the business buildings he saw many open windows and balconies filled with people. He filed in behind the crowd and walk toward the east tower.

Augustine attempted to view Old Waiz on the mountainside as they walked toward the Bridge of Miren. She had hoped to cross the bridge and see the Pallas River, but it became apparent that the Old Waiz inhabitants largely comprised the crowd on the west side of the bridge. Thankfully, Corwin led her and Sebastian straight to the wall that ran beside the river. Both curiously peered over the wall. Augustine didn't expect the river to be as far below as it was, and leaned over for a closer observation. The Pallas River was wide, wild, and raging. *Certainly not for swimming.* The stone walls built on either side of the river began at its bank and stretched all the way up to where they were standing. The walls continued alongside the river throughout the city of New Waiz.

Corwin took them along the wall until the three filed into their seats. The stone stadium-like seats were situated on either side of the towers right behind the river wall. She hadn't asked Corwin how he came by their tickets, but guessed they had prime seats as she noted the massive crowd standing around them. The middle of the tower, or the bridge's entrance, was also crammed with people standing outside. At first she was frustrated at not being able to see past the bridge's entrance; however, she soon realized she had a clear view of the Bridge of Miren and both councils.

On the bridge, the two orders sat facing each other on rows of wooden benches. Each side had a podium turned toward their side of the crowd. For the most part she could only make out the backs of those representing the council for Old Waiz. She was not surprised to see that many on the council were balding older men. Sitting across from them was a much younger group of men. A few had salt-and-pepper hair, but almost none of them were fighting baldness as yet.

Several yells from the opposing side turned Augustine's attention to the stands directly across from her. *Oh, their clothes are beautiful*, she thought, as she eyed the women. As the shouts grew louder, Augustine found the opposite side fashionable but a bit rude. She saw the New Waiz crowd was much larger than the crowd where she was sitting.

When she thought she heard what they were saying, she leaned towards Corwin and whispered, "Are they jeering at us?"

"It would seem so," he said, with a hint of irritation in his voice.

As Augustine eyed the Old Waiz crowd, she wondered if just sitting with them was making a gross political statement. The balconies behind her were full of people holding hand-painted signs. She squinted for a better view and saw several signs painted with slogans such as "The King is Dead," as well as other posters that demanded, "Out with the Old—In with the New Waiz."

Seeing these expressions made her feel nervous, and she immediately tugged on Corwin's sleeve. "Corwin, is this—" She stopped when Sebastian turned his head up at her. "Are we safe?" she mouthed, while gesturing towards Sebastian and making sure he did not see her.

Corwin was very aware that danger was close by. However he also knew that Joel had to be here. Corwin was only here to find him … he had to find him.

Corwin patted Augustine's hand reassuringly in response. He had decided not to tell the other two he was looking for a needle in a haystack, but against all odds they had met Joel before, and Corwin was sure they would find him again. He scanned the crowd. *We need him.*

As Joel approached the east tower, he was surprised as to how much the structure reminded him of Differe. However, these towers were much more magnificent in their setting, free of ice and snow and with a glittering blue river below them. Joel watched the councils enter through the grand archway and studied the carved out window at the top of the tower. *Where are the stairs?*

His thoughts were interrupted by a slap he received on his back.

"My man! How's New Waiz life treating you?"

Joel was pleasantly surprised to see his dancing street escort. "Oh, just fine."

"You see your sunrise this morning?" he asked eagerly as he brushed back a lock of hair with his hand.

"Yeah, got in a little trouble in the bottoms," Joel said sheepishly.

"What? Idiot! I told you to stay up top," he warned, as gave Joel a friendly whack on the back of the head.

"I made it. Watchmen were there."

"Who?"

"Kendrew."

"Oh, good bloke. Lucky for you he was there to save your skin."

Joel nodded as they both chuckled.

"Well, you've at least chosen the right side today. Literally and figuratively. Come on, let's move closer."

Joel followed his friend's neon blue shirt towards the river wall, and he soon became thankful for his height. He didn't think his friend could see a thing over all the heads standing in front of them.

"Well, better late than never, but at this rate we'll have to stand. No more room in the seats."

"Wish we could have that view." Joel pointed to the tower window.

"Aye, but no one can have that view. The towers are completely blocked off. Even the Watchmen aren't allowed up there."

"What?" Joel asked in surprise.

"Yeah, well, actually, it's not that they aren't allowed up there, but more so because they can't get up there."

Joel looked at him even more puzzled.

"Look," the young man pointed into the center of the archway behind the council. "No door to get in."

"So, the tower's just for looks or something?" Joel let out in disappointment, thinking the structure was even more Differian than he had thought.

"No way. I think there's a way up, all right. Just hasn't been found yet," he said mischievously.

Joel pursed his lips and nodded in agreement, knowing full well he had seen a light in the east tower the night before.

He squinted hard through the sun's bright rays that were beating down onto their assembly. He attempted to scrutinize the tower, searching for any concealed passageway someone might have overlooked, but he saw nothing. He raised his hand to his brow to shade his eyes.

"Here," his friend said as he handed Joel a pair of binoculars. "I don't think you'll find your secret door with these, but you can fill me in on what you see. I'm obviously at a disadvantage here," said the young man, gesturing upward at Joel's height.

Joel inspected the tower window and shook his head. *Nothing. Maybe I was seeing things last night.* He soon noticed the structure standing behind the tower across from him. It appeared to be an old hotel. Though the hotel was not nearly as high as the tower, its length spanned much of the meeting area. The balconies provided a perfect viewing place for the meeting. Joel saw that the crowd on the opposite side was a mix of Old and New Waiz citizens. Most of the balconies, however, were filled with New Waiz inhabitants. *Interesting. I wonder which side they're on?* he wondered, as he scanned the building.

Just before looking away, Joel spotted one room with an empty balcony. The door was open and its curtain was blowing in the wind. He stared at the doorway, thinking the open door was a bit odd. *I must be seeing things*, he reasoned with himself when he thought he saw something sway inside. He kept his eyes on the curtain and soon whispered, "There it is again." He waited still another few minutes, and the next time what he thought he saw was confirmed. Joel realized with each breeze that he was watching a piece of fabric being blown along with the curtain. The fabric was green, and he knew it was a cloak.

CHAPTER 23

AUGUSTINE WATCHED AS additional councilmen trickled onto the bridge from either side. She noticed that the councils did not mingle but stayed each to their own side, shaking hands with only those around them. Eventually all sat down, and when they did, both sides of the crowd went silent. Corwin looked at the two of them and held a finger to his lips.

Augustine searched around for the source of the sound she heard next. She knew it did not sound like a horn or trumpet, but she could not see what was producing the loud sound. The instrument blew several times, and then she saw two men from opposing sides rise from their seats. The crowds erupted into applause and cheers at this gesture. The two men met at the podiums that were facing one another and shook hands amicably.

"Well, here goes," Corwin sighed as they sat back down.

Augustine sensed a greater and greater tension brewing the longer she sat on the stone bench. The councilman from Old Waiz turned his podium to face her side. Augustine tugged on Corwin's shirt at the same time Sebastian elbowed her.

"Augustine! Look," Sebastian whispered.

"Sh!" someone seated around them chided.

She nodded her head vigorously at Sebastian to indicate she saw what he was referring to.

By this time, Corwin had turned toward them again and was urgently pressing his finger to his lips.

Augustine stammered and silently mouthed, "That's the mean old man!"

"Who?" Corwin mouthed back.

Augustine swung her head back and forth to make sure no one was watching them. "The mean man from the trail."

"Oh," Corwin mouthed, while nodding his head that he understood.

The head of New Waiz's council also turned to face his crowd. Augustine was, of course, unable to see his face, but noted that he was one of the older men in their group.

The "mean man," as Augustine had dubbed him, spoke first after the shouts of welcome from the crowd died down.

"Citizens of Waiz, New and Old, welcome." He then turned to acknowledge the New Waiz side. "Welcome to the great towers, the Bridge of Miren. Just as the name 'Miren' stands for peace, may this assembly bring continued peace among us." He turned and held out his hand to give the other man the floor.

"Welcome, New Waiz!" The crowd across from them went crazy at the New Waiz councilman's exclamation until he waved his hands for them to stop. He turned just slightly toward her side and nodded. "And welcome, Old Waiz." Those surrounding her met his welcome with silence. "May commerce and progress continue to flourish between our great cities," he paused, then quickly asked, "Reports?" to which the Old Waiz councilman responded, "Proceed."

Augustine soon found her mind wandering as different councilmen from each side gave a range of reports regarding topics such as agriculture, water, and education. The reading of the reports almost resembled a competition to Augustine, as it seemed each side tried to "one up" the other when their stats were listed. *I feel like I'm at a tennis match*, she thought, as her head bobbed back and forth between the speakers.

When the reports on religion and "principles," as they called them, were brought forth, there was no more pretension about the so-called peace between the cities. Differences were the only commonality being demonstrated.

"How can you call yourselves citizens of Waiz yet have no respect for religion, the religion that this sacred place was founded upon?"

Augustine looked up and saw that the podiums were now facing one another as the two council heads began to argue.

"We are citizens of *New* Waiz. We are not bound to the old ways," the younger man argued in arrogance.

"Yes, your religion is commerce and progress. It will leave you and this city empty!" the old man cried in rebuttal.

"On the contrary, progress means more, not less, old man." He shook his finger at the other speaker. "If you do not wish for us to be called your citizens, my council is ready to forfeit that title."

"Separation of governments is not the answer!" The two were furiously yelling and wiping sweat from their brows.

"What about the king?" Joel heard someone yell from the Old Waiz crowd as he carefully approached their side.

"He's dead!"

"He's gone!"

"He's not around anymore!"

Joel heard the citizens of New Waiz respond.

"No! The Majestic is everywhere!" the Old Waiz crowd replied in protest.

As the two councils tried to silence the crowds, Joel easily slipped onto the hotel's fire escape ladder with no one noticing. He put the strap of his knapsack over his head and around his chest before he quietly climbed the sturdy old ladder. Just as with his encounter with the Green Cloak before, he thought very little about what he would do once inside the room. *I don't care.* A hot anger began to well up inside him. His only defense was a glass bottle that he had scooped up from one of the dancing streets on his way to the hotel. *I'll just jump onto the balcony and whack him out cold. If those maps are on him, they won't be his for long.*

Joel noticed the crowds had quieted down again as he made his best attempt at having some sort of plan. He listened hard to hear what was going on. "That's the old realm! This is a new realm bringing a new government. If commerce is to be the religion, so be it."

Joel heard more commotion and cheers come from across the bridge.

"Book? What about the book? It's lost, and everyone knows that you are using a replica which might as well be a fake."

Where is Old Waiz? All he heard was the whistles and cheers from the balcony dwellers. Joel looked out toward the seats of Old Waiz and hardly anyone was even stirring. *Come on, say something,* he begged them silently, as he moved within a few feet of the bare balcony.

"Just because we do not see, we do not lose heart. There is progress in the old ways, though it is not demonstrated as hastily. We must come to an agreement! War or separation is not our desire."

"Here! Here!" Joel finally heard the Old Waiz crowd respond.

"Nor it is our desire," he heard the younger man yell over their cheers.

"I have some information regarding *The Book of Order*," the old man declared, and Old Waiz applauded.

That was the last thing Joel heard before he made his leap onto the balcony. As he clung to the iron bars, he heard something whiz past his head. The object moved so fast that he was only able to hear the arrow Andi had shot. As Joel swung his body over the bars and onto the balcony, he heard screams from all around him. He now had a clear view of the bridge and clearly spotted the Old Waiz speaker. *That's the old man!* he realized, as he looked upon the man's bloody chest. Joel stood frozen at the sight.

Reality quickly jarred him to move as he realized all of Old Waiz was turned toward the hotel and gesturing at him. "There he is!"

"That's him!"

"Murderer!"

His heart sank when he saw their shouts were directed at him. *Oh, not good!* He hurriedly dashed into the room with the bottle in his hand. Sure enough, Joel found Andi, in his green cloak, packing his bow and arrows into something.

"You!" the Green Cloak exclaimed. Before the heavily scarred face could grab an arrow, Joel kicked the quiver out of his hand, scattering arrows everywhere.

With no safe exit, Andropolis turned to bar the balcony doors. He was shocked to see the redhead in the room. "You're stouter than I remember," he remarked in a nasty tone.

Joel quickly scraped one of the arrows off of the ground and grabbed the bow. He soon backed Andi against the balcony doors.

"Quite courageous for a kid your age, aren't you? Not to mention stupid," Andi taunted, as he eyed Joel with disdain.

"I'm almost eighteen! I also have the bow and arrows," Joel threatened as he pulled the arrow back tighter.

"Apparently, *you* were seen," Andi said as he nodded toward the shouts at the window.

Before Joel could respond, Andi suddenly thrust him onto the floor. Pinned there and unable to move, Joel heard footsteps making their way to the room.

"Oh, here come the Watchmen. Thanks for the alibi, kid," Andi said, as he patted Joel's face in arrogance. "I'll leave the bow and arrows with you—good evidence." Andi kept his knee planted on Joel's chest as he strapped his quiver onto his arm.

Joel spit in Andi's face, causing him to loosen his grip. Joel then wrapped his legs around Andi and reached under his cloak to grab the hilt of his sword. In a struggle to get loose from one another, both pulled back, and Joel managed to get the sword into his hand.

Andi's eyes first flickered with fear at the sight and then he quickly shook his head. Both jumped at the sound of the footsteps that were outside the door.

"When is this place going to recognize that I am *not* a kid? To the tower!" Joel commanded.

Andi did not budge.

"Show me the way. Now!" Joel barked at him loudly, hoping the fellow had an escape plan in mind.

"What are you talking about?" Andi asked angrily.

"You were there last night," Joel insisted. "Get us out of here, and I won't kill you."

Joel had no intention of killing anyone, but hoped he and his extra pounds looked convincing. He knew that for some reason this fellow feared seeing him brandishing a sword. "I'll also be taking this. Seems a little important to you," Joel hissed, as he took the quiver.

Andi looked furious but Joel also saw defeat in his face. "You're nothing without your sword, are you?" Joel sneered. "And this quiver looks quite valuable. Too bad it's mine now."

Andi smirked at him. "All this fuss for a trip to the tower? Or is it really a few simple maps you're after?"

"You may not have the chance to find out." Joel gestured toward the sound of pounding fists heard outside the door.

"Open in the name of the king!"

Joel watched Andi spit on the ground in response to hearing these words.

"I'm no shot," Joel continued as he nodded to the bow. "Your skills, however, will certainly blow your cover."

The continued banging from outside the room fueled the tension between the two. Andi hung his head and mumbled, "I'm prepared to die for the Order, but not by some kid."

Joel tried to stay focused on Andi, but his nerves were escalating as both sets of doors sounded as if they were about to be ripped apart.

"Come on, then. Get me the maps, and get us out of here. I promise I'll spare you," Joel ordered him.

"Yes, but the Order will surely kill me if I take you through—" Andi stopped short when he saw a blade slip through the door. "All right, I can at least hide us," he sighed bitterly as he strode over to the room's walk-in closet.

The closet ceiling was covered with old square tiles. Andropolis jumped up to hit one and moved it slightly out of place.

"I'll be needing your sheath," Joel demanded, and Andi turned back to him, irritation covering his face.

"I'm about to save your skin."

"Would you prefer I leave your quiver and sword for the others?"

Andi growled as he undid his belt and thrust it at Joel.

Joel hurriedly put on the belt and slipped the sword into its sheath. Joel watched Andi use the metal hanging bar to help pull himself up past the tiles. Andi grasped something beyond the tiles and pulled himself out of sight. When Joel attempted to follow him, he slipped off the metal bar a few times before being able to grasp inside the attic. He was surprised when a hand clasped onto his arm and helped pull him up. Once both were inside, Andi slid the tile back over the hole, which gave Joel just enough time to redraw the sword.

Neither spoke as they listened to a group of Watchmen search the room below. Joel wondered why they did not search the attic until he heard one say, "How about the attic?"

"There's not one anymore. All closed in for better insulation."

I bet that's one of New Waiz's cronies saving this guy's tail. Both sat in silence for over an hour until the baffled officials finally disbanded and left two guards at both entrances to the room.

After the room below became silent, Joel whispered into the darkness, "What's our way out?"

"Probably the roof or another room. Watchmen will be searching everywhere."

"Do you have the maps on you?"

Joel's question was met by a long pause. "No," Andi finally said in a sharp tone.

Joel sighed. "And I was so hoping to part ways with you."

"What are they to you, anyway? They're not that important. They're not even yours," Andi accused him.

Joel did not answer. *That's why I have to get them back.*

"All right, well, perhaps one belongs to you," Andi admitted.

"Either way, I'd say at this point an exchange is in order. You have four maps that belong to me, and I have your sword and quiver."

"And just why would you expect me to believe you'd surrender my weapons during such an exchange?" Andi quipped.

"An empty quiver is hardly worth anything to me," Joel said, while sensing a look of indignation on Andi's face. "And, on top of that, I have no real need for a sword. I'm not fighting for a particular side."

"You say that as if you think I'm on the wrong side," Andi said matter-of-factly.

"You did just kill an innocent man," Joel replied, and more silence followed.

"Ugh, come on then. Let's try to get out of here," Andi muttered.

Joel could barely see Andi stand up through the darkness. He walked across a few beams and swiftly removed a black tarp from an old skylight. The bit of light shining into the attic made Joel wonder if they should wait until dusk or nightfall before trying to escape. Andi obviously had a different plan in mind. He opened the skylight and threw the black tarp onto the roof and then waited behind the opening.

"No commotion ... no one is watching this side of the roof. Stick to the beams." He motioned to Joel. And with that, he pushed himself through the skylight and onto the roof. Worried that the Green Cloak would get away, Joel promptly crossed the beams and pushed himself through the skylight.

The blow Joel took to the head upon reaching the rooftop knocked him off balance and caused him to drop the sword. He fell flat on his back and close to the gutters. He saw that the roof above the attic was flat, but that the portion past the gutters went into a steep slant off the building. As Joel rolled onto his side, he saw he and Andi were on the backside of the building. This was opposite from where the council meeting had taken place, and the streets below were empty.

When Joel struggled to get to his feet, Andi lurched toward him. The sword was far from both their grips, so Andi improvised. He ripped Joel's knapsack strap from Joel's chest to his neck. "You may have put on a few extra pounds, but you're still no match for me," he hissed as he pinned Joel against the ground.

Joel panicked as he tried to gasp for air. He somehow found a smidgen of free movement in his arms and reached forward to push Andi off of him. The two young men began to rock back and forth as they expelled their force against each other.

Joel glanced up at Andropolis' heavily scarred face. *Here, I'll add another,* he thought, as he gasped for air. He rolled the quiver from around his back and whacked Andi in the face. The blow sent Andi flying past the gutters and onto the roof's slant. Joel rolled over onto all fours and found Andi scrambling for a grip as he slid down the side of the roof.

Joel knew Andi had landed when he saw a green cloak dodge into a nearby barn down the street. There were a few hours of daylight left, and Joel rolled back onto his back to breathe for a moment. As he lay there in exhaustion, he knew he would have to track down this green monster. He kept a close watch on the barn as he changed into a different pair of clothes. With great disgust, he pulled on his gray school robe in order to conceal the sword and quiver.

Once Joel reached the street, he wondered if the meeting had continued or if everyone had fled to their homes due to the murder. He circled around to the back of the stretch of buildings so he would come at the barn from behind. As he studied the structure, he realized all the windows and doors had been shut. Frustrated, Joel wondered what he should do, as he knew the Green Cloak would be looking for him.

He silently approached the barn's back door, still feeling greatly exposed in such broad daylight. His spirit quieted upon hearing the dozens of cattle locked inside. He squinted to look through two slats in the wooden beams and easily found the Green Cloak amidst the cattle boarded in the stalls. The young man was perched by the door on the opposite side. Joel smoothly made his way inside the barn. *Thanks to you,* he nodded at the cattle, which called back to him in reply. When the Green Cloak's hood was in range, Joel did not draw the sword but the glass bottle.

Hours later, Andropolis awoke with a huge knot on his head and a bit of blood coming out of his mouth. As he rolled over in a state of confusion, he saw his sword in his sheath and his quiver in the corner of his eye. Both pieces lay near where he had been lying unconscious. Andropolis quickly reached into the pockets of both his cloak and his pants. The young redhead had made his exchange. *All the maps are gone!* He put his hands on his aching head. *I can't believe I forgot to leave them in the tower like Marcell asked.*

He reached to belt himself with the sword and then tenderly grasped for the quiver. As he pulled it near, he realized the item felt mysteriously heavy. Andropolis could see that it had been filled with some sort of dark substance. Curious, he bent down for a better look. One whiff of the filling caused him to gag. "That little chicken hoe … he filled it with cow turds."

Isabelle finished putting the last bandage on Sarah's wounded flesh. "These are deep," she said sadly.

"Well, I was there longer than usual this time." Sarah moved slowly as she rebuttoned her shirt and helped Isabelle repack the medicine basket. "Thankfully for me, I have this." Sarah pointed to the basket. "This is one of the few useful things I kept after we left Moonstruck," she said as she turned to smile at Isabelle.

Shame flowed strongly over Isabelle as she listened to the woman's words. *How can she smile at me? I just dressed the wounds that I caused.* She hung her head in despair.

"Isabelle, guilt and shame suit you just about as well as the infirmary would suit me. Stop that," Sarah said, as she tenderly raised Isabelle's chin. "Forgiveness doesn't look back. It gives us the opportunity to move forward into more grace." Sarah gave her a wry smile as she looked more deeply into Isabelle's face. "I see shame is already losing its power over you," she said as she brushed her finger against Isabelle's dark scar.

Isabelle tried to look away, but the middle-aged woman still held her face.

"You are even more radiant in the natural, my dear."

Isabelle blushed at the compliment, and Sarah turned to lock up the medical supplies.

"They let you keep your key?" Isabelle called out.

"Yes. I'll still be teaching. And you? Do you have yours?"

Isabelle pulled it out from underneath her shirt, saying, "I'm surprised Holt hasn't taken it from me."

"I'm not surprised. There's more to him than meets the eye, I think. What happened in my absence?"

Isabelle relayed every event in great detail. Her tears flowed as her emotions spilled out, and her hands danced throughout her speech. She said her greatest bewilderment during all the events she related had occurred during her escape back to library. Isabelle also told her about the events of earlier that day and about the letter she had written to her dear friend.

"How did they convince you to write such a letter?" Sarah asked as she combed through her light brown hair.

"I was unafraid to go to Moonstruck. I even asked to go after they took you away."

Sarah raised her eyebrows and nodded in approval at the young lady's courage.

"They threatened to expel Holt and then—well—they took my locket."

Sarah gasped as she covered her mouth in shock. She reached toward Isabelle and let out a compassionate murmur. "I'm sorry."

"But I wrote the letter to make it sound as unlike me as I could, almost in code. I promise I tried to give every indication that I was fine," Isabelle assured the woman.

Sarah flashed her a knowing look and sighed, "I believe they'll see through that, Isabelle."

"Joel will come back for me if I write a desperate love letter. You know that," she said, her blue eyes displaying great fear.

Sarah paused and looked out into the classroom. She finally nodded in agreement. "Yes, love is as strong as death and makes us do foolish, radical things sometimes."

Both sat in silence for a while, thinking about what to do next.

"Sarah, I have an idea," Isabelle hesitated.

"I'm sure it's good, don't be afraid. Let's hear it," Sarah encouraged.

"I've known that I was Joel's bait since I found my school file. How'd you know I would go down to Moonstruck, by the way?" Isabelle looked into her dark brown eyes curiously.

"My dear, I didn't put it there, but I can assure you that they let me know it was missing while I was detained. If you'll remember, I was a little too tied up to have retrieved your file," she said, while letting out a small laugh.

"That's hardly funny. Well, who else would've known to use the flour? I'm confused."

Sarah waved her hand at Isabelle to move on. "Go on with your idea."

Isabelle sat puzzled for a moment, but quickly shifted her thoughts back to her plan. "Okay, well, I've been reading over many of our old lessons on Waiz. I believe it exists, and I'm ready to go. I want to be free just as Joel and I planned. Can you help me escape?" Isabelle asked, trying to sound as mature as possible.

"What if you can't find him? It's a big place," Sarah answered as she ran a hand over her smooth, fair-skinned face.

Isabelle shrugged in response.

"What about your mother, Isabelle?" Sarah asked softly.

Tears crept to the corners of her eyes as Isabelle thought about her mother. She sighed and closed her eyes, letting the tears trickle down. As she sat there, all she could see behind her eyelids was herself writing the fake love letter to Joel.

"They have taken everything I have," Isabelle started, "including my relationship with my mother. I literally have nothing to lose at this point. I can't say that I have any real reason to stay."

Sarah was just about to ask her another question, but Isabelle leaned forward in urgency.

"But, Sarah, I must get out. I must get away to warn Joel. You're right; they're going to ask for a more convincing letter. That's the reason I must leave; he can't come back here. I won't let him risk his life for me, and you know that's what he'll be risking. Will you please help me?"

Sarah answered her by first handing her a cup of hot tea.

"Now, that is a much better reason than your first response. A desire for freedom will get you only so far, but a love for another ... that kind of drive and determination will see you through many dangers."

"Will you come with me?" Isabelle pleaded.

Sarah chuckled and patted Isabelle's hand. "If I was supposed to be in Waiz, I'd be there already. No, you will do this journey on your own. Just as many have done before you."

"You always knew Joel would go without me, didn't you?"

Sarah nodded, "Very seldom are freedom seekers ready at the same time." She winked at Isabelle. "Everyone goes at their own pace, for their own journey," Sarah paused to take a sip of her herbal beverage. "In your case, you're more ready than Joel was. We planned his escape over a long period of time, but yours we must do in a great hurry."

Isabelle nodded in understanding.

"You were good to go over the old lessons. We will do a limited review of these into the night," Sarah commended her and poured her another cup. "Above all else, remember not to leave your personal file behind. Do not destroy it until you have read through it completely. There are many things about your past you need to know," Sarah instructed her intensely.

"I hate the past," Isabelle muttered.

"Do not despise a good teacher, Isabelle."

Isabelle shrunk back at her rebuke and nodded obediently, but could not help adding, "But you just said forgiveness doesn't look back."

"Don't confuse forgiveness and wisdom. Forgiveness doesn't look back, but remembering is necessary for wisdom. Examining your memories through the lens of forgiveness is essential for obtaining wisdom."

Isabelle was surprised when she found herself agreeing with her teacher's statement. Her natural tendency would have been to roll her eyes.

"Grab some more candles and drink up that tea. You will need to be awake the next few hours."

CHAPTER 24

AUGUSTINE HAD GROWN uncomfortable long before the arguments broke out at the council meeting. The sides had started throwing things at one another, and she felt the restlessness rapidly growing around her. She held Sebastian's hand tightly as the tension within her mounted. So when the side of Old Waiz watched the arrow fly into the old man's chest, Augustine reacted with a loud shriek.

She felt Corwin cover her mouth and loudly whisper into her ear, "Look away, dear. Tell Sebastian to look away. Once it clears out, go to the tavern at the top of this hill."

She was so afraid that she started shaking as the tears climbed to her eyes. "Look away, Sebastian! Corwin says to look away," she told him, noticing that he was grossly engaged in the murder scene.

When she saw the people in front of her begin to turn around and point behind her, she quickly turned her head toward the hotel. Her jaw dropped when her gaze reached several flights up the building. She turned to reveal her shock at seeing Joel to Corwin, but he was gone.

She scanned over all the seats in panic. She did not see him on the bridge or anywhere else close by. "Oh, no!" she began to cry.

Shouts of "murderer" and other accusations turned her attention back to the hotel balcony just in time to see Joel scramble inside. Sebastian looked up at her wide-eyed and then frowned upon seeing her tears.

"What's wrong? Are you hurt?"

"No! Corwin—he's gone!" Augustine said in a panic.

"Augustine," he patted her hand reassuringly. "He'll meet us at the tavern. He went looking for Joel." He nodded toward the hotel.

"What? Why!" she cried out.

Sebastian shrugged. "I think the whole reason we came to New Waiz was to find him."

Augustine looked at the hotel in confusion and then to the bridge, where a sheet was being drawn over the old man. *He better not be looking for him. He's a murderer.*

Suddenly, both watched as the Old Waiz Council began to weep on the bridge.

"Augustine, the seats are clearing out enough for us to move," Sebastian said as he jerked his head toward the hill.

"Yes, let's move. A riot is probable at this point."

She hoisted him on her back and walked well away from the crowd before she set up his chair.

She slowly pushed him up the hill in silence.

"What's wrong with you?" Sebastian threw his head back towards her.

She stopped pushing the chair in disbelief. "Do I need to remind you that we just saw a man get murdered, and that this place appears to be on the brink of an all-out war?"

When he didn't respond, she began pushing him again. "It's just … this place isn't what I expected it to be. This Waiz was supposed to be great and glorious, but it's … it's lost that. It's divided and void of the power I'd hoped it would have, and the peace that I longed for."

"That was deep." Sebastian's sarcasm seemed to make light of her comment.

"Well, *you* asked," she defended.

"Yeah, you're right, I did."

After more silence, Sebastian sighed. "Augustine, Corwin wouldn't have brought us here if there wasn't something good for us—some hope."

"Yes, and he tells me that takes faith and all that," she replied, rolling her eyes.

"He's right, you know?"

"Well, it's hard to see any good in this situation," she complained.

"Um, the definition of 'faith,' please, smarty pants?" He laughed in response to her silence. "Ha! No answer! You're mad at me for being right. The definition, if you please," he demanded.

"So what? It has nothing to do with sight. Let's talk about something else."

Sebastian grinned. "How about Joel?"

Augustine let out a groan.

"He couldn't have killed that man, Augustine," Sebastian said. His tone was serious.

"I'm surprised you'd defend him in any manner due to the way you've acted toward him lately."

"I miss him," he said quietly.

Augustine rolled her eyes from behind him again. "I'm not asking again why you're mad at him."

"I'm not anymore," he answered.

She stopped again and bent down toward him. "What? Why not? And what caused this sudden change?"

"I—I talked to Corwin, and he persuaded me to forgive Joel."

Augustine sighed, "Well, you're one for secrets. I have to say that I'm glad, though. That anger didn't suit you—a very foreign friend, indeed."

"Yes, it was making me feel terrible inside and out."

"Yes, I was afraid of that. I should've scolded you, but ..." She trailed off.

"I told Corwin I was angry at him." Sebastian fidgeted with his hands. "After talking through it with him, I realized I could only deal with myself. Staying angry was making me sad, and I was losing a friend."

"What about deserving forgiveness? Did he say Joel deserved it?" Augustine asked suspiciously.

"No, nothing like that. He didn't discount that Joel had done wrong. He said, 'Forgiveness doesn't release that person from their wrong; they have to address that themselves. But it releases you from being wronged and all the negative emotions the wrong has brought,' or something like that," he shrugged.

"Ha! Yes, that sounds just like him."

"You should've scolded me. Joel did wrong, but how I react is my own choice. I'm sorry."

"Look, I think we're nearly there," Augustine said, deflecting his apology.

"Yep, I see it!" Sebastian exclaimed.

"So, do you feel better?" Augustine asked in concern.

"Yes. Can't you tell?"

"Yes, you are much your old self again," she smiled as she patted him on the back.

To Augustine's surprise, Corwin opened the door to the tavern when they reached the top of the hill. It was obvious he was trying not to laugh when he received a look-that-could-kill from her.

"I'm sorry, dear. Come in, and we'll talk about everything over a few cups of tea."

She put her hands on her hips, unafraid of displaying her displeasure toward him.

Sebastian cleared his throat and hinted at Corwin, "Tea would be nice, but a few pastries along with it could go a long way."

"Oh, would they now? Augustine?" As Corwin waited for her to respond, he looked as if he was trying to hide his amusement.

"Well, I suppose sugar and caffeine is a start," she admitted.

"Yes, what we've experienced was quite traumatizing. A few extra sweets might help."

Augustine stared at both of them in disgust. "Sweets do not make you leaving us okay. This entire situation is not funny."

Corwin nodded gravely. "You are right, Augustine. Come in, there's much to discuss."

After the group had settled around the table with drinks and sweets in hand, Corwin spoke in a soft, low voice. "I'm very sorry you children had to see the effects the division of the city has caused."

"How long have the two cities hated one another?" Augustine asked as she nibbled on her pastry.

"'Hate' is too strong a word, as many still have family in both cities, and even still, most continue to retire to Old Waiz. It's much more of a power struggle between the two cities. The councils have been at odds since they divided," Corwin said, then took a gulp of coffee. "New Waiz has proposed separation from Old Waiz for the past couple of years, which has helped to consistently grow the animosity between the cities. Old Waiz has refused to separate, insisting on keeping unity, keeping *The Book of Order*, and keeping to the old—"

"That the Majestic still exists," Augustine interrupted him.

"Yes, exactly. The old ways, the old doctrine. Though New Waiz respects the Old Waiz belief system, its leaders want something entirely new and separate. Because of the deep traditions of Old Waiz, the only way for separation to become remotely possible is to bring it about by force."

"So you think they murdered the councilman?" Augustine asked and became even more upset when Corwin nodded. "Do they honestly think this will bring about a peaceful separation? Do they think Old Waiz will not respond to this?" Augustine asked, while thinking New Waiz was acting horribly wrong in their "new" ways.

"Well, if Old Waiz sticks to many of the principles in *The Book of Order*, they will not retaliate. New Waiz is well aware of this and was confident enough to play their hand this way today," Corwin surmised.

Sebastian spoke up. "I know he's dead and all, and I should probably be respectful, but he really was a mean old man."

"Sebastian!" Augustine cried out in judgment.

Corwin chuckled at the little boy's honesty. "Well, Clovis was a bit cranky toward foreigners, but as you can see, the younger folks treated him quite poorly."

"Was he the head of the council? Is that why he was the one that was shot?" Augustine asked as she brushed a wavy dark strand from her face.

"Yes, he was. The council also makes up part of the Order. So you could also say he was head of the Old Order."

"Who will become the head now?" Augustine fired another question at him.

"Ah, Augustine, that is a very good question."

Augustine saw a flicker of anger flash across Corwin's tan face.

"You have a suspicion, don't you?" she said as she looked into his dark, brown eyes.

"Yes, but it's just a guess at this point." Corwin shrugged.

"Is Waiz going to war?" Sebastian asked, and Augustine cast Corwin a worried glance.

"Children, I mean, young people," he corrected himself when he saw Augustine's annoyed face. "I hate to break the news to you, but there has been a war going on here for a long time, long before it was called 'Waiz.'" He sighed. "But more on that later. Even if a physical war breaks out here, I remain unmoved that I was to bring you here."

"Why? It's far beyond glorious and hopeful," Augustine said in a tone peppered with irritation.

"Augustine, there is always hope. You must remember that at all costs."

She looked away from him, aggravated at having been chastised again on the subject of hope. She soon remembered Corwin's previous absence and sharply turned her head back. "Where were you?"

"When?"

At first she was flustered by his casual tone, but she quickly found her tongue again. "Well, for starters, I'd like to know where you were on the first trip when you left us with Joel. *And,*" she continued with her blue eyes bulging, "then today when you just ran off during a *murder*!"

He responded calmly, "The first trip, I was in Differe."

She drew back from him in confusion, realizing Joel had been right about the chocolate she had brought him from Corwin.

"I needed to find out some more information," he stopped there.

Augustine felt her eyes flash as she continued berating him. "What about my other question?"

Corwin sighed and looked into his coffee mug.

"Come on!" She groaned and slapped her hand on the table. "Are you serious? He chose to leave us. Also, did you by any chance realize that he murdered someone today?" she asked, clearly exasperated by his actions.

"Augustine, I can't explain everything here, so I do not expect you to understand. But yes, I was looking for Joel. *And,* he didn't choose to leave you prior to the incident at the shop."

She frowned at Corwin, knowing he was right.

"How did you know he would be here? How did you know he would shoot from the balcony?" Augustine asked, while feeling extremely baffled.

"I didn't. Mr. Rutherford told me that Joel was interested in the meeting, but that he felt Joel was even more interested in finding the Green Cloak who attacked him in my room."

"What an idiot! Why in the world would he want to find him?"

Corwin turned from her flabbergasted expression and made a sideways glance to Sebastian.

"All right, enough of this. Enough secrets!" Augustine cried at both of them.

Corwin waved his hand to calm her down and motioned to those around them. He pulled his chair closer to the table and so did the others.

"Green Cloaks are spies for the New Order. My guess is that spy took something of Joel's that night he found him," Corwin said in a whisper.

"But he was looking for your things," Augustine said, puzzled.

Corwin nodded. "Yes, but neither I nor my things were there. And I just bet a young apprentice wouldn't dare arrive back from an assignment empty-handed."

"What would Joel have of value?" she asked softly.

Corwin shrugged. "I'm not sure, but without going into detail, Augustine, we have to find him. We need him."

"How did you find him today?" She shook her head at him in disbelief.

"By mere chance. I knew he was headed this way the night he left the shop and figured, well, why wouldn't he join in one of the biggest events of Waiz? I suppose though, it was really more of a hope than a guess."

Augustine stared back at him, dumbfounded.

"Things keep happening to bring him back to us, don't they?" Sebastian piped in.

"Yes, and I believe it is no coincidence at this point." Corwin's expression was grave as he took Augustine's hand. "Augustine, I raced toward the hotel when I caught a glimpse of Joel. There was no time to spare. I'm sorry for leaving you and Sebastian."

"It's okay, I knew you'd meet us here," Sebastian said as he smiled at him, but Augustine's hardened expression did not break.

"Well," she said, as she drew her hand away from him.

"Listen, I'm certain that there were two people in that room. I believe one was wearing a green cloak."

Augustine and Sebastian both looked at him in shock.

"Honestly, I can't imagine that Joel could shoot an arrow that well," Corwin said.

Augustine put her head in her hands as she sat in continued disbelief.

"Augustine?" Corwin prodded her gently.

"So you think—you think Joel happened to find the spy, and the spy killed Clovis?" she asked, as she raised her head to meet his eyes.

"That is my hope."

"That's an awful lot to hope for," she sighed in exhaustion.

"Augustine, I know I have not earned the right, but I need your trust. I need for you to trust me."

She knew as she looked into his eyes, that he was still very much the same man whom she had spent most of her younger days with in Differe. She had held his heart then, and she was certain she held it now.

Augustine made a reluctant jerk of her head in agreement, and as she did, she heard an all too familiar voice in her head say, "You trusted him before, and he left you." But she told herself she was going to ignore it.

"We must find Joel," Corwin continued once Augustine responded. "The cold season is coming, and time is running out for Sebastian."

She shot Corwin a bewildered look, but she soon heard her brother's sweet voice.

"I know. We've talked about it."

"What?" she questioned the two of them furiously but did not give them the chance to answer. "Oh, I suppose that Joel is to be our savior?"

"No," Corwin said softly, as if attempting to cool her anger. "But he is vital."

"Why?" she asked, as she propped her hand under her chin.

"You need something … I also believe he needs it, too."

Augustine looked at Sebastian, feeling angry and hurt. *Why does he seem to already know all the information Corwin is relaying?*

"Where is this 'something'?" she asked as she turned back to Corwin.

In the most serious tone of the day Corwin said, "It's at the Temple of Differe."

"No, you can forget it. He'll never go back there."

"Augustine, we have to try, or at least see if he can help us," Sebastian pleaded with her.

She could not resist the resolve and worry plastered onto his little face. "Yes, fine. Okay."

"So, my question to you two is, after spending several weeks with the redhead, where is he?"

The two siblings glanced at one another and thought hard.

"Assuming that he escaped, I'd imagine he's long gone from here, particularly since he's a prime suspect for murder," Augustine mused.

"Yes, I would think that, too. It will take some time for the news about the murder to travel to all the kalonas," Corwin said thoughtfully.

"Yes, I'm sure he's headed back to Old Waiz," Augustine said with certainty.

"Mr. Rutherford's shop?" Corwin asked.

"No." Both turned their heads to the sound of Sebastian's voice. "I know exactly where he's headed."

Andropolis stood in the corner of the New Order's meeting room. He watched as wine and liquor flowed into every man's cup. After several minutes of socializing, their leader, Emil Marcell, tapped his glass.

"Attention, everyone. I would like to propose a toast to Andropolis Fidel. You have performed well, apprentice. You have brought a new era of reigning and power to New Waiz, much like your father did before he departed, well, into his demise. You have honored the Order and now we honor you."

"Here! Here!" all the men of the Order cheered as Andropolis came forward.

Andropolis had waited most of his life for this moment but did not feel the pleasure he had hoped for. He nodded his thanks and drank to his toast with the rest of the men.

"Ah, that being said," Marcell began. "This power will not come without cost. War is now upon us. I believe Old Waiz will fight."

Gasps sounded throughout the room.

"This was expected?" one man questioned firmly.

"Indeed. We have measures in place, and allies are at hand. We will be unstoppable," Marcell boasted.

"That's a bold statement," said the gruff voice Andropolis had come to know.

"I suppose, but a message is to be hand delivered to Differe in the next day or so. I have no reason to believe that they will not join our cause."

"Andropolis, will you do this as your final duty as apprentice?"

Sounds of awe and a few congratulations rang out from the men surrounding him.

"You mean, I am to be promoted to a member?"

"Precisely," said Marcell as he stuck out his hand.

"Yes, sir. I can go this instant," Andi said breathlessly as he shook the man's hand.

"Good heavens, the letter hasn't even been written yet. So hasty!"

A few of the men chuckled at Andi's impulsive response, and he sheepishly backed away from Marcell.

"It's all right, Andropolis, I appreciate your enthusiasm. Perhaps tonight or early morning; I will keep you informed."

The older man with the gruff voice moved toward Marcell. "Seems to me that Differe would make a pretty poor ally. It's so far away and their government can barely support itself as it is. Plus, most of Differe doesn't even acknowledge our existence."

Marcell laughed arrogantly at this comment, and the rest of the men followed his lead, though Andi thought their laughter sounded nervous.

"Their government is entirely weak I agree, but I am not speaking of them. We are forging a much higher alliance."

CHAPTER 25

A S THE DAY drew on, each lumbered toward their separate destinations until dusk. About this time, both Joel and Andropolis were hit with exhaustion from their fight. Andropolis leaned his head against the window of his train compartment and drifted off into a dreamless sleep. Joel, on the other hand, journeyed upward along a forgotten path until his legs felt like pieces of dead weight. When he could no longer ignore them, he stopped beside the cool stream he was following for a drink. *It's getting dark, anyway.* He glanced toward the sky.

Though he'd walked along the main road in the darkness the night before, he was uninterested in doing so again on such a rugged, unfamiliar path. He had followed a stream that he found on his museum map up from the Pallas River. He was sure this time that he was headed exactly where he wanted to go. *What's one more day?* He looked for a spot to make camp for the night.

He worked in the remaining sunset's light to quickly gather a pile of leaves and brush. "That looks good," he said proudly as he studied his cushioned and insulated bed. He pulled out all the little maps before he threw his knapsack down to serve as his pillow for the night. He lay down and squinted in the fading light to study the writings. He wondered if he would even find the others again so he could return the maps. After a few moments, he put them on his chest and closed his eyes. Heavy breathing quickly followed, and soon all he could hear was the gentle water flowing down the creek next to him. A few owls began hooting in the air above, and nature's night sounds echoed all around him.

How could just one sound bring such a sweet peace? he mused, but was quickly reminded of Isabelle's voice. It was as if his surroundings were singing to him, not in a human voice, but in some sort of bizarre, nighttime lullaby.

This is why I have no friends ... thinking thoughts like these, Joel thought, slightly chastising himself yet still enjoying the uniqueness of sitting under the stars with the sounds of the earth around him. "The ocean sang me to sleep last night; now it's the mountain's turn, I guess. Maybe I don't need Isabelle after all," he sighed, feeling strangely content.

He had found the Green Cloak and retrieved his and Sebastian's maps. *Not that I'll see him again.*

"Murderer!" he heard the shouts of the people echo in his head.

"Yeah, what am I going to do about that?" he mumbled. *Can't hide at the farmer's.*

For some strange reason, though, he felt safe tonight. Maybe it was because he believed he was at least on the right side. He had fought against the Green Cloak, whose side obviously advocated murder. *What a confusing place. What did Sarah tell me? I need to try to remember everything she said.*

Sarah and Isabelle skimmed over information about the city of Waiz. Most of the night they spent going over the temple grounds and formulating the best time and passage for escape. Sarah rolled out plans of the grounds, marking each exit and dotting each Templin hideout.

"How do you know about these hideouts?" Isabelle asked.

"I've had plenty of time to study these enemies," Sarah replied as she poured over the plans.

"I've never heard you call them that."

Sarah let out a long sigh in response to Isabelle's comment. "Well, I suppose it's not the individuals themselves, but rather the beliefs that control them that are the real enemies." She raised her head up from the plans. "I believe with all my heart that they hear voices, too. Just like Joel, and just like you."

"I don't hear them anymore," Isabelle said, realizing she sounded defensive. "I mean, I never heard anything like Joel did."

"Don't think I'm comparing them to you, dear. For you and Joel were actually able to discern that the voices were not your own thoughts."

Isabelle gave her a puzzled look.

"The guards are well deceived," Sarah said as she grabbed another pen.

"I don't think Holt's deceived," Isabelle muttered, then continued on about him. "I think the desire for his father's approval is what drives him. I don't really think he believes all this 'truth' stuff."

Sarah nodded, but quickly returned to the map of the grounds.

"But I guess he doesn't believe in Waiz, either," Isabelle shrugged in sadness.

"Isabelle," Sarah said in a surprisingly stern voice. "You stand on the brink of your destiny! Would you let some young man steal that from you? You will venture on alone to freedom, or you will stay here alone in chains."

"Both sound bad when you put it that way," Isabelle whined.

"The voice you heard the night you left the library—you've heard it before?"

Isabelle nodded, wondering what that situation had to do with the one at hand.

"Tell me about it," Sarah encouraged.

Isabelle thought a moment. "Well, there isn't much to say, really. When I'm in something like that, an impossible circumstance, I—well, I—" she paused, too embarrassed to go on.

Sarah rose and moved toward Isabelle's chair. "Don't be afraid," Sarah said as she patted Isabelle's hand.

Isabelle turned her blushing face away from her listener. "Well, it sounds crazy, but I talk to ... well, it's not talking to myself but sort of like that. I talk to something, but it isn't like the other voices," she sighed in frustration. "I don't feel like I'm making sense."

"Go on, what happens?" she heard Sarah ask.

"Well, many times it—this thing, answers me. Not for anything trivial, really, but bigger questions, like how to get back into the library."

"It is a good voice," Sarah said softly.

"I really just hear myself talking," Isabelle shrugged.

"Do you think it's you answering yourself? Do you, Isabelle? But no, you already said you're not talking to yourself," Sarah mused aloud while answering her own question.

"No, I can't think that quickly on my feet. It's something else, just in my mind's voice." Isabelle suddenly threw her head back and laughed empathetically, "Oh, I sound more and more like him."

She saw Sarah nod in agreement.

"Sarah, are we the only ones that feel and hear these things?" Isabelle inquired.

"As I said earlier, I think everyone is listening to something."

"Then why doesn't it affect them as it has us?" Isabelle asked as she looked pleadingly into Sarah's brown eyes.

"They don't discern that it's not their voice, their thought. Also, because they lack this discernment, unlike the two of you, they don't realize they have power over it. They're completely unaware that they are controlled by these thoughts, feelings, and voices. Joel always hated the voices because he realized they were trying to control him. He fought back, and they fought back. He has a war going on inside him."

"Me, too." Isabelle said.

"Me, three, Professor Louis, four; Professor Dark, five; Holt, six; and so on. All of us are in the struggle."

Isabelle was surprised at the compassion she heard in Sarah's voice as she named the others.

"Why does no one say anything, then?" Isabelle asked, as a tear fell down her cheek.

"Very few recognize their own free will, their own ideas, their own power," Sarah smiled sadly.

"Why did you send Joel to Waiz?"

"To find the source of his good voice. It is war. He needs something good, something for him on his side. And, in every good fight, weapons are needed," Sarah answered.

"But it's just about him getting well in his mind, right? To become sane ... to not be crazy anymore?" Isabelle asked, looking a little bewildered as she awaited Sarah's answer.

"Isabelle, we are all involved in this fight. I believe that even Waiz is on the brink of war," she said as she closed her eyes. "Differe is sure to be involved."

"What! Why? Well, how?" Isabelle became more confused, and her freedom felt even more distant as their conversation progressed.

Before Sarah could open her mouth Isabelle raised her hand. "Wait, answer the first question. Directly, please."

"Joel thinks he's in Waiz to be free from the temple and to find freedom from the voices in his head. Direct enough?" Sarah chuckled.

"And, is that true? Is that why you sent him there?" Isabelle knew Sarah was not telling her everything.

"Yes, his freedom is my first priority and greatest desire for him. I dearly love that boy. You must not question my love for him, Isabelle."

Isabelle crossed her arms against her chest in silence.

"It would be unfair to Joel for me to tell you more, for he does not even know his true identity and destiny."

"And *you* presume to know?" Isabelle questioned, as she felt herself becoming heated.

"I sense an emotion in you that you haven't felt toward Joel in a long time," Sarah pressed.

"Don't change the subject," Isabelle said tersely.

Sarah chuckled again. "Hm … little Isabelle always standing up for Joel. Whether his enemy was a bully, a hospital nurse, or a mean voice, you never cowered."

"If you—if you have sent him there in hopes of him becoming some heroic savior for your precious city," Isabelle paused, trying to tame her anger, "If you have sent him to his death to pave some freedom path for troubled minds, so help me I will—"

"Don't continue this tirade, Isabelle. You know you'll regret it," Sarah interrupted her.

Isabelle bit her lip; she had hurt this woman enough. "I'm sorry. I don't know what came over me. I know you love him and only want what's best for him."

"Don't question that again," Sarah said firmly.

"Yes, ma'am," she nodded.

"Also, Isabelle, it would interest you to know that Joel is not alone," Sarah said as she rose to pour herself another cup of tea.

"How do you know that?" Isabelle looked at her in shock.

"Don't you remember how I know so much about Waiz?" Sarah let out.

Isabelle shook her head as she motioned for Sarah to pour her another cup.

"Well, then do you remember the picture that I had inside my desk drawer at Moonstruck?"

Isabelle paused to think. "Well, yes, it was of a little girl beside the bluest river I'd ever seen. I remember loving to look at the color of the water."

"That's the one. The little girl is me, and I'm standing by the Pallas River."

Isabelle shot her look of disbelief. "You're from Waiz?"

Sarah nodded. "Yes, and I have many contacts from here to there. Joel has been mostly on his own, but his coming was expected."

"Have you—have you—heard anything about him lately?" Isabelle sputtered out.

Sarah shook her head. "Too dangerous to communicate, and even so, I've been in Moonstruck."

"Oh, right," Isabelle said sadly.

"These people, will they know to warn him about the letter?" Isabelle looked at Sarah with pleading eyes.

"I don't know," Sarah sighed. "Let's discuss what you'll need to take with you. I suspect you will leave within the week."

Andropolis slept through most of his train ride to Differe. He exited the train at a stop just short of Crossroads Train Station. As he braced his body for the cold, he pulled the hood of his cloak over his head. *This is miserable.* He trudged toward the station house. He had been to the city of Differe before, but never to the temple. With the current temperature nearly below freezing, he hoped he would not have to stay in the city long.

He sat shivering on an old bench for half an hour before his temple escort arrived.

"Just you? Any luggage?" the driver asked.

"No luggage," Andi replied as he shook his head.

The man soon noticed his shivering, "The Order doesn't make your robes for this kind of weather, eh?"

Andi shook his head no again.

"All right, then."

A minute later the two were driving down a snowy road.

Another half hour passed before they approached a heavily guarded gate. Andi eyed the white marble as the driver spoke with the guards and he gazed up at the large pines lining both sides of the drive as they passed through the entrance. Though the tightly planted trees blocked most of Andi's view, he was able make out a dark, heavily wooded area just beyond the saplings. The vehicle soon drove up a large hill, and near the top the driver stopped.

"Here's the best view," he yelled back at Andi, just as the young man noticed the large clearing.

Andi cocked an eyebrow as he overlooked the landscape. At the bottom of the hill, the forest separated around a large frozen lake. Then right in the center of the grounds, across the lake, was a pristine building that held a magnificent steeple at its peak.

It's no castle.

"That's the temple chapel there, straight away," called the man as if reading Andi's thoughts. "Just past those are the dormitory halls, classrooms, offices, the infirmary, and such. The place has everything, really. It's a self-sustaining kingdom of learning."

Andi shrugged but admitted to himself that the grounds appeared both impressive and exquisite. *But unbearably cold.*

He was about to tell the driver to go on, but a white blur sliding across the lake distracted him first. "What is that white thing?" Andi asked as he leaned toward the window.

"Hm?" the driver squinted.

"That ball of white fur across the lake," Andi answered.

"Oh, that's the headmaster's pet. We call her Big Sasha. She's a white beast, really. Not many of her kind around anymore. She's a rare beauty."

Andi watched as Big Sasha ran and then slid on her hind legs across the ice. From his view, the beast just resembled a very large white bear.

"Interesting. All right, let's move on."

The driver obliged him and continued until they arrived at the temple grounds.

Just as Sarah had predicted, Isabelle was called out of class the next morning.

Of course—Holt, Isabelle thought, when he interrupted her second class to get her. She knew where they were headed, and both walked in silence down the hallway.

Just before she thought they were about to walk toward the headmaster's building, Holt motioned for her to stop. He pulled out a key and unlocked the door to her right. He opened the door for her and nodded for her to go inside. Before she could turn around Holt forced her and himself inside the small closet, then swiftly locked them inside.

Her squeals were quickly concealed by Holt's large hand. He towered over her as he pinned her against the wall. She tried to move but could not budge under his force.

"Shut up, Isabelle, and listen closely," he said in a low voice.

His tone frightened and intrigued her, so she quickly went silent and became still.

"Just like with Joel, *you* are my assignment. Do you get that?"

Isabelle did not move, yet wondered exactly what he meant.

"I study you, Isabelle. I watch you. I know where you are at all times."

Fear flooded over her. *How much does he know?*

"If you so much as sit the wrong way at your desk, I'll notice, and I'll go straight to the headmaster. Your activity is quite important to him these days."

Why is he trying to threaten me? she wondered, still confused.

"So," he began slowly, "let's recap the last few days. A visit to Moonstruck, the temple alcove, oh, and let's not forget the headmaster's office, the foreign map section of the library, and the music room—all night last night." He cocked his head in front of hers and let go of her mouth.

"So what? I had to right my wrong," she said confidently, even though she was terrified.

"Really? Then why would you need plans to the grounds?" he asked as he raised them to her face. "Oh, and look here, the exits and guards are strategically marked. I wonder why that is?"

She lowered her head in defeat.

"Oh, let's also not forget your pitiful attempt at a love letter to your pal Joel," he mocked her.

"Well, looks like I'll have another chance at that. Isn't that why you really came to get me out of class?" she asked in a direct tone.

He finally backed away a little. "Yeah, and this one better be convincing."

She shook her head at him in disbelief. "What has gotten into you? I should've let them expel you," she hissed.

"I'm not a fool, Isabelle. You're planning an escape, but I can't let you do that."

"Because I'm your assignment or because I'm the bait?" she lashed out at him.

"It is against the Temple Order and—"

"Screw the blasted Order. You can lock me up over and over again, but I'll just keep trying to get out. I *am* getting out of here," she said with as much force as she could muster.

"And what about Ms. Harte? Would you send the lady to her death for your freedom?"

"Leave her out of this! Don't mention her to—"

"Oh, Isabelle, but I saw you with her all night last night. I'm really supposed to report that sort of thing," Holt interrupted her, continuing in his arrogant tone.

"What do you want?" she sighed.

"Bait," he said seriously. "You have to stay here until I catch Joel. You know he'll come back for you, and when he does, I'll be ready for him this time."

"So, what you really want is Joel?" she asked coldly.

"Yes, but to get him I need you, which means I need you to stay here," he replied.

"And once you have him?" she looked into his brown eyes.

"I'll let you go. I promise."

"That doesn't mean much anymore," she said with disdain.

"I promise on the Langston name. I'll help you get out."

He sounds sincere, Isabelle convinced herself. She nodded in agreement. "And if you don't, I'll personally tell the headmaster that you knew of my plans and did not report them. I'll also tell him about the library."

"Fair enough. Write a letter today that will get him back here, and you'll get your freedom," Holt instructed.

"And Sarah?" Isabelle questioned.

"I'll keep her confidence, but you know that she'll be a suspect, either way." Isabelle knew that was true. She lowered her head and grimaced, "What if he doesn't come back? I chose you, remember?"

She heard him swallow hard. "Write a good letter. And, in the meantime, in order to keep your little secret, here's my history paper," he said smugly. "Consider it being just like old times."

Isabelle was furious. "Except for the blackmail part," she said.

"I need this by tonight."

"Fine!" She grabbed the assignment and stuffed it into her schoolbag.

"What were you saying earlier about 'they should've expelled me'?"

She stood up and slung the bag over her shoulder. "They said they would expel you if I didn't write the letter." She was pleased to see that he looked speechless. "So, you shut up, Holt, and listen closely. I hate you, and you will not hurt me again."

Both trudged toward the headmaster's study in silence. She dreaded hearing the headmaster's berating that she was sure was coming. *Soon I'll be free of him. But how soon? I won't let Sarah give up her life for me.* She realized there was a great chance they would kill Sarah if she and Joel both got away, especially if Holt failed to keep his word. *I'll have to tell her that he knows, but she'll still send me, anyway.* Isabelle sighed heavily as the two stood outside the headmaster's study.

"Oh, you saw my little pet. Yes, she's guarded the grounds here for several years," they heard the headmaster chuckle. "It is an honor to receive such a request, young apprentice. You say Marcell himself sent you? Of the New Order?" they heard the headmaster ask through the heavy, wooden door.

"Yes, sir. It would bring great pleasure to the New Order to form an alliance with your power and wisdom. War is upon the city of Waiz. Old Waiz is likely to join forces with the Southern Regions. We hope to form strong allies with the north first, as the Order feels it would be best to surround our enemy," spoke an unfamiliar voice.

"Sounds strategic and merciless. I should like to hear more of these plans," the headmaster replied. "Oh yes, I almost forgot. If you will excuse me for a moment, I need to exercise some of that wisdom you mentioned on one of my students."

A few moments later Isabelle and Holt were called inside the study. Andropolis stood tucked away in the far corner of the room. He was sure the two students were unaware of his presence. He could not help but to be interested in this place. There were no such places in Waiz, no fancy temples or prestigious schools. He wondered if indeed Differian education was better or just pompous. He watched as the headmaster approached the young man first.

"So, Hertz tells me your father was furious to learn you failed your first assignment."

Andi watched the young lady's head turn toward the young man, who lowered his gaze to the floor.

"Pity. I wonder who bothered him with such news?"

Andi watched the headmaster wait for him to respond.

"Yes, sir. My father and I are most grateful to Your Honor for allowing me another chance."

"Yes, I shall soon find out if my graciousness was worth extending to you," the headmaster said condescendingly. "And," he continued in a stern voice, "If Joel returns then you will be able to complete your first assignment."

He then walked over to address the girl. "Isabelle, do you know why you are here?"

Andi saw that it was now the girl's turn to look down. He found her strikingly beautiful—small, willowy, and graceful.

"My patience wears thin," the headmaster snapped as he thrust a piece of paper in front of her face. "What is this?"

The junior Templin moved toward her and shook her arm.

"The letter. It's the letter you asked me to write," she spit out.

"No, this is your poor attempt at following orders. Is it not?"

The headmaster's question was met with silence.

"Is it not?" he asked more forcefully.

"Yes, sir," she mumbled.

Andi watched as the headmaster began walking in a patronizing circle around her.

"Yes, I asked for a convincing letter, one from your heart, one that was not written in code, my dear, but according to my orders. Since you seem incapable of writing this yourself I have constructed a letter for you. Copy this down and do not change one word. Understood?"

"Yes, headmaster."

Andi wondered if the headmaster would succeed in making her cry.

"Good. You are both excused."

As the headmaster flicked his fingers at the students, Andi marveled at the man's confidence. *If he's that commanding with his students then it's no wonder Marcell wants him as a force for war.*

CHAPTER 26

HOURS LATER ANDROPOLIS had succeeded in winning an ally for the New Order, though he was not thoroughly convinced that the headmaster had been entirely surprised at this request. Andropolis had briefly explained the basic action plans the New Order proposed and how Differe's role could affect the coming challenges. He received a token from the headmaster to give to the New Order as a symbol of their alliance.

Andi felt things had gone well enough for him to perhaps deserve his new official title. So when the headmaster asked a small favor of him, he was more than happy to oblige him.

The young man Andi had seen earlier soon led him down a snowy path. He discovered the kid was a junior Templin and that the young lady was his "assignment."

He decided not to ask him any questions about Isabelle, but simply stated, "Fine, I just need to get the letter."

"Here. She's in there." Holt pointed to a door and headed in the other direction.

Andropolis was puzzled for a moment but figured the room was open and quickly pushed on the door. He entered the room cloaked and hooded.

Isabelle was startled by his appearance at first. *What is that?* She shuddered as Andi's tall, sturdy figure drew closer. *He's not a Templin.* She eyed his deep green cloak and the hood that almost completely covered his face.

When he was standing right beside the desk where she was writing, she looked over his robe for an emblem. His silence frightened her, but she eventually spoke.

"Excuse me, sir, forgive me." She shied away from him then started again. "Is this letter for you?"

"It is."

Isabelle recognized his voice instantly as the one she had heard outside the headmaster's office.

"But I will not be delivering it, if that's what you truly want to know."

She nodded, still looking down.

"Are you finished?" he asked shortly.

"Just. Yes, sir, just finishing a few small corrections," she replied, then fumbled over the paper and dropped her pen. She gasped in horror and hurried to find it. She felt the man kneel beside her, and as she looked up at him, she saw his hand was drawn.

"Oh, please, I'm sorry! I didn't mean to be so clumsy," she cried as she held her hand near her face, bracing for a hit. To her surprise she felt something warm grab her shaking hand. A hard piece was softly placed in her hand, and she slowly opened her eyes to see the man pressing the pen back into her grip. She caught a glimpse of his dark eyes for a brief moment before she returned to her desk.

"Thank you, sir."

She keeps thinking I'm going to strike her. He was baffled by her behavior. *She's terrified of me—and it's not because of my face.*

Andi was used to most females shuddering at him, but his hood was still covering his head. As he sat in the desk across from her waiting for her to finish, he watched her pull a few golden strands of hair behind her ear. He saw a faint scar drawn across her cheek. Though it was faded, he could tell the scar had been deep. He was not sure why, but an anger burned within him as he studied the scar. The thought of someone harming this beautiful young woman infuriated him.

"I'm finished, sir," Isabelle said, as she held the letter up in her hand, and Andropolis quickly shook his feelings away.

When Andropolis neared her desk again, she stood up. "Please, the headmaster said a Templin was to deliver this letter. If I do not obey his wish, I—" After looking around the empty room, her next statement sounded robotic. "I will get only what I deserve."

"What have they done to you?" he questioned.

"Who are you?" she asked curiously.

"I'm not a Templin," Andi said defensively. "I am a council member from the New Order of Waiz." He saw her eyes flicker in recognition at the mention of the city. "I'm going back to Waiz today. As a small favor, I promised your headmaster that I would personally give this letter to a Templin. That is all," he said in a very official tone.

He moved closer to her and tried to reassure her before he took the letter from her hand. "It's all right. Your letter will be safe with me. I promise to get it to a Templin. The headmaster will have what he wishes," he said gently.

He saw tears form in her big blue eyes, and she was barely able to utter, "Thank you, sir. You are very kind," as she placed the letter in his hand.

"I hope to go to Waiz someday. Is New Waiz the right side?" she whispered.

He watched her courageously spill her words, and as she did her breath lit up the air around her mouth. He nodded his head partly in response and partly to keep from seeing things. In all his years of service, being in this room with some sort of victim from this place made him question his allegiance for the first time. *Am I on the right side?*

She sighed heavily when he did not answer, but to his amazement she moved toward him, unafraid to look up under his hood. His dark eyes locked onto her mouth. The light her breath was exuding was becoming brighter. He noted that with each exhalation the air around her became more lit. And suddenly the air and light began encircling her, but he knew she could not see it.

This was not atypical for Andi, but he usually hated "seeing things" and tried to dismiss the thoughts as his imagination. This time, though, he felt mesmerized by the girl's beauty and light. He did not want to tear his eyes away from her but instead wanted to wait to see what would transpire.

She raised her hand to wipe a tear from her face. He was just barely aware that she was studying his tanned skin, dark curls, and deep scars. Nothing else was happening in his mind besides Isabelle's breath creating more light each time she breathed. He watched a minute more until the light became still and flickered out.

Andi backed away then and suddenly noticed the instruments around the room. "A music room," he said.

"Yes, sir. It's my favorite room on the grounds."

He smiled, realizing that for the first time in his life he had made sense of something he saw. "Well, perhaps you will come to Waiz sometime. The concert hall could always use another soloist."

She cocked her head at him in confusion. "Oh, the headmaster told you that I sing," she guessed.

"No. He told me nothing about you," Andi smiled.

"Then how?"

Andi suddenly felt he could be free with her even if she did not fully understand. "I see it, Isabelle. It is a good voice." And with that he left the temple.

Isabelle sat in Sarah's office, while she picked at her dinner.

"What did he mean by 'I see it'? You *hear* a voice. And was he talking about my voice or *the* good voice?"

"I don't know, my dear. He sounds very interesting, though," replied Sarah.

"I couldn't get a good look at him. His green cloak was hooded," Isabelle remarked, as she wrinkled her nose at the sweet potatoes on her plate.

"Hmm ... he works for the Order."

"Yes!" Isabelle exclaimed and went on before Sarah could continue. "He came to make an alliance with the headmaster. Your inkling about Waiz was right. War is coming."

"Well," Sarah waved her hand, "Those two sides have been at war for a long time, and it will hardly solve the real issues at hand."

"What are you talking about? Can you at least *try* to speak plainly?" Isabelle urged.

Sarah laughed at her request. "All right, I'll try. The true war is within, just as we talked about last night. That war must be won before any true peace will reign."

"Right, but at this point I just want to get out of here before it starts," Isabelle muttered, silently asking herself, *what is she going on about?*

"While we're relaying the news of the day, I noticed that the plans went missing this morning and then mysteriously reappeared this afternoon," Sarah said as she laid them in front of Isabelle.

"Yes, I know something about that. Oh, great," Isabelle scowled. "I have exactly two hours until I have to turn in Holt's paper."

"Doing his homework again?"

"Blackmail."

"Doesn't sound like him," Sarah said as she shook her in head in disapproval.

"He's changing," Isabelle said sadly. "Into a Templin. Into his father."

"What happened, Isabelle?" Sarah asked, as she pointed to a smidgen of jam stuck on Isabelle's cheek.

"Oh, thanks," Isabelle said as she wiped her face. "Well, his father found out about Joel escaping. The way the headmaster mentioned it made it sound like Hertz told him, just to fuel Holt's fire. And it worked, let me tell you. No more 'Mister Nice Guy.' I should've had him expelled," she said.

"Isabelle, you can't believe they would've actually expelled him. It was probably only a tactic to get you to comply with their plan."

Isabelle took a moment to ponder her statement before answering, "That makes me furious, but I'm sure you're right." She then told Sarah about Holt pulling her into the closet.

"I didn't understand what was wrong with him until I found out his father knew of his failure. He's desperate now. He'd do anything to get Joel back," Isabelle shuddered.

"Oh goodness," Sarah sighed.

"Ha! I wonder how he'll feel after he's failed his first two assignments," Isabelle snapped.

"Isabelle, may I remind you that hurt and revenge are not your reasons for leaving."

"Yes, but they do produce satisfying consequences," Isabelle let out in response to her reproach.

"And where would you be if I had reacted in such a way?" Sarah eyed her and Isabelle quickly looked away. "You must control your emotions with truth, Isabelle. He has deeply wounded you just like his father has deeply wounded him."

"So now he's excused for his behavior?" Isabelle asked bitterly.

"No, I'm just showing you that he has no other choice but to give you what's been modeled to him," Sarah replied in the same soft tone she had been using.

"He has a choice," Isabelle grumbled.

"He is controlled, Isabelle. Don't you see it now? He's controlled by approval, hurt, fear, and many other things. You must rely on truth," Sarah instructed again.

"Now you sound like the temple. Truth, truth, truth," Isabelle said as she pushed her plate away in anger.

"No, that's the wrong kind. Real truth brings freedom, not control. Why are you going to Waiz?"

Isabelle's sulky expression was met by Sarah's stern gaze, so she answered the woman's question. "To seek Joel's forgiveness and to protect him from the temple's plot."

"And?" Sarah was not letting up.

"To help him stay free and even become free myself."

Sarah nodded in approval and the two stared at one another in silence.

"What is your fondest memory of Holt?" Sarah asked seriously.

Shocked at the change of subject, Isabelle shook her head in refusal. "What? No. I don't want to think about him anymore."

Much to Isabelle's dismay, she watched Sarah's expression harden, letting Isabelle know she was not going to drop the subject until she answered.

"Fine," she shrugged as she struggled to think of anything remotely good about Holt for the next few moments. "Well, he used to take me to the clock tower at night. We would stay up there until we nearly froze. He'd bring me hot chocolate, and I'd help him study." She felt herself start to smile. "Small bits of ice would hit the bells. They'd start going 'ding, ding.' I'd ask him if he wanted me to sing. He always said, 'No. I don't need to hear you sing to think you're beautiful. I just have to look at you.'"

She stopped the memory and felt her heart warm slightly as she looked up at Sarah. "It's one of the few times I felt like someone desired me not just because I could sing. Everyone always says I have this beautiful voice, when I—me," she pointed to herself, "I want to be the one that's beautiful."

Sarah smiled. "Remember this memory, Isabelle. For that is the 'free Holt.' That is who he truly is when uncontrolled and free, bringing out the best in you."

Isabelle nodded as tears sprang to her eyes. "I'll try."

"Also, don't wish others harm, or you'll be just like them, controlled by bitterness and hurt." Sarah patted her hand as she gave her a tissue.

"I do wish him freedom then, but I can't give it to him," Isabelle cried as she looked to Sarah for approval.

"You're right, but you can give it to yourself and help keep Joel's. We need a way to ensure you can get your file before you leave. Let's go over the plans again. There's no time to waste."

CHAPTER 27

JOEL HAD SHIVERED throughout the night as he dozed off and on. He had not expected the temperature to drop as dramatically as it did. He, like the other two, had sold most of his Differian clothes, but thankfully had kept a pair of wool socks, corduroy pants, and a long sleeve shirt. He wondered if the cold season had come. After a few hours of walking, the sun warmed the trail before him, and he soon stripped back down into short sleeves. His mind was quiet. *It feels strangely silent.*

He approached the road that led to the Marcell House. He cautiously stayed close to the side road that was nearest to the woods. He was so on edge that when the chapel bells rang out he jumped. He laughed at his over-anxious nerves. *Ha! Just bells, Joel. Just bells.*

He turned toward the sound and remembered it was Sunday. The kalona's square was empty, but he was sure this was because the chapel was full. *Perfect!* He assumed this meant no one would find him snooping about the old house.

As he neared the Marcell House, Joel realized he was walking in the opposite direction from where the murdered man had directed him to go on his last visit. It was strange to think that the man was dead, since he had been very much alive just a few days before. *Unfriendly or not,* Joel shook his head, *it was an unfair way to end.* Joel had not experienced the death of anyone besides his mother. *And that was enough*, he thought, while trying to push the thoughts of death away.

He did not have to push too hard, as he soon came upon what he thought must be the historic place. A low chain roped off the property and Joel easily managed to pass over it. He stopped to look at the structure. The Marcell House resembled an old, broken down barn. The wood on the outside was splitting with age and rotting. "Nothing glorious about it," he let out to himself.

The roof was high and steeply slanted. Joel was able to make out a group of bells in the roof's highest point. The bells were cracked, and Joel wondered if they had even moved in the past hundred years. He carefully stepped onto the porch, hoping he would not fall through the floor. The wood creaked and groaned at his every step, and he was relieved when he made it to the door. He jiggled the handle and was surprised to find there was no lock on the door. *I guess anyone's welcome once you cross over the chain,* he smirked, as he pried open the old, wooden door. He left the door open to allow some sunlight into the room.

He walked down from the porch and onto the building's dirt floor. Joel noticed that the floors appeared to have been kept and were swept clean. He first went to look up into the bell tower, and discovered a mass of knotted ropes hanging from above. To his left was a small, bare platform, and over to his right as well as in front of him were rows of pews. Both the platform and pews were roped off, and Joel found the fact that the wood had survived absolutely remarkable.

"Well, that's it, then. Literally just a meeting place," he sighed, having hoped for something more. He looked around for artifacts or inscriptions, something that would give him a clue in his hunt for a caychura.

Is there a way to climb the bell tower? He glanced around for a set of stairs or a ladder. All he found was the pile of ropes hanging from the tower. Joel walked over to them and gave one a firm tug. Though old, the ropes felt sturdy enough to hold him. He dropped his bag and swung on the ropes to ensure that his observation was correct. *Not so much as a sound from the bells. Let's see what's up there.* Climbing the ropes was harder than he had imagined. *Of course.* He felt his hands becoming blistered.

Once he reached the top, he found that the windows encircling the bells had a ledge just large enough to hold him. He shifted his weight back and forth and eventually gathered enough momentum to swing himself onto the ledge. As he tumbled near the window he saw several large black birds scatter around the outside of the tower and fly inside. As he and his new companions sat in the top of the tower, he peered outside into the sun.

Joel had come to Waiz to be free of the temple and its laundry list of rules; however, his deeper desire had always been to be free of the voices he had heard since he was a child. As he gazed back at the birds, he decided to tell one of them his story.

"I've been tormented all my life by these horrible, debilitating voices, these things that I can't see," he said aloud in frustration. "The temple told me they didn't exist—you know, that they were all my imagination. So, the professors, the doctors, the headmaster, they all told me that I was crazy. In fact, they told the whole temple, even my dad," he shuddered, "that I was crazy, but here I am talking to a bird, so who knows." Joel shrugged and smiled. "My friend, Sarah, she was mostly my teacher, she—she helped me get here. She helped me escape. And well, actually, she was born here.

"I have no idea why she stays at the temple," Joel sighed heavily to the cooing stranger. "She told me to explore the whole city once I got here, to learn its history and what not. 'There's much value in it,' she said, or something like that, anyway. Come to think of it, she sounds a lot like Corwin. Hey, you probably know him," Joel pointed at the bird. "He's also from around here. So, there you go. That's why I am sitting here trying to figure out how Waiz started. How did this city house some Majestic king?"

The bird flapped at him in response.

"Yeah, I know, *that's* crazy. She didn't really mention much about him before I left. Not that I would've really cared; I was so just ready to get out of there," he said, nodding to the birds. "Sarah told me about the king as a child. 'He's the good voice and can take away all the bad voices,' she told me. Funny thing is, I actually believed her. I think it's probably because I mostly wanted it to be true. Have you ever seen a king around here? You've been around for a while, I guess?"

The birds stared back at him in silence.

"No, you're too smart to fall for some tale like that," Joel said as he watched a few more birds fly into the tower.

"Good to see you. You made it just in time for the rest of the story," Joel acknowledged the newcomers. "Isabelle, she's this girl, well, it's a long story, but she used to talk to something. I don't know what it was, but she claimed it answered her. She couldn't see it, just like I can't see my voices ... but it was a voice, I think," Joel mumbled. "And, well, I didn't think she was nuts. Um, yeah, I obviously didn't have much room to talk," Joel admitted. "But for some reason, I've thought about it, her, her 'voice thing' or whatever, since I've been here. It's just such a different place—the people being so kind, I mean, look at you all, even the birds are different. So ... I've been thinking," Joel stammered. "Maybe believing in this thing or trying to talk to it is like seeing a therapist or something, which never helped me, either, but I can't help wondering if because I'm in Waiz now it's different. What if—what if this good thing—this voice, this good voice—would do something?"

He leaned his head back against the tower's wooden frame and closed his eyes. He quickly peeked back at the birds and said, "Okay, you're my witnesses. Here goes."

Joel closed his eyes again, and his heart began to pound, mostly out of his feeling of complete awkwardness. "I'm alone, and no one can hear me," he assured himself and swallowed hard. "Okay, um, thing or king, or really, whatever lived in the caychuras, if you're still here, my name is Joel. My friend, Sarah, sent me to find you—I think. I'd really like to find a caychura if they still exist. I think they do," Joel paused, and hated being met with silence. "I'm not sure if I'm talking to the air or something, but if it's real, I'd really like to know. Please."

Joel reminded himself that if he was talking to a king he should probably be polite and truthful. "I'm just trying to figure out if the stories are true. I'd like to know you, if you're real, but just so you know, I have ulterior motives. Hey, at least I am honest," Joel said as he shrugged. "So, I've had these tormenting voices since my mom died. I've heard—well, I think if you're real you could probably help me. I just want to be free." When Joel was met with silence again, he sighed and opened his eyes.

He was shocked to see that the wooden frame surrounding him had become completely black. He shuddered when he realized the tower was now full of the black birds. As he looked around, Joel felt as if the birds were staring him down and letting him know he was in their territory. His jaw tightened as he tried to brush off his fear and convince himself, *they're just birds.*

He sat up to reach for the rope, and as he did, one of the dark flyers suddenly darted toward him.

"Hey!" he retorted loudly. He swatted the bird away and reached for the rope again.

He received the same response from the bird, and this time two more gathered with the first one. Nervousness set in as Joel glanced around and saw he was surrounded. He tried for the window, yet was met by another angry group. Now he was not sure what to do. If he went for the rope again, he was afraid he would get his eye poked out. He leaned back again, confounded and afraid.

Corwin, Augustine, and Sebastian arrived near the Marcell House by norrac and were briskly walking down the street.

"We must hurry before the service gets out," Corwin said.

"Why?" Augustine asked as she pushed the wheelchair.

"A few reasons, but the main one being that the old house is closed to everyone on Sundays. I also would prefer not to be bothered by anyone today. This kalona is generally unhappy to see any visitors. After it receives the news that Clovis is dead, which I doubt they know yet, they will surely be suspicious of any characters such as us," Corwin replied, motioning for her to quicken her pace.

"Joel knows this, too, I bet. He won't stick around long," Sebastian piped up.

"I believe that is also true. In fact, he might—" Corwin stopped in mid-sentence.

The other two followed his gaze toward the Marcell House.

"Oh, it's kind of decrepit looking," Augustine said as she squinted at the building through the sunlight.

"The tower, Joel's in the tower! Augustine, take Sebastian up that hill, get him as far away as you can. Now! Go!"

Augustine's heart raced, having never seen Corwin so alarmed, not even at the murder the day before. The two watched as he darted toward the house.

"Augustine, look! The tower is swarming with crows," Sebastian pointed.

She saw the black objects and quickly noticed something was different about them. "No, they can't be crows," she said slowly. "They're huge!" she exclaimed, running his wheelchair onto a shady hillside across from the place.

"This is far enough! Why don't you take me inside? I can help!" Sebastian let out.

"No, I have clear instructions not to," she countered.

"Well, at least go and find out what's going on," he pleaded, looking behind his chair at her. "Go on. Go on! I'll be fine. There's no one out here. It's Sunday, remember?"

She sighed and nodded. "Okay, seriously, stay here. I'm putting you behind this tree, and I better find you in this same spot when I get back."

He nodded and watched in awe as his always-so-proper sister dashed down the hill and across the street.

Augustine ran faster than she knew she could run. She burst into the old house and yelled, "Corwin! Corwin! Where are you? Oh!"

She ducked as several of the large black birds she had seen outside darted down towards her. She ran over to the bell tower and saw dozens of birds swooping and diving. "Shoo! Ah!" She screamed as the birds whizzed past her face. "Corwin!" She glanced around for him and instantly heard his voice above her.

"Augustine! Back away! Get under the pews!"

There was no time for her to argue or try to discover if he had found Joel. She rushed to the furthest set of pews and swiftly slid under them. She lay still, hoping that the birds' eyes would not find her in the dim light. She quivered inside as the sound of the birds' screeching echoed throughout the building. She closed her eyes when she heard a loud banging. *What on earth is he doing?* she wondered, as her heart pounded in agony. After enduring several minutes of these torturous sounds, Augustine realized they were finally fading away.

She opened her eyes again when she heard Corwin's voice. "Augustine?"

"I'm over here, under the pews, like you told me."

"Good girl. Stay there."

She turned over onto her side and saw Corwin climbing down the bell ropes with a limp body in his hand. She gasped at seeing the body. It was covered in bloody holes that appeared to have been pecked into its clothes and flesh.

Corwin looked strangely unharmed, disheveled perhaps, but not injured. He laid the body out on a pew, and Augustine screamed when she saw a bird swoop down behind him. The body shook, yet Corwin turned swiftly while sweeping something metallic through the air towards the bird. Augustine watched in awe as the bird fell down dead. The others lagging behind it squawked in fear and immediately flew away.

Augustine now saw that Corwin was carrying a long sword. He thrust it into the ground near the body and sat down. She could tell he was calm but waiting for something.

"Corwin," she whispered. "May I come out?"

Corwin looked toward the sound of her voice. "I can't even see you."

She crawled out from underneath the pew. "Over here."

"Ah, good hiding spot," he said as he stood up and walked towards her. "Are you all right, dear? Where you're standing probably hasn't been touched in—"

"Corwin!" she screamed, pointing behind him.

The limp body had risen. It had red hair, and Augustine was certain it was, indeed, Joel. Both she and Corwin started toward him, and Joel quickly leapt for the sword. Corwin put his arm out to stop Augustine when Joel pulled the sword from the ground. All watched as the sword's blade began to glow in his hands, turning into a white, blazing light. Joel shook his gaze from the light and bolted toward the door. Right before he reached the door, however, the light shattered, and the hilt of the sword disintegrated in his hand. He stood in the doorway for a moment, looking both awestruck and defeated.

When Joel heard Corwin make a move toward him, he took off toward the hillside. Joel somehow managed to lumber up toward the mountains. Blood was pouring from every wound, and every hole was burning as if the beaks of the birds had been tipped with poison. He stopped briefly to inspect the holes. Red blood was flowing out from the wounds, but the skin surrounding the holes had turned black. He grimaced and sighed as he heard a voice. *Who is that?* he wondered, aware that he was too exhausted to fight another enemy.

He moved cautiously toward the sound and made out the word, "Help!" He was surprised to hear it was a child's cry, which made him all the more uneasy. *Kids aren't up here. This is a trap!*

"Please, don't leave me. I'm over by the tree," the voice pleaded through sobs.

Joel looked toward the tree but could see no one. He searched over the ground and grabbed the only makeshift weapon he could find, a long, thick stick.

"I see you! I'm on the ground," the voice cried.

Joel did not see another soul. "Who are you?" Joel called out, keeping his distance.

There was a pause, "Joel, is that you? It's me! It's Sebastian."

The familiarity of the little fellow's voice suddenly came back to him. Joel ran toward the tree and almost stumbled over his young friend.

"Oh, sorry," Joel said while picking himself up. "What happened to you?"

"Why didn't you know it was me?" Sebastian answered his question with another one, while wiping his eyes on his shirt.

"Well," Joel pointed to his bloodied skin and clothes. "I think I was a little too freaked out to recognize your voice."

Sebastian nodded. "What happened—"

"No, you first," Joel interrupted him.

"Well, we came up here looking for you."

Joel raised his eyebrows in surprise.

"Yes, Corwin really wants to talk to you."

"About the murder?"

"What? Oh, no. He doesn't believe you did it."

Joel straightened, "He's right; I didn't do it. All right, go on."

"Okay, well, Corwin saw the crows, or whatever they were, and ran like a madman toward the house. He shouted at Augustine to get me as far away as she could." He paused as he watched Joel bring his wheelchair back over to him, then he continued. "So Augustine put me over here, and I told her to go see what was going on inside. I wanted to go, too, but of course, she had to follow Corwin's orders."

Joel nodded in understanding.

"I told her to go on so she could find out what was happening. So I was just sitting here waiting when all of a sudden a bunch of older kids, obviously skipping chapel, found me over here."

Joel found this part of the story hard to believe. *What older kids would be up here?* he silently questioned, yet the sight of Sebastian's tear-stained shirt made him keep his mouth shut.

"I did my best to distract them from the house. I tried to be nice to them," Sebastian said and looked down.

Joel gritted his teeth; he knew from his personal experiences all too well where this story was going.

"They just started taunting me, making fun of me. They even threw some rocks at me," Sebastian said angrily as he showed Joel a fresh scratch on his neck. "They made sure I'd be stuck here. They closed up my wheelchair and threw it after they knocked me out of it." Sebastian looked down in humiliation and big tears welled up in his eyes again. "Do you know what it's like to be made fun of? To be handicapped?"

Joel gingerly picked him up and put him back in the wheelchair. After he set the little boy's feet on the footrests, he put his face directly in front of Sebastian's. "Yes, my whole life. Sebastian, I may have the use of my legs, but I know what it's like to feel handicapped."

"I'm sorry I became so angry at you, but . . . I saw you in the barn the morning we talked about the Green Cloak. You got some scroll from behind the wooden slats. I thought you were lying to me about not having my dad's maps."

Joel put a hand on his head. "So that's what that was all about! I wish you would've told me. My knapsack is at the meeting place along with the scroll from behind the slats. I'm sure Corwin will get my bag, and you can see for yourself what's inside. Maybe you can crack the code. I haven't been able to interpret any of the writings on the papers inside the scroll. But here, before I forget." Joel reached into his pocket and handed him the maps.

Sebastian became wide-eyed when he saw his father's maps. "How did you get them back?"

"It's a long story, but they're all accounted for. I never meant to keep them. I just had kept them and one other in my pocket since the night we left the train station."

"I know. I'm sorry," Sebastian said sincerely.

"Yeah, me, too," Joel replied.

"Do you forgive me?"

Joel was puzzled by his request. "Forgive you?" Joel shook his head. "You said you were sorry."

The little boy's demeanor did not change, so Joel finally said, "Yes, all right, I forgive you."

"Will you stay with us?"

"No. I can't. I gave you back the maps," Joel sighed.

"Please. We want you to stay with us," Sebastian pleaded.

"You weren't looking for me just to get the maps?" Joel asked in surprise.

"How would I have known you'd gotten them back? Please, talk to Corwin."

"I can't, Sebastian. He can't help me. If ... if," he paused, then lowered his voice, "if the king, the Majestic, still exists, I have to find him. He's the only one who can help me."

"You're still looking for a caychura?" Sebastian asked.

Joel nodded. "I'm headed up there," he said as he pointed to the steep, rocky mountainside.

Sebastian seemed to understand there was no use in trying to convince Joel to stay. "Well, I'll make a deal with you."

"What's that?" Joel asked as he watched Sebastian pull a dark brown, tattered document out from underneath the back of his shirt.

His pale face broke into a mischievous grin when he held the item up in his hand. "You didn't get all my maps."

"Apparently not," Joel said and could not help but grin back.

"If you find him, and he can help you, then promise me you'll ask him if he can help me, too." He held out the map, and just before Joel was about to grab it, Sebastian pulled it back. "You have to promise!"

"I promise," Joel agreed, and with that Sebastian handed over the map.

"Augustine is going to kill you," Joel said as he looked over the contents.

A map of the mountainside's most sacred places were etched in faded red ink across the old paper.

"She hasn't killed me yet and besides, I don't think she believes in the king or caychuras."

Joel nodded.

"Well, go on then. What are you waiting for?" Sebastian asked, making a wry smile.

"Yes, I—" Joel paused, feeling conflicted, not wanting to leave the little boy. "I will keep my promise, Sebastian."

"I know."

Not long after Joel had left in pursuit of a caychura, Corwin and Augustine made their way up the hill toward Sebastian.

"What happened to you? Are you all right?" Augustine cried upon seeing his dusty clothes and disheveled appearance.

"I had a little fall, but I'm fine," he said, as he gave Corwin a sly wink.

"I hate both of you. What happened here?" she demanded.

"Oh, Augustine, 'hate' is a strong word," Sebastian responded in jest.

"I have plenty more."

"Augustine, Joel had several of the maps your father had given you," Corwin interrupted. "Sebastian had given him three at Crossroads in order to help you find me. The Green Cloak took them from Joel the night he was in my room." He waited to allow her time to process this new information. "He didn't tell Sebastian what had happened, but I suspect his second run in with the spy had something to do with wanting to get them back."

Sebastian held them up.

"Ah, very good," Corwin said, clapping his hands.

"Did you get his knapsack?" Sebastian asked.

Corwin swung it from around his back.

"He said there were a few more in there."

"Well, well, that makes him a thief and a liar, just as I suspected," Augustine sputtered, clearly furious with both of them.

"Not anymore. He returned them and told me the truth," Sebastian stated.

"We need to find him," Corwin said.

"Why? He's clearly mad, or did you not see him in there?"

"Augustine, hold your tongue, as you are fully aware I had to disclose a weapon to rescue Joel. It's not madness. Where do you think he went?" Corwin asked, turning back toward Sebastian.

"That's easy. To find a caychura." The little boy smiled up at him.

"Great. Just great," Augustine grumbled.

"Did you give him my map?" Corwin asked quietly.

"Yes, but he was headed up the mountainside, anyway." Sebastian shrugged.

Augustine fell to the ground in frustration and covered her face with her hands. When Corwin tried to put his hand on her shoulder, she jerked away from him.

"How much more haven't you told me? Have I proved myself so untrustworthy that you can tell Sebastian more than me?" she cried out as tears began to run down her cheeks.

Corwin bent down beside her and attempted to look into her teary blue eyes. "I know it's been a long few days, but we must make this journey," he paused, and thoughtfully stroked her hair. "Augustine, you are so strong for your brother, so determined and focused. I haven't wanted to burden you with all of this or distract you from your duty of caring for him. You already have so much on you with him as your responsibility." He sat down on the ground next to her and put a hand on her shoulder. "But it is time to tell you what happens next."

"Corwin … what is that?" she asked as she pointed to his sword, which apparently had reassembled itself shortly after Joel had left.

"A *rhydid.*"

Her eyes widened and then narrowed in anger. "You've had one all this time."

He nodded and gently grabbed her hand before she could move away from him. "Only Joel can take you to get yours. It's at the Temple of Differe. He's our hope; I believe we were destined to meet him."

She looked at him. "Why can't I go alone?"

He smoothed away the tears streaming down her face and whispered, "You don't like being alone." After taking a deep breath Corwin began again. "Sebastian's doing poorly in even the slight coolness here. I fear his body would not survive another exposure to Differe. Augustine, he mustn't be left alone, so I cannot go with you. Joel has gotten out before, and I believe he could get you there, as well as back again, safely. He also greatly needs what you're looking for."

She shuddered in response to his plan. "I can't. You should've seen him collapse at the store. I'd be afraid to go with him. Also, like I said at the tavern, if you haven't noticed, he seems to despise the temple. I doubt he'd return, especially with someone who's been," she stopped and took in a sharp breath, "quite unkind to him." She sighed.

"He looked worse today, though. He also clearly wanted my rhydid. I think he may just be desperate enough to go back," Corwin encouraged her.

"Where will he go first?" Sebastian asked.

Corwin pulled out Joel's scroll. "I'm pretty sure I have a good idea, but let's see what we have here. In any case, we will all need to change. It's going to be a rocky climb."

CHAPTER 28

JOEL HAD A significant head start, and with Corwin's map in hand, he easily navigated toward the mountain caves. The air became cooler the closer he got to the mountainside and gave him goose bumps. His body felt more ragged with each step, but when he looked down at his wounds, he saw that most of the bloody holes had dried.

When he approached the foot of the mountain, he studied the map and determined that in order to get to the caves he would have to climb the mountain's rocky terrain. "That's one good reason to have lost my knapsack," he said.

The area appeared abandoned, due to chapel, he guessed. Though the rocks were bare, Joel didn't think he would be noticed. Still, he moved forward with great caution, intently searching the area for anything that remotely resembled the dark birds or anything else unfriendly. After he looked for a few moments, he squinted and thought he could make out the outline of one of the caves.

Got to be as good as any. His eyes searched for any he may have missed. The climb proved not too treacherous, as the cave had obviously been visited in ages past. There was still somewhat of a path, but even so the climbing and pulling was exhausting to Joel's wounded body. When he finally reached the mouth of the cave, he sat down just inside the opening for a rest.

Nothing special, he thought, seeing no drawings or inscriptions on the cave's walls. He glanced behind him toward the darkness inside and grimaced.

"I forgot about not having a light. Oh well," he muttered. "I didn't come this far not to go inside." He eventually pulled himself back up, ready to find something.

"Hello!" he called out, yet only heard his echo in return. His voice changed to a small whisper as he walked further inside. "King, if you're here ..." Joel wasn't sure what else to say.

His heart pounded in the darkness and silence that surrounded him, but he kept walking. After he had walked far enough to lose sight of the opening he heard Sarah's voice in his head: "Ask. Just like the temple people, pray."

Over the course of the last few days, he had begun to remember much of what she had told him about the king. She had never called him "the Majestic," just "the king of Waiz." He remembered her saying something about him being dead but his spirit living on. These thoughts were getting confused with the information he had heard about the Majestic.

Are they the same? he began to wonder.

"Ask, like the temple people, pray," he heard her voice command again.

The thought of doing anything like the temple people brought repulsion to his heart. He sighed and tried to push past those feelings, as well as his own stubbornness. He stood still and then closed his eyes.

"Are you here? I've come to find you. I need your help. I want to be free."

His whispered prayer was met with silence. His injured body's energy was fading, and Joel felt his soul wearing out, as well.

"It wasn't supposed to be like this. This place, Waiz, it's supposed to be glorious, peaceful, free, a place where people can dream. It's at war. People are being murdered. They're drunk in the streets. There's stealing. Sebastian is still sick. And I'm—I'm still crazy!" he burst out in frustration and anger. "Where are you, oh, King of Waiz? We need you!" he yelled.

He sighed in defeat at the deafening silence, and whimpered out once more, "We need you."

This cry was met by a slight warm breeze that blew past his face. The breeze caused the hairs on his arms and neck to stand on end. When the breeze grew stronger, Joel became too afraid to speak. *Something heard me. Something's here.*

Just as he finished this observation, a deafening boom bursting with sound and light blasted through the cave. The light from the explosive sound blinded him. Joel fell to his knees and covered his face with his hands to shield his eyes from the light. He felt the warm winds continue to rush past him, but he noticed the wind itself made no sound.

Suddenly he heard what sounded like dozens of mirrors shattering all around him. The sounds grew louder with each passing moment and it soon sounded like hundreds of tiny glass shards were clinking against one another. In addition to the glass, Joel thought he heard an ensemble of thousands of concert bells and chimes ringing. The sounds were captivating, and within a few minutes a chorus of beautiful singing caroled out. The voices were more heavenly then any of the singers he had heard at the temple.

To his surprise, his body began to shake in response to the melodious voices. At first he panicked, unable to move and too petrified to open his eyes. Joel sensed no hands on him, and it was as though the shaking was involuntary. Though shaking, he was still able to focus on the singing voices; they became more and more beautiful as their sounds harmonized with the bells. As they grew louder, Joel's body seemed to shake even more violently. Through the shaking Joel was only able to make out one word in their song.

My name. I hear my name. They're singing about me? Is this song about me? he asked himself in disbelief. He continued to hear his name called out and could not help basking a few minutes in what seemed to be his glory.

Eventually his body went completely stiff, and he fell against the cave's floor. His already jittery heart raced as he felt something tight wrap around his body. He thought the tightness felt like a cord of rope. When he attempted to move his hand to touch the object, his hand lay still and became wrapped to his side. Whatever the object was, Joel determined that it was illuminated. When he cracked his eyes to catch a glimpse of the rope, all he saw was golden light radiating below his chin. The rope tightened around him until his body was no longer shaking. The song then turned to shouts that Joel could hear but not understand. He knew whatever they were saying was good, and he did not need to be afraid. He was held tightly, but not in chains.

As he lay there, his thoughts turned to his most recent victories: escaping from the temple, making a true friend, having his first job, and defeating a trained official of the New Order. He sighed, deeply contented.

Then suddenly all around him went dark. Joel was rattled when he felt the rope turn into thick metal chains. He moved his hand under the cold metal bands that began pressing into his skin. He opened his eyes and saw a pair of red, X-shaped eyes glaring back at him. The creature's red eyes glowed, revealing its gray, emaciated skin and hideous, mouthless face. As soon as their eyes met a black hole opened, and though the hole was not a mouth, high-pitched screams escaped. Joel had heard these screams before, but had never seen the source of the blood-curdling sound.

More furious that his song had been interrupted than he was frightened, Joel instantly thought, *two can play at this game.*

"Shut up! I don't belong to you!" he shouted unafraid, in the creature's face.

It shook its head furiously, causing its very few dingy, stringy hairs to fall into its face.

Soon, just like with the birds, more came, with the smaller ones gathering behind the larger ones. Joel could only make out their faces due to the darkness. Though mouthless, the creatures appeared to have a V-shaped nose just south of their eyes. A shape that Joel could not make out was marked above each eye.

Now surrounded and firmly clinched in chains, Joel seethed at these screaming monsters for stealing his time of glory. Joel gathered all the vigor he had left inside him, and screamed back at them in anger, "I don't belong to you!"

Just then, Joel realized he could still hear the faint sounds of his song over the creatures' screams. He breathed hard while trying to listen intently and block out more of the awful noise.

As he tried, as if on cue to distract him, the creature stopped screaming and spoke to him. "You belong to no one—not even your own family," its raspy voice harassed him.

The others joined in and repeated in unison, "You belong to no one."

"No," Joel reasoned softly as he heard his song in his head. "No, you're wrong."

His voice was drowned out by the creatures' chanting and screaming.

"No, I do." He tried to think of how to win the argument. "I belong—I belong—"

"To no one!" the creatures continued to call out.

Joel mustered up his last bit of strength, looked the creature defiantly in the eyes, and yelled, "No! The king of all Waiz! He is here and I belong to him!"

Joel watched the red eyes flicker at his statement.

He lifted his head to listen hard for the song still being sung over him. "I hear—I hear his song for me," he said aloud.

The creature pressed something sharp against Joel's throat and scoffed, "He will not save you. You are nothing to him."

Joel leaned his head back onto the ground, away from the arrow. He felt his body beginning to slightly shake again. "So, you admit he exists," Joel said as hope and confidence rose in his spirit. "No, *you* are nothing to him," he accused the creature. "And he—he—"

Joel faltered as the shaking had started again, and his teeth chattered this time, making speech difficult. He knew the shaking was from something earlier, something good, so he pressed on with the words inscribed on Corwin's map. "He promised—he promised—to love me—."

As he did this, something thick yet unseen descended upon the group. The host of creatures screeched loudly, and Joel shook in his metal cocoon. The darkness lifted again as a golden light began to fill the cave. The light brought a soothing warmth, and Joel peeked to make sure the creatures were gone before he fully opened his eyes. The cave went completely silent, but his head did not.

"There's an inscription above you. Read it aloud," said a voice, his voice. *But that's not me.*

He blinked his eyes and saw a passage written above him on the cave's ceiling. He began to feel flushed as he lay there looking at the words.

"What's the matter?" the voice asked, still speaking in his voice in his head.

"I—I can't read. Well, I used to, but I can't read very well anymore," he spoke aloud in response.

"Just seeing if you would admit it."

"What?" Joel said a little defensively.

"No, really, I wanted to tell you that you do not see as others see. Now when you read, you will see the truth. Look between the lines."

Joel obeyed this voice and squinted at the words of the passage. He was astonished that, at closer observation, he was able to make out a perfect picture of an armed warrior fighting. The passage instantly became clear to him.

"Every warrior needs weapons to fight his enemy," he read aloud.

"Very good."

"Sir, will they come back?" he asked almost in a whisper to the voice in his head.

"Yes, and even stronger, but so shall you be."

Joel sighed, not feeling reassured.

"They are only as strong as you allow them to be. The power to cast them aside lies within you," the voice went on.

Joel cringed at the thought of facing any such creatures again.

"Why are you afraid?" the voice asked, as if reading his mind.

Guess that makes sense. You're in my mind. Joel sighed again, thinking this was just as crazy as listening to his bad voices.

"You haven't answered my question," the voice reminded him.

Well, I believe you're real, or I couldn't, well ... I'd be sitting in this cave in silence, but I am in silence.... Joel was interrupted before he could continue.

"I am here, Joel, and I am speaking. You are not in silence; you are listening, which takes being still."

Joel hurried to answer the original question. "I suppose I fear the cost.... Yes, that's mostly it. I can't imagine I'll be stronger without a cost," he admitted.

He almost thought he heard the other voice chuckle as it answered, "Ah, yes, your freedom. That is what you asked for. If that's truly what you want, it will cost you nothing, yet it also will cost you everything." There was a pause and the light began to fade. "I promise you freedom, which I will give you freely in return for your faith. To reap the benefits of your freedom, you must do what I say."

An hour later, Joel awoke from a deep sleep. He wondered if his whole experience in the cave had been a dream until he tried to move. With his body still in chains, he did the only thing he could think of. "Help! Please help me!" he cried out.

After a few minutes of this, he was astonished to hear footsteps running into the cave.

"We hear you! We're coming!"

Corwin soon came alongside him and fumbled over the chains. "Stand back," he told Augustine as he gave her Sebastian.

Augustine trembled in fear. All watched as Corwin drew out his magnificent sword and cut through Joel's metal prison.

"How'd you find me?" Joel coughed, as he sat up and stretched.

"I was looking for you, and you have my map." Corwin helped prop him up, and Joel nodded at him in understanding. "The king sent me."

All three of them looked at Corwin in shock.

"This keeps getting weirder," Joel said weakly then asked, "Is he—is he still here?"

"Yes, but not in the way you just encountered him," Corwin said as he thrust some water down Joel's throat.

Joel wiped his mouth and then lowered his voice, "Are they still here?"

"No. They can't stand his presence. Or this." Corwin gestured towards his sword.

"I heard him, I think," Joel said before he gulped some more water. "I heard him in my head—in my voice."

Corwin nodded and smiled at him. "Sounds better than the other voices you're accustomed to hearing, doesn't it?"

Joel shook his head, feeling completely exhausted. "How will I tell the voices apart?" he sighed.

Corwin patted his hand. "More talk later. Augustine, I will need you to do what I asked."

At this, Joel watched Augustine hoist Sebastian onto her back, and Corwin moved to pick Joel up.

"No, I can move," Joel protested. Then he tried and realized he could not. "What's wrong with me?" he asked, panicking.

"We'll have plenty of time to talk at my mountain house. Just rest," Corwin instructed.

By the time the group reached the mouth of the cave, Joel had drifted off into deep sleep again.

"Augustine!" Sebastian tugged on her neck.

"What?" she whispered.

"Look at Joel."

"He looks exhausted."

"No, look! The holes from the birds," he paused as she caught on in disbelief, "They're gone."

CHAPTER 29

JOEL SAT UP with a start then almost immediately went back into a sleepy daze as he leaned back against the worn leather couch. He looked down and found a worn geometric-patterned blanket wrapped around him. The couch sat in front of a large red brick hearth that had a blazing fire glowing inside it. The mantel above the fireplace held several wood framed pictures. As he gazed at it, he got his first glimpse of the plethora of taxidermist's art placed throughout the den. A cozy kitchen sat off to his left and behind him was a set of dark-stained wooden stairs. He was sure there was more to the downstairs, but this was all he could see from the couch.

Corwin's mountain house was rustic yet colorful and his décor was bizarre, exotic even. *He must have been to tons of places.* Joel approached the fireplace while still wrapped in his blanket. The pictures, to Joel's surprise, were of people, rather than places. One was of a young Corwin down at the Pallas River with a bald-headed man and a dark-haired young woman. The next frame held a large group of travelers that appeared to be standing on what resembled a snowy mountaintop. The third was a picture of the same dark-haired woman with Corwin in front of a train. The last picture was of a little girl playing with Corwin in the snow.

Joel's eyes lingered on the last photo. "Augustine?"

"That's right."

Joel was startled by Corwin's voice.

"Here. Drink this," Corwin said as he shoved a hot coffee mug into Joel's hand. "It will perk you up."

Joel nodded as he took the mug.

"I'm their uncle," Corwin said as he pointed to the picture.

"All right," Joel replied, fully understanding that there was much more to say on the subject. "Where are they?" he asked.

"Resting, also. I think everyone was worn out from the climb, among other things," Corwin mused.

"Uh, thanks for helping me," Joel said, as he glanced down into his mug.

Corwin nodded in reply. "Have a seat."

Joel plopped back down on the couch, and Corwin sat down across from him onto a thick, oversized, leather recliner.

"Joel, in return for my helping you, do you think you could answer some questions now—about you?"

Joel nodded without hesitation at the man who had rescued him. The hours of restful sleep seemed to have had a sizable calming effect on Joel's soul. His body relaxed even more with each sip of warm liquid.

"I'd like to guess first before you answer."

Joel shrugged in response.

"You're from the temple, and somehow, outrageously managed to escape. I believe you grew up in Differe and knew how to get to the train station, but probably didn't know much about the inside of the place since you used Sebastian's map for direction."

Joel was about to answer the bearded man's assumptions, but Corwin continued before he could open his mouth.

"I assume you're important to the temple, or they would not have noticed your being gone so quickly, meaning, I was surprised the lady from the inquiry desk knew your name. I also suspect someone from the temple helped you escape and made sure the picture sent out for your warrant had brown hair."

Joel waited this time as he watched Corwin take a sip of coffee. Corwin swallowed then let out a chuckle. "I feel at this point it's only fair that I answer your first question that you asked me. Do you remember what it was?"

Joel reflected on their first meeting for a moment then smiled and said, "How'd you know where the train was?"

Corwin nodded. "Waiz is old, older than Differe. As you may remember, Theodore Waiz found a kalona upon his arrival. Once Differe became the thriving metropolis that it is," he said with sarcasm, "they feared losing residents to the glorious city of Waiz and promptly built Crossroads on top of the original train stop Waiz had built. Since I'm from Waiz and have only ever traveled by that train, that's how I knew where to find it. To those not looking for it, like the lady from the inquiry desk, it's, well, forgotten." Corwin stopped to take another sip from his mug.

"Let's see, where was I? Oh yes, we met you on the train. You had just left the temple but seemed half-starved," Corwin said. "You're looking healthier these days. Anyway, I think you came hoping to find freedom here. I suppose just not having rules felt pretty good," he said with a wink, then went on, "You took up residence at the Hallie farm."

Joel's eyes widened at him in surprise.

"He's a friend of mine. I'm from here, remember? So, living on the farm, and working with Haskell at the store. By the way, he says you're quite the singer, chef, and poet. Does the temple appreciate such talents?"

The scowl that soon overshadowed Joel's face answered Corwin's question.

"I thought not. I heard of how you cared for those two while I was gone," Corwin said as he pointed upstairs. "Very admirable, Joel. I also heard about Sebastian's maps going missing and then being miraculously recovered. Why did you do that?"

"Question one?" Joel asked.

"Depends. How many do I get?" Corwin grinned, and Joel rolled his eyes.

"I never meant to keep the maps. I just forgot about them after we got on the train. I have a tendency to keep things that are valuable in my pocket rather than my knapsack, in case I should lose the bag. The Green Cloak just happened to see them and grabbed them. I just went to New Waiz because, well, you heard what happened at the shop," Joel said while looking away from him. "I couldn't go back there, so I left for New Waiz. I had a little money saved. I wanted to go to the meeting," Joel sighed and shrugged his shoulders. "I honestly just happened to see the Green Cloak."

"You still haven't answered my question. Why did you retrieve the maps? Why did you go after the Green Cloak?" Corwin leaned forward as he asked again.

"Uh, well, because," Joel stammered as he felt himself turn the shade of his hair and sputtered out, "Because it was the right thing to do."

"Your integrity is extreme."

"It's all I have," Joel muttered.

"So, in the name of duty then, rather than love and friendship, or maybe revenge?" Corwin questioned him.

"Whatever. Who are those Green Cloaks?" Joel asked, as he turned his gaze back towards Corwin.

"Apprentices of the New Order, or spies."

"He had a large scar on his face," Joel said as he ran his fingers across his cheek.

"Hm … Andropolis. Yes, I've known him since he was a small boy," Corwin said as a pensive expression crossed his face.

"Ando-what?" Joel shot him a puzzled look.

"His name. Andropolis."

"He shot the old man," Joel told Corwin and motioned to his knapsack that sat by the fireplace. "I kept a few of his arrows. I could've taken his quiver, too, but he seemed pretty attached to it."

"Yes, it was his father's, but we are still talking about you. So, Joel goes to the Marcell House. Why?" Corwin asked, redirecting the conversation.

"I was looking for something," Joel muttered.

"Did you find what you expected?" Corwin asked with a hint of suspicion in his voice.

"No. What were those things?" Joel asked as he looked into the man's dark eyes.

"Guards," Corwin answered, and Joel could tell by his serious expression that Corwin knew exactly what "things" Joel was referring to.

"Sorry, what? No, I mean the birds! They were birds." Joel grimaced as he thought of the dark flyers again.

"Strange birds, wouldn't you say? They guard the bell tower. The bells have not been rung since they started guarding it," Corwin said matter-of-factly.

"Just what are they guarding it for?" Joel asked, not sure if he believed the man's answer.

"To keep the bells from ringing," Corwin answered.

"But I wasn't ringing the bells," Joel argued.

"You were on their territory apparently doing something they didn't like," Corwin explained.

"I was just—I was just talking out loud," Joel muttered, feeling embarrassed again.

"To yourself?"

"Well, sort of. Maybe trying to talk to the king?" Joel could barely squeak out the latter part.

"You shouldn't be ashamed to say it. Look at you—no holes." Corwin pointed at him.

Joel stared at his body in disbelief. "How? When?"

"After we left the cave," Corwin said as he put his mug down on the wooden floor.

Corwin watched Joel reflect and piece things together in his mind.

Joel's eyes narrowed as he asked, "Those birds. Are *they* their masters? I mean, are the creatures with the red eyes their masters?"

Corwin clapped his hands. "Bravo! Yes, in a way."

"Did I find a caychura, Corwin?" Joel asked, not sure he wanted to know. "If they're like that cave, I don't want to find any more."

"I'm the one asking the questions right now. Did you find the king?" Corwin asked in a tone all too casual.

"I think so," Joel said, unsure and flinching a little.

"Well, when you decide you're sure, then I will say, yes, you found a caychura."

Joel's mouth opened in surprise, but he soon laughed in the face of Corwin's grin.

"That was my map," Corwin let out. "I asked Sebastian to give it to you."

"That little liar! He can sure fake a good cry," Joel said in mock annoyance.

"Don't blame him. It was my idea." Corwin winked at him again.

"Why did you want me to find it?" Joel pressed him.

"Me, first," Corwin said again. "Why did you want to find it?"

Joel sighed then finally admitted, "Everything you have guessed at this point is right except for me being important to the temple. I was an outcast there. I went to that prison at my father's request after my mother died." Joel took a slow breath before continuing. "I heard horrible, tormenting voices in my head after she died. No one could help me. The temple assured my dad they could 'cure' me, but all they did was put me in a dungeon called 'Moonstruck.' If you're not sure what that means—"

"Insane," Corwin interjected.

"Right. Anyway, they kept me down there for years, trying to make me 'better'—convincing me and everyone around me, even my dad, that I was crazy, that I suffered from some mental illness. By the time I got out and attended classes, I couldn't even read anymore. I was—I was so brainwashed, thinking I was crazy, which meant to me *stupid* as well." Joel clenched his fists in anger. "My classmates were merciless. I got beat up and stolen from by those with better names and better standing, which means just about everyone else there. In addition to that, I had a standing appointment with the Templins for a weekly flogging. Their tactics varied between verbal berating, physical beating, and humiliating tasks. Yeah, and this is when I was trying to comply," he said when he saw Corwin shake his head in sadness. "So I decided to fight back and ended up rebelling in every form I possibly could against their ways.

"I was starving," he said, as he looked directly into Corwin's face. "I ate whatever scraps were left in the back of the kitchen. I had one person in authority who stuck by me ... when she could, anyway. She helped me get out, like you guessed. She's from here and she told me I could be free in Waiz. I think she must've thought the king was still alive and that the city hadn't divided." Joel stopped and sighed in frustration. "She said he—the king—could take away the tormentors. If you haven't noticed, they're debilitating. Try having moments like that during class or chapel."

As he finished, the young man's shoulders collapsed, and he looked away from Corwin, surprised at how much he had voiced to the man. "I wanted to find a caychura to find the king, see if he was real—if he could help me. I want to be free, if it's possible."

The crackle from the burning wood in the fireplace was the only sound heard in the house as Joel finished. The two sat in silence. Joel patiently awaited the man's commentary and was surprised when Corwin asked him another question.

"What did you discover?"

Joel paused to think through his answer. "I guess—" he started but was interrupted.

"You must decide, Joel," Corwin coached him.

"Okay, then," Joel said in annoyance and then hesitated before he continued. "He is real, but so are they. I don't get it at all."

"To answer your question, I wanted you to find the caychura so you could find him. Once I saw those blasted holes the birds left, I knew your search was vital."

"But it was—it was just a voice. I didn't see him like I saw those creatures," Joel shuddered.

"They're called *mouthpieces*. Did you notice how they appeared to have no mouth?" Corwin asked.

"Yeah, it was weird. I could still hear them, though, and sometimes a black hole opened on their face." *Sarah was right. We all hear voices, but how did I see them?*

"Have you always seen them?" Corwin asked, as if reading his thoughts.

"No. That was the first time, or the first time it was that real. I didn't really know what to do. I just screamed back in their faces," Joel said, his voice expressing his hatred of even talking about the creatures.

"Sounds like you were ready to see them. Anytime earlier, and you may have been too afraid to yell back," Corwin speculated.

"You said something in the cave, something like 'the king told me to find you.' What did that mean?" Joel looked at him in curiosity.

"Just what I said," Corwin answered.

"He talks to you?" Joel asked in disbelief.

"Sometimes," Corwin said softly.

"Well, how do you know it's him?" Joel asked, suddenly filled with intrigue.

"Easy, and yet not so easy. One voice speaks lies—one of the mouthpieces—and the other voice speaks truth."

Joel rolled his eyes in aggravation. "I've had enough truth crammed down my throat. Ugh, I saw that *Book of Order* deal. How could I have any more to learn after having been at the temple? I don't want any more 'truth.'"

"Well, some truth comes from experience, conversing like we are, books, music, art, and the list goes on. Unlike your temple, where truth is compartmentalized to just books and intellect, the king's truths are in everything, and his truths speak to us all the time."

"This is so odd," Joel sighed and tried to stand up.

"By the way, does the word *warrior* mean anything to you?" Corwin asked.

Joel slumped back onto the couch and remembered the words etched on the cave's ceiling. "Yeah, 'Every warrior needs a weapon.'"

"I know where your rhydid is. This," Corwin said, as he pointed to his sword. "I know where your weapon is, Joel. It will help you defeat the mouthpieces and get your freedom."

"Where is it?" Joel asked halfheartedly, assuming obtaining such an object would be no small task, if, indeed, Corwin really knew where one was.

The seriousness of Corwin's expression assured Joel whatever Corwin was about to say was true, and all his doubt instantly melted away.

"Augustine's is also with yours."

Joel was obviously surprised by this interjection but remained all ears when Corwin spoke again.

"While I was away and you cared for my niece and nephew, I was in Differe."

Joel was still listening intently, but was very pleased to hear that his suspicions had been correct.

"I spent a few days in the historic library. There were actually several of the old books with images of rhydids and their whereabouts in Differe. I could not go to the location to see for myself if the swords were there, but I know you will know."

Joel straightened on the couch in amazement. "How?" Joel asked.

"Have you been to the scared alcoves in the temple chapel, Joel?"

"Yeah, I hid near one before I left." Joel nodded slowly.

"Was there a sword in one?" Corwin asked.

Corwin waited with an eager expression on his face as Joel tried to remember the artifacts in the alcoves. Recollection soon flooded over Joel's face. "Yes, there's a sword there, but it can't be a rhydid. It's encased in glass and sitting in some sparkly sheath. The professors said it's just a remnant from, I don't know, some saint or something."

"Do they like the sheath?" Corwin asked.

"Oh, yeah. They made it themselves," Joel replied.

"They're covering up something. You *are* important to them. They know within you is great power, and they tried to beat it out of you. They're trying to cover up your destiny, Joel. That sword is yours!" Corwin exclaimed.

Joel sat there for a moment in utter astonishment and then shook his head angrily at Corwin. "You're crazy. I'm not going back to the temple!" he cried.

Corwin's voice was gentle. "It's the only way to get your rhydid and be free," he pleaded.

"Why is it there? I bet you didn't get yours there." Joel said, sounding suspicious and frustrated at the proposition.

"Why do *you* think it's there?"

His questions were becoming annoying to Joel.

"What?" Joel's anger rose to the surface. "Because I have to face my fears, my past. Is this what this is about?"

Corwin did not move a muscle.

"No way. I'm not going back. There has to be another one," Joel said matter-of-factly, as he stood up and walked over to the fireplace.

When Corwin's silence persisted, he turned around and said, "Fine. Say it is my rhydid, but what about Augustine? Why is hers there? There's only one sword in the alcove."

"Her reason is between her and me, but what is important for you to know is that Sebastian remains in the care of his sister. He is the real reason for my urgency. He will die without that rhydid in her possession."

"You take her, then," Joel demanded. "I'll stay with him."

"Joel, you got out before, and I believe you can do it again. I wouldn't even attempt to try such a feat so blindly," Corwin explained.

"I have a map you can have," Joel responded.

"But *you* need the rhydid," Corwin urged him.

Joel sighed, feeling worn out all over again. He closed his eyes and wondered if he really could complete such a task. He thought about all the obstacles he would have to endure … again.

"What will I do if they come?" he asked Corwin when he opened his eyes.

"The voices—the mouthpieces—will come in many forms. The greatest battle with them though, lies between your ears," Corwin explained, as he pointed to his head. "They love to accuse you. A thought that starts with 'you' is typically a sure way to detect them."

"Huh?" Joel asked.

"If I was thinking about myself, why would I say 'You are so stupid' instead of 'I am so stupid'?"

"Bad grammar lessons?" Joel joked. "So, a 'you' thought, that's a mouthpiece?" Joel asked, as he contemplated his observation. "How did you know that they don't just scream at me?"

Corwin just smiled in reply as he lit his pipe.

"I don't think I want to know this, but something controls these mouthpieces, right?"

Corwin removed the pipe from his mouth. "Yes, just take off the ending of the word."

"'*Mouth*.' It's called 'the Mouth'?" Joel asked, thinking it was quite a mild name for such a horrible thing.

"Yes, he controls them and uses them to control people such as yourself."

Joel shook his head in confusion. "Let's just stick with his minions for now. Okay, if I hear 'you.' How else do I detect them?"

"Well, remember that the 'you' thought is followed by some lie, something negative." He pointed at Joel with his index finger in order to drive home his statement. "Sometimes their location is obvious, such as in an evil place or practice. You will find them there most certainly. Sometimes you can feel their presence of terror just like you felt the king's presence. Occasionally, they will show themselves. Some like you can see them at times."

"It would be nice to find someone who can see them all the time," Joel mumbled.

"There are some who can, but they're very rare. Most people think they're crazy, so they are led to believe that themselves."

"Sounds familiar," Joel said sarcastically.

"On the contrary, and more importantly, the king's voice will be more distinct in your head. It will be a thought that is always good towards you, towards him, and those around you. Typically it's a thought that's brilliant, simple at times but brilliant, and one that you wouldn't have conjured up on your own. His 'you' thoughts are always good toward you, even when they're a little chastising."

Corwin grinned, and Joel thought of how the voice had at first asked him to read the inscription in the cave.

"Can I talk to him like I have talked to the mouthpieces?" Joel asked hesitantly.

"As if he's real? Yes, though I warn you it's not for the faint of heart. It takes practice. Practice to hear, to listen, to discover his truths, to filter through the lies." Corwin chuckled. "And he's very mysterious. The mouthpieces are easily located, whereas his presence is everywhere, though it seems elusive at times. His answers may vary from a whisper, to a shout, to a puff of smoke."

For emphasis, Corwin blew a puff of smoke from his pipe as he finished the thought.

"Going back to the temple is the only way?" Joel questioned wearily as he rested his arm upon the mantle.

"When I was in Differe, I was being watched by the Templins. I cannot go back because they know what I was studying. They would track me straight to the temple, knowing I wanted the rhydid. I guarantee that even they know it's real. Please consider going."

"No," was Joel's hasty reply.

Corwin sighed in disappointment.

"These rhydids hold power?" Joel asked, turning back towards Corwin.

"Yes, great power, power that you need. Look at you! If those holes were still there you'd barely be functioning, Joel."

Joel was just about to refuse again when Augustine's screams echoed throughout the house. Corwin's eyes darted upward toward her voice and they both raced up the stairs toward Sebastian's room. The scent of leftover food met their senses as they entered the little room. Augustine was holding, rocking, and shaking the little boy all at the same time.

"Sebastian! Look at me, Sebastian!" was her terrified cry.

Corwin knelt down next to the bed and began to check Sebastian's breathing as he pried him from Augustine's arms.

His pale skin appeared to have a bluish tint, and Joel watched in horror as Sebastian gasped for breath. Augustine was crying as she patted his limp hand.

"Joel! Joel!" Corwin startled Joel out of his mesmerized stare. "I need you to go out toward the river, behind the house, and get a handful of alabaster. It's an herb that has blue buds, so it's easy to spot. You should be able to find some a few steps from the house. Don't go into the woods! Can you do that?"

Joel replied with a slight nod, still unnerved. *I've never seen anyone like this. He looks worse then I do during my attacks.* He glanced at Augustine's teary eyes as Corwin coaxed him again.

"Joel, Joel! Go now! Hurry."

Once Joel could feel his feet beneath him again, his adrenaline kicked in, and he was out the back door in no time. He ran as quickly as his legs would carry him over the rough mountainside terrain, slipping and sliding as he went, all the while carrying the image of Augustine's face and the terror he had heard in her voice in his mind. He realized that for one of the first times in his life, he could be the one to help instead of being the victim.

"Okay, I'm close to the river," he said as he heard the sound of rushing water nearby. *What am I supposed to do?* "Get the herb. Yes, get the herb. Blue buds," he coached himself aloud. *I've got to hurry. What if? No, stop. Don't even think that. Just find the alabaster.*

His eyes scanned the forest floor and easily spotted the blue buds. "Gotcha," he said as he raked up a handful.

As he reached for another sprig, suddenly, just as in the cave, all of the hair on his neck stood up. He heard a branch snap, the rustles of the leaves around him, and then Augustine's screams echoing all around him.

Is it in my mind? Instead of waking to reality, Joel became paralyzed with fear as he realized in his haste he had gone against Corwin's instructions and into the forest.

"You're too late, Joel," he heard a voice say behind him.

"That's probably the wrong herb," said another.

"You're too late, Joel," a few more voices mocked.

"You stole from him. He doesn't want your help," still another taunted him.

"Should've listened to Corwin, Joel. Now who'll save you? Who'll save Sebastian?"

The mouthpieces had come, and, almost as a natural reaction, Joel felt himself reach for a weapon as he turned to face them. To his dismay, he found only an empty pocket.

The six ugly creatures blocked the path before him as they stared at him with their glowing red eyes in horrible delight. Each figure had a long narrow face with narrow-slit, X-shaped shaped eyes. A black right triangle was fixed just above each eye against the creatures' pale gray faces. A V-shaped nose and a few dingy strings for hair were the only other features on the mouthpieces' heads.

Joel was alarmed to find that the mouthpieces had bodies the colors of camouflage green and brown, resembling towering, hard-hitting soldiers. Their appearance was more than threatening, and as Joel reached into his pocket and found nothing, each proudly displayed its gaping black hole while shouting out more lies and screams. As the verbal attacked heightened, Joel crashed onto the forest floor.

CHAPTER 30

AUGUSTINE SAT ON the porch while Sebastian, Joel, and Corwin all lay sleeping inside. The sun was going down, and the beauty of the sunset brought some comfort to her.

There has to be another way. She sighed. *But how can I find out?* The question had bothered her since the night before when Corwin had explained where he thought her rhydid was. She wondered how he could be sure of the object's location. *After all, Corwin found his information in some old books in Differe.* Though she knew very little about rhydids, Augustine felt a deeper urgency and much greater pressure to set out for one following Sebastian's episode from a few hours before.

"I can't go all the way back to Differe," she sighed. She stood up from her chair with an idea. "But I can find some old books!"

She ran all the way to Mr. Rutherford's shop. By the time she arrived, Augustine had run out of steam and she bent down to gasp for air. Because the temperature had dropped so dramatically over the last several days in Old Waiz, Augustine saw each puff of air that she expelled from her lungs. She rang the bell, rubbing her hands together between each tug to keep them warm. She waited, and when there was no answer after a few rings, she peered through the windows.

The light's on. You can't ignore me today. She rang the bell more vigorously.

She soon saw a startled Mr. Rutherford jump up from his counting chair and head for the door. She quit ringing the bell when she saw Mr. Rutherford eye her from the window. She thought it best to wave and smile in hopes that the friendly gesture would ensure that he would open the door to her. Augustine felt relieved when he finally unlocked the door and asked her to come in.

"Miss Augustine, I thought you'd made your way to New Waiz," the man said as he beckoned her to come inside, and she noted the obvious disdain in his voice when he uttered the new city's name.

"Ah, but I'm glad to see you," he said as he gingerly squeezed her hands then added, "Missed these little hands." He smiled and nodded toward the piano.

"New Waiz didn't suit us." She shook her head at him. "I'm glad to see you, also. I have missed playing," she said.

"How's Sebastian these days?" Mr. Rutherford inquired.

"Oh, he's fine," she lied.

They both paused, causing an awkward moment of silence to pass between them.

"Uh, did you come to play the piano, dear?" he asked as he moved back toward the counter.

Augustine shook her head and then panicked inside. She had not thought of how to go about asking Mr. Rutherford for what she needed.

"Well, I'm just back in town, and I know it's late, but I wanted to see you."

The man smiled at her but she knew he was no fool. He instantly raised his eyebrows at her in curiosity.

"I was hoping I could look around for a moment," Augustine managed to squeak out, while dodging his scrutinizing gaze.

"Anything I can help you with?" he asked.

Come on, be brave. Be brave for Sebastian, she told herself. "Well, actually, yes, I do need something. I was wondering if you had heard of it or had any books on the object. I think it's quite old."

"You came to the right place, then. I have lots of books on 'old somethings.' Here," he said, as he led her to a chest of books. "Look, here are some of the books of old. They used to be in the schools, but New Waiz, well ..." His voice trailed off as he flipped through the pages. "Oh, and here's some ancient maps of Old Waiz. Look here, sketches of the sacred stones. Have I ever shown you mine?"

She shook her head. "Sacred stone?" Augustine was puzzled as she looked upon a drab piece of blue gravel that hung around the man's neck.

"The museum had some, remember? Corwin has not told you about our sacred stones?" the man asked in surprise.

I think he's failed to mention quite a few things, but she only answered, "No, sir."

"Oh well, it's all history. This is just a piece of history now," he sighed sadly as he tucked the rock back under his shirt.

"Yet, you seem to hold it with hope," she observed.

"See anything you're looking for, dear?" he asked, obviously wanting to change the subject.

"These are wonderful. I'm an avid reader," she stated as she quickly picked up one of the books to thumb through. *Be in here. Be in one of these,* she pleaded silently as she flipped through the pages. "Do you mind if I look through these a moment?"

"Of course not, I'll be over here counting," he said as he walked away. "Usually don't work late on Mondays, but I'm missing my help," he called behind him.

"Joel?" she questioned, as she frantically searched the pages. Her anxiety and stress mounted as she quickly flipped past each page. Her hands began to tremble under the pressure she was feeling.

"Have you seen him lately?" Mr. Rutherford asked in response to her question.

"Yes," she said absentmindedly and then quickly corrected herself. "I mean, no. Not really since Corwin returned."

"I would very much like to know if he's all right," he called out in genuine concern.

Augustine shrugged, now too engrossed in her search to answer.

"Augustine? Do you know if he is all right?"

"Ah! There it is! Here," she almost yelled from excitement but caught herself. "I mean, wow, would you tell me about this, Mr. Rutherford?" she asked, as she made her way to the counter.

He straightened his red glasses and walked around the counter again. He squinted at the page then said, "Oh, yes. That's a rhydid." He took the book from her for closer examination.

"Yes, a rhydid, I've heard of it," Augustine said in feigned innocence.

"Have you, now?" he replied while not taking his eyes off the book.

"Oh, I would love to get one to take to Sebastian. I'm sure he would be fascinated by it. Don't you think?" she gushed at the bald headed man.

She jumped when he snapped the book shut and took a step nearer to her.

He narrowed his eyes and asked in a low voice, "Is this what you came to find, Miss Augustine?"

"No, sir, I—I wasn't looking for anything in particular," Augustine stammered in fear, as she stepped back from him.

He soon had her backed into a corner and feeling terribly afraid.

"Thank you for letting me look at your books. Now I really should be going. Can you show me out?" She added, "Please?" when he did not budge at her request.

She tried to move past him but he caught her shoulders.

"Who sent you? Who are you working for?" he asked suspiciously. He continued to interrogate her.

His voice rose with each question until tears came to her eyes and she was shouting back in his face, "No one, sir! Please! I'm with no one! I'm with Corwin, my uncle, Uncle Corwin!"

It was at this statement that the man finally appeared to be pulled out of his dark demeanor. He silenced himself and let her go of her shoulders. He sighed as he backed away and wiped his forehead.

"I'm sorry, Miss Augustine. Outsiders are not trusted around here, especially when seeking out old things. The Old Order also suffered an enormous loss at the last meeting, as you may well know. I fear I'm overly suspicious. Forgive me."

"I—I don't want anything. I need to go," she stammered, as she tried to rush past him.

"I'm so sorry, dear. Here, take the book," he pleaded, pressing it into her hands.

She could tell by his pained face that he was truly sorry.

"So many want to use the old things for new practices," he mused. "See if you can come up with some good ideas." He smiled.

She was almost to the door when he called back out to her, "Augustine, wait. I have something important to give you."

She stopped and watched him pull a letter from under the counter.

"This is addressed to Joel," he said hesitantly. "Corwin will want to see this. Tell them an official came looking for Joel. I told the fellow he had worked in my shop."

Corwin was waiting for Augustine on the front porch when she arrived back at his house. She looked up at the stars and grimaced before she reached the stepping stones that led to Corwin's porch. Though she hung her head in shame as she trudged up the porch stairs, she still managed to see Corwin's pipe dangling from his mouth as he walked over to her.

"You are a brash child," he said in a frustrated tone.

"I'm, sorry," her voice faltered in response to his reproof. She felt his strong arms reach around her just as her tears began to fall again.

"There, there. I know why you went," Corwin said as he patted her hair compassionately.

She buried her head further into his embrace, and both were quickly reminded that their last embrace had also taken place on a front porch.

Corwin cleared his throat and instructed, "But you must learn to trust me, even when I don't tell you everything."

"Blind trust," she cried, her voice muffled by the fabric of Corwin's shirt.

"Yes, but the source is good. I'm always after your good," he said.

She sighed. "I want to believe that."

"Well, that's a start. How was Mr. Rutherford?"

"Very suspicious. He gave me this book. It has some information on rhydids."

Corwin nodded as he rested his chin on the top of her head. "You can read it on the train. Now, do you understand what you must do?" he asked in a serious tone.

"Yes. Did you convince him to go?" she murmured.

"I would like for you to ask him," he replied.

She jerked her head upward from underneath his chin. "No."

He nodded back towards her. "Yes. This will be your first opportunity to show kindness to him. Until it becomes natural for you." He smiled.

"Ugh," she muttered. "Oh, I have a letter Mr. Rutherford gave me before I left. It's addressed to Joel."

"Interesting. I will let you give that to him, also," Corwin said, as he pressed the letter back into her hands.

"Let's get this over with," she grumbled. She made a move to go inside, but Corwin quickly caught her arm.

"Let's stay here a while. He is thinking, and I have secrets you'll need to know for your journey."

She brightened for the first time in days, and he could not help but smile widely back at her.

"Yes, only you and I will know them. Joel will need your help when the mouthpieces come. You'll be his secret weapon."

A while later, Augustine entered the house without Corwin and walked softly over toward the couch where Joel sat.

"Hello," she said, as she sat down in Corwin's enormous recliner.

"Hello," he answered, his voice devoid of emotion.

"How are you feeling?" she asked softly.

"Fine ... considering."

Augustine flashed him a tentative smile. "Yes, you've had quite an eventful past few days."

Joel nodded and then both were met with the deafening sound of awkward silence.

"Thank you for trying to get the alabaster," Augustine said hastily in order to break the silence.

Joel looked away from her. She bit her lip and chided herself for saying the wrong thing.

"At least you tried," she said as she attempted to console him.

Joel met her face with a silent glare then looked away again.

"Have you seen him yet?" she asked gently.

He shook his head.

"Well, you should. He's always anxious to spend time with you. Makes me jealous sometimes," she admitted.

Joel turned back toward her and looked into her blue eyes. "What do you want? Quit dancing around whatever it is you're wanting to say."

She drew back a little, startled at his directness, then made her request. "All right, I want you to take me to the Temple of Differe to get my rhydid."

Joel sighed sharply in obvious irritation.

"I can't do it without you. I—as much as it pains me to say it, I need you." Augustine couldn't help thinking, this is a new low for me. Pleading with him feels worse than begging for Sebastian's medicines at the hospital.

Joel shook his head at her in continued frustration.

"Please. Please, Joel. I know you may not want to do it for me, but please do it for Sebastian."

He put up his hand to stop her. "Augustine, it's not that—" He stopped and closed his eyes. He ran his fingers through his flaming hair and groaned as he opened them. "I'm not sure you can do it with me. I'm not really qualified."

"Corwin isn't qualified to be a parent, but he took us, anyway," she reminded him.

Joel frowned. "Have you seen what's happened to me lately? In the past few days I've passed out three times, been mugged, um, 'pecked at,' I guess you would say. I'm not exactly scoring a great track record."

"Yes, but you're not scoring zero, either. You escaped from the temple, helped us find Corwin, got a job, you learned to milk goats and make cheese, for crying out loud. You beat up an official of the Order. Get that sword, and you'll conquer the rest of it," she urged.

Joel rolled his eyes at her speech. "We don't even know what the swords do."

"The king told you to get one. Isn't that enough? Corwin believes in you, so I believe in you."

Augustine's eyes let him know what she said was true, but it didn't seem to matter. Joel had not been able to muster even an ounce of belief in himself after what had happened when he went to look for alabaster.

"Besides, at this point you need a weapon. You know you're hunted here."

He returned her admonishment with a baffled stare.

"Joel, I went to Mr. Rutherford's shop to find out if there was another way to get my rhydid. Quit giving me that look. I already got it from Corwin," she continued. "Listen, he said an official came looking for you. He told them you had worked for him, and the official left you this letter."

She held it out to him, and he immediately noted the emblem on the back.

"Templins," he muttered under his breath as he ripped open the letter.

The letter's contents surprised and dismayed him. He sat back in disbelief as Corwin entered the room.

"Joel, do you mind if I see the letter?" he inquired.

"I don't know," was the shaky reply.

All three jumped at hearing a few small coughs from upstairs.

"Augustine, tend to Sebastian, please," Corwin instructed, nodding at her.

When the two were left alone, Joel spoke first. "I have to go back," he announced.

"Change of heart?" Corwin questioned.

"My friend's in danger," Joel replied seriously.

Corwin cleared his throat. "Joel, I don't even have to look at the letter to know it's bait."

Joel looked at him in shock. "What?"

"They," Corwin pointed to the emblem, "are trying to get you back."

"Great. So I just concede and fall right into their trap?" Joel asked, furious.

"No," Corwin soothed him. "You go on with your plan, but you cannot take their bait." There was a long pause between them. "You must promise me, Joel. Listen," he lowered his voice. "Sebastian will die without this help. You go in as we discussed, get your rhydids, and that's it."

Joel sat there with the letter in his hand remembering how cold Isabelle had been at their last meeting. He knew in his mind Corwin was right, but his heart could not help but hope for one fleeting moment that the sentiments expressed in the letter were true.

"Right. It's bait," Joel said. "I promise, Corwin. I will keep my word."

"I believe you will. You must know the fact that there is bait makes this journey all the more dangerous. They'll be expecting you, waiting for you," Corwin informed him.

Joel nodded. "I'm hunted here for murder and there for rebellion or maybe insanity," he said, trying to sound as if he were joking.

"You're a wanted man," Corwin agreed.

"I prefer to use the word 'popular.'"

Corwin shook his head. "Your sense of humor is amazing in these circumstances, Joel. It will always be of help to you. Now let's get down to it. You can get back in, I'm sure of that, but there's something important that you need to know. The Templin spies and New Order spies are everywhere at this point, but, so are the others like me. If you need help, it, or rather the person, will find you."

"How will I know to trust them?" Joel asked, searching his friend's face.

"How did you know to trust me?"

Joel thought for a moment. "You had my ticket."

"That's right. I had what you needed. By the way, how were you able to read that letter just now?" Corwin asked.

Joel just smiled at him.

The three decided it would be best to follow Joel's previous escape plans, just in reverse, which would mean going into the temple grounds at night. This would require Joel and Augustine to take the earliest train out of Waiz to ensure they would arrive on the outskirts of Differe by dusk. If they could, the plan was to move the night they arrived, but, just in case, Corwin suggested the group meet back at his mountain house in no later than five days. If his place, for some reason, seemed unsafe, they would meet back at the cave.

Augustine and Joel packed very little. They took only his knapsack and a backpack, filling them with food and water, as well as extra hats, gloves, and socks. Corwin searched his closets and found warm coats and clothes for them to wear for the journey. "Joel, look at you. You've put on enough weight to fill out the coat I wore at your age," Corwin stated in delighted surprise. Corwin also already had two train tickets to Differe that he had purchased on his way back to Waiz. He gave Joel a wad of money and instructed that the two would have to purchase their own return tickets.

By the time they had finished preparing for their journey, only a few hours of night were left before they had to leave, yet both were restless and unable to sleep. Augustine was just about to tiptoe into Sebastian's room to kiss him goodbye when she heard a voice outside his door.

"Sebastian," Joel whispered while slightly shaking the little boy. "You awake?"

Sebastian moaned in response.

"How are you feeling?"

"Sleepy," Sebastian yawned.

"Listen, I'm going away for a few days, and Augustine is coming with me. I wish you could go with us," Joel said, then stopped to think of what he should tell his little friend. "I met the king, Sebastian. He is real.... I'm going to get something that will help you," he concluded, though he felt unsure how much he could promise.

When the little boy did not move, Joel figured he had already fallen back asleep. "I don't want to go, but you must've heard that I wasn't able to get you the alabaster when you needed it. As much as I don't want to go, I think of that moment, and ... well, I never want that to happen again. So I just wanted you to know that we're leaving, but we'll be back in a few days."

Just as Joel was about to stand up, he felt Sebastian's little arms wrap around his neck. Neither spoke during the embrace, and Joel let the little boy hold onto him for as long as he wanted. Joel realized he had almost forgotten what a hug felt like.

Finally Sebastian let go and said, "Take care of her."

"I will."

As he lay back down and pulled the covers up again he whispered, "Promise you'll come back for me."

"I promise."

The train headed to Differe was surprisingly full of passengers, forcing Joel and Augustine into a compartment with an older couple. They had no privacy to carry out their plans of going over the temple map and talking through ideas. Augustine had also wanted to look through Mr. Rutherford's book.

"Since it's just 3:30 in the morning, would you mind if we turn out the light and pull the shade?" the older woman across from them asked.

Both Joel and Augustine nodded respectfully. Each of them fell fast asleep in no time.

A few hours later, a bright light dancing back and forth over Joel's eyes woke him up. The shade was bouncing off the window, causing the early morning rays to splash into his eyes. The ride was bumpy, and, to his amazement, he saw that the clock already said ten o'clock in the morning. He also noticed their neighbors were gone. When he looked down he saw a mass of dark curls under his chin.

Augustine must have slumped over. He felt her head lying on his chest. He knew she would be mortified to find herself in this position, yet he was unsure of what to do. Her heavy breathing indicated she was still in deep sleep. He gingerly propped up her body with one hand and swiftly moved out from underneath her. He grabbed a blanket from overhead and stuffed it into the corner of the seat. With both hands he gently laid her down, being careful to position her head on the blanket. He sat back across from her and peeked at the landscape outside.

Sunny day. He turned back to look at her. *She's sleeping like a baby.*

He had never known another girl like her. He had observed at the barn and at Corwin's place that getting ready took them both about the same amount of time. He wondered if taking care of Sebastian had caused her to have to learn to get ready in a hurry or if she simply did not care for all the "fussing" other girls did in front of the mirror. *Doesn't really matter, though, she's still a knockout*, he thought, all the while reminding himself that he still loathed her in many other ways.

The next big bump woke Augustine up, and Joel grinned at her surprised face.

"Enjoying some rest?" he called out to her.

"Where's the older couple?"

Joel shrugged his shoulders in reply as he watched her stretch.

"Ten o'clock. Wow," she said as she rubbed her eyes. "Guess we missed breakfast."

"Lunch will come around in an hour," Joel said.

Augustine nodded toward him while tugging her small pink bag out of her backpack. Joel watched her pull a small toothbrush out of the bag.

"I'll be back," she said as she snapped the bag shut.

"I'll be here," Joel said with a touch of irony as he pulled up the shade.

She opened the compartment door, then turned back toward him. "Thank you for the pillow ... and thank you for coming," she blurted out through gritted teeth.

Joel chuckled at her behavior, but only after she was out the door. "Corwin must have told her to play nice," he said. He smiled at the seat across from him and thought of her sleeping again.

She's like one of those white bears. All peaceful and tame when asleep, but watch out when she wakes up.

His smile quickly faded when he realized something he had forgotten about. Something he had not had to encounter during his escape. *Oh no, Big Sasha.*

CHAPTER 31

EUNICE, RAINER, AND Isabelle, please gather up the assignments from your rows and bring them forward."

As Isabelle turned hers in, Sarah slipped her a torn sliver from a piece of paper with the words, "Meet me at lunch," scratched onto it.

Isabelle promptly arrived at the music room at twelve noon and awaited Sarah's instructions. When she entered, Isabelle spoke hastily. "I'll need an assignment or reason for seeing you. Holt's right outside the door."

Sarah nodded and lowered her voice. "Listen carefully. You must leave tonight."

Isabelle's eyes widened in surprise.

"They've found Joel, or are at least sure that the letter was delivered."

"How do you know?" Isabelle asked, as feelings of deep remorse and guilt washed over her at the mention of the letter.

"The headmaster always takes the opportunity to boast, even if the information is confidential. He simply cannot help himself," she replied, with irritation in her voice. "Can you gather what you need this afternoon, dear?"

Isabelle bit her lip, then answered, "Yes, I think so."

"All right, just as we talked about, here's the school map. I will leave the gate open for you. Isabelle, you must leave through Moonstruck to ensure you get your file and the rest of the maps. Do not leave without it," Sarah stated urgently.

"Joel," Isabelle started.

"Forgot his in his great haste," Sarah interrupted her. "It would look too suspicious for me to be near Moonstruck tonight, so I cannot meet you. Unless I come to find you, the gate will be open," she instructed.

Isabelle trembled and shot her a bewildered look.

Sarah firmly grasped her shoulders. "You can do this. Love conquers all."

"That's a temple truth, Sarah." Isabelle rolled her eyes at her.

"Putting truth into practice is what makes it powerful, Isabelle. Here's your opportunity to move beyond just having mere knowledge of truth. Again, do not forget your file. Oh, and here," she smiled as she pushed something into her hands. "This is your new solo to learn for Sunday chapel next week."

Isabelle nodded. She looked down and smoothed her robes. "Sarah, I—"

The woman caught the blonde's fidgeting hand and embraced her. "I'll miss you, too."

Isabelle laid her head on Sarah's shoulder and whispered, "Thank you. Thank you for not giving up on me."

Sarah responded by giving her a tight squeeze.

"And thank you for sacrificing so much for me. I will find him, Sarah. I'll make sure he stays safe."

Sarah patted her face and pushed her away. "They'll miss you at lunch. Go."

Holt seemed surprised when a beaming Isabelle ran up to the column he was leaning against.

"Look at this! A solo for Sunday chapel. The headmaster is giving me another chance! It's beautiful," she gushed as she looked over the music.

Her smile faded a little when he said nothing in response. "I know you don't care, but," she paused and shrugged her shoulders, "I have no one else to tell."

"No, that's great. I'm glad you have something to keep you busy," he said halfheartedly.

"Thanks. I may skip my last class to start practicing." *And so I can pack.* "Well, my desk in the kitchen is waiting for me."

Sarah smiled as she watched Isabelle and Holt make their way to the cafeteria. *Good girl, that was quite convincing.*

At first Augustine and Joel did not have much to say to one another, which made the rest of the morning pass by slowly. When Joel would try to ask her a more personal question, such as, "How did you get the name 'Augustine'?" she would reply with, "How did you get the name 'Joel'?"

Small talk was hardly either one of their strong suits. Neither one cared much for it, so by the afternoon most of their conversation consisted of the plan, the layout of the temple, and so on. This leg of the trip actually went faster than both would have liked, with each feeling their nervousness build with each stop and start of the train. So, when Joel finally said, "This is our stop," Augustine practically jumped to her feet.

"Wait, where is this?" she cried, as she looked out the window.

"We're not going to Crossroads," Joel said calmly. "This is the outskirts of Differe. It'll be much easier to access the temple woods and gardens from here."

"How are there gardens in the freezing cold?" Augustine asked, as she strapped on her backpack.

"Uh, there's not. They're just called that, I guess." Joel shrugged as he patted his knapsack and looked around the compartment to make sure they were not forgetting anything.

The two walked onto a small outdoor platform, which appeared to be the only object in the heavily wooded area. Augustine noticed a clearing in the trees following the snowy embankment in front of them.

"This is in the middle of nowhere," she said, while pulling her hat over her ears.

"Yep—works well in our favor. Come up here," he said as he turned to climb the hillside. "There's a road we need to find."

The snowy powder was several feet deep, and after Joel was halfway up the side he glanced behind to see how Augustine was fairing. She was wading through the snow with tremendous effort, but when he stopped to help her she motioned that she was fine.

"I've done this before. Just been a while."

Eventually the two trudged their way to the top and headed down a long, neglected, icy road.

"We're going to get off this road right down there," Joel said as he pointed to a bend in the road.

"All right. Then what?" Augustine asked, wondering if they should be nervous about walking so openly near the temple grounds.

"Well, we got here earlier than I planned, so we'll have to hide out for a while," Joel sniffed. He cupped his hands around his nose and chin in order to give his face a blast of warm air.

"Right. Well, will we wait in that underground place? The one we're going to in order to reach the grounds?" Augustine asked breathlessly as she marched down the road behind him.

Joel couldn't help but notice how hard he was breathing, also, and figured having to wait might prove to be an advantage, giving their bodies time to acclimate to the altitude and colder temperature.

"Uh, no, we can't hide there. It's too close to the temple. We'll have to hide farther away than that, but I know a place. It's a cave, close to the lake. You'll be able to see where we're going tonight."

"A cave!" Augustine shot back.

Don't start this, Augie. "Okay," he stopped and looked off the road. "All right, time to go into the woods."

Joel carefully led Augustine into the still, quiet woods. The deeper they went, the more shaded their path became. The shade provided by the lofty, snow-laden trees also, unfortunately, brought on much colder temperatures. After a few minutes Joel heard Augustine's teeth begin to chatter.

"Augustine, you okay? Need a break?" he asked, as he turned around.

She did not meet his eyes, but quickly shook her head no, so the two pressed onward in silence.

With each step Joel tried to remain focused, keeping Sebastian fixed in his mind, seeing the writing and image on the caychura ceiling and remembering Corwin's words of affirmation and instruction. *I can't afford to let any negative thoughts come between my ears,* he told himself, as he blinked and saw Sebastian's face.

After several hours of trekking through the snow with hardly a word to each other, Joel felt silly when he turned back to Augustine and held a finger to his lips. He then motioned for her to stop following him and wait. When she nodded that she understood, he gave her his knapsack and cautiously moved toward a high incline of boulders.

When Joel was sure it was safe for both of them to climb up the rocks and go into the cave unseen, he motioned her over to himself. Once both were in the narrow cave, they decided to stay near the opening for light. Joel gave Augustine her water and both immediately plopped down on walls that faced each other to quench their thirst for a few minutes.

"Are you doing okay?" he asked when she gave him back the water.

"You don't have to keep asking. If I'm not, I'll let you know," she said matter-of-factly.

Joel knew she was right, but felt annoyed at her response, just the same. *She has no problem making her needs known. That's for sure.*

"Sorry, I know you're just trying to be courteous," Augustine said, sounding remorseful.

"Nah," Joel said, and Augustine jerked her head up at him. "I was just trying to be *nice*."

She smiled at his poking fun at her choice of words then looked toward the frozen lake outside.

"What is this place?" she asked.

Joel grabbed the school map from the knapsack. "Well, right above you is the main road to the temple. This is the hot spot on the road," Joel nodded above them. "All the new students stop here their first day. It has the best view," Joel said, as he pointed out over the lake and toward the chapel.

Augustine moved toward the mouth of the cave and gasped when she stood up. "I can't believe it—the temple chapel."

"Um-hm," was Joel's unimpressed reply as he spread out the map.

"I've never seen anything like it. Magnificent," Augustine said dreamily as she looked on with awe. "I have lived in Differe all my life and never seen anything like it," she marveled again. "Joel, how long will we be on the temple grounds?"

"Only long enough to get our rhydids," Joel replied.

"Do we have to stay in this cave until tonight?" she asked in a tone that clearly conveyed her displeasure at the idea.

He looked up at her and said, "At least until dusk."

"We can't go sooner? Just hide and wait until dark?"

"We've been over this, Augie. We're sticking to the plan and going in tonight," Joel said directly.

"Well, I'm just asking. Just because your way worked the first time doesn't mean it's the *only* way," she argued.

Seriously? He breathed a sigh of exasperation.

"It's going to be well below freezing by tonight," she said as she wrapped her arms around herself.

"Augustine, we can't go until tonight," he repeated, though he understood that the temperature was a valid concern.

"Why?"

Her attitude was forcing his patience level to new heights, but he tried to remain calm and remember her feelings, as Corwin had instructed.

Very hard to do. "Augustine, there are a lot of stupid things here. A lot of things are backwards. The minute we step onto the temple grounds, the Templins will be alerted that we're there."

She sat down and looked over his face.

"In truth," he paused and gritted his teeth, "They will know that you're there or, at least I think they will."

"Me?" she pointed to herself, still obviously confused.

Joel nodded, not sure what to say next.

"Because I'm an outsider? But I'm from Differe," she replied defensively.

"Uh, yeah, I know. The alarm is not for outsiders, exactly." He sighed. "It goes off when anyone who was not accepted to the temple steps onto the grounds." The silence that followed in the next few moments was deafening. "Augustine?"

"Yes, yes, I understand," she said, as she rose and moved toward the mouth of the cave again.

His eyes followed her, and he noted it was snowing again. For the first time, he felt truly compassionate toward the girl. He had seen her take care of her invalid brother for weeks now, but had never felt any sympathy toward her for having to endure such a weighty task.

Was she ever just a kid? He wondered if she, like so many others, had to grow up entirely too fast. Joel knew rejection was a horrible tool of the voices, or "the mouthpieces," as he would now call them. Perhaps the tough, independent exterior she displayed was a protective mechanism. He had always figured it was a façade. She had been rejected by the temple, and he had deduced by Corwin's picture and her lack of mentioning her parents that there was something wrong with her family dynamics. *Where were her parents? Why did she barely seem to know her Uncle Corwin? Why did she look nothing like her brother?*

He looked back down toward the map and remembered having to encounter his own fair share of rejection in this place.

"If not dealt with properly, rejection becomes a breeding ground for distrust and suspicion." He heard Sarah's voice in his head.

He would love to see her, but remembered his word to Corwin. *In and out,* he reminded himself as he gazed at the back of Augustine's silhouette. *Maybe I just figured out why her rhydid is here.* Why did retrieving these swords require them to face their painful pasts, Joel wondered, then began marking places on the map again.

"Joel. Joel!" Augustine whispered urgently at him. He rose quickly to see what was the matter.

"What," he whispered.

She pointed to the center of the lake.

"Oh, you've found the headmaster's pride and joy, Sasha. That's why we were very quiet before we came up here."

Augustine was mesmerized as the large white beast ran and slid over the icy lake.

"She's his precious pet and helps guard the grounds. Apparently she has a pretty keen sense of smell. She's a special type of white bear, a hybrid."

Augustine squealed in dismay. "A hybrid? The hybrids are supposed to be the most ferocious! I thought they had died out."

"*Almost* died out," he corrected her.

"She is beautiful," Augustine said, as Sasha's white fur shimmered against the setting sun's rays. The playful beast even seemed to have a smile on her face as she pranced in the snow. "Watching her from here makes her seem harmless," Augustine mused.

"Yeah, and so does that." Joel pointed in the direction of the chapel. The light was beginning to fade behind the chapel, making the structure appear even more glorious.

"We'll go inside there?" she asked softly.

"That's where the rhydids are," Joel answered.

She laughed sadly. "Typical storybook feature—weapons in the most beautiful place in the world, almost dreamlike."

"Uh, yeah, or nightmare," Joel added quickly. "Come here. I need you to go over the route with me."

"Why are you asking me? I don't know anything about this place." Augustine shrugged, barely able to pull her eyes away from the chapel.

"I want you to know how to get in and how to get out," Joel told her, while also hoping she would read some of the words on the map for him.

"Joel, we're leaving together," she replied firmly.

Dusk fell rapidly within the next few hours. Joel felt comfortable enough to move out an hour after he had observed Sasha venturing toward the headmaster's residence.

"She's probably feeding. The headmaster has his own house across the lake," he told Augustine as he pointed to the far left. "So, we should be safe. Either way though, no talking."

Augustine nodded in understanding, and he could see the anxiety on her face.

The two easily climbed down the boulders and hiked to the edge of the tree line that surrounded the lake. The fierce wind and falling snow nearly blinded them as they walked along the edge of the frozen lake. After fifteen minutes, Joel could barely feel his feet or see his hand in front his face. He turned to his right. If they went further into the woods, he was afraid their vision would become even more obstructed. When he turned to his left he noticed that the air on the lake was much clearer than what they were facing on the edge of the woods. The moon was rising and darkness was swiftly descending upon them.

I don't think we can be seen. He was not able to make out any landmarks on the other side of the lake. He threw his hand over his head in the direction of the lake to show Augustine he intended to trudge that way.

The two had marched and slid across the lake for half an hour before Joel felt a tug on his sleeve. He looked back at Augustine, whose face was red and chapped from the cold. She motioned to him that she needed a drink. He pulled out the water bottle and grimaced when he realized it was frozen solid. He shook his head at the bottle, and she waved her hand to gesture she was okay.

Joel was putting the bottle back in the knapsack when all of a sudden Augustine jerked his arm and started shaking it. He searched her fear-filled eyes and knew something was wrong. Joel looked over her head, and to his horror, saw Sasha bolting across the lake.

Maybe she doesn't see us, he hoped.

"She's moving faster! Oh! She sees us! Joel, what do we do?" Augustine shrieked as Sasha headed toward them.

Run, his head told him. "Run! Augustine, run! Don't look back!"

He watched her take off across the ice toward center of the lake, and his head screamed at him, *this is stupid! You can't outrun this thing.*

Joel started picking up icy blocks and throwing them behind him at the white beast.

"All right, King, Corwin said I could talk to you. Sorry, can't really talk now, but I need a little help," he gasped as he raced across the ice, stopping every time he found an icy chunk of ammunition.

To his great dismay he soon watched Augustine slip and fall spread eagle across the ice in front of him. He whispered firmly to himself, "Get up, Augie. Come on, get up."

He then moved closer to the shoreline in hopes of keeping Sasha as far away from Augustine as possible. Once she scrambled to her feet again, she looked around for him. When she found him, Joel motioned for her to keep running.

Augustine shook her head. "Wait, Joel, look!" she shouted as she pointed toward the tree line behind him.

Joel turned just in time to see the white ball of fur dodge off the ice into the woods. Joel dropped the block of ice in his hand. *Why would she stop?* As his icy chunk hit the lake's surface he heard a loud crack. "Oh, no," he whispered, as he looked around them in terror.

"Augustine, don't move!" he yelled at her, but it was too late.

He heard the ice cracking all around them as he moved closer to the shoreline. By the time he reached its edge, Augustine had plunged under the lake's icy surface. The moon hanging over the chapel lit the lake just enough for Joel to be able to see several holes forming in the ice.

"Augustine!" he yelled as he anxiously searched for movement among the holes. "Augie! Splash, so I can hear you!" he called out to her.

He heard a scream and a splash from the nearest opening in the ice. Joel immediately slid down onto his chest and carefully moved across the ice, asking the king for help once again.

"I'm right here! Just reach out and grab my hands," he commanded Augustine as she thrashed in the freezing water.

After a few attempts, Joel had Augustine's arms and pulled her out of the water. He dragged her cautiously across the ice to safety. He was panting furiously by the time he pulled her into his arms.

"Augustine, Augustine, can you hear me? Are you okay?"

Though she nodded, Joel could feel her whole body convulsing in reaction to the cold shock.

"You're going to be okay," he said breathlessly yet confidently in her face. "I'm going to carry you. Just stay with me, okay? Stay conscious."

Joel ripped off her backpack and threw it over his shoulder. He wondered what he should do as he stood up with his wet companion in his arms. The beast was smart, as she had put them in both the wrong direction and in danger.

As Joel glanced around himself in frustration, his eyes caught something in the distance. There was a light up ahead, and though it was in the opposite direction of where they needed to go, he discerned it did not appear to be a trap and started moving toward it. His heart raced as he ran with Augustine bouncing up and down in his arms. Though she was shaking violently and rolling her eyes beneath him, hope rose in his spirit as he neared the light. He was relieved when he reached the edge of the woods on the opposite side of the lake. He was just about to cross into the woods when suddenly Sasha dashed right onto his path.

"Sasha, move. My friend needs help," he said half pleading and half commanding.

The large creature growled at him, digging her razor sharp claws into the snow as she disregarded his request and continued to block him from the light.

This is it. We're going to be eaten alive, he thought, as he stood there defenseless with Augustine lying limp in his arms. *Move toward the light.*

In a desperate attempt to follow his instinct, he tried to move past Sasha and she in turn lunged at him. Joel closed his eyes and braced himself for the blow.

When nothing happened, he opened his eyes and saw a cloaked figure standing between him and the beast. He watched in awe as the person held a blazing golden rhydid up in his defense. Sasha paced before them, obviously unsure of what to do.

He heard the voice from beneath the cloak say, "You saw the light from my house up ahead. Go, and I will meet you there."

Though Joel was alarmed upon seeing a cloak; he did not think it looked official. But the rhydid was more than enough proof for him that this figure was a friend and not foe. He hurried to obey as he realized Augustine had quit moving. He was able to see the light again when he crossed into the woods carrying Augustine and past Sasha. The closer he got to the light, the weaker he became.

Just before approaching the property where the house stood, Joel felt his insides quake. He froze as he felt their presence descend upon him. They were here—the mouthpieces. Eerie whispers began drifting out into the cool air around them.

"Augustine, oh, no. Augustine, they're here!" he cried, not even knowing if she could hear him anymore.

Thankfully, she could. She moved her lips close to his ear and did exactly as Corwin had instructed.

CHAPTER 32

A S THE MOUTHPIECES locked Joel in his tracks, he began to
hear Augustine whispering into his ear. He could not make out
what she was saying, but whatever it was distracted his mind from the
mouthpieces, and he felt himself step forward. By the time he was to
the door, she was nearly shouting in his ear.

"It's okay. They're gone," he cried in both bewilderment and triumph
as he slammed the door behind him.

She smiled up at him. "Good," she said, just before he watched her
eyes roll into the back of her head.

"No, Augustine. Augustine."

He searched around the cabin for a bathtub and quickly made for
one he saw at the top of the stairs. He laid Augustine's limp body in
the tub and turned on the water. He hastily removed her hat, gloves
and boots as the tub began to fill. After he removed her coat, he felt a
tap on his shoulder.

An older woman nodded at him. "I can take it from here. You need
to warm up yourself. There's a shower downstairs with a clean robe
inside. You can hang your wet clothes by the fire."

Joel instantly recognized the woman's voice as being the one from under the cloak. He hesitated as he looked back down at Augustine.

"She needs you to take care of yourself," the woman said, as she hoisted the leather holster around her waist that securely held her rhydid.

Joel nodded as he rose to leave.

An hour later, Joel sat cross-legged on an oversized bear rug in front of one of the largest fireplaces he had ever seen. Once he was assured that Augustine was going to be fine, he ate a bowl of hot soup and talked with the old woman. She referred to herself as "the housekeeper." She explained that there were several old properties surrounding the school and she was in charge of their upkeep. Then suddenly she stopped.

"I will not be asking, nor answering, any more questions. When I put this fire out, it will be time for you to go. Sasha should reside at the headmaster's for the rest of the night. Do you understand?" she asked, looking closely at his face.

"Yes, ma'am," Joel replied respectfully and added, "And thank you for your help."

Though he wanted to ask her a thousand questions, such as, "Where were you when I was escaping?" he realized that the longer they stayed with her the more danger they would put the woman in.

She nodded and headed back to the kitchen.

The house was nothing more than a small, sparse cabin built from heavy logs. In fact, the rug was the only object to sit upon in the den. In the downstairs there was the tiny bathroom where Joel had showered, a kitchen, and the den where he was sitting. The kitchen area held a sink, tiny stove, and one cabinet. Joel assumed there was probably a bedroom in addition to the bathroom upstairs as he glanced at the ceiling above him.

He was drinking a steaming cup of hot chocolate and once again looking over the map when he heard a familiar person clear her throat. Augustine sat quietly on the floor in front of him, and he glanced up to see that her hair was just starting to dry.

"Well, I'm not going to ask if you're okay," Joel said, just before he looked back down at the map.

"Fair enough," she said and took a delicate sip from her hot mug. "Joel?" She rarely said his name in such a soft tone.

He cocked his head up at her. "Yeah?"

"Thank you for saving my life."

Joel was completely caught off guard. He sputtered out, "Sure."

He watched her lie down on her side and prop her head up with her hand.

"Can I help?" Augustine inquired.

Joel shook his head. "Nah, we're leaving together, remember?"

She nodded her head in earnest, yet still peered over the map as she lay across from him.

I guess I did save her life. This act had apparently changed her demeanor toward him. He could feel it, so he finally could not resist asking her something.

"Augie?" he said gently.

She glanced up at him, her face still reddened by the bitter cold.

"Why is your sword at the temple?"

He watched her shoulders droop in defeat; he could tell she was too tired to put up her guard any more.

"I wasn't chosen to go to the temple. I'll have to live the rest of my life knowing I'm—I'm uneducated and ill bred. Or," she sighed bitterly. "Just not good enough. I believe the students here call people like me a 'reject.'"

Joel watched as she gazed intently into her cup. He was surprised to see her sad face change quickly into a smile.

"But, I guess I was chosen to care for Sebastian ... or, at least that's what Corwin and my father used to say."

"Trust me, you got the better end of the deal," Joel concluded before deciding not to press her for a more specific answer.

She nodded. "Why do you hate it so much?"

He cringed inside, and still having some strength, left his wall up. "Too much homework and stuck up kids," he shrugged.

Augustine was not stupid, and Joel was sure she knew he was lying, but for some reason she let the moment pass.

"Joel?" she said again in the same soft tone.

"Augie?" he mocked her slightly.

"Can I ask you a question?" she asked as she began pulling at the fur on the rug.

"Yeah?"

She looked toward the door and then back toward the rug. "Do you ever get tired of having so many secrets?"

Joel took in a deep breath to ponder her question. He knew she was not prying for information, for he now understood that she had secrets of her own. He breathed out hard and said, "Yeah."

"Are you having to face some secrets you wished you could've forgotten by coming back here?" she asked, still without looking up.

"Yeah," he responded again.

"Me, too," she said quietly. There was a long pause before she asked her next question. "Are you wanting to kill any of your secrets?"

What is she talking about? Joel wondered, but he answered, "Yeah."

She finally raised her eyes to his. "Is that the only word you know?" she asked with her usual Augustine attitude.

He paused to act like he was thinking and then grinned. "Uh, yeah."

She rolled her eyes at him, and he returned to memorizing the Templin hideouts on the map.

A little while later, Joel jerked himself awake, shocked that he had fallen asleep. It was well into the night by now, and seeing that the fire had gone out, he knew it was time to go. There would be no turning back this time. He was sure he could get Augustine out and had made up his mind that if he was needed to create a distraction he would stay behind. He knew they would have fifteen minutes on the property before the barrier alarm would sound.

He nudged Augustine, who was sleeping curled up into a tight little ball as if trying to conserve warmth. She sat up and rubbed her eyes. She glanced over toward the fire then looked around for the housekeeper. She nodded toward Joel that she understood it was time to go.

Joel concentrated on getting the map and supplies back into their bags. He did not want to leave any evidence behind. The housekeeper had saved their lives, and he did not want to risk putting her into any more potential harm. She had promised to distract Sasha as best she could during the night if the beast caught their scent again.

Joel quickly grabbed their clothes off the line from in front of the fireplace. He threw on his bottoms and stuck his head through his shirt. He jumped at the sound of scratching and quickly forced his head through the hole to locate the sound's source. He soon found Augustine brushing her teeth. She knew she had startled him and stopped for a moment when their eyes met.

Joel could not help but laugh. "Of course—you're brushing your teeth," he chuckled.

She opened her eyes widely and shook her head vigorously in order to communicate, "Yes, of course I would be brushing my teeth."

She spit in the sink then said, "For the love, we're going to the temple. I thought I might at least brush my teeth." She turned back to him and eyed his mouth suspiciously. "When was the last time you brushed your teeth?"

Joel shrugged.

"Here." She pointed her toothbrush at him.

"You aren't serious?" he balked.

She gave him a look that let him know she was, indeed, quite serious.

He thought for a moment. *I probably won't run into Sarah. Definitely not Isabelle—but maybe it wouldn't hurt.*

He laughed again as he took the brush from her hand. "Okay, but let's not tell anyone we shared a toothbrush. Makes us sound a little—"

"Desperate? Joel, I'm pretty sure the way we look gives that fact away."

Joel brushed his teeth, completely thankful for the rest they had gotten at the old cabin. It seemed to put them in good spirits. He loved that they both even seemed a little lighthearted, considering the unknown dangers from the task that lay ahead of them. He zipped up the map in her bag then headed toward the door.

"Do you have the map out?" Augie asked, as she put on her backpack.

"I won't need it, Augie." He put his hand on the door handle. "I lived here the last twelve years of my life."

"Then why have you been pouring over it for so many hours?"

He turned toward her deadly serious. "I was making sure the paths and Templins were marked perfectly just in case—" he stopped short and moved toward her. "Promise me you won't fight me, but just do as I say. Corwin has put you in my care. You have to promise me, Augustine, you'll do what I tell you, even if I tell you to leave."

Joel knew her well enough to understand that she hated feeling defeated. He could see the hope evaporating from her face as the lightheartedness they had felt moments earlier faded away.

"We're leaving together," she said indignantly.

Joel stood before her unmoved.

"Okay," she faltered. "Not like I have a choice."

"No, you do," he said.

"I said 'okay.' Yes, okay." She hissed defensively at the look he was giving her.

Joel nodded. "All right, then, just like before, we're keeping quiet and moving into the shadows until we're underground. Tug my jacket if you need anything."

She nodded as she watched him swing open the door and let the cool air flow into the cabin.

The icy wind fought hard to force them back into the cabin within the first few feet of their journey. Thankfully, both were covered in bearskin coats that the housekeeper had left hanging by their clothes. Joel hated wearing such a garment, feeling the sight of him in it would only give the headmaster another reason for wanting to skin his own hide. *But the warmth is amazing,* he admitted to himself.

Joel turned back every few minutes to check on his companion. He flinched each time he noticed how loud their boots sounded as they crunched through the deep snow. He wanted to believe Augustine would actually do everything he asked without question, and so far, she had done fairly well, *for her, anyway,* in this regard. Still, he felt on edge, all the same, knowing how desperate she was to get the rhydid for Sebastian. The responsibility Corwin had given him was beginning to feel overwhelming.

So much for this being easy. He decided he'd best keep a close eye on her. *She's probably terrified in this pitch black.*

Joel heard Augustine copy his pace and noted she kept only one step behind him. She was careful not to bump into him as he stopped every so often to take a breath and look back at her. During one stop, Joel wondered if she was reminded of them traveling down the dark stairwell to get on the train to Waiz. *Was that only a few weeks ago?* The adventure of a lifetime had started and it was continuing with the petite, argumentative brunette following him.

Just as with the map back at the cabin, Joel decided to go over every detail of his plan over and over in his head while they walked. Sasha, unfortunately, had already caught him off guard, and he wanted to be ready for any more surprises, even if it meant taking alternate routes.

Stupid Templins. Everywhere. He grimaced, while thinking back to the X's marking their locations on the map. He quickly reminded himself that he had slipped past them before and that this time some king had summoned him back here. He was going to get something that belonged to him—that was his.

"Don't forget who's on your side, who has asked this of you," he heard Corwin's voice saying in his head.

After Joel checked on Augustine again, he realized that he knew this part of the path so well he had barely been paying attention to his footsteps. After slipping and sliding over the snowy ground for about another half hour, he put his hand up.

There's the boulder. Joel went forward and pressed against it only to discover that it was encased in a block of thick ice. He huffed out a loud sigh in annoyance.

Augustine drew closer to him. "What's wrong?" she whispered.

"Hey, you got anything sharp in your bag?" he whispered.

She thought for a moment and then said, "A nail file, maybe a pair of scissors."

Joel nodded and pointed to the rock. "Okay, whatever you got. Try chipping through this."

When he started to walk away, Augustine broke her vow of silence and cried out fearfully, "Where are you going?"

"To look for something else to help us break through that. Keep working," he instructed.

"Well—well, please don't go far away."

If the darkness was not enough, being alone in such an unfamiliar place terrified Augustine. "Joel? Joel!" She turned around and strained her eyes in the direction her companion had gone. "Great. I don't know where I am, and then there's only a hybrid bear out here," she muttered to herself as she snatched the pair of scissors from the travel-size first aid kit.

About ten minutes later, Joel had yet to return. By this time, her sheer panic and her weariness from the force she was exerting to chip away at the ice had caused her to break out into a full-fledged sweat. Her nerves were on edge, so she naturally jumped when she heard footsteps again.

Joel waved his hand quickly when he approached to indicate it was just him.

"Good job, Augie," Joel let out as he examined the boulder. "Now let me try this," he said and motioned for her to stand back.

412

Augustine watched as he lifted a gigantic silver claw over his head. She shuddered at the object as it shone against the moonlight. With a few blows, the ice broke off the boulder, and Joel removed the pieces in no time. She jammed the scissors into the backpack then waited for his instructions.

Joel was feeling somewhat encouraged at this point, having actually tripped over the claw. His heart thudded against his chest as he heaved the boulder away and lifted the iron lid. As he climbed into the old tunnel, he fought all the emotions that began to flood back to him. "Didn't you just get free from this place? Why in the heck would you go back to this prison? Do you remember what they did to you? Do you remember how much you hate this place? If they catch you—"

"Stop!" he said aloud to the accusations. "I hear all those 'yous.' I choose not listen to you, but to follow the king's orders."

"I agree," he heard Augustine whisper.

And with that, he pushed the thoughts aside. "Let's do this."

Joel felt much like he had felt the night he had left, with his heart pumping and adrenaline flowing; only this time, he had a partner. He smiled at the irony. *How can two very different people need the same thing?*

He was not alone in this tunnel for one of the few times in his life. The old, dim lighting splashed across Augustine's terrified face. Joel cast her a mischievous grin to calm her spirits.

"This is your tour of the temple, 'Joel style,' which I can assure you is the least boring of all the tours around here."

She nodded, appearing too nervous to smile. He grabbed her shaking hand, and off they flew down the underground tunnel.

When they reached the end of the tunnel, Augustine saw that there was a locked gate and all was dark beyond its iron bars. Joel quickly pulled out his key and unlocked the gate. He turned the iron handle and put a finger to his lips.

How did he get a key?

Since she was not supposed to talk, Augustine began making a list of questions in her head for their train ride back to Waiz. She watched as he quietly pushed the gate open. He held his hand up and signaled for her to wait outside the gate. She watched him disappear into darkness once again.

Within a minute, light poured into the room before her, and Joel was back to beckon her inside.

"Okay, we're safe. No one's here," he said.

She walked inside feeling slightly relieved at his news, then slowly eyed her surroundings. *This is a bizarre room.* Half of it held bookshelves from floor to ceiling and the other half resembled an old classroom. Iron bars encased the classroom, and a large sign hung above the room.

"Moonstruck," she said aloud, looking a little bewildered.

"Yep, this is where they bring all the crazies," Joel said playfully, indicating to her that he assumed she knew the word's meaning. "I got to know it very well," he said, cross-eyed and in his best rendition of a mental patient's voice.

"Stop that," she chided him. "You're freaking me out! How on earth did you know about this place? It's perfect for getting in," she exclaimed, beaming at him.

His humorous expression faltered as he turned to check the locks. "Rejects don't get in, Augie, but if you do get in and they don't want you, they bring you here."

He turned back, briefly displaying silly eyes in her direction, but she knew all the playfulness in his voice had dissipated.

"Wait here. Oh, the restroom's over there if you need it. We'll have to hurry once we leave here."

As promised, she did what she was told. She quickly used the restroom then waited near the classroom. She eyed the chalkboard as well as the lockers then found herself wincing as she discovered that some of the chairs in the room contained constrictive straps. She walked past the wrought iron door to take a closer look at the desks. She squinted at the old, dusty wood and saw there were actual names imprinted upon each one. She wondered if Joel had been teasing or telling her the truth earlier.

Sure enough. The desk third from the right had his name carved into it. *No last name.* She checked to see if he was on his way back from wherever he had gone before she slowly lifted the lid of his desk. She was amazed to find an enormous leather-bound file like the ones housed right outside the room deep inside the desk. Highly intrigued at this point, she hesitated only for a moment before opening it.

There it was. *Joel's temple file.* She thumbed through grades, letters, and other paper documents. *Why did he leave this here?* Her heart raced, fearing Joel would walk in at any moment. She did not have near the alone time she wanted with this file. *I need to know about Joel, for Sebastian's sake,* she reasoned, before snatching the file and shoving it into her backpack.

As she closed the lid, her eyes caught a glimpse of an old, frayed picture of what must be Joel and his parents, as well as an empty jewelry box. She carefully took the picture and slipped it into his file.

She was just zipping up her bag when Joel surprised her from the dungeon's door. "Enjoying yourself?" he asked sarcastically.

She shook her head no fervently, feeling quite uneasy that he may have seen her.

He shrugged, and it was then that she noticed he was covered in snow. "Told you it wasn't glamorous."

"That or you've proved to be a very poor tour guide," she said with a hint of sadness in her voice.

"That might have something to do with it," he replied bitterly to the tone in her voice.

He shot her his serious look again, and she knew what was coming.

"Augie, okay, remember what you promised. And no matter what, even if I tell you to leave," he reminded her.

"Yes, I promise," she finished for him.

"We're going up the Moonstruck trail, like we talked about. I just checked the courtyard around the temple chapel and it looks quiet. We're going in through the chapel window, remember? The old latches won't set off an alarm."

"No, my presence has done that," she said flatly.

"The temple chapel should be dark and empty," Joel continued.

As he watched her put on the backpack, he still did not understand why she seemed so dejected about not being at this place, especially after seeing Moonstruck. He had tried to explain as many details along the journey to Augustine as he could remember for at least two reasons. He hoped this would eliminate the need for her to open her mouth to ask questions, and, just in case he was staying behind or if they were to be separated, he wanted to make sure she could find her way out. He did not have a "Sebastian" at home in his care, so he had resolved that no matter what, he would make sure she got her rhydid to her brother.

"No talking from this point on. I will lead you exactly where to go," Joel commanded, and Augustine nodded in submission.

Both grabbed their bags and headed for the stairs. Just after Joel opened the black iron door that led to the first level of Moonstruck, he turned back to Augustine. She was trembling. He grabbed her hand and smiled widely at her.

When he just stood there and started swinging their clasped hands back and forth, she shot him a puzzled glance.

"So," he rolled out slowly. "How's about we show the temple what rejects are made of?"

CHAPTER 33

JOEL LED AUGUSTINE up the stairs to the house portion of Moonstruck Asylum. He barely gave her the chance to glance inside what resembled an empty, rundown metal shop before he took her out the back door. He cautiously rounded the house and guided her up to a clear, snowy trail.

Halfway up the well-worn path, Joel stopped dead in his tracks. He thought he heard movement ahead, so he waited to see if his suspicion was correct. *Surely not the barrier alarm already?* He had hoped they would have more time.

He swiftly shoved Augustine off the trail and jumped into the snowy brush after her. He put his hand over her mouth and whispered into her ear, "Someone's coming down the trail."

She nodded.

Joel felt the blood in his temples beating steadily. *Come on, we're so close. We can't get caught.* He sent a reminder to the king that they needed to get going.

He had spoken to unseen creatures since he was five years old, but it still seemed odd talking to something other than himself. In fact, the whole ordeal that had led him thus far had done nothing but fuel the idea that he really was insane.

He held his breath as they heard footsteps approaching. *Maybe it'll be Sarah*, he hoped, trying to keep positive as Corwin had admonished.

Soon Joel made out a willowy figure walking quickly down the path toward them. He peered at the figure through the moonlight and noted the long blond strands that were flowing out from under her hat. His heart skipped a beat as he immediately recognized her. There was his bait right in front him. He frantically removed his hat as he jumped onto her path.

"Isabelle?"

He knew he had startled her but was sure she instantly recognized his hair and face.

She looked at him entirely confused. "Joel? What—what are you doing here?" she whispered and moved closer. The unexpected relief that washed over her face made him smile as he reached toward her. *She must want me to get her out of here.*

Before Joel could answer Isabelle's question, a dark flash darted past him, yelling and flailing her arms. Augustine threw herself onto Isabelle, knocking them both onto the snowy ground. Joel watched in horror and confusion as Augustine straddled Isabelle and pinned her to the ground. Augustine began roughly shaking Isabelle by the shoulders, all while tersely uttering the words, "I hate you!" over and over again.

This is crazy. She's gone mad! Joel came to his senses when the sounds of Isabelle's pleas for mercy became louder than his thoughts of utter confusion. He swiftly reached forward and forcefully pried Augustine off of Isabelle. Augustine fought Joel for a moment, but soon was overpowered by his strength.

"Enough! Enough!" he ordered Augustine as he held her still. He grabbed her chin tightly with one of his hands. "Look at me. Look! Get your backpack, and wait over there." He nodded toward the bushes.

Augustine angrily pushed his hand off her chin and marched toward the bushes.

Joel turned back to Isabelle. She was pale and shaking. He grabbed a breath and reached down to help her off the ground. He quickly scanned her face and limbs for injuries.

"Are you okay?" He could tell that she was just as much in shock as he was. Relieved as he was at seeing her, he noticed she was not in robes.

"Isabelle … are you running away?"

"Joel, it's a trap. You have to get out of here. It's a trap! They'll catch you," she said urgently. "I was leaving to come warn you. The letter, it was to—"

"Yeah, I know. I'm not here for you," he said more directly than he would have if he had had time to think about his response.

An awkward silence fell between them as he watched a puzzled and hurt expression come across her face. Eventually, she looked down.

"I mean, if I could, I'd rescue you, but you look like you're doing pretty well all by yourself."

She looked up and shook her head at him.

"Listen," he sighed. "I'm sorry, but tonight's not your night. We need to get something, and they'll be out looking for us. They'll find you," he paused, painfully aware that precious time was ticking away with every breath, "They'll—they'll hurt you." He took her hand. "I'm sorry."

Tears welled up in her eyes as she pulled her hand away and ran her fingers through her hair.

Great. Two crying girls, he thought, but he only said, "Don't cry, Bella."

He closed his eyes in frustration, wishing he could invite her along, but this was his and Augustine's journey, and judging by what had just happened, taking Isabelle along would prove more than disastrous. Above all, Joel had to keep his word to Corwin.

I can't take the bait, he told himself as he felt Augustine come up behind him.

He looked over his shoulder. "Not a sound. You keep to your word, and hold your tongue," he snapped.

He focused back on Isabelle for a moment. "Do you have your robe?"

She nodded.

"Good. Put it back on so they won't be suspicious. Do you have a good excuse for being out after hours?" he asked hastily. *Augustine and I have to get moving....*

She nodded again.

"I'll give you a few minutes' head start. Bella, if you think you can risk it, go straight to Sarah and tell her to meet me in the chapel. Please, Bella, can you do that for me?"

Before she answered, Isabelle turned her attention to Augustine. She seemed to study her for a moment before focusing back on Joel.

"Joel, I'm—I'm sorry for—"

He cut her off, knowing there was no time for this. "It's done. Get Sarah for me."

She nodded and pulled on her robe as she headed back up the trail.

Joel's expression darkened when he turned to Augustine. He was unmoved by the face that was stained with tears of hate and reddened from cold and humiliation. Joel understood that she had not been taught how to control her emotions as students at the temple had been. At times he had found the honesty of her emotions refreshing, but the tension from the dangers surrounding them made her lack of self-control completely intolerable.

"I don't want any answers right now, but can I expect *anything* of that nature out of you again tonight?"

She hung her head and shook it.

Joel blew out a breath of hot air and snatched his knapsack from the bushes. As he grabbed Augustine to head up the trail, he watched her eyes lock onto his. He was furious when he saw that she was about to start a "But I—" phrase.

"No," he headed her off harshly. "I don't want excuses. You'll do exactly what I say. Don't speak one word until I tell you. Is that clear? For crying out loud, Augustine, keep your mouth shut and think of Sebastian."

Joel's mind raced in confusion as to what had just transpired between the girls. He vehemently told himself to focus back on the task at hand. The minute he was sure Isabelle had managed to have enough time to cross through the courtyard, he motioned for Augustine to quicken her pace.

When they reached the courtyard gate, he stopped her. Joel gazed at the spotlights for a few moments to determine the strategic pattern in which they were flowing. Thankfully he and Augustine were able to dodge the lights just as well, if not better, than he had before as they made their way over the grounds.

He reached for the window and gently pried it open. *Still unlatched. Just like I left it.*

He gave Augustine a leg up, and she reached through the window and pulled herself over the sill. Joel immediately followed, leaving the window cracked as they both scrambled to their feet. Joel pulled Augustine to the front of the chapel by her wrist. Just as he suspected, the only lights lit inside the place were those glowing around the front left altar.

Though Augustine was incredibly annoyed at Joel for yanking her down the aisle, she could not help but feel that she deserved this type of treatment. Once they reached the front, he sat her on an ivory pew. Much to her disappointment, she was not able to make out much of the chapel in the dark. She was surprised that the room's temperature felt nearly as cold as it did outside. The ceiling was high, with a stained glass dome in its center. In the dim light she could only see the rows of ivory pews behind her and the plush red carpet that was under her feet. She sat on the hard pew, feeling a bit disillusioned by the sight of it all. She had expected a place burning with glory and power and least a little more warmth. She propped her hand underneath her chin and gazed at the altar in front of her.

As her eyes scanned the area for Joel, she soon raised her head in awe. Just beyond the clergy platform near the back left, she saw something radiant, something like she had anticipated finding in this place. A small gold lantern hovered above the glass case that held her prize. There sat the rhydid, luminous and in all its grandeur. The sword was lying horizontally in the most brilliantly crafted sheath she had ever laid eyes upon. The sheath was adorned with blazing crimson and shining silver, which crisscrossed all the way down the blade. Augustine stood up from the pew in wonder just as Joel approached the sacred alcove that held the magnificent object.

When the two heard a knob turning from the nearest side door, they scrambled to hide. Joel slid behind the closest set of organ pipes, and Augustine ducked under the pews.

As Joel tried to sneak a peek at the intruder from his hiding spot, he heard a soft, familiar voice. "Joel … Joel?"

He came out straightaway. "Sarah, I'm up here by the rhydid—I mean, the sword," he said, not knowing if she knew about rhydids.

Sarah hurried toward him. "Isabelle just told me you were here. What are you doing here? Oh, and who is this?" she asked as she bent down and eyed Augustine under the pew.

"Never mind. Sarah, is this the only sword at the temple?"

She turned slowly from Augustine and cast him a puzzled glance. "Well, that's the only one like that one."

"There are no others?" he pressed her.

"Why are you here?" she asked again.

"Why aren't you answering me?"

Augustine stood to her feet and Joel watched Sarah look back and forth between them, as if thinking through her answer.

"Is this yours?" she asked him, pointing to the sword.

Joel shook his head at her for eluding his question again. He hated being in this room; it was anything but a sanctuary to him. He forced out his answer as emotions from the past flooded back to him, along with tormenting memories.

"Yes, it's mine, but I need one for her," he sighed. He looked at Augustine and motioned for her to move toward him.

All froze when the side door opened again, yet were quickly relieved when they saw Isabelle enter the sanctuary alone.

She walked toward them carrying a brick. "I thought you might need this," she said, as she motioned to the glass case. "You'd better hurry. They know someone's here who ..." her voice trailed off as she nodded in Augustine's direction.

Joel took the brick from her hands.

Isabelle fidgeted with her robe. "How's Sebastian?" she asked, not looking at Augustine.

All the brunette did in response was stand expressionless before her.

Joel, though thoroughly confused again, answered Isabelle directly. "He's fine. I asked her to keep quiet. Thanks for this." He waved the brick at her. "Now both of you get out of here."

"Please, can't I come with you?" Isabelle pleaded again.

Pretty sure we've been over this. He was fuming inside that so much time had been wasted. "No, not this time. She'll get you out," he replied as he motioned to Sarah.

"Will you wait for me in Waiz, so I can find you?" she asked softly.

He could hardly believe the change in her voice and demeanor toward him. He made himself focus intently on the rhydid encased before him.

"If I can get out of here ... Sarah, I don't have time for this. Get out of here."

"Isabelle, go now. Joel is safe as long as he doesn't take the bait. Go!" Sarah said.

"Tell him about the Green Cloak," Isabelle called out to Sarah as she turned to leave, and with that, she fled without another word.

"Joel, no, I'm staying to help. I'd risk my life again to see you free," Sarah said to Joel's cold, stone gaze.

He patted her heavily scarred arm. "You've risked enough."

"Do it. Hurry," she said while motioning to the glass.

With one blow Joel shattered the glass, setting off a blaring alarm. Augustine and Sarah braced themselves for his next move. Joel brushed the glass away and closed his eyes as he placed one hand on the hilt of the sword and the other on the sheath. The flaming sparks that ignited around the sword as he drew the rhydid from its sheath sent him sprawling to the ground amongst the broken shards.

He opened his eyes to behold his rhydid, his weapon. He did a double take in disbelief, as he was not holding the glorious sword he had envisioned, but a small dagger. He looked at Sarah in confusion and then noticed Augustine was running to the altar. The sword had somehow mysteriously replaced itself, and his first thought was the same as Augustine's. She looked at Joel and he looked at Sarah, as the loud sirens continued blaring.

"Get it! Now!" Sarah yelled.

Joel nodded to Augustine, whose grip ignited similar flames. He held his breath as he waited for her to take it, but Augustine's hand did not budge.

"Oh, no," he groaned, as Augie struggled to pull the sword away from the sheath. He jumped to his feet and rushed to grip the sword with her. The force of both of them pulling on the object eventually sent them flying backwards, back to where Joel had landed earlier. With his eyes open this time, Joel saw a shining beam of light in the shape of a sword being pulled out of the sheath. The light soon flashed and left a dagger identical to Joel's in its place. The two looked at one another, perplexed.

Joel shook his head and motioned to Sarah. "Sarah! You need this! Get one! Take it! Do it! Do it to fight!"

"I will, but get out of here!" She carefully approached the altar and pressed her hand onto the rhydid. She stumbled a bit as her hand gripped the sword, yet no flames ignited this time. Bewildered, she looked at them.

"What is it?" Joel asked.

"Go! It's nothing!" she commanded.

"Your hand!"

"Yes, it's stuck. They'll catch you! Go!" She waved her other hand at them.

"What!" He rushed towards her in dismay, remembering the bizarre effects the rhydid had displayed when he had tried to take Corwin's. He reached up to pry her hand off.

"Joel, look at me! You have to go!"

He continued jerking at the sword, ignoring her.

"Joel, listen to me, listen! They're going to catch you! Take her!" She looked pleadingly toward Augustine. "Please! Please go, and get your file! It's where I left it!" she smiled and touched his face with her free hand. "Go!"

He nodded. He grabbed Augie by the hand and turned off the lights, making the whole sanctuary pitch black.

He and Augustine jumped out the window and ducked into the shadows as he watched the headmaster and Templin guards run toward the front of the chapel.

During all the commotion Joel felt his confidence slightly increase. *Getting away might be easier than I thought.*

After the group moved past them, he and Augustine sprinted to the courtyard gate. They continued their run down the snowy path back to Moonstruck.

Joel figured most of the junior Templins and guards would be heading towards the chapel, so in order to save a few seconds he ran toward the front door of Moonstruck. He knew the door might be locked, but it was old, so he figured that between the two of them, they could force it open.

Or, he thought as he approached the nearly rotted wooden front porch, *I'll try sticking the dagger in the lock.*

He motioned for Augie to stand back when he reached the door. Joel leaned on the door. To his surprise, it instantly opened, sending him flying through the doorway right into the trap Holt had set for the temple reject.

At first, Joel struggled against the prisoner-type chains that bound his feet and hands.

"Moonie!" Holt cried out in delighted surprise. "I wasn't expecting you." He flashed Joel a sinister smile. "But you'll do just fine. Guess the others didn't think you'd be smart enough to get back here." He gave the chains a rough tug, sending Joel's face to the floor. "What are you doing back here, anyway? Nobody missed you," he scoffed.

When Joel met his questions with silence, Holt grabbed a wad of Joel's hair at the back of his head. "I asked you a question," he hissed in Joel's face.

Joel felt for his dagger, but much to his chagrin realized he must have dropped it outside the door.

"I suppose I should call the Templin guards, or the headmaster, rather—he'll be very pleased to see you." Holt squatted down next to him. "They can wait a minute, though. First, I'll have a little fun with you," he whispered haughtily as he kicked Joel in the stomach. "That's for defying the temple laws then having the arrogance to come back here." A punch flew through the air and found Joel's face. "That's for your stories," Holt continued as he gave blow after blow. "And that's . . . well, that's for being alive."

Before the beating began, Augustine had grabbed Joel's dagger, which had fallen behind him during his entrapment. She quickly ran toward the back door. She figured that, since it was the way they had come before, there would not be any traps set for her. She sighed when she reached the door and realized it must have locked behind them. So, thinking like Joel, she swiftly thrust her dagger into the dead bolt. The locks turned immediately, and she carefully nudged the door open just in time to see Joel receive his first blow.

At first she could not believe what was happening. Then she recalled how much Joel had hated this place. It all made sense to her now. *This was what the temple had been to him—a beating.*

At Holt's last blow she decided she could stand for no more. Though she didn't know how to use the rhydids exactly, she knew there was power in them. So while their enemy was taking a breath to gather up steam for his next blow, Augustine burst in the room, waving both daggers.

"Ah, nice company you're keeping these days." Holt cocked his head in Joel's direction and turned back to Augustine. "So, you're the trash that set off the barrier alarm." He leered at her in a way that made Augustine feel extremely uncomfortable. "Though you are quite pretty for a reject. What do you call girls like her?" He cast a glance back toward Joel. "A 'double-take,' right? 'One look is not enough.' Or is that just what you wrote in your journal about Isabelle?" Holt snickered at him.

Joel began swinging wildly at his opponent as he struggled to get to his feet.

"Easy, Moonie. Gosh, gotten a little thick, haven't you?" Holt taunted, as he jerked the chains again, pulling Joel's legs out from underneath him.

"Hey, girl, do you know why I can him 'Moonie'? Cause he lived here—in this place—most of his life." He gestured around the room. "'Moonstruck.' Do you know what that word means?"

After waiting a moment, he grinned and then took the opportunity to chastise her. "Oh, sorry, I forgot you weren't smart enough to get into the temple."

Augie seethed inside, turning so hot that she could have taken off her coat.

"The word *lunacy* gets it origin from the word *moonstruck*."

Augustine looked over at Joel, who was bleeding from his nose, mouth, and above his eye.

"Oh, he didn't tell you that you were hanging out with a lunatic, a crazy?"

Augustine she had heard enough. She boldly took a step forward as she held the daggers out in front of her.

"What?" Holt mocked her. "You gonna poke me with those itty bitty daggers?" He then noted she was serious, and looked at her aghast. "Wait, you're as crazy as he is," he said and started towards her with a set of chains that had been piled up in the corner of the room nearest to him.

Augustine didn't flinch. She thrust the daggers out toward him, breaking the chains he had intended to wrap around her completely in half.

Holt stopped and stepped back stunned. She quickly thrust the daggers toward him again. Holt took another step back and threw his hands up in bewildered surrender.

"Easy." Holt motioned with his hands. "Hey, it's okay," he said, as she walked over to Joel while keeping one dagger aimed right at him.

She stuck the other dagger into the lock pad of Joel's chains. Sparks flew as the chains fell to the ground, and Joel stood to his feet.

Joel stared at her with eyes widened in surprise. He took his dagger from Augustine then strode over towards Holt. He put his bruised face near his nemesis's ashen complexion.

Holt started to squirm and squeaked out, "Please don't hurt me." Pleasure and satisfaction peeked through the bruises on Joel's face as rage coursed through his veins. He drew in a deep breath and wiped his bleeding mouth. He gave Holt a death look after he saw fresh blood on his hand.

He was confused when Augie motioned for Holt to hold out his hands. The young man winced and braced himself for pain, but instead felt metal clasps around his wrists.

Joel raised his eyebrows at her cleverness as he saw she had just chained him to the wall. The two turned to leave.

"Isabelle's hurt, Joel. I know you got her letter. You can't leave her. She needs you!" Holt cried out after him as he left the room.

Joel stiffened at the lie, but knew he could not say he had seen her. "You help her then. She chose you, anyway."

"Fine! Go on then. We'll find you in Waiz," Holt threatened.

Joel stopped on the stone staircase. *Is there any truth to that threat?* He didn't have time to answer his own question because Augustine clutched at his arm. She shook him back to the reality that Templin guards were chasing them and time was valuable. They ran down into the dungeon and Joel threw his keys at Augustine, who scurried over to unlock the gate. He headed over to his desk.

Surprise and disappointment stopped Joel for a moment when he discovered the desk was empty. He shrugged then searched his locker. After finding nothing again, he slid over to Isabelle's locker and was surprised to see it held her temple file and several scrolls. *She's a smart girl. She'll find these when she's ready to leave.* Augie stood waiting in the tunnel as Joel walked through the classroom once more. He locked the gate back again then both continued a hurried walk through the underground tunnel. When the two were back out in the snowy woods again, their nerves heightened. The Templin guards were not only hunting them, but also they knew that somewhere in the darkness Sasha waited.

CHAPTER 34

MEANWHILE, BACK IN the chapel, as soon as Sarah was sure Joel had made it to the edge of the courtyard, she loosened her grip on the sword and ran out the back door straight to her private music study. She carefully locked the door behind her and made her way up to the attic. She decided to hide amidst all the commotion that was soon to occur, in hope of giving herself and Isabelle a safe alibi. She had used the attic often as an escape from the world around her. She sat down near a time-worn trunk. She unlocked the old case and gingerly took out an object wrapped in cloth.

After Isabelle had told her about the Green Cloak, Sarah had realized that war was a real possibility. She believed it would come on all sides, and decided it was high time to dust off a small, dull-edged sword that had been locked away for quite some time. She also reached deeper into the chest and took out a treasure, several cigar boxes full of bound letters that she had encouraged Joel to write every week to his father.

"It's time your father knew the truth," she said aloud.

As Sarah sat tucked away in the attic, a frenzy was taking place in the chapel sanctuary. The guards examined the shattered glass and were puzzled over the situation.

"But why wouldn't they have taken the sword, Your Excellency?"

"I am not so sure they did not," the headmaster spoke gravely as he stroked his chin. "Where is Sasha?"

"At the far side of the dam. She should be near the old river house."

"Good. I have a feeling the fugitives will head that direction. She is sure to pick up their scent," he mused, then snapped to attention. "Is anyone stationed at Moonstruck? And where is Ms. Harte?"

For half an hour the fugitives continued at a hurried pace. Both could feel their adrenaline wearing off and exhaustion beginning to set in. Joel deliberated about stopping at the cabin for a rest. Augustine had been obedient to his command and had not said a word since their discussion on the trail. He wondered how she was holding up but dared not speak, fearing Sasha or the Templin guards might somehow hear him.

There will be time to talk on the train. He felt the dagger in his hand but had not had much time to think about the rhydid until now as they continued to trudge through the snow. He realized he knew very little about the tiny weapon. *And just why is it so small?*

This was not the first time Corwin had been guilty, at least in Joel's opinion, of leaving out important information. He was baffled somewhat, knowing that if the mouthpieces decided to reappear, he really did not even know how to use the thing. He did not want to take the time to stop at the cabin, but the longer they walked, the more he questioned if he could go all the way to the platform without a rest and something hot to drink. He hoped his wounds were not much to worry about, but he also knew the housekeeper would know what to do.

"Augie, Augie," he whispered loudly to get her attention. "I think we need to stop at the cabin. I—I might need a rest." He was certain she had noticed his ragged breathing and slowed pace since reaching the woods.

He soon heard the river that flowed into the lake and figured they had to be fairly close. He searched across the landscape, yet was unable to make out any light from the cabin, only observing more snow and darkness. As the two began crossing the portion of the river that was nearest to the lake, a large crack resounded around them.

Joel turned toward the lake. *Oh, come on!*

As the two glanced around, trying to locate the direction the sound had come from, Joel knew that this time the sound was not from the ice.

"Augie, run straight! The cabin will be straight," he whispered weakly to her.

The sound of objects cracking and groaning drew nearer once they reached the embankment. As they slipped and sloshed their way up the side, Joel was able to make out the framework of the cabin about ten yards in front of them. He pointed the cabin out to Augustine as they reached the top, and, as he did, a mist of hot air blew across them.

Both slowly turned their heads, eyeing Sasha just a few feet away. Joel hastily thrust his dagger out toward the beast.

Augustine finally broke her silence and whispered, "Joel, what are you doing?"

He kept his eyes locked on the beast. "I'm just doing what the housekeeper did," came his muffled reply.

"Yes, but she had a sword," Augustine exclaimed, fear in her voice.

The animal stared back at them, taking in slow heavy breaths as if to communicate that she was waiting for them to make the first move.

Joel remained unyielding. "Remember your promise, Augustine. Run on three. Ready? One, two, three—run!"

Augustine took off, not looking back and unaware that Joel had stayed behind. Once she got to the cabin, she practically broke down the door to get inside.

"Hello, Hello! Um …" She realized then that she did not even know the housekeeper's name, though she was not sure it mattered, since the cabin looked as though it had been vacated years ago. Fresh snow was falling onto the table in front of her from a hole she saw in the roof above.

"This can't be the same house," she said aloud, then quickly searched for a place to hide.

Joel hoped Augie was on her way to safety. He knew the beast had noticed her, so Joel swiftly hurled a large chunk of ice toward the bear.

"Hey! Over here, Sasha!"

The beast instantly focused its attention back on Joel and started lunging toward him. Joel held out his dagger in defense, and the beast stopped. Sasha cautiously came near until she was close enough for him to touch. She sat still again; then, with her jaws clenched, she hissed in his face.

Unsure of what to do, Joel trusted his instincts. He reached out with his dagger and lightly poked the white bear on the tip of her nose. Sasha instantly jerked back and rubbed her snout. Once the pain appeared to have subsided, she narrowed her eyes and let out an angry roar. Joel starting backing away, feeling less confident that his dagger would be able deliver him. Sasha heard his foot crunch against the snow and growled louder as she bent down toward him.

"Uh-oh," Joel said right before he took off running. As he darted toward the cabin, he felt the beast right on his tail. He was certain he could not outrun her.

But maybe I can outsmart her. He dashed onto the path that led to the cabin. The path was narrow and overgrown; he hoped Sasha would be too large to get through the brush and trees.

"Ha!" Joel yelled when he heard Sasha's footsteps stop behind him. He looked over his shoulder to see her large body blocked by a thick set of trees.

Joel burst into the cabin and was taken aback by its decrepit state. He shrugged, having fewer expectations at every juncture. "Augie, where are you?" he called out.

"I'm hiding upstairs!"

He reached the top of the stairs to find her hunched over in an old bathtub.

He rolled his eyes. "Augie, get out of there! She'll tear the roof off first."

"Fine! Where do you suggest we hide?"

Both became suddenly distracted by the fierce howls coming from just outside the cabin.

"Come on," he urged, as he helped her out and up.

The two ran downstairs, and Joel spotted the large fireplace. Augustine looked at the door as she heard the beast begin to claw the side of the house.

"The fireplace! Come on. She can't knock that down," Joel commanded, as he raced inside the brick opening.

They hid on one side, scrunched together and holding onto each other. They heard the beast continue to strip away the wood on the little cabin. As they stood in the ashes, Joel thought Augustine might squeeze the life out of him. Both were startled when the scratching abruptly stopped.

"Sasha, my darling girl, have you found something?" Joel heard the headmaster ask. There was a pause and then the man spoke again. "Yes, she's found something around here. Search the cabin. Tear it apart if you have to."

"Wait! Headmaster, look! A light! See there, just across the river?" asked Hertz Marlis.

"Yeah, the light's moving!" cried out a few more Templin guards.

"Yes, it is moving," the headmaster let out slowly. "Go on, Sasha. We will follow you. The cabin or the light?" he instructed her. "Ah, there she goes; she must have picked up their scent again. Come let's catch these thieves."

Joel felt Augustine shudder at the man's sinister voice. He pried her off of him and stepped out from the fireplace after all the footsteps were out of earshot. He instantly sank to the cold, snowy, wooden floor.

"Sorry there's nothing hot to drink," she said softly as she stepped out behind him.

He gave her a weak smile. "Yeah, but I can at least sit in safety for a minute. Seems like it's been dangerous every second since we met, huh?"

She shrugged. "Playing the piano in Mr. Rutherford's shop isn't too dangerous."

He breathed heavily and closed his eyes. "Augie, you've got to understand something now."

He felt the corners of his mouth with his tongue, sure they were cracked and caked with dry blood. He was surprised to find her right in front of his face when he opened his eyes. Then he saw that she was examining his wounds. He grabbed the hand that was moving towards his eye.

"You were seen with me. From now on they'll be looking for you, too."

Augustine frowned as she looked down toward the floor and let the reality of this truth sink in.

"Before we go to the station, we've got to—" He stopped mid-sentence while fixing on a dark smudge of ash that had gotten on her cheek.

"What?" she asked self-consciously, touching her face.

Joel dragged himself back toward the fireplace and grabbed a couple of old coals and ash. "Here, cover your skin in this," he instructed.

He removed his hat and rubbed the dark ashes into his hair until he saw in the reflection of his dagger that his hair had turned to a blackish color. Before he moved the ashes to his skin, Augustine managed to wipe most of the blood off his face.

"These cuts will need dressing," she said, grimacing at the sight of them.

"Later," he muttered.

He then also covered his face, neck, and hands with the dark ash. While Augie was obediently covering her olive skin with the dark soot, Joel rummaged through his bag and pulled something out.

He snatched off Augie's hat. "Here." He threw a knitted cap at her. "Put that on. It's bigger, so tuck all your hair up in there, 'August,'" he grinned.

Once they resembled two dark-skinned teenage boys, they crept out the door and then moved rapidly through the woods toward the road. They traveled with their daggers out, knowing that Sasha may have rediscovered their scent by now. The dark night sky was beginning to brighten when Joel spotted a small country store down at the end of the service road they had found at the edge of woods. The store was located right next to several train tracks, and Augustine pointed to a sign hanging above the bottom window on the building.

Joel turned to her and let his guard down. "What does it say?" he asked sheepishly, and braced himself for her reaction.

She eyed him curiously and said, "'Purchase Train Tickets Here,'"

They approached the country store cautiously, searching for any temple security. Joel knew purchasing tickets was risky. *But we really don't have a choice.*

"Where to, young man?" the sleepy ticket master asked, while casting the two an odd look.

Joel surmised the look was probably due to their peculiar appearance, covered with ashes and wearing bearskin coats.

"Uh, doesn't matter. Two tickets, please," Joel sputtered, which further caused the man to eye them strangely.

He took a sip of coffee then asked, "All right, how about Facilis, then?"

"Fine," Joel said quickly while continuing to search his surroundings for any sign of temple employees.

"Thanks," he said, as the man handed him the tickets. He then turned to "August" and gave him a ticket.

Just as he had instructed on the road, the two separated and sat on different sides of the open-air platform while they waited with the crowd. As the minutes passed, Joel's insides churned as he saw a Templin slowly walk onto the ground in front of the platform. The guard eyed the crowd with fierce scrutiny. Joel's heart raced as he watched the official march promptly over to Augustine.

"Hey, you, boy, have you seen any other students here today?" the guard inquired.

Augustine shot him a puzzled look and spoke out in a low tone, "Gee osh tuk bey?"

Gosh, she's quick on her feet. He slipped to the back of the platform.

"From Galanne, never mind," the guard waved past her.

Joel crouched behind a bench until the man left.

After half an hour, Joel crept up behind Augustine and whispered, "Where do you think the train is?"

"How about down through those trees? Right past the tracks. Look."

The sun coming up allowed Joel just enough light to see the ticket master heading in the direction Augustine was referring to.

"He has a bag. He's headed somewhere," Augustine observed, as they watched the man disappear into the trees.

"Okay, let's follow him. Wait!" He grabbed her. "Let's go once this train finishes pulling up. No one should notice us crossing over the tracks."

During the commotion of the train unloading and reloading with passengers, the two easily slipped past the tracks and into the woods on the opposite side of the platform. Once inside the woods, they nearly slid down the ravine that led in the ticket master's direction. They were relieved to spot him and another train track after they reached the bottom.

The ticket master motioned for them to cross over the tracks. When they were within earshot, he pointed to an approaching train and said, "I wondered if you'd be headed this way, since you didn't care what your ticket said. I don't know how you two know about this train, but," he paused and turned toward them, "you must be both brilliant and brave. I commend you."

"Is this the train to Waiz, sir?" Joel asked.

The man nodded his head and chuckled as he gestured at their rhydids. "So young. You'll *see* many things with those."

"What else do we not know about these?" Joel asked, slightly annoyed.

"Not much due to their size," the man laughed again. "Oh, but don't worry," he said upon seeing their confused looks. "They'll grow with more time."

"Er—you mean they grow?" Joel asked.

The man shrugged and gave Augustine a wink.

Joel shook his head good-naturedly at the man's lack of answers. *Waiz people are so odd, but also so intriguing.*

"Ah, here. These might help," the man said as he lifted two leather straps out of his inside coat pocket. "These are sheaths."

Joel shook his head, refusing to take one.

"Don't be afraid," the man encouraged. "These are merely to keep the rhydid safe, not to conceal it or devoid it of power."

Augustine reached forward and took a leather piece. "Corwin has one," she said to Joel.

Joel nodded and took the other.

"Thank you, sir," he said as Augustine politely nodded her thanks. *Corwin's right. The enemy is everywhere, but so are we.* He watched the train approach with hardly a sound.

Once safely on the train, the two found an empty compartment. Both were grateful it would be just the two of them inside; there was so much to talk about. Having one pair of clean clothes left, both agreed they would clean up and meet back for breakfast.

While Joel sat waiting for Augustine as she finished showering, he replayed the night's events in his head. He held up his dagger. He had really not even had a chance to look at it. The hilt was a dull gold with magnificent sketches etched upon it. He ran his finger over the grooves of the drawings. He slit his hand after he touched the blade's side and then cut himself further when he ran his fingertip over the blade's point. He remained puzzled about its size, but did not allow his confusion to bother him much. He was so satisfied that he had his and Augie had hers.

The compartment door sliding open distracted him from his thoughts. Augustine, clean and beautiful, moved into his line of vision.

He found himself unable to respond right away when she said, "Sure feels good to be clean."

Joel nodded, unaware that his mouth gaped open. When he found his voice again he said, "Oh, yeah. I think I used two bars of soap just to scrub the first layer of soot off."

"Yeah, me, too. How's your face?" she asked, with compassion in her voice.

"Oh, this?" he pointed to his puffy eye and slashed cheek. "It's not so bad." He shrugged.

"Does it hurt?" she winced, as she moved her hands near his face.

"Only when I think about it," he sighed, squinting as her ring reflected sunlight into his eyes.

"I'm sorry. Will you let me doctor it now, please?"

He nodded and leaned his head back.

As she bandaged his face tenderly for the second time since he had known her, he asked, "How do you know how to do this?"

"Use your head," she laughed.

"Huh?" he jerked away to look at her face.

"Joel, who's my brother?" she asked, then pulled his chin back toward her. "I've had lots of opportunities to be around nurses—lots of practice with taking care of people."

He smiled, feeling even more gratified that she had a rhydid attached to her hip.

Breakfast came shortly after she finished bandaging his face. The two enjoyed something hot as much then as they had at the cabin a few hours earlier. The food put Joel back in rare form, and he was soon standing in the compartment and clinking a knife against his glass.

"Ladies and gents, I'd like to propose a toast to the most brilliant and brave girl I know," he said, borrowing the words that the ticket master had spoken over them. "She may not choose the best hiding places, and she may not bear frozen temperatures well, especially when she's wet—"

"What?" she scoffed.

"But, let me finish," he paused and waved his hand. "Not only does Augustine have the most clean teeth in all Differe *and* Waiz, but," he stopped to take a breath then uttered out in a lower and more serious tone, "She can break chains with a single blow and keep her word." He lifted his glass high in the air. "To Augustine."

She beamed back at him and then the two drank accordingly.

"Ahem, now do I get the floor?" Augustine implored as she stood up.

"It's all yours. Take all day if you need to. I know it's pretty hard to know when to stop talking about me," Joel said, as he relaxed back into his seat.

"Watch it. I know lots of big words, remember?"

"How could I forget? It's a little frightening," he said, pretending to be scared.

"Even though Joel is—" Augustine started, and Joel cringed jokingly.

"Stop, you're messing me up!" she laughed, then attempted to start again. "Even though he is stubborn and secretive at times, I'd still like to honor my friend Joel.... Now that I'm allowed to talk."

Joel straightened upon hearing the word *friend.*

"He rescues damsels in distress, fights off beasts with his bare hands, and the dagger doesn't count," she continued, as he waved the rhydid in front of her. "Navigates through darkness, and faces his fears."

Joel raised his glass, thinking this was the end of her speech.

440

"Furthermore," she said as she held up her dagger, "I declare in the name of the king, who I think might exist, that Joel is *not* crazy."

"You sure about that?" Joel interjected, beginning to feel slightly uncomfortable at her tribute.

"Let me finish," she commanded. "But that he is completely sane and full of truth. He has proved himself trustworthy."

As she sank back down to her bench, they drank again.

They were all smiles as they went over the past few weeks they had spent together. Augustine pulled out the book Mr. Rutherford had given her, but as soon as the food was taken away their eyes became heavy. Joel suggested that they rest until dinner.

After he pulled the window shade, Joel saw big tears forming in Augustine's eyes. He wondered how she went so quickly from silly to this. As the tears spilled over onto her cheeks, he reached over to her.

"Augie? Hey, it's over. It's all over. We're gonna be back in Waiz soon, and you'll get to see Sebastian. He's going to be fine now."

"Yes. Yes, you're right. I know," she said while attempting to wipe her tears away.

"Corwin and I will be there to keep you safe. You don't have to worry." He smiled at her.

She nodded and smiled faintly back at him. After a long pause, she wiped her face again and then asked, "Are you ready to go to sleep?"

"Uh, sure," he answered, willing to do anything to get her to quit crying.

After they had lain in the rumbling darkness for a few minutes, Joel heard Augustine sniffle. He sighed, wishing he knew what would make her feel at ease. He was surprised when she suddenly called out to him.

"J ... Joel?"

"Yes?" he replied softly as he sat up.

"Isabelle was supposed to have your ticket."

Joel didn't say anything, but laid his head back down. *The ticket? What ticket?*

Then he remembered. Stunned, he asked, "The one at Crossroads?"

"Yes," she whispered and began to cry again.

Great, it wasn't supposed to be me. He wondered if she was crying because she wanted to be with Isabelle or if it was because, like the temple, Isabelle had not chosen her. He felt the dagger at his side and shook his head. *No. This was always supposed to be mine.* He hoped its power could somehow take away all the pain they had both encountered in their lives.

"Augie, go to sleep. It's been a long day, or night rather," he said quietly.

He was content that they had completed their mission, but not at ease. He knew war was brewing. *Isabelle mentioned a Green Cloak.* He believed that could only mean one thing. The temple would be involved in the war between the cities of Waiz.

Andropolis overlooked the Pallas River as he stood in the tower above the Bridge of Miren. He wore his crisply pressed new cloak. The distinguished New Order emblem glittered on the front of the fabric. As he ran his finger over it, he recalled Marcell's words: "You have served your side well. You have honored your family, and so, we honor you."

Stealing the maps, performing the murder, making the temple connection, delivering some letter of importance—in his mind a new cloak seemed hardly the right payment for all his efforts. On the train ride back to Waiz, he had had more than enough time to ponder the murder, the seemingly evil headmaster, and the coming war. He also had not been able to get the poor girl at the desk out of his mind. Since that day, he had dreamed of Isabelle every time he had closed his eyes. His conscience was paying a dear price to be on the side of the New Order. As he swung the payment he had secretly kept for himself around his finger, he could not help but wonder, *Am I on the right side?*

A NOTE FROM THE AUTHOR

TIME IS VALUABLE.

I'm honored you would choose to give me some of yours by reading the first installment of *The Waiz Chronicles*. Sorry to leave you hanging like this. In my opinion, unresolved endings make reading a series worth the effort. So again, forgive me, but I think I've come up with a way to make the wait for book 2 less excruciating. To ease your anticipation and discover more about *Escape From Differe* as well as updates about the upcoming release of book 2, visit my website at www.mikelynbolden.com, or join *The Waiz Chronicles* Facebook fan page. For those wanting a more personal reply to the information listed above or for advice on writing and/or publishing, please e-mail me at mikelyn@mikelynbolden.com. I'd love to hear from you. Thank you in advance for your interesting comments, thoughtful questions, and challenging critiques. Each of these expressions helps me to produce better writing and a more well-rounded story.

A humble and most grateful thanks to all those joining in on this grassroots effort by helping spread the word about *The Waiz Chronicles* on blogs, Facebook, and Twitter, as well as by providing me with opportunities to speak about the series. To the wonderful people who've touted the story to book clubs, bookstores, schools, libraries, churches, coworkers, mailmen, folks at the checkout line, passengers on planes, or anyone else in your world, much appreciation. You make this series worth writing.

On a more serious note, I hope this story has enticed both your senses and your heart, entertaining you as well as moving you beyond reading to experiencing. As you see yourself through the lives of these characters, as I have, may hope arise at this revelation: You are not alone … and perhaps, you're not crazy.

ACKNOWLEDGMENTS

I ONCE HEARD Dolly Parton refer to her songs as her children. I didn't understand what she meant until I completed this book. There have been many, many folks involved in the birthing of this project.

First, thank you, Mom and Dad. You raised me to believe I could do anything. That core value provided the courage needed to pursue this venture. Thank you for your continual support and patience. I pray I will live out your heart—that your ceiling will be my floor.

Steve and Cindy Strickland, the words "thank you" cannot even begin to express my gratitude for your life-changing mentorship and prayer support. You have created a massive domino effect. The world thanks you.

Jaime and Andrew Sharp, thank you for demonstrating the true standard of vulnerable community ... on steroids. You have supported, loved, baptized, and prayed relentlessly for me. You are some of my greatest treasures.

Lyndsay and Jeff Rutherford, thanks, Jeff, for giving the shopkeeper a name and lovingly sharing your wife's time for this project. Lyns, we were destined to be friends. Thank you for your impeccable editing skills, constructive feedback, and encouragement on my dark days.

To the initial group of readers, I can *never* thank you enough for the time you invested in this project. I have an outstanding story because of you!

Jerome Daley, last year a close friend told me that everyone needs a coach. He was so right. Your insight and direction were invaluable on this journey. You not only helped produce a book, but redefined what my life should look like. Thank you for your counsel in the ways of rest, intentionality, and well, soul space. Thanks to you, "life" doesn't run me anymore.

Tom Kimball, what are the chances? Thank you for being a risk taker and pursuing a total stranger. Your expertise pushed this project to new levels. This journey has brought many surprises and you are one of my favorite ones.

Blair Thompson, you nailed it on the first try. Thank you for sharing your brilliant creative talent on this project. Your camaraderie as a fellow "cliff jumper" has encouraged and inspired me.

Mark and Jeannie Broadway, thank you for using your gifts to capture the true me. You both have a natural flair for bringing out the best in your subjects.

Bekah Davis, thank you for believing in me. May you receive a beyond your wildest dreams return on your investment.

A special thanks goes to Rachel Hendrix, Hannah Miller, and Troy Fountain for taking the time to endorse this project. The passion you each exude has served as a catalyst to fuel my own. Blessings on you all!

A *huge* thank you to my team at WinePress! Because of all of you, this book has morphed from a word document to a creatively crafted masterpiece. Thank you for all your hard work and answering my numerous questions along the way.

Ryan & Elizabeth, Colleen & Kurt, Lindsey & Anthony, and Craig, I couldn't ask for a more loving immediate family. Being connected with all of you has helped me move past my insecurities towards this dream.

To Clara Grace, Camden, Mason, Mollie, and all those yet to come, may these words compel you to proclaim liberty to the captives and freedom to the prisoners.

Donald and Sally, thank you for giving me your son, without whom this book would not exist. Well done, in modeling a good marriage for us to follow. I am honored to be your daughter-in-love.

I would be remiss if I didn't mention a few other names: Larry & Mary Bolden, Jason & Amy Sharp, Grant & Elizabeth Faulk, Brett & Shawn Hemphill, Eddie & Kelly Coker, Brannon & Ann Payne, Jack & Linda Holmes, Ricky Gordon, Kelli Gettinger, Laura Krämer, Anna Uzzell, Emily Smith, Becca Broderick, Emily Gross, Stephanie Wright, Cindy Woodcox, Scott Fain, Brittany Sumlar, Sarah O'Keefe, Paxton Tharp, Stephanie Holder, Mary Kate Gilbert, the Labor Day Group, my SAMC Co-Workers, the Wiregrass Church Guest Services Team, my Wiregrass Church Smallgroups, my AU Family, all my "Speech" Gals, DCF, and Bethel Church. Also, thank you to those youth pastors, churches, youth and college ministries, teachers, schools, bookstores, book clubs, bloggers, and magazine writers who graciously agreed to help promote the story even before there was a means to get it published.

Now, I always save the best for last.

Marby, where do I begin? This whole thing started after you boldly spoke truth I didn't want to hear. "*You are afraid.*" Thank you for your relentless pursuit to love me well, and drive me to wholeness. Your tireless efforts on this project—working two jobs along with me—spoke volumes of love and sacrifice. Your encouragement, dry humor, and lack of complaining continually kept me going. What we've achieved in nearly eight years of marriage, I'm convinced some rarely get in a lifetime. You are my favorite.

To my Daddy God, Fiery Best Friend, and Ever Present Help, Your presence has ruined me for anything else on this planet. Thank you for setting me free.

WinePressPublishing
Great Books, Defined.

To order additional copies of this book call:
1-877-421-READ (7323)
or please visit our website at
www.WinePressbooks.com

If you enjoyed this quality custom-published book,
drop by our website for more books and information.

www.winepresspublishing.com
"Your partner in custom publishing."

CPSIA information can be obtained at www.ICGtesting.com
Printed in the USA
LVOW120555271112

308768LV00004B/4/P